# I will agree, but only if you kiss me.

The thought came unbidden, a whisper from deep in her brain. Her gaze darted to his mouth, those full lips that flirted and cajoled every time they parted. What other feats could his mouth and lips perform, if needed?

*Stop, Mamie. You've been listening to Florence too much.*

She let her lids fall and tried to calm her racing heart. Chauncey. He was her future husband, the only man she should be lusting over. Desire for Frank Tripp was a complication she could not take on right now.

A finger swept under her chin to turn her head—and her eyes flew open. Frank was openly studying her, his stare hot and intense, with the gentle press of his finger holding her in place. The air in the carriage turned charged, an electricity that seemed to jump between them like alternating current. Her heart thumped in her chest, so loud she was certain he could hear it.

"Do we have a deal, Mamie?"

There was that deep grating tone again, the one she'd not heard him use before tonight. "Yes," she heard herself whisper.

### By Joanna Shupe

# THE Rogue OF Fifth Avenue

### ∾ UPTOWN GIRLS ∾

# JOANNA SHUPE

AVONBOOKS

*An Imprint of HarperCollinsPublishers*

THE ROGUE OF FIFTH AVENUE. Copyright © 2019 by Joanna Shupe. All rights reserved. Printed in the United States of America. No part of this book may be used or reproduced in any manner whatsoever without written permission except in the case of brief quotations embodied in critical articles and reviews. For information, address HarperCollins Publishers, 195 Broadway, New York, NY 10007.

First Avon Books mass market printing: June 2019

Print Edition ISBN: 978-0-06-290681-6
Digital Edition ISBN: 978-0-06-290682-3

*Cover illustration by Jon Paul Ferrera.*
*Cover photograph by Michel Legrou/Media Photo.*

*To Queen Bee and Drama Queen.*
*Thanks for all the gray hair.*

# The Rogue of Fifth Avenue

# Chapter One

*The Bronze House*
*Broadway and Thirty-Third Street, 1891*

He spotted her immediately, as he always did.

Frank had a preternatural ability to spot Marion "Mamie" Greene in any room, no matter how crowded. She was a beauty, perfectly put together with the most expensive accessories. Tonight, her coppery brown hair was adorned with diamond combs, her evening dress cut indecently low.

Christ, her décolletage was a thing of beauty from this high vantage point.

However, it was her smile that caught his attention. Always her radiant smile. It lit up a room far better than Edison's incandescent bulbs. Her plump dark red lips were a sharp contrast to her creamy skin and her white teeth gleamed in the gaslight. Just then, she won and started clapping, joy etched on every square inch of her face. She laughed and loved life more than any other woman he'd ever met, drawing attention better than a moth to a flame.

This evening was no exception, it seemed, judging by the crowd surrounding the two Greene sisters. Mamie and her sister were the center attraction tonight from their spot at the roulette table.

Dear God, a roulette table.

As he stared down at the floor of the city's most luxurious casino, the Bronze House, he lamented the turn his evening had taken. This was not the first time he'd been summoned to a casino or gaming hell to rescue a client—in fact, the request came much more often than he'd like. As attorney to many of the city's richest, most prominent men, Frank had done any and all manner of things to keep clients out of trouble.

Nothing illegal. Just . . . creative maneuvering.

Frank's mind did not work in straight lines, black-and-white. No, considering his upbringing and childhood, he'd learned how to plot and scheme. Dodge and weave. *Survive.* Talents that had made him very rich after school. Very rich indeed.

So he did not mind being summoned to solve a problem and save the day. Especially when he was being paid handsomely for it.

This particular client was different, however. This marked the third rescue in four months—rescues Frank hadn't confessed to his client.

He'd kept these rescues a secret because they involved the client's eldest daughter. A daughter who, if Frank were being completely honest, he liked. She was unconcerned with dance cards, matrimonial prospects and other society nonsense. Instead, Mamie spoke her mind and let nothing—and no one—get in her way of accomplishing her goal.

He admired that. In fact, he operated in much the same manner.

However, his interest in her was unhealthy. He was not a "court the uptown Knickerbocker princess" man. He was a "fuck the gorgeous chorus girl until dawn" sort of man. Mamie Greene did not fit into his neatly crafted life, one he'd carved for himself atop buried secrets. It was time to be done with her.

No more bailing her out from seedy establishments. Tonight he would retrieve her and take her home to Duncan Greene, her father, and let him deal with her from now on. Which was exactly what Frank should have done the last two times he'd found her out in the rougher side of town. Instead, her smile and sass had caught him by surprise, charmed him, and he'd believed her when she promised never to return.

All lies.

The reckless female had no idea what disaster she courted by visiting a casino, the dangers that lurked in every corner of the Tenderloin district. Vice and sin reigned here, with corrupt policemen looking the other way. Any number of ills could befall her south of Thirty-Fourth Street.

But he couldn't keep doing this, no matter the insane desire to watch over her.

"Thank you for your expeditious arrival."

Frank started at the sound of a voice directly behind him. Turning, he found Clayton Madden, the shadowy owner of the Bronze House, standing there. Appropriate Madden should lurk in the darkness; not many had met the man, as he preferred to keep an inconspicuous presence in the city. Madden stuck out a hand and Frank promptly shook it.

"Of course," Frank said. "Thank you for alerting me to her presence."

Madden jerked a chin toward the casino floor. "She brought one of her sisters this time."

Women were not allowed inside the Bronze House, yet somehow Mamie managed to get inside. "Why did you let them in?" Frank asked, not taking his eyes from her.

"I have my reasons."

"They could lose a great deal of money. Worse, they could lose their standing in society."

Madden's lips quirked. "I assure you, neither of those outcomes concerns me. What does concern me is the crowd they've attracted. If men are standing and gawking then they aren't gambling. It's one of the many reasons we don't permit women to play here."

Frank shot Madden a glance. "Figures you have a financial reason for wanting them removed."

Madden crossed his arms over his chest. He was about the same height as Frank, a little over six feet, but bulkier. Rougher. A scar ran through his right eyebrow, another on his chin. He wore an impressive black suit with a black vest—his usual attire. "Greene and I don't exactly see eye to eye. I'll be damned if his girls win a dime at my club."

"You could refuse them entry."

Madden stroked his jaw, staring at the pair below. "I could," he said cryptically.

Frank didn't bother to seek more answers. Madden was notoriously tight-lipped and it hardly mattered. The Greene sisters had no business coming here, and Frank was dashed glad Madden had notified him when Mamie arrived. "Well, I'll collect them now. Greene passes on his thanks."

"Come now, Tripp. We both know you're not telling your client about these little outings."

Frank gritted his teeth and thought about denying it. There was no use lying, however. Madden was right. "That ends tonight. I'm done with favors. He can look after her now."

Madden chuckled under his breath. "Keep telling yourself as much. By the way, I wish to hire you for a bit of consulting. My lawyers are giving me a hard time on one particular issue, but I'm told you might be able to help."

Frank nodded. "I have time tomorrow, if that works."

"That'll be fine. Come by at four."

Mamie won another round and threw her arms around her sister as the crowd applauded. Frank gritted his teeth and considered pummeling each man encouraging this outrageous behavior.

Then it happened. In fact, if Frank had blinked he would've missed it.

Clever, delicate fingers darted into the inner jacket pocket of a bystander and withdrew a money clip. The stack of greenbacks then disappeared into the folds of Mamie's evening gown.

Madden whistled softly. "Not bad. Where'd an uptown girl learn to dip like that?"

Jesus Christ. Frank could not believe his eyes. Her father would have a stroke if he knew. "I must get down there—"

"Hold up." Madden's hand landed on Frank's arm. "Dark suit on her left."

Sure enough, Madden was right. With Mamie's back turned, the man next to her took the opportunity to pour the contents of a small vial into Mamie's champagne glass. Frank's body went rigid, ice filling his veins. "What the hell?"

"Fucking bastard. Leave him to me." Madden started for the staircase at the end of the long balcony.

Frank had no intention of waiting. He had to intervene before she drank that champagne. Without thinking, he threw his legs over the side of the railing, then twisted to hold on to the ledge with his hands. He lowered himself until he was hanging on by his fingertips. A high-stakes craps game was about an eight-foot drop beneath him.

He let go.

His feet hit the table, which rocked under his weight but held. Gasps erupted, chips flying every which way, but he ignored them and remained focused on the man to Mamie's left, the one who had poured an unknown liquid into her drink. Fury made it impossible to look anywhere else. He jumped to the floor, wincing at the sharp pain in his ankle, and lunged for the roulette table.

The man looked up just as Frank hurled across the baize. They smacked together and went down hard, the man taking the brunt of the fall. "What were you hoping to accomplish?" Frank snarled, shaking the other man. "Were you waiting until she passed out and then you'd offer to see her home?"

"Wait." The man put his arms up to shield himself. "I did nothing—"

Frank hit him in the face. "You are a goddamned liar."

Hands suddenly lifted Frank off the floor. He struggled to break free, to tear that drugging bastard apart with his bare fists, but whoever held him was too strong. Out of the corner of his eye he caught Mamie and her sister a few feet away, their wide eyes taking everything in.

"You're done, Tripp." It was Bald Jack, Madden's right-hand man, holding Frank. "Madden wants you out."

"But this man deserves—"

"And he'll get it. Madden will see to it personally."

Frank calmed immediately. Whatever justice Madden doled out in private would be a hundred times worse than what Frank could accomplish here on the main floor. Bald Jack carefully set him on his feet, and Frank smoothed his hair and tried to catch his breath. The bastard on the ground moaned, blood pouring from a cut on his cheek. Frank resisted the urge to add a kick for good measure. Instead, he nodded at Jack. "Pass along my thanks."

"I will. Now, you best take the ladies out of here—"

"I'm not leaving," a feminine voice cut into the conversation. *Mamie.* Frank would know the husky tone anywhere.

He pinned her with a look. "You are indeed leaving, Miss Greene. Your sister, too. This is not a safe place for either of you."

Mamie marched closer, her brown eyes snapping fire. "I'm up two hundred dollars, Tripp. I am *not* leaving."

Frank clenched his hands and dug deep for patience. The maddening woman. Had she any idea of the danger she'd narrowly avoided? She could have been assaulted or raped . . . or worse.

Bald Jack stepped in when Frank faltered. "Mr. Madden asks that you and your sister depart immediately, miss. He also insists you refrain from entering this establishment again."

She pressed her lips together, her chin rising. Frank expected her to argue with the huge man, but she surprised him by saying, "Fine. Allow me to collect my winnings and I'll be on my way."

"Um, Mamie," her sister Florence said behind them, gesturing to the table. The chips collected at their places had disappeared. Another patron had used the distraction as an opportunity to steal whatever winnings the girls had accumulated.

"Where are our winnings?" Mamie stalked over and began searching, as if the chips had merely been misplaced. "They were right here."

Florence shrugged her shoulders.

Bald Jack lifted the injured man and shoved him toward two of Madden's employees, who quickly took their quarry and disappeared. "Now, you three," Jack said to Frank and the Greene sisters. "All of you out. Let's go."

"But we've been robbed," Mamie complained. "Our winnings were stolen. I had over two hundred dollars."

"All due respect, miss, we cannot pay out without chips. Otherwise every man here'd claim he misplaced a stack somewhere. You need to forget about the money and head toward the exit. Immediately."

No one won an argument with Bald Jack, at least

none that had lived to tell about it. Frank could sense, however, from the set of Mamie's chin, that she was determined to try. He decided to intervene, as had been his original intention in coming tonight.

Striding forward, he took Mamie's elbow and began towing her toward the exit. "Come with me."

She struggled but he held fast. "Release me this instant, Tripp."

A large hand settled on Frank's shoulder, shaking him roughly from behind. "No manhandling the ladies. Madden's orders."

Frank resisted the urge to pull free. The last thing he'd ever do was hurt Mamie. "I am not manhandling her." He raised his hands in the air to show his innocence as they continued on. "I was merely assisting her to the door."

Mamie let out an irritated scoff and went ahead, her silk skirts twitching as her bustle swayed. He tried not to stare at the swoop of her shoulders, the arch of her back . . . the curve of her backside.

Tried . . . and failed.

The girl was dashed dangerous.

MAMIE CURSED HER terrible luck.

First, she and Florence had barely made it out of the house earlier. Their father discovered them sneaking down the corridor and Mamie had been forced to lie about attending the opera. She hated lying to her father. His disappointment would be unbearable if he learned the truth.

Then once at the Bronze House, a strange man stationed himself by her side at the roulette table, breathing down her neck for hours . . . and then her two hundred dollars disappeared.

Worst of all, Frank Tripp had arrived. Again.

Her skin pebbled with awareness. She could sense his stare directly between her shoulder blades, but she ignored him as they trudged down the front steps and into the cool New York evening. She loathed him, a man so polished and smooth he put that bronze door behind her to shame. Yes, he was absurdly handsome and charming, but he wielded the qualities like weapons, flirting shamelessly with every woman he encountered and cozying up to the men for favors. He always got what he wanted, with everyone hurrying to follow his orders the second they left his mouth.

He was slippery. Evasive. Baffling.

And most infuriating, the only man Mamie could not figure out.

She had a knack when it came to men, always had. They were easy to talk with—and even easier to manipulate if one knew what she was doing. Unfortunately, most girls hadn't the first clue.

In general, society girls were taught confusing lessons about the opposite gender:

*Be nice, but not too nice or he'll think you are desperate.*

*Smile, but not too wide or he'll think you are daft.*

*Pay attention to him, but not too much or he'll think you are loose.*

*Be firm, but never argue with him or he'll think you are a shrew.*

Complete flimflam, in Mamie's opinion.

Men were simple. They liked cigars, horses and bosoms—not in that order. As well, they liked women who listened and asked them questions. They liked to feel important.

Take her almost-fiancé, Chauncey Livingston. They'd known each other forever and the man could not be more transparent if he were a window. Chauncey kept the same routine every day. He ate the same foods, caroused the same spots. There was absolutely no mystery, and being his wife would hold the same predictability.

Frank Tripp, on the other hand, defied all her rules. He was a veritable enigma. Upon some investigation she'd learned he had no routine. Belonged to all the clubs and attended them randomly. Hardly smoked or gambled. Caroused in all parts of the city. Plus, he cut her off nearly every time she opened her mouth, and he'd never peeked even once at her bosom.

A bosom that was, as she'd been told, quite remarkable.

Florence leaned over as they approached the street. "Your errant knight looks none too pleased."

Mamie gave an unladylike snort. "Hardly a knight. More like a fire-breathing dragon."

"Then best to let you get burned while I find us a hack."

"Coward."

Florence chuckled and continued to the street, head swiveling as she searched for a ride. Within seconds, Tripp appeared at Mamie's side, a scowl on his striking face. Ignoring the fluttering in her stomach, she went on the offensive. "Was it necessary for you to ruin our evening?"

His eyes narrowed sharply. "You mean was it necessary to save you from assault or violation? A man poured some sort of liquid in your drink, likely a drug to incapacitate you. You are welcome, by the way."

"You mean the man on my left who took a vial out of his inside jacket pocket?" She had the pleasure of watching Frank's mouth fall open in surprise. "Yes, Tripp. I saw him. I would not have touched the champagne glass again and had plans on moving tables to escape him. But yes, thank *you* for saving *me*."

A hack rolled up to the curb, so Mamie lifted her skirts and made to move around him. "Wait," he said, shooting a hand out to block her path. "You're not taking a hack. I will escort you home."

"Not necessary. Florence and I are perfectly capable of seeing—"

"It's not up for negotiation, Mamie. Get in my carriage." He pointed to a glossy black vehicle up the block.

"Why?"

He cocked his head. "So that I may take you both home. Are you not listening?"

Lord, the man was intolerable. Using clear logic was the only way to deal with him. "This is the third time you have bounced me from the Bronze House, correct?"

"Correct."

"And on any of those other occasions did you see me to my front door?"

The side of his mouth hitched. "No, I did not."

"Furthermore, did you not call me a 'bored, spoiled child' during our last meeting?"

He didn't bother to hide his amusement as he crossed his arms over his chest. "Yes, Your Honor, I did. Is there a point to all this?"

"You don't care for me and the feeling is definitely mutual—"

"That's not true. Would I give up my evening plans and tramp down here for someone I didn't care for?"

"Yes, if you thought you might lose a client."

A muscle jumped in his cheek as he frowned at her. "If this is about your father, then why haven't I informed him of these excursions of yours?"

Actually, she'd wondered the same herself. "I assume it's part of some elaborate scheme you've concocted. You never do anything without benefit to yourself, I've been told."

"Says the woman who pilfered a money clip from that man in the crowd."

Now it was her jaw that fell open. He saw her swipe the money clip?

"Yes, Mamie, I saw it," he said, answering her silent question. "And while I mean to learn precisely why you are out robbing swells in casinos, I'd prefer to do so from the comfort of my carriage. Come on."

Not robbing, she wanted to tell him. At least not the way he assumed. More like redistributing. These uptown men had more money than sense while those downtown were starving and living in squalor. Young women and men who sold their bodies for coin. Matchstick girls with their glowing, rotting flesh. Babies covered in dirt and filth. Men angry and violent over the lack of opportunities afforded them.

Mamie never kept what she took. She gave the money either to a charity or directly to a tenement family herself. There were too many needy families in the city, and the charities were oftentimes more concerned with temperance and religious conversion than distributing aid. Mamie would rather not see any restrictions placed on relief, which was why she traveled downtown herself a few times a month.

Not that she'd tell Tripp any of this. Only her sisters knew . . . and Mamie meant to see it stayed that way.

She lifted her chin and stared Tripp down. "Unless you are prepared to kidnap me—and my sister—then I think not. Now, thank you for ruining my—"

Before she could blink, Tripp bent and swooped her off the ground, his arms sturdy and unforgiving around her. Mamie let out a shriek and struggled in his hold. "Tripp, for God's sake, put me down!"

The blasted man ignored her and started for his carriage. Another man walked toward them, his curious gaze taking in the scene of a tall man carrying a well-dressed woman along Thirty-Third Street. "Help," she said to the stranger. "He is kidnapping me."

The man shot a concerned glance at Tripp. However, the lawyer never broke stride as he answered, "Wife's had a bit too much champagne, I'm afraid. I am seeing her and her sister home. Come along, sis." He threw the last part over his shoulder and Mamie was horrified to see a grinning Florence hurrying to catch up.

The stranger continued on his way, not intervening. "He's lying," Mamie called to the man's back. "He is a consummate liar. Every word out of his mouth is a fabrication."

"How's this for a truth? You are a pain in my backside," Tripp muttered.

"I could say the same of you—and put me down. I am able to walk. I promise to come with you."

"Forgive me if I don't believe you."

She stiffened and pushed her palm against his shoulder. Heavens, he was sturdy. "I've never broken a promise in my life."

He made a rude noise in his throat. "Is that so? You promised not to gamble again the last time I caught you. You also promised not to visit casinos, saloons, dance halls, brothels, opium dens or any other disreputable destinations. And yet, here you are."

Well, yes. She had promised those things—but only because she hadn't planned on getting caught. She sniffed. "I crossed my fingers when I made those promises."

"I rest my case."

"That makes two of us, then. I never believe a word you say." He lied for a living, after all.

*He hates you. He thinks you are a spoiled society girl, flitting about with no purpose except to cause trouble.* Fine. Better if everyone believed as much. Otherwise, she'd never be able to help those in need, those with the misfortune of being born on the wrong end of town.

So perhaps she and Frank had more in common than she originally thought. They were both liars.

That realization didn't bother her nearly as much as it should have.

He stepped aside and let Florence board first. "Traitor," Mamie hissed at her sibling, only to hear Florence's laugh as she disappeared inside. Tripp then placed Mamie on the ground. "After you," he said with a sweep of his arm.

*I shall not talk to him. I owe him absolutely nothing.*

Resolved, Mamie ascended the steps and climbed into Tripp's carriage.

# Chapter Two

❧

$\mathcal{H}$er resolve lasted only a few seconds.

As soon as the wheels began turning, Frank scowled at her. "Have you a death wish? Why are you so very eager to find trouble?"

Florence snickered but Mamie kept her gaze trained on Tripp. "I do not answer to you."

"Wrong. Unless you'd like for your father to know precisely what you are about, tell me why you are pinching money clips at casinos."

"Threats? Really, Tripp. I had thought better of you."

He leaned in, the lines of his face stark in the semidarkness, his eyes glittering with intensity. "When it comes to getting what I want, Mamie, there is nothing I will not do."

Perhaps it was the words or the husky promise in his tone, but a shiver of excitement worked its way down her spine. Had he been flirting with her? No, that was ludicrous. The man loathed her. "Tell my father, then. Go on and tell him all of my exploits." She angled toward him. "If you do, I will inform him of the other occasions you pulled me from that casino—occasions you failed to mention to him."

He drummed his fingers on his knees, his gaze fixed outside on the buildings as the silence stretched. Florence elbowed Mamie and gave her a wink of approval. Mamie tried not to smile. Tripp clearly thought he could best the Greene sisters, but they had faced tougher foes.

Mamie, at twenty-three years old, was the eldest and most respectable Greene sibling. It was her duty to marry well and be seen in society, a role she'd never questioned as it had started before she could walk. Her path in life was preordained, her marriage decided upon in an understanding between the Greene and Livingston families when she and Chauncey were babes. While becoming Mrs. Chauncey Livingston was not her ideal future, Mamie had agreed on the condition that her sisters would be free to choose their own paths—a pact her sisters knew nothing about.

Florence was two years younger than Mamie and a constant source of vexation to their parents. With no interest in conforming to society's rules, Florence spoke her mind, escaped the house nearly every night and kept a stash of bawdy books under her bed. To date, she'd turned down four marriage proposals.

Their youngest sister, Justine, was two years younger than Florence. She was to debut next spring, though she continued to fight her mother on such a "waste of everyone's time and money." A suffragette and do-gooder at heart, Justine would much rather take to the streets in protest or collect for charities than pay afternoon calls to "old women with narrow minds."

Even though they were all different, the three Greene girls stuck together. Mamie would do anything for her sisters and they in return for her.

"Perhaps I'll tell your fiancé instead," Tripp said, regaining her attention.

Would Chauncey even care? They led completely separate lives at the moment, a last gasp of freedom before the shackles of marriage descended. "Go ahead. I doubt he'd believe you."

"Mamie." Tripp dragged a hand through his perfect hair. "You must realize stealing is wrong. If you are caught, you'll be arrested. Your family will be humiliated."

"No, because if I am arrested I shall send for *you*. Then you will arrive and work some of your lawyer magic." She waved her hands like the conjurer she'd seen perform last year. "I'll be released in no time at all."

"How are you so certain I will ride to your rescue?"

"Because my father would be very disappointed if his oldest daughter sent for his lawyer and said lawyer ignored the message."

Tripp shook his head, his lip curled in what was most likely disgust. "You are not my client, Mamie. My loyalties are to your father, not you."

"Then why are you trailing me all over town, insisting I depart these fine establishments?"

He threw up his hands. "You are talking in circles."

"Ha. How does it feel to be on the other side?"

"Perhaps I'll refuse your father's business, refer him elsewhere. Wash my hands of the Greenes once and for all."

Now that surprised her. Would he really? Her father likely paid Tripp handsomely, but so did every other swell, tycoon and crime lord in the city. He could hardly need the money.

"Ah, my little rebellious dove. I see you never contemplated such an outcome," he said, his voice smooth with superiority. It had Mamie digging her nails into her palms.

"I am not your little anything—and I think you are bluffing."

He shrugged. "Sweetheart, you're looking at the best bluffer in the city of New York, perhaps the entire state. In fact, there are those who say I've turned it into an art form. But I rarely bluff in relation to my own clients. I tend to be brutally honest when I am being paid to advise them."

"Yet I am not your client, as you have repeatedly stated."

She watched a muscle jump in his jaw. Excellent. If he thought to run verbal circles around a Greene, he was mistaken.

"This is not getting us closer to discovering why you are working as a pickpocket."

"Give it up, Mr. Tripp," Florence said, finally joining the conversation. "Mamie has always done as she pleased. No one is able to talk her out of anything."

Mamie thought about elbowing her sister but couldn't fault Florence for telling the truth. Besides, better Tripp learned of Mamie's stubbornness now.

"And you are aware, I suppose," Tripp said to

Florence, "of what your sister is doing, of the danger she faces? That makes you an accomplice."

Mamie didn't appreciate the vague threat behind those words. "No one is on trial here, Tripp—"

"Not yet anyway," the lawyer murmured.

"And you are worrying for nothing. I'm very good at what I do."

He snorted—actually snorted!—and said, "Madden and I both spotted your clumsy move from the balcony. You couldn't have been more obvious."

"Clumsy! That is—"

"Wait, you met Mr. Madden?" Florence said, leaning in with wide eyes. "What's he like?"

Mamie paused, her anger shifting to confusion for one brief second. Why was her sister inquiring about the infamous casino owner?

"I hardly know him," Frank said, "but he's not a man to be trifled with . . . which is why you two must never return to the House."

The order was unnecessary. Mamie wouldn't gain admittance to the casino ever again, not after tonight's fiasco. "You were spying on me from the balcony?"

"Hardly spying. Merely observing for a few minutes while Madden and I chatted. Then I noticed the man spiking your drink with God knows what while you were robbing the customers blind."

Would he ever stop beating that particular drum?

"How does one get up to the balcony?" Florence asked it innocently enough, yet Mamie knew her sister all too well.

"Florence," she said in warning. "We should discuss this later."

"Oh, you're no fun." Florence angled toward the

window and fixed her stare on the passing buildings.

"See." Frank gestured toward Florence. "You are corrupting your poor sister."

Mamie smothered a laugh at that idea. Florence needed no corrupting. Indeed, she was the one who had corrupted the other two Greene sisters. "Why must you always assume the worst of me? You hardly know me."

"Call it intuition guided by history. Do I have your promise to cease these excursions and stealing from others?"

For once, Mamie gave it to him straight. "Absolutely not."

"Damn it, Mamie—"

"We're almost there," Florence said and pointed. The Greene mansion loomed just up the street. Mamie was vaguely disappointed. She hadn't had this much fun in one evening in quite some time.

Yet all that fun could come to a disastrous end if Tripp informed her father of what had happened.

She folded her hands and kept her shoulder relaxed as she faced him. "What do you plan to do?"

He stared at her, his thoughts cleverly cloaked behind his flat expression. She couldn't begin to read his intentions. Her heart pounded beneath her corset, a staccato of panic that her efforts to help others may very well be stymied because of this maddening man. Perhaps she should've confessed all to him, appealed to his sense of justice, rather than antagonized him.

When it came to Frank Tripp, however, Mamie couldn't seem to help herself. He brought out the worst in her.

*It's because you find him appealing. And intriguing. And intelligent. And—*

Oh, for heaven's sake. She needed to cease that line of thinking immediately. Heat spread over her skin and she looked away, unable to hold his gaze.

He was her father's attorney and a thorn in her side. That was all.

A fist thumped on the roof and Tripp called out to his driver, "Take us to the servant's entrance." She cast him a quick glance and found him still watching her. His lips twisted in a self-satisfied smile. "You live to steal another day, Miss Greene. However, I will get answers from you tomorrow night. Shall we say Sherry's at ten o'clock?"

She blinked. "You are blackmailing me into having dinner with you?"

"Yes, it appears that I am."

"Even for you, Tripp, this is a new low. I won't do it."

"You most definitely will." His eyes darted toward her mouth before he captured her stare once more. "I get what I want, Mamie. Never forget it."

Undoubtedly he intended the words as menacing. Instead of fear, however, warmth settled in her belly as she snuck into the servant's entrance a few moments later.

THE BRONZE HOUSE appeared quite different in the daylight. With the afternoon sun pouring through the overhead skylights, one could hardly miss the expensive cherry furniture, gilded accents and exotic rugs. Frank had seen upper Fifth Avenue drawing rooms shabbier than this.

He continued to follow Bald Jack across the casino floor, past the silent roulette tables. That only served to remind him of Mamie. God above, that woman. Erasing her from his mind today had proven near impossible. Thankfully, some urgent requests from clients had distracted him . . . until now. What caused a gorgeous woman from a prominent, wealthy family to pick pockets? Was it the thrill? And where had she learned such a skill? There were no thieving classes for society ladies that he was aware of.

Frank had represented clients in all sorts of various predicaments over the years. These days, he focused on high society clients, which meant mostly delicate personal and financial cases. But he had defended murder, theft, kidnapping and everything in between. He'd even represented a woman being sued because her cat reportedly kept a neighbor awake at night. He'd truly seen it all in his eight years as a lawyer in New York City.

At least he thought he had.

A woman of Mamie's background and social status, a thief? It made no sense. Duncan Greene was a generous man, something Frank had personally witnessed time and again. If Mamie needed money, why not ask her father?

*Because the money needs to remain secret.*

So, was it a hop habit? A lover bilking her for cash? Blackmail? Frank vowed to receive an answer tonight at dinner—an appointment he was anxiously anticipating to an absurd degree.

Truthfully, his anticipation had more to do with the woman herself than gaining insight into her criminalities. She challenged him in a way that both infuriated and intrigued him at the same time. In a world of glittering diamonds, Mamie was a fiery ruby, a flame that burned brighter than anything else around it.

She was also unattainable. Nearly engaged to the Livingston scion, Mamie belonged to a rare social circle that included few and excluded many. Her future did not involve a lawyer born at the wrong end of town. He'd gone to great lengths to hide his Five Points past, create a history acceptable to his fancy clients. A woman like Mamie, one who certainly never did as she was told, could bring down everything he'd built.

Still, even with that reminder, he would take her to dinner. Perhaps it was the small boy in him—the one who'd grown up in filth and violence, the one who'd yearned to escape uptown—who wanted to sit in the city's best restaurant with the most desirable debutante and have the whole world take note.

Or perhaps it was the man who'd fantasized about her for the better part of three months.

Bald Jack stopped in front of an ornate wooden door. They had traveled deep into the building, far from the casino floor. Jack turned the latch and threw open the panel, then gestured for Frank to enter.

Clayton Madden sat behind a huge walnut desk, his head bent as he scribbled with a pen. "Have a seat, Tripp."

Frank did as ordered, while Jack quietly retreated and closed the door. Madden put down his pen and looked up. "Thank you for coming. I hope to not take up too much of your time."

"It's quite all right. I'm always happy to provide advice when requested."

"I'll get right to the point. Your reputation paints you as a problem solver. I have a problem that needs solving."

"Which is?"

Madden rested his elbows on the desk and steepled his fingers. "I wish to build another casino, a little farther north on the East Side. I found the perfect spot and bought all the necessary land, save one plot. That owner refuses to sell to me. Some do-gooder has convinced her to hold on to the property." He said the words with a good deal of derision and Frank suppressed a smile.

"I need this last plot of land," Madden said. "It's smack in the middle of the damn block."

Frank lifted a shoulder. "So make her a better offer."

"My offer has been above fair market value. I refuse to go higher." He leaned in. "I want to take her to court."

"On what grounds?"

"I had hoped you might suggest the grounds."

Frank shook his head. He could not fabricate laws. "If she owns the home and hasn't broken any zoning violations then you have no case."

"What if I threaten her with legal action, no matter how bogus, to waste her time and money. Not to mention the embarrassment. She would still need to defend herself, even against a frivolous suit."

Ah. No wonder Madden's lawyers were objecting. "In theory, yes. What is costly for her, however, is also costly for you. Why not start construction on either side of her? My guess is she won't appreciate the noise or the chaos and she'll move."

Madden's expression shifted into something hopeful and devious. "Build around her house?"

"Sure. Have your plans drawn up, get your permits. Then start demolition. I predict she'll move before you break ground on the casino."

"I like it. Even by annoying her I have won." He pointed at Frank. "I like how you think, Tripp."

"Thank you. By the way, I know a great architect. She's the best."

"She?"

"Mrs. Phillip Mansfield. Responsible for the new Mansfield Hotel."

Madden flipped open the lid of the enameled box on his desk and withdrew two cigars. "Ah, I've heard of her. I do appreciate a woman who shakes things up. Speaking of women, how did Greene take the news last night?"

Frank merely pressed his lips together.

The edges of Madden's mouth curled as he trimmed the cigars. "You didn't tell him. I am shocked," he said, his tone suggesting the opposite.

As Madden lit a cigar, Frank tried to defend himself. "I have merely postponed the conversation. Miss Greene and I are having dinner this evening, at which point I'll learn what these outings are all about."

"You assume they have a purpose?" Madden handed the unlit cigar to Frank. "These bored society girls love to go slumming downtown. See how the other half lives."

"You're not exactly downtown," Frank pointed out as he pocketed the cigar for later. "If they wanted that, they'd travel to the Bowery." Frank had grown up not far from there, where he'd gained firsthand knowledge of downtown squalor. Memories that haunted him still, ensuring he'd do anything and everything to never return there.

Madden exhaled a long plume of white smoke. "The sister is an expert at roulette. Craps, too. She was up two hundred and thirty dollars by my count."

High praise coming from the owner. "So the story of the stolen chips was true."

Madden shrugged. "I never saw any chips disappear."

The liar. Madden knew everything that went on in his club. "Where would Florence Greene learn to gamble like that?"

"I couldn't say. Seems both the Greene sisters have secrets."

"Any chance you'll tell me about your squabble with their father?"

Madden puffed on his cigar and then tapped the ash in a dish. "Seeing as how you represent him, I think it best if I keep those reasons to myself."

"Fair enough. I don't need conflict of interest charges brought against me." He checked his pocket watch, then rose. Another client awaited, this one downtown, before he needed to return home and bathe for his dinner appointment with Mamie. Ignoring the sizzle that slid through him at the thought of seeing her, he said, "I have another meeting, unless there was something else?"

Madden got to his feet. "No, you have been most helpful." The owner reached into a drawer and pulled out a fat stack of cash. He held it out to Frank. "Thank you for your time."

Frank waved away the money. "I'll bill you—"

"Nonsense. I hate to be indebted to anyone, even for a short period. Take this, and if it's not enough then see Jack for more."

Frank accepted the payment. He'd worked with enough men of Madden's ilk to know that arguing was futile. Refusing their generosity only angered them, a complication Frank didn't need at the moment. "Thank you. Good luck with your project."

"I don't need luck." Madden put his cigar between his teeth. "I own a casino. I am the goddamn luck."

WOMEN WERE NOT supposed to play billiards. Well, there was no law prohibiting women from playing . . . but there might as well have been. The billiards room in nearly every fancy home was located far away from the common areas used by women. It was the goal, by segregating these male domains, to shelter ladies from the smell of tobacco and ribald language. To allow men a place away from the rest of the family, where they could drink and commune with other men.

In the Greene household, however, the three sisters spent more time in the Moorish-style billiards room than hardly anywhere else. Their father never played and the girls had taken over the space as their own.

That afternoon Mamie skipped paying calls with her mother to play a match of fifteen-ball pool with her siblings. The rules were simple: the player who reached sixty-one points first won the game, and whoever won best of three games collected the pot of seventy-five dollars. The second game was underway, with Justine easily handling the first. The youngest Greene sister, if not for her love of charities and being born the wrong gender, could have had a thriving career as a professional billiardist.

Mamie hadn't given up just yet, however. She was determined to win the money and divide it between the many struggling families she knew downtown.

Florence studied the table and debated her shot. "Shall I sink the nine or try for the ten off the rails?" Justine opened her mouth, but Florence threw her a quelling look. "Do not answer. I'm merely thinking aloud."

Justine held up her hands and remained silent. Florence lined up and tried for the ten ball . . . only to miss the pocket. "Hell," she cursed.

Justine slid off her stool and strolled to the table. "You cannot carom to save your life. You never correctly judge the distance."

"Please stop giving advice." Florence dropped into a chair. "No one likes a know-it-all."

"Or a sore loser," Mamie pointed out before popping the rest of an almond macaroon in her mouth.

Florence reached over to snatch the last macaroon off the tray. "Why did I let you talk me into putting up my last twenty-five dollars? I was saving it for something."

"Like another trip to a casino?"

"Oh, that reminds me." Justine lined up and took a shot, sending the cue ball flying over the green baize. "How was your excursion last evening?"

Mamie said nothing, not certain where to even begin, and Florence took the opportunity to weigh in. "We won over two hundred dollars, a fight broke out, someone drugged Mamie's drink and our chips were stolen."

Justine sank another ball. "Goodness. Glad you were both unharmed. What was the fight about?"

"Frank Tripp dropped from the ceiling to attack the man who drugged Mamie's champagne."

"Frank Tripp?" Another ball fell into a pocket. "Daddy's attorney?"

"The one and only. He carried Mamie to his carriage—"

"That is quite enough, Florence. Justine does not need to hear every detail."

Justine moved to the other side of the table. "Yes, Justine certainly does. Why on earth did he carry you?"

"He insisted on driving us home. I was more inclined to hire a hack."

"You should have seen it," Florence said. "Tripp jumped down from the balcony like an avenging angel, ready to pummel this man. Then he wouldn't leave Mamie's side. I think Tripp is sweet on our eldest sister."

Mamie's stomach fluttered. "You are ridiculous."

Justine missed her next shot. Frowning, she waved at Mamie. "Your turn. Put me down for twenty-four points, Florence."

In studying the table, Mamie saw Justine had already claimed the balls with the highest point values. That would make winning more difficult. She aimed for the seven ball first.

"I am not ridiculous," Florence said as Mamie leaned over the table. "I saw the way he looked at you when you weren't paying attention, like he was a starving wolf and you were a sweet little lamb he planned to bite."

Mamie's hand slipped at that, the tip of her cue digging into the baize. "Dash it, Florence."

Florence and Justine both snickered, which had Mamie's blood rising. She leaned on her cue and faced her sisters. "I have no interest in him. I only agreed to share dinner with him tonight because it was the only way to keep him from telling Daddy."

"Keep who from telling me what?"

Mamie swung around at the deep voice and found her father in the doorway. Oh, dear. How much had he heard? "Hello, Daddy. I thought you were downtown today."

At six feet tall and over two hundred pounds, Duncan Greene commanded every room he entered. His family, one of the oldest and most prominent in New York, had built a shipping empire that now spanned the globe, an empire their father now directed. Before marrying their mother, he'd been an amateur baseball player, a boxer, hammer thrower and swimmer. Their mother said Duncan had been the only man capable of sweeping her off her feet, both literally and figuratively.

He strolled inside the room and thrust his hands in his pockets. "Returned early. I thought we might have tea together. I've been missing my girls."

Florence ran to him first and their father opened his arms wide, enveloping her in a fierce hug. "Hello, Flo." Justine was next, receiving the same larger-than-life embrace. Mamie waited until last. She and her father had always been the closest, possibly because he had no son on which to dote. So he'd doted on Mamie instead, making sure she would carry on the Greene legacy.

He held her tight and pressed a kiss to the top of her head. "Marion, do you have something to tell me? Perhaps you could start with why you lied about attending the opera last night."

She let out the breath she'd been holding. The opera had been a poor lie, one she'd been forced to think up on the spot. "Because we went to a party, Daddy. Mother would not approve of the family and you know how I hate to put you in the middle of these silly social squabbles between us."

He grunted. "You let me worry about your mother. I don't like lies, no matter the reason. Now, where are you going this evening?"

"I'm having dinner with Mr. Tripp at Sherry's." Undoubtedly, someone would see them together and alert her father anyway. Better to tell him the truth now.

"Frank Tripp, my attorney?" He angled to see her face. "I wasn't aware the two of you had more than a passing acquaintance."

She lifted a shoulder in what she hoped came off as a casual move. "He was at last evening's party and asked me to dinner. I had no reason to refuse." *Because he blackmailed me.*

"Girls," he said to Florence and Justine. "Give your sister and me the room."

Pool match forgotten, both the younger Greene sisters hurried into the corridor, where Florence cast a last worried glance in Mamie's direction before disappearing. Her younger sister undoubtedly feared Mamie would tell their father everything. Florence should know better. Mamie had no intention of telling her father about their trip to the casino, ever.

Her father released her and walked to the tray of small sandwiches and sweets. He selected two smoked salmon sandwiches and popped one in his mouth. "I have known Frank Tripp a long time," he said after he swallowed. "And I like him—as my lawyer. That does not mean I want him for a son-in-law."

*"Daddy!"*

"Mamie, you are old enough to understand how these things can happen. But Frank is not of our world. He's not Chauncey." He finished the other sandwich in one bite. "Do you get what I am saying?"

Yes, quite clearly. Her father thought Frank Tripp a brilliant lawyer but not good enough for his eldest daughter. His concern was unfounded, however. "You have nothing to worry about. I'm not interested in Frank Tripp."

"My dear, he could sell water to a drowning man, he's that persuasive."

"Well, he won't persuade me. You know Chauncey and I are still promised."

Her father shook his head. "Won't matter to Tripp. If he wants you, he'll move heaven and earth to have you—not that I will grant my consent. You will marry Chauncey, no matter what happens."

"I know. We've discussed this a hundred times."

"I just need to make sure you don't forget it. We made a promise to the Livingstons and I don't think I must remind you what that promise means to me."

She rolled her eyes and parroted the words she'd

heard so often. *"It's the joining of two of the most prestigious families in New York as a favor to the man who once saved my life in the war."*

"That's no small debt, Marion. And Chauncey will make a fine husband. You've known him your entire life. It's not as if I'm sending you off to England to marry an old stodgy duke or a philandering earl."

The idea gave Mamie chills. At least she would live near her family after her marriage. "Don't worry, Daddy. I won't disappoint you."

"That's my girl." He leaned in and kissed the top of her head. "You're my favorite, you know. But don't tell your sisters."

She smiled and patted his chest. "I wouldn't dare. Your secret is safe with me."

"I love Florence and Justine dearly, but I don't care who they marry. You, on the other hand, are different. You are the one who will carry on the Greene legacy by marrying Chauncey. Don't let Frank Tripp—or any other man—try to convince you otherwise because I will not bend on this."

# Chapter Three

$\mathcal{H}$e had arrived first.

*Damn*, Mamie thought as she was led through Sherry's crowded main dining room. She'd purposely come fifteen minutes early, hoping to beat Tripp here. The additional time would have allowed her a chance to compose herself and calm her nerves before seeing him.

The crafty man had robbed her of that chance.

He stood, straightened his cuffs and threw her a wide smile. His black-and-white eveningwear perfectly complemented his handsome features. The vest and coat highlighted his wide shoulders and flat stomach, with the white bow tie and collar contrasting his dark hair. His blue eyes were sharp and shrewd, but never cold. No, they burned and sparked, as if his legendary ambition and intelligence heated an internal forge visible in his gaze.

Curious eyes in the dining room tracked his movements, guests angling to get a better view of Frank Tripp. He was a man that women noticed and men either admired or feared.

*If he wants you, he'll move heaven and earth to have you.*

She swallowed at the reminder of the words, her tongue suddenly thick in her mouth.

*Oh, this is ridiculous.* She hadn't been nervous around a man in her entire life. She certainly wouldn't start now.

Drawing herself up, she strode closer to him. His stare remained on her face, not once dipping to appreciate the care with which she had dressed tonight. Arriving from Paris only a few days ago, the cream silk evening gown was heavily embroidered on both the skirt and revealing bodice.

She remembered once asking her mother why they dressed for every occasion, even when no one else was around to notice. Her mother had said, *We dress for ourselves, for how it makes us feel, not to impress anyone else.*

Well, tonight Mamie felt beautiful, powerful and more than capable of standing up to one cunning lawyer.

"I was certain you wouldn't come," were the first words out of his mouth. "Seeing how you routinely break your promises."

Her nerves evaporated. This was familiar ground, trading barbs and nursing the resulting anger inside her. "Are we to start with insults, then? I had assumed we'd wait at least until the first course had been served."

Though he didn't appear chastised in the least, he lifted her gloved hand and brushed his lips over her knuckles. "Miss Greene, how beautiful you are this evening."

Goose bumps rushed over her skin. "I would thank you for the invitation but as I had no choice in the matter . . ."

He chuckled and held out a chair for her. "It seems we both have trouble holding our tongues. What would you say to a truce?"

She lowered herself into the seat, taking care not to crush her bustle or train. Waiters began moving about the table, and champagne was quickly uncorked and poured. Tripp lifted his glass and Mamie followed suit. "A truce," he said.

"A truce," she answered and tapped her crystal to his. They both sipped and she purposely looked away as he drank. She didn't need to watch his lips pressed on the delicate glass, his throat working as he swallowed . . . Was the room always this warm?

He placed his glass on the table. "I received an interesting cable from your father tonight."

She fought to hide her surprise, though the tips of her ears burned. "I apologize. He overheard me discussing tonight's dinner with my sisters."

"No need. I'm quite familiar with Duncan's bluster. What did you tell them?"

"Tell who?"

"Your sisters. What did you tell them about tonight?"

"That you had blackmailed me into coming."

"That's all?"

He was angling for something, yet she had no idea what. "If you had hoped we waxed poetic over your multitude of charms, rest assured we did not."

"That is merely because you haven't yet experienced my charms."

*Yet?* Was he . . . ? What did he mean, exactly? Mamie lunged for her champagne, desperate to cool her insides. Was there not any fresh air in this blasted restaurant? "Putting your charms aside for now, what of my father's cable? What did it say?"

Tripp shrugged. "That you are promised to Livingston in a long-standing agreement between two important families. He values my insight as his lawyer, et cetera. Exactly what one would expect."

She drained the rest of the champagne in her glass. "He told me you could sell water to a drowning man."

Tripp laughed at that, the lines of his face easing, making him appear younger and more carefree. And yes, more handsome, dash it. "I've never tried so I could not say. Tell me, what about Livingston appeals to you?"

"You cannot be serious."

He held up his hands as the waiter refilled their glasses. "Are we not to make polite conversation? I genuinely wish to know. What is it about a man like Livingston that interests you?"

This was hardly polite conversation. "It's none of your business. And I have known Chauncey all my life. The decision for the two of us to marry was made years ago."

"And you never complained? Never considered refusing?"

Of course she had, years ago. But her father would never relent. "It's a good match. Our families are close and he is the type of man I'm expected to marry."

Tripp's mouth fell open before he quickly shut it. "A ringing endorsement if I ever heard one. Are you not bothered by the rumors of actresses and opium dens?"

Actresses? Opium dens? That hardly seemed

like the Chauncey she knew, a man more interested in sailing and horses than vice. She studied Tripp's face to gauge the veracity of those wild claims . . . yet she saw no sign of falsehood. *The man is a practiced liar. Believe nothing that comes out of his mouth.* "We are not yet betrothed. Chauncey is free to spend his time as he sees fit."

"Ah, yes. That brings us to how you are spending your time—"

Black-coated waiters returned with plates. They served Mamie first. She stopped the waiter with her hand. "What is this?"

"A bisque of shrimp."

"I didn't order it."

The waiter looked at Tripp then back to her. "The gentleman has preordered your dinner, miss."

Without asking her first? Mamie took a deep breath. "Please have this removed. I have an aversion to shrimp. Mr. Sherry knows my dinner preferences. Tell him it is for Miss Marion Greene. If you would ask him to bring me those items instead, I would be most grateful."

The waiter nodded and took the soup away. "And you, sir?"

Tripp rubbed a hand over his jaw. "Take mine away as well and just bring two of everything in Miss Greene's order."

The waiters disappeared and Tripp shifted in his chair, his expression contrite. "I apologize. I had no idea you hated shrimp. I only thought to save time by ordering in advance."

Save time . . . and make decisions in her stead. "I'm quite capable of speaking my own mind."

"So I'm gathering," he murmured. "Look, this

dinner has clearly started off on the wrong note. I apologize. May we begin again?"

Two apologies? She hadn't expected that. "If I agree then will you drop this inquiry into my affairs?"

"You mean your stealing?"

She sucked in a harsh breath and cast glances at the neighboring tables. Thankfully, no one was close enough to overhear them. "Have a care, Tripp. I've not yet agreed to start over."

"And neither have I. Remember, I know your secret. And if you wish for me to keep said secret then you'd best explain yourself."

She would do no such thing. "Would you believe kleptomania?"

"Not even under oath."

She narrowed her eyes at him. "What is the purpose of this dinner? For you to pry into my life? Or to pass judgment and cast aspersions on my character? Because I had thought we called a truce."

The lines of his face sharpened as he leaned in. She imagined this was what he looked like when handling a difficult witness in court. "I told you I wanted answers, Mamie, and I mean to have them."

God, his arrogance. Her heart was pounding in her chest, every angry beat a reminder of how much she disliked him. "I am not on trial, Tripp—and I owe you absolutely nothing."

Seething, Frank lounged in his chair and watched as Louis Sherry fawned over Mamie. The restaurateur had arrived moments ago with the first course to apologize for the mistake with their order. Then he promised to bring her all her favorite dishes tonight.

Frank had absolved the owner of any wrongdoing, of course, but Sherry wouldn't hear of it. He prided himself on service and couldn't bear the thought of any customer leaving unsatisfied. While Frank respected Sherry for the dedication to his guests, he mostly felt annoyed at the interruption.

Annoyed because he still hadn't received an answer on the reason behind her theft.

Annoyed because he'd erred badly this evening—and he hated to fail.

Annoyed because she looked exceptionally beautiful.

Annoyed because he had minded propriety instead of reserving a private suite for them.

He downed the rest of his champagne. A private suite with an unmarried woman who was the daughter of his client and who hated everything about him? Had he lost his damn mind?

There was no denying his fascination with Mamie. Fascination . . . and attraction. Yes, he was drawn to her. Not that he could act on it, but she was a spark that lit something inside him. He hadn't experienced it before, this burning obsession, and certainly not with a female who loathed him. Who fought him at every turn. So why this one?

He had to forget her and move on. New York City was full of women, all of various shapes and colors. Finding a companion for a night or two hadn't ever been a problem before, though it had been a while for him. A month, perhaps? He needed to dedicate more time to the endeavor, he thought as his gaze unwittingly drifted to Mamie's décolletage. *Oh, fuck.* That view did not help matters whatsoever.

He quickly shifted toward the windows. *Stop*

*staring at her.* She was the daughter of a client and not some trollop on display at a dance hall.

He needed to visit Mrs. Wright's on West Twenty-Seventh Street and work this . . . restlessness out of his system. Tonight.

"What has put you in such a sour mood? Unable to lie to any judges today?"

He met her amused stare. "I'm hardly sour."

Exhaling, she picked up her soup spoon and sampled the cream of artichoke soup. "I won't answer your questions. I suppose that leaves us at an impasse."

Frank nearly snorted. He'd never been at an impasse in his life. No, he was paid—quite handsomely—to maneuver around impasses. A very good thing, too. Seeing as the direct approach was clearly not working with Mamie, he'd need creativity and cunning to deal with her. Patience. Skill.

All that at which he excelled.

Growing up with nothing, Frank had learned early to play the long game. He'd spent years studying diligently, taking odd jobs, saving money, working through college. High marks had earned him an apprenticeship with an established attorney, where even more saving and studying had been required. No one gave you anything free in this life and the best rewards came as a result of hard work.

So he could wait for answers. He'd slowly chip away at Mamie's resistance and build her trust until she told him everything.

"I suppose it does," he lied and began eating his soup. "Tell me about your family. Your sisters. What are they like?"

She blinked, possibly confused at his easy capitulation, but answered. "Well, you've met Florence. My father calls her the hellion."

"Why?"

"Because she believes rules don't apply to her. She's fearless."

"And you follow the rules?"

The edges of her mouth turned up slightly before she sipped another spoonful of soup. "To you, it might seem like I do not. However, believe it or not, I'm the responsible one."

"I don't believe it, actually." He reached for his champagne glass. "Nothing about what I have observed over the last six months demonstrates responsibility."

"You caught me in unexpected locations on three occasions. The rest of the time I'm playing dutiful daughter, society debutante and charity worker."

"An unproven claim," he could not help but return. She flashed him an angry glare and he held up his hands. "I apologize. Undoubtedly you are right and I have misjudged you." Not likely.

*Patience, Frank.*

"And what of the youngest Greene sister, the one who has yet to come out?"

"Justine." A fond smile softened her expression. "She is the best of all of us. That girl will change New York City one day."

"How so?"

"She sees the good in everyone. A do-gooder by nature. Wishes to make the world a better place."

He cocked his head and studied her. "You admire her."

"Yes, I rather do. It's hard not to, really—though

she did take me in a game of billiards for twenty-five dollars earlier today."

"You play?" That surprised him.

"A bit. Our father hardly uses the billiards room so it's become our clubhouse of sorts. What about you? Do you play?"

"A time or two." A lie. Frank had practically paid for college using his pool-playing skills. No need to recount those sordid tales, especially as he'd told everyone he came from a wealthy family.

Black-coated waiters arrived to clear the soup bowls as she asked, "What of your family?"

A heaviness settled in his stomach, one that had nothing to do with food. "Happily living in Chicago," he lied.

"Is that so? What does your father do?"

Toast points topped with caviar were placed on the table, but Frank hardly noticed. *Dead from alcohol after beating his wife and family for years.* "My grandfather made some money out in Dakota. Copper mine." The falsehood tripped easily off his tongue after so many years.

Her gaze narrowed slightly. "And where did you go to school?"

"Yale."

"Was any of that the truth?"

He stilled. No one had ever seen through the stories he told to protect himself. No. One. "Why on earth would I lie?"

"I don't know." She shook her head. "But your eyes . . . they dimmed when you were just speaking. I get the sense you're not telling me the truth."

Panic gripped the edges of his chest, squeezing.

He could only imagine telling her the *real* story of his childhood.

*Well, you see, I grew up in a shack down off Worth Street. In fact, a tenement would have been a palace in comparison. There were seven of us packed inside, practically on top of each other in the filth and grime. One brother died on the streets in a gang fight. Another brother was nearly killed in a factory machine accident. My two sisters . . . Well, let's just say they were put to work early. Me? I hustled and studied. And, thanks to the generosity of a saloon owner who pitied me, I made it out. I changed my last name and went to a boarding school as a charity case. Once there, I never looked back.*

He studied his soup as if memorizing it. "I'm due for a visit, is all. My mother's been after me for the better part of six months to come home."

She heaved a sigh. "The Greenes may be rich but we are not stupid."

He was beginning to see that. Not that he ever thought her stupid, per se, but she was far more complex than he'd given her credit for. But he still wasn't telling her the truth.

No one knew his history . . . and no one ever would.

"But I will let it go," she said, popping a piece of toast and caviar in her mouth. "For now."

He couldn't help it: he chuckled. "I'm beginning to think you are the lawyer at this table. I feel like I'm on the witness stand."

"Without even trying, I might add. Imagine if I actually devoted my energy to the task." She appeared all too pleased with herself, with her eyes sparkling and a wide grin on her face. The verbal sparring between them excited her as well, and that knowledge slipped under his skin to wrap around his insides, heating him everywhere. If she were not the daughter of a client or twenty-three years old and unmarried . . . the two of them might have had a great deal of fun together in bed.

But she *was* those things and to pretend otherwise was foolish.

Frank had gone to great lengths to distance himself from his childhood, Five Points and the rest of the Murphies. What was he supposed to do, invite those miscreants to Fifth Avenue for tea? Yes, he secretly kept tabs on them. Sent money to his mother anonymously. Had even bailed his brother out of the Tombs a few years back. However, that part of his life was over. He had a different future mapped out for himself—and it didn't include a bunch of thieves, lowlifes and alcoholics.

Nor did his future include a blue-blooded wife. One who would expect honesty and fidelity. Frank descended from a long line of men who hadn't been capable of staying with a single woman. He'd seen firsthand what cheating had done to his mother, how it belittled and shamed her. Women coming around the shack looking for their father, some with small babies. God only knew how many children Colin Murphy had fathered.

What wealthy family would hire him if they knew? His career would be over if his lower-class upbringing became public. His clients and partners in the firm believed he'd grown up in privilege, as they had. He'd concocted an elaborate backstory that included money, private school and an elite university. There was no going back on that now, not unless he planned to walk away from everything he'd built.

And he loved his life far too much to ever leave it . . . or let someone destroy it.

MAMIE COULD BARELY restrain herself from digging for more information. Frank had obviously lied; she'd been around him enough to recognize the signs. So what had he been lying about? Yale? Chicago? The copper mine? All of it?

She wanted to reassure him that stories of a less than ideal childhood would not shock her. While her own upbringing had been full of love and comfort, her visits downtown had certainly opened her eyes to the struggles other families faced.

More than a year ago, Mamie had asked Justine to suggest a charity endeavor for her. There were only so many balls, trips to Newport and operas Mamie could take. She'd longed for something more, a way to help people less fortunate. Justine had suggested the Sixth Ward Advancement Committee, which assisted needy families around Five Points.

Through the committee, Mamie had seen the awful conditions of the tenements, the small confines crammed with too many bodies. The children, most of all, broke her heart. Forced to earn wages at an early age, they seemed far older than their years. Most did not escape but went on to hold low-earning or dangerous jobs as adults. Hopelessness permeated every alley, every street lamp and every cobblestone.

The Advancement Committee wished to convert those they helped to Christianity, even though many families practiced other religions. Mamie had protested, asking why aid could not be provided freely, why a religious stipulation must be placed on receiving charity.

She was asked not to return to the committee meetings.

So, she began lending aid herself. She chose families rejected by the Advancement Committee and Florence had taught her the basics of how to pick a pocket. Yes, she stole to acquire the aid money, but where was the harm in taking something that would never be missed and giving it to someone in desperate need? Those in the top stratum had so much, while others near the bottom had nothing. It was righting a wrong based only on circumstances of birth.

She studied Frank over the rim of her glass. He was so perfectly attired, meticulously groomed. Nothing out of place. The most expensive fabrics and accessories. Yet he was not Chauncey, who dressed similarly but was bred in laziness and privilege. Frank was rougher, with an edge that spoke of determination and drive.

It was such an edge that interested her.

"Why did you pursue law?"

He leaned back, champagne glass dangling from his fingers. Guests carried on conversations around them, the main dining room boisterous and bright. Mamie hardly noticed. Frank consumed her attention, almost as if the two of them were alone tonight. It was strangely intimate, though they dined in a very public place.

"I wished to make a difference, I suppose."

"And have you?"

"I like to think so, at least in the lives of my clients."

"Like my father?"

"Yes."

"What sort of legal assistance has he required over the years?"

"You know I cannot answer that, Mamie—"

"Evening, Tripp!"

A couple now stood next to the table. They were well dressed but Mamie didn't recognize them as members of high society. The woman, a statuesque blonde, appeared to be in her early thirties while the gentleman was considerably older.

"Phillips." Frank rose and shook the man's hand, then turned to the wife. She lifted her hand and Frank dutifully kissed the back of it. "Mrs. Phillips."

"Frank," Mrs. Phillips drawled, "how nice to see you. It has been ages."

"Indeed." Frank moved back and addressed the husband. "Mr. and Mrs. Phillips, may I introduce Miss Greene?"

Mr. Phillips smiled kindly at Mamie and bowed. "Miss Greene. This scamp is treating you well, I trust."

"As well as can be expected," she returned. "We are speaking of Mr. Tripp, of course. Good evening, Mrs. Phillips."

The wife frowned at Mamie, barely giving her a nod, before smiling broadly at Frank. Suspicion prickled along the back of Mamie's neck. She'd witnessed jealousy in other women before. Had something transpired between Mrs. Phillips and Frank at some point in the past?

"How was Vienna?" Frank asked Mr. Phillips.

"Boring," Mrs. Phillips said before her husband

could answer. "We're so glad to be returned to New York."

"Now, it wasn't as bad as that." Mr. Phillips leaned in closer to Frank. "I had quite a number of meetings. You know women. They hate to have too much free time on their hands."

The look Mrs. Phillips sent Frank from beneath her lashes said much about how that free time had been spent. Frank's reaction was nearly imperceptible but Mamie caught the slight twitch of one eye. He thrust his hands in his pockets and angled away from Mrs. Phillips. It was a very subtle, but deliberate, snub. Interesting.

"I do need to see you," the man said to Frank. "Perhaps you could come around tomorrow."

"Yes, please come to the house," his wife put in. "We would both *love* to visit with you."

Frank kept his gaze trained on Mr. Phillips. "My day is booked tomorrow. However, if you'd visit my office around noon, I could squeeze you in between appointments."

"I'll do so. Thank you, Tripp." They shook hands and Mr. Phillips smiled at Mamie. "Enjoy the rest of your evening, Miss Greene."

"I shall try. Good evening to you both."

The other woman said nothing, merely let her husband lead her through the crowded dining room. Mamie watched them go as Frank resettled in his chair. He reached for his champagne a little too eagerly.

"So, you and Mrs. Phillips were lovers."

Frank choked in the middle of drinking, liquid dribbling down his chin. "Damn it, Mamie."

Ah, so it was true. She smoothed the napkin on

her lap and tried not to feel disappointed. After all, she and Frank were nothing to one another, not even friends. Frank flirted and cajoled as easily as he breathed and he was certainly pleasant-looking. Women would naturally gravitate toward him. Though she'd never heard of him linked with one particular woman, he was certainly not spending his nights alone.

"Does it bother you?" He'd recovered and was now studying her face. "Meeting a woman I've known intimately?"

"Don't be ridiculous. I don't care about any of your women. I am appalled you would ruin another man's marriage, however."

He returned the glass to the tabletop, his lips twisting into a mischievous smile. "For the record, that friendship ended before she married. As a rule I try to avoid relationships with married women, especially when clients are involved. But she has been rather persistent and it's hard to remain polite while representing her husband. Now, does that restore your faith in my character?"

A bit . . . not that she would admit it to him.

She arched an eyebrow. "Are you seeking praise for resisting something that any decent person would know is wrong? If so, I fear you'll be disappointed."

He leaned in, one arm resting across the table. "My dear Miss Greene." His deep voice caressed along every one of her nerve endings. "We've already established that neither of us is a decent person. That means we're on the other side, the one with the sinners. And I promise it's a lot more fun over here."

# Chapter Four

Was she a sinner?

The idea haunted Mamie as Tripp's carriage rolled uptown. He'd insisted on driving her, refusing to allow her to hail a hack at the conclusion of dinner. Instead of their usual banter, however, they'd each turned pensive on the journey, lost in their own thoughts.

Mostly she wondered about the state of her soul. Yes, stealing was morally wrong and she did steal. But was it wrong if she stole for a noble cause? She had justified her actions as benevolent over the past year . . . and now Frank Tripp had her doubting herself.

Curse him.

She lifted her chin, determination settling in her spine. Let him think what he wished. She was on the side of justice, doing her small share in helping those less fortunate. If Frank ever paid attention to anyone other than himself or his fancy clients, he'd surely see that her actions were justified. The extra funds meant everything to those families.

"You've gone quiet," he said. His long limbs

were relaxed, his body sprawled in the spacious carriage. Dark hair had fallen over his brow in a rakish manner. He reminded her of a ruler from days gone by, all confidence and grace on his throne. The only thing missing was a woman at his side to feed him grapes. "Are you so bothered I wouldn't see you off in a hack?"

"Ordering my meal for me, not allowing me to see myself home . . . I do not wish to be controlled. I'm not some ingénue who must be coddled."

"Some consider such behavior gentlemanly."

"The twentieth century is almost upon us, Tripp. Women are working, living on their own. Soon we'll have the vote."

He whistled softly. "A suffragette. How progressive."

She nearly rolled her eyes. Yes, shocking that a woman should want the same rights as a man. "You don't know everything about me, it would seem."

"True, but I do wish to learn more."

The way he said it—a low rasp in his throat, like silk whispering over skin—caused a shiver to work its way down her spine. Why must this particular man affect her in such a manner? Chauncey was bland tea compared to Tripp's rich and complex Bordeaux.

She had to put a stop to this, now. If he continued to flirt with her, she might be tempted to flirt back . . . and there was no telling where that would lead. Someplace dangerous, for certain.

"I'm afraid you shall remain disappointed, then," she said. "You demanded one dinner, which has now concluded. There is no reason for us to cross paths in the future."

"Ah, but this is a small city. Undoubtedly I will see you again."

Small? The idea was ludicrous. The city seemed tiny only because Tripp kept trailing her about. "You must stop following me. I'm tired of having my evening ruined because you show up."

"I am attempting to protect you. Clearly, you are unaware how dangerous this city is for some."

"Oh, I'm well aware of the dangers of the city." She'd seen drunken fights and children living on the streets. Women with no choice but to sell their bodies in dirty alleyways.

All the more reason why her visits downtown mattered.

He exhaled and stared at the window, his fingers drumming on the silver knob of his cane. His profile showcased a chiseled jaw and sharp cheekbone, an elegant, well-shaped nose that perfectly complemented his features. Though she hated to stare, he was a difficult man to ignore.

"Very well. I had only thought to keep you safe, but I withdraw my assistance. You are now on your own."

Tripp, capitulate? She hadn't anticipated he would give up, at least not without more arguing. Had he meant it? "Thank you—and I appreciate you not informing my father about any of this."

"I never agreed to that."

She blinked, unsure she'd heard him correctly. "I held up my end of the bargain. I came to dinner. Keeping silent is the very least you could do."

"Wrong. If I had wished to rid myself of you, Mamie, I would've informed your father ages ago. What I would much rather do is strike a bargain with you."

A bargain . . . with the slipperiest lawyer in Manhattan? "Why on earth would I agree to any sort of bargain with you?"

"Because you wish to pursue your adventures. I think you know what happens if you don't agree."

Her father. Mercy, that threat was losing its teeth. "What is this bargain?"

He shifted toward her, his fierce stare focused on her face. "Should you find yourself in a situation that is dangerous, leave. Immediately. Do not risk your safety, Mamie. Whatever it is you're doing, it's not worth injury or death."

Oh. That was unexpected. She warmed everywhere, heat building under her skin to melt her insides. One would almost think he carried some sort of torch for her. He didn't, of course. They hardly knew each other, and his life was filled with chorus girls and widows, if the gossip columns were to be believed. Perhaps he considered himself more of an older brother figure to Mamie.

Pity. She had no need of an older brother. And her feelings regarding Frank were far from familial.

*I will agree but only if you kiss me.*

The thought came unbidden, a whisper from deep in her brain. Her gaze darted to his mouth, those full lips that flirted and cajoled every time they parted. What other feats could his mouth and lips perform, if needed?

*Stop, Mamie. You've been listening to Florence too much.*

She let her lids fall and tried to calm her racing heart. Chauncey. He was her future husband, the only man she should be lusting over. Desire for Frank Tripp was a complication she could not take on right now.

A finger swept under her chin to turn her head—and her eyes flew open. Frank was openly studying her, his stare hot and intense, with the gentle press of his finger holding her in place. The air in the carriage turned charged, an electricity that seemed to jump between them like alternating current. Her heart thumped in her chest, so loud she was certain he could hear it.

"Do we have a deal, Mamie?"

There was that deep grating tone again, the one she'd not heard him use before tonight. "Yes," she heard herself whisper.

The side of his mouth hitched, a flare of male satisfaction lighting his gaze. He dropped his hold on her and before she could blink he rapped on the roof. "Here!"

The wheels slowed as the vehicle pulled over. Was he getting out? "What about seeing me home?"

"My driver will ensure you arrive safely. Remember our bargain. Good evening, Miss Greene."

And he disappeared out the door and into the dark Manhattan night.

WITH FOURTEEN RESPECTED attorneys on staff, the law offices of Thomas, Howe, Travers & Tripp bustled during the daylight hours. The firm occupied three floors of a nine-story brick and terra cotta building downtown near the federal court building. One of New York City's most prestigious firms,

THT&T handled everything from murder trials to patent filings. Frank was the newest and youngest partner attorney but also the best known around town. It helped that he moved easily in high society, and he'd made friends with reporters at just about every newspaper in the area.

Once off the elevator, he nodded at various employees along the way to his office. This floor handled mostly civil cases, with the more serious criminal cases worked on upstairs by Thomas and Howe. Frank avoided the murder trials whenever possible; he'd seen enough of that in his youth. No need to relive those horrors all over again now.

His secretary, Mrs. Rand, stood at his approach. "Good morning, sir. I have placed the morning papers on your desk."

"Thank you. When is my first appointment?"

"Mr. Jerome is coming in at nine thirty. The material is on your desk to review."

"You are an absolute gem, Mrs. Rand." He continued into his office, removed his coat and dropped into the leather chair. One of the newspapers was open to a specific page his secretary wished for him to see. Closer inspection revealed it as the society page, one of Mrs. Rand's little jokes. She liked to ensure he never missed his column mentions.

BEAUTY AND THE BARRISTER . . . Spotted together last night at Sherry's were two of the city's well-known luminaries, Miss G_____ and Mr. T_____. The lady sent back her first course and requested another dish. Was it not to her

liking or had she changed her mind? One wonders if she may also change her mind regarding
her betrothed as well.

Barrister? Really? A solicitor would've been a
fairer comparison. Frank could hardly believe the
lack of imagination in the society writers. Couldn't
write directions to their own homes.

He wondered if Mamie had seen the blurb. Of
course, her father would be furious over the attention. Frank would find a way to explain it, if need
be. Besides, there were far greater things to worry
about this morning.

Like how he'd almost kissed her.

Worse, she had wanted him to.

He'd bedded women from Brooklyn to the Bronx,
Morristown to Massapequa, and beyond. Since the
age of twelve, he'd been able to recognize desire on
a woman's face, the heat in her eyes. The way her
breathing hitched and the thrumming of her pulse
in her neck. Mamie had stared at his mouth like it
was pistachio ice cream on an August day.

No doubt he'd been staring at her the exact
same way.

As the night wore on his craving had grown
worse. What had started as a quickening of his
blood at dinner had turned into a semierection
in the carriage. Christ, he feared what might've
happened if he hadn't hopped out halfway uptown. Would he have come in his trousers at
Seventy-Second Street?

Mamie had been jealous of Abigail Phillips,
though she covered it well with a lie. Frank, how-

ever, spotted lies as easily as breathing. A product of his upbringing, he supposed, with abuse and neglect the only constants in his sordid life.

This was why he'd cut Mamie loose. No more would he follow her around town, riding to her rescue at the first sign of danger. She was growing into an unhealthy obsession and there could be no future for the two of them. Better he forgot about her and moved on. She was welcome to visit every two-bit dive, casino or dancehall. He no longer cared.

*You must stop following me. I'm tired of having my evening ruined because you show up.*

She was right. It was past time for this to end.

He tossed the newspaper aside. Work awaited him, including the papers he needed to ready for his first meeting of the day. Mamie Greene was in his past.

He was nearly ready for his first appointment when a knock sounded. His secretary poked her head inside the room. "Sir, Mr. Greene is here to see you."

Shit.

The meeting was impossible to refuse . . . and he wasn't all that surprised by it, either. Frank took off his reading glasses and slipped them in the top drawer of his desk. "Show him in." While waiting, he stood and put his coat back on.

Duncan Greene was an imposing athletic man. He'd been raised in privilege but one would never call him "soft." If you found yourself in a taproom brawl, you'd certainly want Greene on your side. But Frank had grown up around plenty of men more terrifying than Duncan Greene. If Mamie's father thought to intimidate him, Greene would be sorely disappointed.

Greene entered, a brown derby in his hands. His suit was impeccable, perfectly tailored. That he'd come to Frank instead of issuing a summons spoke volumes about the timeliness of this conversation.

"Good morning, Duncan." Frank held out his hand. Duncan shook it in a crushing grip, one so hard that Frank nearly winced.

"Frank. Thank you for seeing me."

"Of course. You know my door is always open for you. Have a seat and tell me what's on your mind." As if he didn't already suspect.

"I was in the neighborhood this morning so I thought I'd stop and have a chat." Duncan lowered himself into the armchair across from Frank's desk. "We're both busy so I won't waste any time. I wish to know your intentions toward my daughter."

Intentions? Jesus. "It was one dinner, Duncan."

"One dinner noted in every society column this morning. I've already had a visit from Mr. Livingston, the father of Marion's betrothed. He is equally concerned."

The two older men should instead concern themselves with Mamie's habit of stealing money from strangers at casinos. A dinner at Sherry's hardly equated with gambling and larceny. "Concern that is totally unfounded, in my opinion. We ran into one another and she mentioned a fondness for Louis's artichoke soup. I offered to escort her." The lies fell easily from his tongue.

Duncan's gaze studied Frank carefully, and Frank fought the urge to shift in his chair like a guilty defendant. "Marion's story was of a similar thread." He tapped his fingers on the armrest. "You may already know this about me, Frank, but it bears repeating. I don't care for attention, not for myself or my family. The Greene name has always been associated with respectability and, as my eldest daughter, I expect Marion to follow decades of tradition."

Frank nearly snorted. Mamie bucked so much tradition that Duncan's head would spin if he ever found out. But it wasn't Frank's job to inform his client of this. He needed to reassure Duncan, agree to whatever Duncan demanded and get on with his damn day.

Duncan was one of New York City's most powerful men. One word from him and no one above Thirty-Fourth Street would work with Frank ever again. He could kiss his legal career goodbye. And Frank hadn't bowed and scraped since escaping the poverty of his youth only to throw his vast fortune away on a woman.

Yes, Frank could still find clients—downtown thugs always seemed to require legal representation—but the prestige was in representing the blue bloods. Dining in the best restaurants. Having his name in the gossip columns. Invitations to the best parties.

All that would disappear if Frank disregarded Duncan's wishes.

Did that make him vain and shallow? Yes. He readily admitted it. He liked money, liked having a big house on Fifth Avenue. The club memberships and box at the Metropolitan Opera House. Hell would freeze before Frank returned to a life of poverty.

"I have no intention of pursuing any further contact with your daughter, Duncan. You have my word."

Duncan dipped his chin. "Excellent. While I'm here, I want you to take care of something else for me. Livingston and I decided to push the children and set a date. Let's get a settlement drawn up, something that puts aside money for Marion in case Chauncey bungles the whole thing. Also include a clause about infidelity. I don't care what he does after I have some grandchildren, but he best settle down and do his duty for the first ten years."

A sharp pain dug into Frank's ribs, even as he nodded and wrote all this down on paper. "Not a problem."

Duncan rose, putting an end to the meeting. He looked around at the bare walls. "Surprised you don't have any paintings or your degree hanging up. Where did you say you went to school again?"

"Yale," Frank replied. "Just never got around to getting the damn thing framed."

"I understand. My paper from Harvard is in a trunk somewhere in our attic. Some of your clients might find the degree impressive, though. That way, they'll know you didn't attend University of Delaware or Boston College."

God forbid. There were only three or four schools good enough for these high society types, which was why Frank would never admit his degree had been from Allegheny College. "Good point. I'll look into having it framed," he lied.

"Excellent." Duncan stared hard into Frank's eyes. "And I don't mean to imply that you're not worthy of Marion. However, she's been promised to Livingston for years. His father is a close friend of mine. We'd like the two families permanently joined."

Distaste crawled across Frank's skin. Duncan spoke of Mamie as if she were a commodity. Something to be bartered and traded. Not uncommon in Greene's circle but repugnant all the same. Perhaps this was what Mamie wanted as well. Who was Frank to quibble with destiny? "I understand. Don't worry, I'll ensure she's well taken care of. Legally speaking, of course."

Suspicion crawled over Duncan's face. "Yes, legally speaking. Because any man who tries to get in the way of my daughter's future is a dead man." He jammed his derby on his head. "And I would really hate for that dead man to be *you*."

MULBERRY STREET RAN through some of the worst parts of the Lower East Side, with the notorious Five Points intersection at its south end. Mamie tried to avoid that area whenever possible, even in the daylight. The Sixth Ward was dangerous at all hours, which was why she kept to the northern side.

The streets here were vastly different than their spacious and clean uptown counterparts. Downtown, thoroughfares were jammed with people of all backgrounds, along with pushcarts, horses and goods for sale. Musty paper and dirty rags littered the alleys, providing makeshift pallets for those without permanent shelter. Laundry hung from windows, and in the summer it wasn't uncommon to see fire escapes being used as beds.

When large groups began immigrating here, blocks and streets quickly turned into neighborhoods based on religious or cultural identity. English was not the chief language amongst the neighbors and shop owners in these spots; instead, one could hear German, Hebrew, Russian, Italian, Chinese and more. Skin color of every shade was represented, everyone trying to find a foothold in this new modern era. Many children ran barefoot, their faces and clothes reflecting time spent mostly outdoors. And when one lived with five or six people in a tiny one-room apartment, who could blame them for not staying inside?

Mamie visited families in five different tenement buildings in and around Mulberry Street. She had chosen each carefully. The wives tended to small children, usually while doing wash or sewing for pennies a day, and their older children worked in factories, shops or on the streets. The husbands of these particular families were either unwell, drunkards or missing. That left the women struggling to keep things together by themselves, and any little bit of money Mamie gave them made a huge difference in their monthly budgets.

She spent a long time at the first home, a Polish family's fourth-floor apartment. The husband was recuperating from a leg injury and the wife had two sick children preventing her from completing her promised work. So, Mamie fed and soothed the children while the wife feverishly sewed. Any offers to aid in the mending were steadfastly refused; the woman wouldn't hear of it.

The next two stops were quicker. One woman grabbed the money through a crack in the door, thanked Mamie and locked up tight. The other wife whispered that her husband was sleeping and accepted the money quietly.

Two policemen loitered outside the adjacent building. Police were not an uncommon sight in the Sixth Ward but one didn't usually see clusters of them. They ignored Mamie as she went inside, too intent on their chatter and cigars to pay her any mind.

She carefully climbed the derelict stairs to the third floor. A bulb flickered in the ceiling, the walls coated with damp. This particular family, the Porters, had troubled Mamie for quite some time. The husband worked on the docks, but whatever money he earned mostly went to his gin habit and not the family. The wife took in laundry, but it wasn't enough to feed their three small children. They'd rejected the Sixth Ward Advancement Committee's efforts to convert them and therefore were unable to receive aid, so Mamie had added them to her distribution list.

What bothered Mamie most were the bruises that often appeared on Mrs. Porter's face and neck, as if she'd been choked or punched. When Mamie asked about them—while in the same breath offering her assistance should Mrs. Porter wish to leave her husband—the wife insisted the bruises were from falls, her own clumsiness to blame.

Mamie didn't believe it.

When she reached the third floor, the sound of wailing children greeted her. There were four apartments on this floor so crying was nothing new . . . but this was more than that. This was gut-wrenching misery, the kind that came from injury or neglect.

Mamie hurried to the Porters' apartment. The door stood open, the cries growing louder. She knocked before peeking in to see—

Three policemen were inside, all gathered around a body on the floor. Was that Mr. Porter? Oh, God. What had happened? Was he dead?

On the far side of the room, two more policemen surrounded Mrs. Porter, who was sitting in a chair, her face as white as flour.

Mamie didn't stop to think, she just went in. "Mrs. Porter, may I be of assistance?"

Mrs. Porter glanced up, blinking at Mamie, and it took a long second before recognition dawned on her face. Angry cuts oozed blood from her left brow and the side of her mouth, her skin swollen and red. She tried to speak but nothing came out.

The men all turned to Mamie. The oldest of the group, likely the highest-ranking officer, approached her. "And who might you be, miss?"

Mamie drew herself up. "I am Miss Marion Greene. Daughter of Mr. Duncan Greene."

His brows dipped, skepticism plain on his face. "Of Fifth Avenue? You expect us to believe that Duncan Greene's daughter would be down here in the Sixth with the filth? What, was Mrs. Astor unavailable today?"

The men in the room all snickered, causing Mamie's blood to heat. "Nevertheless, I really am Miss Greene."

He puffed up, raking her fiercely from head to toe, a slow, intimate inspection meant to demean and belittle her. "Well, no offense Miss Greene, but we don't usually see girls like you down in these parts."

True, but that was hardly the point at the moment.

She'd encountered men like this officer before:

powerful men who believed women were feeble and fragile creatures. In her experience, the best way to deal with fools such as this was to be as direct and confident as possible. Show no weakness.

One of the Porter's small children was sitting on the floor, alone, crying. Mamie went over to pick him up, cradling him close and whispering soothing words to calm him. When the child quieted Mamie returned to where the officer stood. "Will you tell me what has happened, sir?"

"That's sergeant, miss—and I cannot see how this is appropriate for the delicate sensibilities of a proper lady with your upbringing. Perhaps you should find your carriage and return home. I don't think your father would appreciate you down here."

"I'm afraid I cannot do so just yet, sergeant. Mrs. Porter is my friend. I wish to see if I may offer my assistance in this matter."

"Your friend?" he scoffed, his mustache twitching. Then he chuckled and glanced about to make sure his officers heard this as well. "You hear that, boys? Mrs. Porter's got herself some fancy uptown friends."

Anger snaked its way over Mamie's skin, scorching and burning, and she reminded herself to stay calm. They assumed she'd become hysterical and start screaming, grow red faced and irrational. Then they could dismiss her.

However, if she remained logical and even-keeled, they would be forced to deal with her.

"I wish to help her, if possible." The child in her arms started to fuss, so Mamie gently bounced him.

"That's right noble of you, Miss Greene. However, I'm afraid there's naught that can be done for Mrs. Porter. You see, we've just arrested her."

"Arrested her!" Mamie glanced over at Mrs. Porter. The other woman's eyes were vacant and haunted, as if living through a nightmare. "For what?"

The sergeant swept a hand toward the body on the floor. "For murder, Miss Greene. Now, if you don't mind, we have a job to do."

"But . . ." Mamie couldn't wrap her head around it. Could they not see what had happened? "Mrs. Porter has clearly been beaten. If Mr. Porter has been killed by her hand, then surely it was in defending herself."

"That's not an excuse for killing a man, miss. What happens between a husband and wife in the privacy of their own home is not our business and has no bearing on this case. The fact of the matter is that a man is dead and his wife is responsible." He motioned to the policemen by Mrs. Porter. "Take her away, boys."

Mrs. Porter was yanked to her feet and led toward the door. Mamie watched in absolute horror as this hardworking, kind woman she'd known for over a year was marched off to jail. Had these policemen no compassion? No willingness to understand the true facts of what had transpired here?

As she passed, Mrs. Porter dug in her heels to slow down, now addressing Mamie, "My children. Please, see them placed with my neighbor. Tell them I love them."

Mamie nodded. "I will help you. I swear it. Do not worry, Mrs. Porter."

"Move along," the sergeant barked behind them.

"Get her in the wagon. Then tell the others to bring a stretcher for the body."

Mrs. Porter's older son and daughter began to cry as their mother disappeared, the sound breaking Mamie's heart. God, the pain of mothers and children being separated from one another must be absolutely unbearable. She whispered to the little boy in her arms, rocking him back and forth.

"Now, I really must insist you leave, Miss Greene. We need to move this body and it's not a sight for delicate eyes."

God save her from misogynists. "What happens next for Mrs. Porter?"

He lifted a shoulder. "She awaits trial at headquarters, just down the street. Then it's off to the Tombs, I suppose."

Not if she could help it. There was one person who could assist Mrs. Porter, one that Mamie happened to know quite well.

And she was going to owe him a huge favor for this.

## Chapter Five

❧

"You need me to do what?"

Frank stared across his desk at Mamie, who had stormed into his office a moment ago. She was disheveled and flushed, clearly agitated. He tried to quash the little burst of happiness over her arrival, especially as she was upset. This was no social call.

And her request confirmed it.

She snapped her gloved fingers in front of his face. "Frank, pay attention. I need you to represent a friend of mine who has been arrested."

Arrested? "What friend is this?"

"You don't know her. She's being held at police headquarters on Mulberry Street."

At least it was a *she* and not a *he*. "That doesn't make sense. They would only take her there if she were a resident of the Sixth."

"Because she is a resident of the Sixth. She lives on Bayard between Mulberry and Mott."

Frank straightened in his chair. "That's nearly Five Points. How in God's name do you know someone that lives down there?"

She put her hands on her hips. "That is the wrong

question to ask. You should be taking notes on her name, the charges against her and how you plan to get said charges dropped. Fast. She has three children who depend on her."

He rubbed his eyes tiredly. It was nearly six o'clock in the evening. He had dinner plans with a client at eight o'clock. There was no time for Mamie Greene, her sass and fire, or her mouthwatering body in a surprisingly drab dress. Nor did he have time to represent some tenement wife who could never afford to pay his rates and was probably guilty anyway.

And still.

This was Mamie asking. He hadn't been able to forget her. Three days had passed since their dinner together and she was so deep inside his head that his cock twitched each time his carriage drove past Sherry's.

He was in a bad way.

"Mamie—"

"You're not allowed to refuse, Tripp. A grave injustice has been done to this woman and you must set it right."

Hmm. As worked up as he had seen Mamie at various points of their acquaintance, she'd never been quite *this* worked up. It seemed she finally needed something from him, something that made her desperate and bossy.

His heart thumped in his chest, desire humming like a swarm of bees in his blood. He was but a man, a man who traded favors and knowledge for a living. Legal expertise was his currency. So, how far was she willing to go for his help? And what did he want in exchange?

*Not that sort of favor, Frank. Remember, she is a lady.*

Nothing untoward, then. But he could ask for something in return. After all, she couldn't expect him to perform this service out of the charity of his heart, could she? His heart held no charity; it had been forced out years ago.

This required a negotiation.

He rolled his pen between his fingers, thinking. "Before I decide to help this woman, to right this grave injustice you speak of, I wish to know what's in it for me."

Her lips pursed, brows dipping low. "What's in it for you?"

"Yes, you know. What will I receive out of this arrangement that makes the endeavor worthwhile on my part."

"The knowledge that you have saved an innocent woman's life is not enough?"

He chuckled dryly. "Mamie, the city's prisons are full of innocent people. I cannot save everyone."

"I'm not asking you to save everyone. Merely one woman who happens to be a friend of mine."

"My caseload is very full." He scratched his jaw thoughtfully. "Perhaps if you spoke to my secretary she might be able to find you some time next week—"

"Fine!" She threw up her hands and let them fall at her sides. "What do you want in exchange, Frank?"

He stared at her, unsure. Part of him hadn't expected her to capitulate so quickly. The other part had expected her to suggest the payment, not leave it up to him.

Dear God, the things he wanted in exchange.

Prurient, inappropriate, dirty things . . . things that would make a Fifth Avenue princess's hair stand on end. *Fuck.*

He cleared his throat. Really, he wished to spend time with her. As ridiculous as it sounded, he liked being around Mamie. She was smart and funny, more insightful than other ladies he knew. If he asked himself why he'd chased her these past few months the answer was to simply be near her.

There might not be a romantic future between them . . . but they could be friends of a sort. He would keep the evening respectable.

But not *too* respectable.

Thinking back to their dinner, the bargaining chip became crystal clear.

"A night of billiards. You and me."

She rocked back on her heels, confusion etched on the lines of her face. "Billiards? You wish to play a game of pool with me?"

"Not one game—many games. Best of seven. And at my home."

"I . . . Frank, I cannot be seen playing billiards with you at your home. That would be . . ."

"Exciting? Stupendous? The most memorable evening of your life?"

Her lips quirked and he thought for a moment that she might smile. Instead, she said, "You have a very high opinion of your company. And what I meant was that it would be scandalous—and not the good kind."

"Worried at what Chauncey might say?"

"More like I'm worried about my father and the rest of society."

"What if I promised no one would see you enter

or exit my home? And my staff is incredibly discreet."

"From generous experience, no doubt," she muttered. "Have I really a choice? Is there any way I could offer something else, something less . . . intimate?"

He thought of her bent over his billiards table, her long torso stretching to set up her shots . . . A shiver went through him. "No, absolutely not. Unless you wish to find another lawyer to help your friend."

"You are the very devil, Frank Tripp." She stared at the wall for a moment, toe tapping while her jaw worked. Raising his arms, he laced his fingers behind his head, ready to wait her out. In the end, she would see there was no use dissembling. This was the price for his help, full stop.

Finally, she faced him, her chin high. "All right, I agree to your ridiculous billiards tournament. Now, get moving. You need to hurry to headquarters and have my friend released."

Satisfaction flooded him, a victory so sweet he had to smother the giddy laughter filling his chest. Rising, he buttoned his coat. "Then I shall do so, Your Highness, and report back to you directly. What is your friend's name?"

"We'll discuss this in the carriage. I'm coming with you."

That got his attention. "Like hell you are. Mamie, you're not traipsing about downtown amongst the thieves and criminals. Let me do this for you."

She glanced heavenward then spun on her heel. "You're wasting time. I'll be damned if I sit home and wait while her fate is decided."

He followed her blindly, momentarily distracted by her use of a curse. *You've seen her pick pockets. She probably knows just as much about the criminal element as you.* Maybe more.

Shit.

"Best of nine," he called to her back. She shot him a disgusted look over her shoulder and he couldn't help but grin widely.

Indeed, he was doomed.

As A GIRL, Mamie had once met Edwin Booth. The famous actor had been very kind to her, shaking her hand and exchanging a few words now lost to the sands of time. What she could still recall was how those around him had treated the actor, as if he were a god sent from Mount Olympus down to Earth. Everyone had vied for his attention, calling and shouting to him, reaching out in the hopes of touching greatness. They'd practically thrown rose petals for the man to tread upon.

Walking into New York City Police Headquarters with Frank was a similar experience.

Upon leaving his carriage, he was bombarded by officers, other lawyers and detectives bellowing his name and shaking his hand. It was relentless. Frank slapped backs and accepted cigars, a smile splitting his face as they made their way inside. The center of attention, everyone's friend. *He loves this. He was born to do this.*

Frank Tripp was a bona fide New York City celebrity.

While this surprised Mamie, it shouldn't have. She read the newspapers, knew of his reputation both in court and out of it. He was part of a law firm, but Frank was the lawyer all men—guilty or innocent—wished to hire. However, she hadn't realized how this affected his everyday life, how average men would scrape and bow for his notice.

It was . . . disconcerting.

He politely held on to her elbow as they entered the building. A woman here was unusual, unless in irons. The Chicago Police had recently allowed a woman in their ranks, but the New York Metropolitan Police remained entirely male, other than a few matrons to assist with the female inmates. So Mamie ignored the strange looks thrown her way and kept her chin high. Nothing mattered but obtaining Mrs. Porter's release.

Once inside, activity buzzed around them. People from all walks of life and backgrounds were there, a testament to the diverse population of the city. Much more diverse than Upper Fifth Avenue.

They stepped to the main counter. An older policeman with bushy auburn sideburns sat behind the high wooden partition. When he glanced up, his mouth hitched. "Well, if it ain't Frank Tripp comin' down here tonight to bless us all with his presence. How are you, Frank? It's been a while." He had the hint of an Irish accent when he spoke.

"Hello, McDermott." Frank was all smiles as he leaned a hip against the counter. "How's that wife of yours? Feeling better?"

The man's expression sobered. "She is, most definitely. Got her sister stayin' with us to care for her, but doctors say she's on the mend, thank God."

"That is good news, then. Please send her all the best from me. Now, the lady and I"—he gestured toward Mamie—"are here to see a Mrs. Porter of

Bayard Street. She was brought in earlier today on suspicion of murder charges." Mamie had filled him in on the carriage ride.

"Miss," the attendant said to Mamie before turning back to Frank. "You aren't representin' her, are you? Bit of a step down, ain't it?"

Mamie opened her mouth to tell the man exactly what she thought of that disparaging comment, but Frank squeezed her arm. She clenched her jaw and remained silent, though it irked her.

"I am Mrs. Porter's attorney," Frank said. "I made a promise and I do intend to see it through."

McDermott slowly shook his head. "I suppose you know your business." Glancing down, he flipped through a registry book on the counter. "Mrs. Porter . . . let's see. She was brought in around one o'clock this afternoon. I'll have one of the matrons fetch her from the other building."

"Excellent, thank you. We'll sit over here and wait." Frank pointed at a bench against the wall.

McDermott waved an officer over while still speaking to Mamie and Frank. "No, no, no. Head to an empty room in the back. It's not as if you don't know the way. We'll have her sent there for you."

Frank shook McDermott's hand, thanked him and led Mamie through a series of corridors. "In you go," Frank said as he pulled open a door. "This is where they bring suspects to question them. We'll wait here for Mrs. Porter."

A windowless room with dirty white walls surrounded her. There were two small wooden chairs, one on either side of a table. Mamie lowered herself into one of the chairs. Exhaustion tugged at her like a physical weight she was carrying. The day had been long and stressful. Considering how terrible she felt, she could only imagine how poor Mrs. Porter was holding up. The woman must be frightened beyond belief.

"When Mrs. Porter arrives, we'll try to get her side of what happened," Frank said quietly. "At her arraignment I'll ask the judge to release her on bail. However, this is a capital offense, so bail is at the judge's discretion."

"Why are you telling me all this?"

"Because you must manage your expectations. This is a long process and much of it is out of our control."

"Not out of your control," she couldn't help but put in. "Considering your reputation."

He put up his hands, palms out. "I'll do my best, Mamie. But she killed her husband."

"Allegedly."

Frank slipped his hands into his trouser pockets and shook his head. "Based on what you've told me, it looks grim. Not to mention it's almost always the spouse in a situation such as this."

While that may be true, she wasn't about to leap to conclusions. "Circumstantial at best. We have no idea if there is proof."

"Mamie, most murderers are convicted on circumstantial evidence." When Mamie started to argue, Frank leaned down closer and placed his hands on the scarred table. "Listen, I don't care if she did it or not. My client's innocence or guilt is hardly relevant. My job is to represent her in court."

"Then how do you choose your clients?"

He straightened, his lips twisting into a smirk. "If I say it's money will you think less of me?"

She'd expected the answer, but it had a whole new meaning for her now. A woman's life was on the line, a good woman with three small children to raise. "So only those who have a lot of money can afford great lawyers?" Like her father.

"You act as though you're unaware of the privilege money brings in this city. You cannot be that innocent. I found you picking pockets in a casino, for God's sake."

Oh, that again.

"Not to mention you are Duncan Greene's daughter," he continued. "There's a whole city out there that you've never experienced, with people of all kinds."

She opened her mouth to tell him what she knew of those less fortunate, but the door parted. A police matron in a plain gray dress led in a pale and disheveled Mrs. Porter. Mamie shot to her feet and clasped her hands to keep from running over and hugging the woman. The matron unlocked the manacles around Mrs. Porter's wrists and brought her to the table. "Sit here," the matron ordered.

After Mrs. Porter sat, the matron told Frank, "I'll wait in the hall. Let me know when you're finished."

"Thank you."

When they were alone, Mamie reached across the table and clutched the other woman's hand. "Are you all right? Have you been mistreated?"

Mrs. Porter swallowed. "I'm fine. How are my babies?"

"With your neighbor. She said between her and the other women in the building they'll be well cared for."

"But they don't have enough money to—"

"Do not concern yourself with that. I've taken care of it. Whatever they need they shall have, I promise."

Mrs. Porter's eyes welled up with tears. "Thank you, Miss Greene. I don't know how I'll ever repay this kindness on top of everything else you've done for us over the past year."

Mamie squeezed her hand. "No repayment is necessary. I know how hard you work. We're going to get you through this." Pulling her hands free, she gestured toward Frank. "Mrs. Porter, meet your lawyer, Mr. Frank Tripp."

MAMIE HAD CLEARLY not lied about this woman being a friend. However, this was more than friendship. Mamie offered Mrs. Porter . . . financial assistance and support. Had arranged for the neighbors to look after the Porter children.

*I don't know how I'll ever repay this kindness on top of everything else you've done for us over the past year.*

What had that meant? What had Mamie done for her over the past year?

And would Frank ever understand this woman?

He reached out to shake Mrs. Porter's hand. "Hello, Mrs. Porter. I am Mr. Tripp, an attorney here in the city. I need to ask you a few questions. Would that be all right?"

She nodded but didn't speak, her eyes wary. Frank had represented only two women in criminal cases over the years, neither in a murder trial. He was suddenly grateful for Mamie's presence here, her ability to put people at ease. It would save him time in building trust with an unknown client. "First, I want you to understand that everything you share with me is privileged information. Meaning, I cannot ever tell anyone. Whatever you say cannot be used against you in court. Miss Greene is here in my employ, so the same rules apply. You may be totally honest with us."

"But I have no money for a lawyer. They said someone from the state would represent me."

"Don't worry about that," Mamie said before Frank could comment. "Mr. Tripp is a friend of mine. I will see that he's compensated for taking your case."

Oh, *Christ*. The myriad of prurient thoughts that went through Frank's brain was positively shameful. Had she any idea of how she affected him?

Likely not, else she'd certainly never discuss compensating him ever again.

"Oh, Miss Greene—"

Mamie held up her hand. "Please, I insist. If not for yourself, then please accept my help for the sake of your children."

Mrs. Porter's shoulders relaxed ever so slightly. Another nod.

Frank took this as his cue. "Now, what happened earlier today?"

The woman's gaze darted between him and Mamie, then she stared at the table. He raised his brows at Mamie meaningfully and jerked his chin toward the other woman. *Help her.*

Mamie touched Mrs. Porter's arm. "It's all right. You may trust—"

"I killed him."

Frank stilled at the abrupt confession but quickly masked his outward reaction. God knew it wasn't the worst thing he'd heard confessed in one of these rooms. Mamie was a different story, however. Eyes wide, she rocked back in her chair, so he put a palm on her knee to steady her.

"Tell us what happened." He kept his voice even, nonjudgmental.

Mrs. Porter nodded and wiped at a tear sliding down her cheek. "He . . . was not a nice man. Not to me. There were times—" She stopped abruptly and let out a shuddering breath.

Mamie reached out once more, soothing the other woman by stroking her arm. "There were times . . . ?"

"When he would use his fists on me. In front of the children. I came to expect it, you know. After he returned home from the gin holes, at least. I didn't mind so much, unless I had to take to my bed to recover." She locked eyes with Mamie. "You see, I made him mad, always after him to stop drinking and help more around the house. I nagged him."

"That does not excuse physical violence," Mamie told her softly. "Nothing excuses anyone hitting you."

Mrs. Porter lifted a shoulder. "He works—worked—hard on the docks. When he came home he wished to be left alone. Sometimes that was hard for me."

Mamie swiped at her own face with her free hand, brushing away tears at learning these details of Mrs. Porter's home life. Frank hated to tell her how common this was, how often some men believed it their right to hit their wives and how often the wives excused it. His own mother, in fact, always defended their father and his violent tendencies. She had chosen that bastard every time, instead of herself or her children.

Shaking off those long-buried memories, he returned his focus to the conversation. "And this morning?"

"He'd been gone all night, came home drunk. I . . . I couldn't stop them from crying." Tears fell in earnest now, misery etched in her expression. "I did everything I could think to keep them quiet. He . . ."

Mamie continued to hold on to Mrs. Porter, giving her strength. They waited, no one speaking, until the other woman was able to go on.

"He started in on our eldest, Katie. She's five. She was crying in the kitchen and I tried to tell her to hush. I begged her." Mrs. Porter's eyes were dazed, the horror returning as she recounted the morning. "When she kept carrying on Roy told her to shut up or there would be consequences. But she still made noise. He raised his fist to her. I . . . I didn't think. I just . . ."

Frank could almost picture it, the scene so vivid in his mind. How many times had it happened in the Murphy household? Fifty? A hundred? Always those big meaty fists raining down violence and shame.

"And so you were defending Katie?" Mamie asked.

He caught her attention and shook his head. The last thing they should do is put words in a client's mouth. It was best if Mrs. Porter struggled through her story, no matter how long it took.

"I had no choice," Mrs. Porter said, her eyes pleading, willing them to understand. "He would've killed her. He was thrice her size, at least. I couldn't let him hit her."

"And then what happened?"

"I grabbed the heaviest pan on the stove and hit him in the back of the head with it. He stumbled, went down on one knee, and that's when I hit him again. Then he fell."

"This was in the kitchen?"

She brushed away more tears. "Yes, sir. Sort of right in the middle of the apartment."

Frank hadn't visited the scene of the crime, but he didn't need to. He'd been in more tenements growing up than he could count. They were all one or two rooms, everyone cooking, eating, sleeping together. "Did your husband rise up again?"

"No, sir. He just lay there. Cops showed up not long after."

That was odd. A domestic disturbance wouldn't generally trigger a visit by the police. So how would anyone have known to fetch the police? He'd need to speak with the neighbors. Establishing a pattern of violence requiring self-defense was their best chance at acquittal.

"What have you said to the police? Did you tell them what you just told us?"

She closed her eyes and swallowed. "No, sir. I was too scared, even when they yelled at me."

"Excellent. That is good news," he said. "Do not speak to them without me present. They may try to coerce you into an admission of guilt."

"But I am guilty."

"Only because you were defending yourself and your daughter," Mamie said. "Mr. Tripp is the very best attorney in the city. He'll get you acquitted, I promise."

While he appreciated Mamie's faith in his abilities, it was always better to prepare clients for the worst. "Mrs. Porter, the next step is your arraignment. We'll go before the judge, hear the charges and try to get you released on bail. That should happen in the next few hours."

"And if I'm not released? What about my children?"

"I'll see to them," Mamie said before he could comment.

Frank walked around to the other side of the table and helped Mrs. Porter to her feet. She was a small woman, with not much meat on her bones. Her face was still swollen with two ugly cuts that had barely scabbed over. Presumably Porter's handiwork. Gentling his expression, Frank said, "Remember, don't speak to anyone but me about your case. I'll ask the matron to come in and get you now. Then they'll bring you to the courtroom later. Have you any questions for me?"

She shook her head. Mamie was suddenly there, knocking him out of the way to take Mrs. Porter into her arms for a hug. He couldn't hear everything Mamie whispered but he heard an apology and a string of reassurances. She promised a quick release from jail. Frank hoped he could deliver on that promise.

First, however, Mamie had some explaining to do.

# Chapter Six

Immediately after Mrs. Porter was escorted out, Mamie watched as Frank strolled to the chair on the other side of the table and sat. He leaned back and placed his feet on the table, legs crossed at the ankle. "The very best attorney, is it?"

Oh, he'd heard that, had he? Well, she wasn't about to expound on the comment. The man's opinion of himself was high enough.

She put her hands on her hips. "I said that for her benefit—not yours."

He brushed his trousers, flicking imaginary lint off the dark blue wool. "Still, these words were said. They cannot be taken back. Hell, Mamie. I had no idea how much you respected and admired me."

Lord, he was insufferable. And handsome. Though the second observation was hardly relevant, it was top of mind after watching and listening to him for the past few minutes with Mrs. Porter. "Do you expect for me to continue to flatter you now that we're alone?"

His lids lowered slightly, lashes sweeping down

to partially cloak his bright blue eyes. "That depends. How badly do you want my help?"

She swallowed. The man was potent. Seductive. A living, breathing temptation in a bespoke three-piece suit.

Dropping into the other vacant chair, she adjusted her skirts and tried to calm her racing heart. "Be serious, Frank. You've already committed yourself to Mrs. Porter's cause. It's clear she acted in self-defense."

"Nothing is clear and nothing is committed . . . not until I get some answers out of you."

This was what she'd feared, that he would insist on discovering more about her secret life and how she came to meet Mrs. Porter. Yet she'd gladly suffer Frank's questions to secure assistance for Mrs. Porter. Without a good attorney God knew what would happen to the mother of three in the city's courts.

"You already have my word that I'll play billiards with you at your home one night. What more could you possibly want?"

"Quite a lot, actually. Let's start with how you met Mrs. Porter."

"A friend of a friend."

His lips quirked and he shook his head. "Mamie, my dear. You seem to think evasion and lies will still work, but they won't. Not with me. Not after I have met Mrs. Porter and heard what she had to say. So how about you are honest with me for once in your overprivileged life?"

"I wasn't lying. Evading, perhaps, but not lying."

He drummed his fingers on the table, not uttering a word. Apprehension crawled over her skin at his silence. Would he really withdraw his support for Mrs. Porter if he didn't hear the truth? Mamie didn't think so, but she couldn't be certain. The risk was not worth it.

If spilling her secrets gained Mrs. Porter's release then Mamie had no choice.

"Fine. One of my sisters knew of a charity organization downtown. About a year and a half ago I learned that some women who seek help are turned away because they refuse religious conversion. I asked for a few names of those refused help so that I might offer it instead. I visit them once or twice a month and bring money."

His feet hit the floor and he leaned forward, elbows on the table. "Wait, you're telling me you—" Understanding dawned and he glanced at the ceiling. "The money at the casino. This was why you picked that man's pocket. You're stealing money from uptown swells and giving it to downtown waifs."

"Downtown families. These women are clawing and scraping to survive, raising children in the worst conditions imaginable. Those uptown swells have more money than they could possibly spend in three lifetimes."

"That does not mean their money belongs to *you*. The money is theirs to do with what they wish. If they wanted to donate it to the needy, they would. What are you, some sort of modern Robin Hoodess?"

"Perhaps I am. You have no idea what these women—" She slammed her jaw shut. How could he possibly know? Not a man who'd been raised in Chicago to a privileged family and educated at a prestigious school. Not a man with a brilliant legal career who lived in a large house on Fifth Avenue.

"What I know is that stealing from others is not the way to help these families. They need much more than the occasional extra sawbuck."

She shook her head. "You're wrong. Money controls everything in this city, and men control all the money. Women like Mrs. Porter are powerless to improve themselves. You think with three children that she can pick up and go off to college? Get a high-paying secretarial job? She is imprisoned by the circumstances perpetuated by our society."

"She chose to marry him and have children, Mamie. The circumstances are of her own making."

"Wrong. Women are given no representation in our society. No votes, no rights. We're nothing. She was at the mercy of that . . . monster. He spent their funds on gin and women. Came home and treated her like trash. What kind of man is that? Not the one who courted her, I can guarantee it."

"Men like Mr. Porter are as common as rats in the Lower East Side. She should have known better."

Mamie rocked back in her chair. "*Known better?* So this is her fault for falling in love with a man who was weak and cruel?"

The lines of his face twisted, an uneasiness she hadn't ever seen before. "That wasn't what I meant. Do not put words in my mouth."

This was a whole new side of Frank Tripp. Yes, he was crafty and evasive, but she'd always assumed him intelligent and fair. This attitude about struggling women and their families staggered her. There could be only one explanation. "Yet I'm able to read beyond what is said. You are a snob."

"Don't be ridiculous," he snapped, though his gaze did not meet hers. "I'm not a snob. I understand what it's like to struggle."

"Are you certain of that?"

"Why are we discussing *me*?" He pointed at her. "We should be picking over your decision to traipse around Five Points dispensing ill-gotten gains."

"I assumed we were done discussing that."

"Wrong, my little thief." He pushed away from the table and stood, thrusting his hands in his trouser pockets. "Have you any idea of the dangers you face on these streets? New York City's murder rate is the highest in the country. Rape, assault, pickpockets . . . Your father would drop over of heart failure if he knew."

Here they went again, round and round with the threat of Duncan Greene. It was like a carousel that never ended. "Good thing he'll never learn of it, then."

"Unless a journalist happens to uncover the story of a Fifth Avenue princess on the fringes of a Five Points murder trial."

Oh, dear. That hadn't occurred to her. She opened her mouth and then closed it. Why hadn't she thought of this before now? She looked up at him. "Will I be called to testify?"

"Definitely not if you're in my employ—which is the only reason you were downtown today, should you be asked. Understand?"

"Is that why you told Mrs. Porter I worked for you?"

"Yes, and I wanted her to speak freely."

"Do you ever tire of spinning the truth to suit your purposes?"

"No, quite frankly. Would you rather I told the newspapers the real reason I took the case? That it was a favor to Miss Marion Greene?"

"I'd prefer it if you didn't."

"Then we are clear. Incidentally, I should point out that I have now saved you yet again after you rushed forth without considering the consequences of your actions."

"If the world finds out what I've been doing, then so be it. What matters is keeping Mrs. Porter from the gallows."

"They don't hang the condemned any longer in New York state. It's death by electrocution."

Good God, that was a horrifying thought. Shocked to death. "Be that as it may, all I care about is saving Mrs. Porter."

The side of his mouth hitched, tiny lines appearing at the corners of his eyes. Lord, he was a handsome devil. "Marion Greene, a crusader. Well, let me see you off in a carriage, Miss Do-Gooder. I've got an arraignment to prepare for."

"Shouldn't I stay? You might need my help."

"Not necessary. I'll handle this all on my lonesome. You'd best return home before you're missed."

She didn't care for the idea but it was probably wise. Not only because her family might note her absence but because time spent with Frank Tripp was dangerous to her overall well-being. Just looking at him—the perfectly groomed hair and classic features, wide shoulders and long limbs—sent her pulse shooting into the atmosphere. The air sparked and sparkled when they were together, a charge that vibrated in her veins, creating a bone-deep desire she couldn't shake.

Did he feel it, too? Was that why he'd asked for a billiards tournament with her as compensation?

He watched her, waiting silently across the room, a slight frown pulling at his lips. Likely he thought she'd put up a fight about staying for the arraignment. She started for the exit instead. The less time they spent together, the better.

He went to open the door for her. Just as his hand reached the knob he stopped. She nearly collided with his back. "Oh, and do not discuss the case with absolutely anyone, *employee*." He glanced over his shoulder to glower at her.

Mere inches separated them, and both were caught by surprise at the proximity. She could see the shadow of a beard on his jaw, each individual lash fanning his eyelids. She also noted the pulse pounding in his neck. Was it her nearness he reacted to, or his general aggravation with her? Hopefully it was the first—because she didn't wish to suffer alone, desiring a man who so thoroughly vexed her.

She stepped to the side, putting more distance between them. "Not a problem, Mr. Tripp. Oh, and seeing as how I am your employee now, I expect a *huge* raise."

THE DOOR TO Frank's office burst open the next morning. Charles Thomas and James Howe barreled in, the two older men not bothering to knock or ask if Frank was busy before dropping into the chairs across from his desk.

Howe and Thomas were two of Frank's partners. Their offices were upstairs, where they handled most of the high-profile criminal cases. Frank didn't see them often outside their weekly partner meeting.

"Have you lost your mind?" Howe asked, tossing the morning's newspaper on Frank's desk. "You took a Sixth Ward murder case?"

Frank had seen the article already. Hell, he'd been the one to contact the publisher last night to ensure the story made the morning edition. Relaying information meant he could control it. "Yes, I have."

Thomas squinted through his spectacles. "Pro bono? You know we don't do that kind of work."

"Not exactly pro bono. I am being compensated." By Mamie. In the manner of Frank's choosing. A hundred cases were worth that bargain.

Not that he would tell Mamie as much. It would only encourage her to rescue more tenement residents.

"And I fail to see why it's a problem," he lied.

Howe lifted a gray brow. "We have worked hard to build our reputation. We represent some of the wealthiest men in the city. Now, we never complained when you took on one or two downtown clients."

Because said clients were all richer than Midas and hated notoriety of any kind. Frank helped them quickly and quietly—a situation that had suited everyone perfectly. Those were not clients the firm bragged about openly.

No, they bragged about clients such as Duncan Greene and the Astors. The Fishes and the Cuttings. The Livingstons and the Van Rensselaers. In other words, the wealthiest and most prestigious families. And the publicity worked because the blue bloods all followed each other like sheep. Same architects, same tailors, same restaurants, same lawyers.

Which was why Frank could not afford to upset the status quo.

And yet, the restraints chafed more and more often these days.

"But?" he prompted when the other two men fell silent.

"But this . . . woman. She's a wife living in a tenement." Thomas recoiled as if these facts were downright horrifying. "It makes us all look . . . lesser."

"I fail to see how that's possible with just one case. We won't lose any business over it."

"Who is compensating you for the time?" Howe asked.

"That's confidential."

Howe cocked his head, almost as if he hadn't heard Frank correctly. "What do you mean, confidential?"

"It means the payment remains between me and the referring party."

Thomas sat a bit straighter. "You know our agreement, Frank. We cannot take cases on our own. All payments must be—"

"There is no money exchanging hands. The payment is of a different sort."

"Ah," Howe said. "Does this have something to do with the woman who accompanied you to headquarters last night?"

Interesting. That piece of information hadn't appeared in the papers. Had they been digging on him? "And how did you learn about her?"

"I had an early meeting with an assistant prosecutor over another case. People are talking about it, apparently. It's not every day you arrive at headquarters to represent a murderess."

He sighed. This was a waste of time he did not have. "If you two will quit sniping at me for doing a good deed I could use your help. It's been some time since I defended in a murder trial."

Howe and Thomas exchanged a quick glance. They'd known each other for more than thirty years and often communicated without words. Whatever message was exchanged, they must have decided to help Frank because Howe said, "Have you been to see the coroner yet?"

"Sending my investigator. I don't expect to learn anything new, however."

"You never know," Thomas said. "What judge did you draw?"

"Smyth."

"Who's your prosecutor?"

"McIntyre. He wasn't expecting to see me at the arraignment, that's for certain."

"He's good," Howe said. "Undoubtedly he expected one of the court-appointed lawyers to defend her. Did they set bail?"

"Denied. They argued her mental state is fragile and she's a danger to her children." Mamie wouldn't be pleased about this. Frank had tried his best, but the judge hadn't given him a chance to dispute the assumption with any facts.

"Probably true," Thomas said. "Those people just don't value human life."

*Those people?* Frank shifted in his chair. Was that what he'd sounded like to Mamie last night, some stiff-necked, unfeeling snob? "What happened to all are innocent in the eyes of the law until proven otherwise?"

"You of all people know how the law works, Tripp. Innocent hardly figures into what we do."

Yes, he was aware. Most of his clients walked a fine line, skirting the law when it so benefitted them. Frank had built a reputation on twisting the facts to excuse such skirting whenever rich clients were caught. It was not a particularly noble path he'd cleared for himself . . . but a damn lucrative one.

"Just plead it out and finish the thing with all haste," Howe said. "Get her to admit what she did and then we can all move past this."

"No, I intend to get her off. I plan to argue that long periods of mental and physical abuse drove her to murder her husband." The strategy had come to him during their talk with Mrs. Porter and it seemed like the perfect argument. Not to mention it was the truth. "The jury will acquit her."

"Perhaps, but the firm will suffer from the publicity," Thomas said.

"And have you considered the drain on your time and resources?" Howe asked. "You cannot honestly care what happens to this woman."

Mamie certainly cared. And while Mrs. Porter's circumstances were tragic, Frank learned long ago not to become emotionally involved in the cases he handled. This one was no different.

"Let me worry about the publicity and my resources, hmm?"

The two older men exchanged yet another look, one that promised this wasn't the last conversation on the topic. After they said their goodbyes and departed, Mrs. Rand brought a stack of papers into his office. "What's this?"

"You asked for the Greene marriage settlement as soon as it was ready." She held out the pages. "Here you are. I checked it against your notes and everything is in there as you directed."

Frank stared at the offering as if it were poison. Mamie's marriage agreement. For marriage to another man. Part of him had hoped the document would take longer than a few days. Damn the efficiency around here. "Thank you, Mrs. Rand. Just leave it on my desk."

"Would you like me to send a copy up to Mr. Greene at home?"

"No," Frank blurted. Mrs. Rand frowned, so he lied, "I'll take it up. No need to trouble yourself."

"Very good, if you're certain."

She strode out of his office, leaving Frank to stare at the marriage settlement on his desk. He couldn't bring himself to touch it, not yet. Touching it meant the engagement was real, not the figment of society's imagination.

*The engagement is real, you idiot.*

Besides, what did he care? Mamie and Chauncey were destined for each other. Frank had no right to her. Never had. This idea of forcing her to spend time with him, whether billiards or dinner, was a terrible one. What had he been thinking?

This business with Mamie had to stop. As much as he was having with her, Knickerbocker princesses didn't end up with men from the wrong end of town, even wealthy ones. They ended up with society scions, fucking nitwits like Chauncey Livingston.

Frank had always kept his career in the forefront of his mind. Success, power and money . . . the New York trifecta. And he'd gained all three. No woman, not even one as intriguing and clever as Mamie Greene, would ever jeopardize that.

"Mrs. Rand," he called. When his secretary appeared, Frank pointed at the legal papers. "Actually, I changed my mind. Go ahead and send one of these to Duncan Greene for review."

THE AFTERNOON SUN had just started to dip in the sky when Mamie exited her carriage at the entrance to Central Park. She grabbed her parasol and walked to the gate, slipping inside.

With little foot traffic today she was able to easily spot her escort waiting by a bench. Chauncey Livingston. Her soon-to-be fiancé. Chauncey appeared a bit pale, his face haggard. Was he ill?

*Are you not bothered by the rumors of actresses and opium dens?*

Frank must have been joking. Chauncey was no deviant. A little flighty, perhaps, but not a bad seed. She'd known him almost her whole life.

More importantly, she didn't need a reminder of Frank Tripp. She hadn't seen or heard from him since the night of Mrs. Porter's arrest four days ago. She absolutely did not miss him or his stupid charm. God knew she certainly didn't miss arguing with him. But no contact at all? It seemed a bit rude.

Not that her feelings were hurt. That would be ridiculous.

It was just, as far as employers went, he left quite a lot to be desired.

At that moment, Chauncey spotted her and offered a small wave. Dressed in a tan linen suit and straw hat, he was every inch the wealthy young man about town. Perfectly at home in his privileged surroundings.

He was always nice. Polite. Almost boring, if she were honest. He hated athletic endeavors and wasn't much for theater or opera. Visited his club each afternoon, dined at the same restaurants. Spent eight days in Newport every summer. He went to London for the Christmas holiday.

No surprises. Utterly predictable.

Just like her future.

*It doesn't have to be. You could have more.*

No, she couldn't. She had decided against that years ago, when she and her father made their bargain. He wanted her to marry Chauncey and she would not disappoint him, seeing as he had no son to carry on the family legacy. Mamie *was* the legacy. She knew this, had been made painfully aware of it her entire life. She would marry Chauncey so that Florence and Justine could marry whomever they wished. Their happiness was worth this small sacrifice.

Besides, it wasn't as if she hated Chauncey. She didn't love him but she was fond of him. And that was more than most society marriages.

Most importantly, there was no rush. Chauncey didn't seem to care how long it took to get to the altar—and neither did she.

"Hello, Mamie." Chauncey leaned in and kissed her cheek.

"Hello, Chauncey. Nice to see you." And it was.

She held no ill-will toward her future fiancé. "I was surprised to get your note."

"It's been some time since we've seen one another, I suppose. I apologize for that." He offered his arm, which she took, and they began to walk the path together. She held her parasol with her free hand.

"I expected to see you at the Vandermeyer costume ball," he said.

Ah. That had been the most recent night Frank caught her at the Bronze House. "I wasn't feeling well and decided to miss it. Was it a gay time?"

"Dashed good fun. Tippy brought a live cat in a bag, let it loose in the dining room." He snickered. "Hilarious."

Mamie frowned. This was Chauncey's world: pranks and parties. Clubs and yachts. Had he ever stepped below Fourteenth Street? Had he any idea of the suffering of most New Yorkers?

Of course he didn't. And without her younger sister's influence, Mamie wouldn't either. Ladies held fundraisers for various causes, but one did not witness poverty firsthand. "That poor cat," she couldn't help but say.

"Aw, it wasn't harmed." He patted her hand. "I forgot how soft you are."

Soft? Frank would have a good laugh at that. "So your note mentioned a discussion. What was it you wished to talk about?"

"Have you spoken to your father lately?"

A bird landed on the path beside them, flapping its wings in the dirt. "I saw him a few nights ago at dinner. Why?"

"Did he . . . Well, I'm wondering if he mentioned our betrothal."

"No." She looked over at him. "Has something happened?"

"There was some talk. Gossip going around. Apparently you went to dinner with your father's lawyer."

He waited and so she confirmed it. "Yes, I did."

"Well, our fathers decided to solidify the betrothal after that. I'm surprised he didn't tell you."

Surprise did not begin to cover what Mamie felt. More like stunned. Betrayed she was not consulted. Despondent that her future had arrived. How could Daddy have done this without letting her know? "No, he didn't."

"My father shared the agreement with me last night. Most is standard language, you know. Your father was very generous. He's planning to buy that old Huntville property on Seventy-Third Street up for sale as a wedding present for us."

Mamie's stomach turned over, nauseated at the idea of settling into her role as a society wife. Overseeing a household, raising kids, tutors and governesses, vacations in Paris . . . It felt like a huge current sweeping her down to the bottom of the ocean. "Yes, that does seem generous," she murmured, her brain struggling to take it all in.

"Indeed." They walked for a few moments, the quiet sounds of nature surrounding them. She sensed he was working up to something.

Lord, how could this have finally come to pass? She had always assumed her father would speak to her first, give her some hint as to what was to come. Get her input on the terms of the agreement. To proceed blindly, without her knowledge, smacked of rashness. Panic. Was her father worried—?

Of course. Her father hadn't liked the idea of her and Frank sharing a night out together. The timing was too convenient not to be connected. Did he believe Frank had designs on her? The idea was ludicrous. She would need to speak with him and clear this up, immediately.

"The thing is, Mamie," Chauncey said. "There are a few clauses in the agreement that are . . . unusual."

She hated that her fiancé was filling her in on the most important document of her life. Why did men discuss these things without a woman's—the bride's—input? Shouldn't she get a say in how her future was signed away?

Swallowing her irritation over patriarchal traditions, she asked, "Oh? Such as?"

"Things like children."

"That's not unheard of, Chauncey."

"He wants one grandchild every other year for the next eight years."

She stopped in her tracks, dragging him to a halt. "He put a timetable on grandchildren?"

Chauncey thrust his hands in his pockets. "Yes. He wants four."

Mamie's jaw fell open. Outrageous. Positively ludicrous. Her father was not shy about his desire for grandchildren, but this was beyond anything she could've imagined. What if she and Chauncey chose to wait a few years, to grow accustomed to one another before starting a family?

A dry laugh escaped her throat. "Why not stipulate the gender of the grandchildren as well?"

Chauncey winced. "Oh, he did that, too. As a request, of course, but hoping for three boys and one girl."

"Good Lord."

"Indeed."

Her father had lost his mind. That was the only explanation for such a clause. "And this was all drawn up in the agreement?"

"Yes, by your father's lawyer."

*Tripp.*

She closed her eyes to absorb the horror. God, what must he have thought, drafting this up? How utterly mortifying. Worse, why hadn't he told her? He'd obviously known about it. So, why not tell her? Or at the very least warn her.

*Because his loyalty is to your father, not to you.*

How could she have forgotten? Money and prestige mattered to both her father and Frank Tripp. Not the wishes of one silly twenty-three-year-old woman.

Something suddenly occurred to her. If Frank had known about this, then why ask for the billiards tournament at his home? Visiting the home of an unmarried gentleman at night could ruin her and jeopardize her engagement. What had he been thinking to suggest it?

"And there's more," Chauncey said, and Mamie's chest squeezed in dread.

"I'm almost afraid to ask."

"There are clauses included about, ahem, infidelity."

She could only stare. "Infidelity? I don't understand."

"If I—or you—are found to have any . . . partners outside the marriage in the first ten years there is a steep monetary penalty."

"How steep?"

"More than I could ever pay without going to my father."

She sighed and rubbed her eyes with her gloved fingers. This whole business was dashed *embarrassing*. "Is it me? Are you worried I might take a lover?"

# Chapter Seven

𝒜 hiss escaped through Chauncey's teeth and he glanced around wildly. "Mamie! You cannot say such words in public."

She gestured toward the empty path. "No one can hear us, Chauncey. And we're to be married. We may speak of such words in private."

"I suppose, if we must. Furthermore, we all know the concern in this particular case lies with me."

"That you will take a mistress?"

Another hiss. "You should not know that word."

Was he serious? Everyone knew that word. And why was *her* infidelity not a concern? Women frequently allowed men who were not their husbands into their beds. Not that Mamie would dishonor her marriage vows by being unfaithful, but why was he so sure she wouldn't?

She waved her hand. "Let's not quibble over the extent of my vocabulary. May I assume this clause is an issue because there already is a conflict?"

The skin of his neck flushed and he dropped his gaze. "Yes, I have a conflict."

So Chauncey had a mistress. Hmm. She waited

for a stab of jealousy to erupt or her stomach to roil . . . but nothing. His paramour—or paramours, as the case may be—did not bother her in the least.

"And you are unwilling to give her up?"

He adjusted his straw hat more firmly on his head. "Hardly seems fair, not when every gentleman in New York keeps one. You're a practical woman. You are aware of how these things go. Ours will be no different than any other society marriage. We'll be happy but respectful. I won't ever flaunt her in any manner to embarrass you."

Was he in love with this other woman? Mamie had assumed mistresses were as exchangeable as handkerchiefs. However, if Chauncey had feelings for his paramour that could negatively impact their marriage. "You wish for me to speak to my father. To have this clause amended."

"Yes." He sagged in obvious relief. "He'll understand, as a man of our world, that it's unrealistic to ask a gentleman to subject his wife to one hundred percent of his bedroom attentions."

And there went her stomach. She fought the visceral reaction to the idea of what "bedroom attentions" with Chauncey would entail. She could not contemplate one percent of his affections—let alone one hundred.

*This is the bargain. This is your path.*

She dragged in a deep breath. "I think you're worried for no reason. My father could hardly enforce such a stipulation."

"Perhaps, but I don't wish to start our marriage with a lie. You know how these things can be discovered. And I lack the funds to pay a penalty this steep."

Children . . . intimacies . . . mistresses . . . Her life had suddenly become surreal. She took his arm and began leading him along the path once more. "What's she like?"

He stumbled then caught his balance. "*Mamie.*"

"If you are unwilling to give her up then she must mean a great deal to you. I would wish to know who holds my soon-to-be husband's affections."

"This is not a proper conversation for us to—"

"Chauncey, please. I'm twenty-three, not some eighteen-year-old miss. You and I have known each other since we were babies. I know you kissed Penelope Van der Meer on the cliffs in Newport."

"We were nine, Mamie. This is quite different."

Not entirely. She felt the same about him now as she had then, like a friendly acquaintance. Their marriage would be a partnership toward common goals: stability, child rearing and status quo. "We must trust each other if our marriage is to work."

"Fine. She's a singer at a club in the Tenderloin."

"Pretty?"

"Gorgeous," he replied quickly, as if he hadn't stopped to think about it. Then he straightened. "I apologize. I never should have implied . . ."

"What? That you find other women attractive?" A mental image of Frank came to her, with his perfectly polished exterior and wide shoulders. The ways in which he filled out a three-piece suit should be considered dangerous in all forty-four states. "That would be a bit hypocritical of me, seeing as I have eyes as well."

Chauncey drew to an abrupt halt. "You find other men attractive?"

Were all males so oblivious, or just the ones born north of Forty-Second Street? "Yes, of course I do."

"I'm uncertain how I feel about this new side of you. You've grown quite bold in the last few years."

Bold? More like enlightened. Her eyes had been opened to the entitlement and waste of her social circle, to the injustice and inequality of their city. How could one's priorities not completely shift after seeing the need and desperation in a mother's eyes when she was unable to feed her children? "You are welcome to not sign the agreement," she told him. "Our fathers will get over their disappointment."

Chauncey was instantly contrite. "I don't wish to back out." He considered her for a long moment. "Do you?"

*Yes.* "No, of course not."

"Good, then it's settled. You'll talk to your father to change those particulars of the agreement and then everything will move forward as it should."

*As it should. Maintain the status quo.* How she hated the very idea of that.

Perhaps her father would reconsider the marriage if they couldn't resolve this issue. Perhaps the whole thing would be called off. Duncan Greene was not known for bending when he set his mind to something.

There might be a way out of this after all, one that wouldn't be Mamie's fault. She tried to hide her hopeful grin. "I'll speak to him just as soon as I return home."

"But carefully," he warned. "I don't wish to upset your father. He cannot suspect I'm unwilling to go along with the proposal."

"Does your father know we are meeting?"

"No. When I complained, my father told me to marry you, sire some children and then do as I pleased."

God, how depressing. "But how am I supposed to object to the clause without letting him know why?"

"You are clever, Maims. You'll think of something."

She certainly hoped so, because marriage was speeding toward her at breakneck speed. There had to be a way for her to avoid the collision without breaking her promise to her father—even if it meant throwing Chauncey under the wheels of the oncoming train.

MAMIE DIDN'T OFTEN visit her father's home office. He preferred his solitude there—one of the last places in his home he could claim solely as his own, he said. So she was unsurprised by the lukewarm reception she received upon knocking.

"Mamie." Her father lowered a stack of papers and squinted at her through his spectacles. "Is it urgent?"

"Hello, Daddy. Yes, I'm afraid it is."

He sighed and tossed the papers on the desk. "Best come in, then. Have a seat."

Mamie loved her father, but he had to be handled carefully. In business, he was decisive and ruthless, unafraid of anything or anyone. At home, he definitely wanted things done his way. Therefore, in Mamie's experience, it was best to let her father think her good ideas were his own . . . even when they weren't.

Getting her father to break this engagement would not be easy, but she had to try.

"Are you terribly busy?" She lowered herself into the chair across from his desk.

"Always, but I'm happy to make time for you when you need me. Tell me the problem."

"I just returned from a walk with Chauncey."

"Excellent." His eyes brightened considerably at that news, his mustache twitching. "It pleases me to hear of you two spending time together."

"Yes, I've always been fond of him. I was surprised, however, to hear that the details of the wedding agreement had been arranged."

"The arrangement is my responsibility, Mamie, one I have ignored for far too long."

"Was there a reason you suddenly moved forward with it?"

"No." He rested his elbows on the armrests and steepled his fingers. "It's past time for you to be married. I preferred not to rush you but it's been nearly five years since your debut."

She didn't believe him. This wasn't about her debut or age. Something deep in her bones told her this was about Frank Tripp. "Should I not have a say in what I'm agreeing to?"

"You are aware that's not how these matters are handled. But you needn't worry—I set aside a large sum of money for you that Chauncey cannot touch. Ever."

Interesting Chauncey hadn't mentioned *that*. All he cared about was the ability to retain his mistress. "That's very sweet of you, Daddy. Thank you."

He inclined his head. "No daughter of mine is ever going to be penniless. Chauncey's a fine fellow but not all men can be trusted. Unfortunately, you often don't learn of the bad seeds until you've eaten most of the apple."

"What of the other clauses?"

"Standard, mostly. Nothing for you to worry about."

"According to Chauncey, there is need for concern. You put a timetable on your grandchildren?"

He shifted in his chair, his big body adjusting to sink deeper into the leather. "It's perfectly reasonable. Better to get them out of the way in the beginning, as your mother and I did."

"You assume we wish for a family right away and that I'm able to conceive."

"There is no need to be crude, young lady. You might talk that way with your mother but I would prefer it if we did not discuss such delicate matters."

She struggled to hide her irritation. He acted as if she'd described the act in gory detail. She longed for the day when women could describe these matters openly with their families. Secrets merely led to ignorance. "I don't wish to be told when to start a family, Daddy. That decision is between my husband and me, no one else."

"Sometimes it's better to state these things ahead of time. Trust me."

"Marriages are different now than when you and Mama were married. We prefer more time to get to know one another—"

"*Get to know one another?* You've known him since birth. Don't be ridiculous. Have children right away, then you may each do as you wish."

This was the opening she needed. "Is that why

you put in an infidelity clause, because you don't trust us?"

"No, I put that in because I don't trust *Chauncey*."

"Has he given you reason to doubt his faithfulness?"

"Of course not. I have no specific knowledge of his . . . tendencies in that area. But I do know men." He waggled a finger at her. "They're not capable of fidelity."

"Including you?"

He snapped upright and shot her a withering glare. "Tread lightly, Marion. You are still my daughter and I am still your father. Do not disrespect me or your mother while you are in this house."

"I meant no disrespect. I'm merely pointing out that you are overgeneralizing. Chauncey's not a womanizing rake. Have you ever heard of him embroiled in a scandal, like fathering a baby out of wedlock or ruining a girl?"

"No, I have not. But he's no stranger to the casinos and dance halls of the Tenderloin."

"Which has little to do with his future as a husband."

"Are you willing to risk your marriage on that?"

No, she was hoping to avoid marriage altogether. To that end, it was time to bring this around to Chauncey's unsuitability. "Chauncey has been honest with me. He said he has many lady friends and has no intention of dropping them merely because we've married. He's asked that we eliminate the infidelity clause altogether."

Her father's lips tightened as he searched her face. "Is this about Frank Tripp?"

She inhaled sharply. How had her father drawn *that* conclusion? "O-Of course not," she stammered. "I barely know Mr. Tripp."

"I see. I'm beginning to understand. You are trying to pin this infidelity clause business on Chauncey when it is really *you* who wishes to abolish it."

"Daddy! How could you say that?"

"Because I'm well acquainted with Frank Tripp. I don't trust him, not with you. Is he filling your head with all kinds of promises for after your marriage?"

She could only stare at her father. Where was he coming up with these accusations? "He's doing no such thing. You have misunderstood me."

"I don't believe I have. If this were about Chauncey, you would demand that clause remain in the agreement. What wife wants her husband to be unfaithful?"

This had taken a disastrous turn. "Chauncey has a woman, one he keeps. And he said he has no intention of giving her up after our marriage."

He reclined and folded his hands on his stomach. "I've known Chauncey's father for over forty years. He and I served as officers in the Sixty-Sixth Infantry during the war. He was the best man at my wedding, and I at his. I trust him to get Chauncey in line in time for your wedding."

"And if he doesn't?"

"Then Chauncey will be found in breach of the marriage contract and you will add to that stack of money I've set aside for you."

"But why risk it? Perhaps we should—"

"Mamie, I will not remove that clause. Not for

you, not for Chauncey and definitely not for Frank Tripp. Are we clear?"

"Mr. Tripp has nothing to do whatsoever with this conversation."

"If you say so," he said, though his tone was less than convincing.

She had bungled this entire meeting. Instead of throwing doubt on Chauncey, she'd thrown doubt on herself. Time to retreat and rethink her plan of attack.

She rose. "I'll let you return to work."

He stood as well, reaching down to straighten his vest. "One last point before you go. I believe you when you say Tripp has nothing to do with this. But Marion"—he paused for effect—"see that it stays that way."

THE AFTERNOON LIGHT was fading as Frank crossed Mott Street. He stepped over a puddle that was most definitely not water and grimaced. Nice to see that Five Points hadn't changed much since he'd lived here. Muck and filth were the building blocks of the Sixth Ward, an area that had been left to its own devices after the rich folk moved farther north.

Gin palaces, saloons and flophouses ruled these streets, with raucous laughter and arguments spilling out onto the walk at all hours. Life was hard below Twenty-Third Street, no more evidenced by the desperate hopelessness that permeated the air here.

*You're too smart to end up dead, Frankie. Go to school. Get out of this neighborhood before it kills you.*

If Mr. Gordon hadn't given Frank enough money

for school, what would have become of him? A b'hoy, stealing and killing in the name of staying alive? Or a newsie, standing on the street in all kinds of weather to sell a few papers? After that, he'd have transitioned to a professional criminal or gone to work in a factory. He'd still be here, miserable and married, supporting kids any way he saw fit.

His chest squeezed, the relief so keen he could not breathe. He never wanted to remember what those days felt like, what they sounded like. The insecurity and the fear. His mother's cries and the grunts of his father as he took what he wanted, come hell or high water.

*She was at the mercy of that monster. He spent their funds on gin and women. Came home and treated her like trash.*

Mamie's words rang true in so many ways. He'd never tell her, of course, but he understood the desire to rescue a woman in that situation. He had tried with his own mother for fourteen years.

"Ho, Tripp!"

The voice caused him to look around. Then he spotted Otto Rosen, the young man Frank often used as an investigator. Otto was stocky, probably not more than six or seven inches over five feet tall, and smart as a whip. He'd asked to take the policeman's examination several times but had been refused on the basis of his Jewish faith. Frank had offered to speak to the police commission on Otto's behalf, but his investigator hadn't wished to "pull strings."

Frank couldn't begin to understand this logic. Pulling strings was the New York City way. Fairness? That was for fools. Yet Otto preferred to proceed by the letter of the law. He'd be granted an examination on merit or not at all. Frank respected the other man for it, even if he didn't agree.

In the end, Otto had gone to work for the Pinkerton Detective Agency. Which, unless a policeman lined his pockets with bribes, was the more lucrative career choice anyway.

"Hello, Otto," he said when he drew close, extending his hand.

The young man grinned and pumped Frank's hand. "You look like you stepped in horse droppings." His accent barely hinted at his Russian heritage, his parents having immigrated to the Lower East Side some thirty years ago. "Fond of our little neighborhood, I see."

"I have nothing against the neighborhood." Merely the memories that haunted him here, which was why Frank made a point never to visit. "Just thinking about a case."

"A case . . . or a woman?"

Both, as it turned out. Why was Otto so damn astute?

"Thank you for meeting me," Frank said as the two of them moved toward the buildings. "You've seen the notes?"

"Read them this morning. I've already been to see the coroner."

"Good. What did he say?"

"Exactly as she said. Two blows to the head from behind. Liver was an unholy mess. Dr. Dobbs said he'd never seen one like it. Estimated Porter had been a heavy drinker for more than a decade."

"That holds up with what Mrs. Porter told the police. Excellent." He jerked a thumb at the building behind him. "We need to speak to the neighbors, find out what they saw, what they heard. Anything Mrs. Porter may have told them about her situation. Past injuries, et cetera."

"Sure, no problem. Want me to get started and report back in a few days?"

Frank grimaced. Normally, yes. He'd usually turn this all over to Otto and wait for the investigator to finish. However, Mamie was involved in this case. He could almost hear her telling him to hurry up, to get Mrs. Porter out of that miserable place. Assisting Otto meant this all moved a bit faster.

Which was what Frank cared about most. The sooner they wrapped up this case, the sooner he could return to his life of parties, women and the law. Mamie Greene would be in his past, just a young girl he'd once helped. And lusted after.

Damn it.

He focused on Otto, who was staring at him carefully. "No, I will help you. It'll go quicker."

"You . . . plan to help? Don't take this the wrong way, but tenement residents are a bit different than your fancy juries."

"I can hold my own, don't worry. The woman who hired me for this case is anxious for the accused to be released."

"I see. Is she anything like that woman headed toward us, the one who looks like a wealthy uptown lady?"

Frank spun toward the street. Dear God. There was Mamie, marching straight up the steps of Mrs. Porter's building. She wore a simple dress but it was clean and new, not stained and patched like the garments one usually saw down here. Her shoes were not worn down but shiny. Her skin was like fine French porcelain, as only those who remained indoors could manage. She didn't blend in down here, not even close. In fact, eyes all around them turned to track her progress.

For fuck's sake, what was she doing here?

He bounded after her before he could even register what his feet were doing. Once she stepped into the vestibule, he caught up, took her elbow and dragged her off to the side. She began to struggle, crying out and kicking to get loose. He ground his back teeth together, too angry at her recklessness to announce himself. Was she trying to get herself killed?

When they reached the stairs, he released her—and she immediately turned to smack him across the face. "How dare you—" She exhaled sharply. "*Frank.* My God. You scared me half to death." Realization dawned, and she shoved his shoulder. "What is wrong with you? Were you purposely trying to frighten me?"

"No. I was attempting to ask you to tea." He rubbed his cheek, now stinging from the flat of her palm. "Nice right hook, Mamie."

"You deserve worse." She straightened the sleeves of her dress and pinned him with an accusatory stare. "Are you following me? *Again?*"

"Believe it or not, I am out working on your case. Remember, that thing you hired me to do? That means you stay home and I fill you in on developments as they happen. You absolutely do not come down to Five Points and wander about on your own."

"In case you've forgotten, I am able to do as I please. I'm here to check on the Porter children and to speak to some of the other neighbors. Hiring you does not preclude me from attempting to learn information on my own."

"Yes, actually. It does."

"Not when I am your employee."

Christ, why had he ever said it? Even in jest it was a terrible idea. "You are my employee in name only, Mamie. You're the employee who must remain uptown. Safe and sound."

She moved closer, her skirts rustling against his trousers, and put out her hand. "I need one dollar, Frank."

The air in the room suddenly burned his lungs, the walls too close. The smell of orange blossom and sweet spices stole into his lungs, a mysterious and complex aroma that was so like the woman herself. Why on earth was she standing so near? He tried to take a step back—and found the wall prevented it. Swallowing, he asked, "What for?"

"It's considered rude to ask a lady about money. You are supposed to provide it, no questions asked."

The front of her generous bosom was alarmingly close to his chest. He would do anything to end this conversation before he embarrassed himself by saying something ridiculous. Or falling at her feet and professing his annoying and inconvenient desire for her.

Shoving a hand into his jacket pocket, he withdrew his billfold and retrieved one bill. He nearly tossed it into her hand. "There. Happy?"

She tucked the money into the depths of her bodice . . . and Frank's knees nearly buckled. The crisp bill that had just been in his palm was now nestled somewhere deep in her magnificent décolletage. Touching all that soft and supple flesh. Holy Jesus.

He might never recover.

She shifted away, putting a healthy distance between them. "Now I'm officially your employee. Let's go."

# Chapter Eight

This is a terrible idea," Frank grumbled under his breath.

"On the contrary, sir." Otto grinned down from the first landing. "I think Miss Greene will put some of the wives at ease. She might help them to talk."

"See, I told you," Mamie said behind him. "Stop complaining, Tripp."

Otto laughed. "I see how it is."

"What you see," Frank snapped, "is a woman who will get herself harmed one day because she doesn't know when to quit."

"Mr. Rosen, has Mr. Tripp told you where he and I first met?"

They started up the second set of stairs. "I doubt Otto wishes to hear—"

"Oh, I wish it all right. Please continue, Miss Greene."

Mamie pushed by Frank to get closer to her audience. Frank thought about complaining, but the view vastly improved this way. He smothered a smile as he watched Mamie's backside sway during the climb.

"I was in the Bronze House. Gambling," she said. "Skills honed in Tenderloin dives for months with my sister, Florence. It may shock you to learn this, but I was able to take care of myself for years before Mr. Tripp arrived to criticize me."

"I don't doubt it. You seem a very competent woman." Rosen's mouth twisted, mirth dancing in his gaze, clearly attempting to stifle his laughter.

Frank glared at the investigator but said nothing. He could leave, of course, find a willing woman for the evening and spend the hours in bed. Let Otto and Mamie handle the inquiries and save himself the aggravation.

Yet he couldn't bring himself to abandon her. The neighborhood was a dangerous one for proper ladies and he wouldn't cease worrying until she'd been returned to the bosom of uptown Manhattan.

"How should we split this up?" Otto asked as they gathered on the landing. "I take the top two floors while you and Miss Greene cover the bottom two?"

"I think we should all start with the neighbors on either side of the Porters'," Mamie said. "They were the most likely to have heard something through the walls. I've met the neighbor on the right when I took Mrs. Porter's children over. We should definitely speak with her."

"It'll go faster if we split up, Mamie," Frank said. "Cover more ground."

"The point is not for this to be over quickly," she replied. "The point is for us to learn as much as we can to help Mrs. Porter. If you wish to waste your time on the fourth floor, so be it. However, I'm starting on the Porters' floor."

Frank sighed inwardly. There was no use arguing with Mamie. Not only was she incredibly stubborn, she also happened to be right. If speaking to the direct neighbors yielded nothing then they could move to other floors. "Fine. Let's start on the third floor."

The first neighbor was an elderly woman who spoke little English. Fortunately, she spoke Yiddish, one of the languages Otto knew well. The investigator quickly interrogated her and ascertained that her hearing loss had prevented her from listening in on the Porters. According to her, they were a quiet family who caused no trouble.

"I hope we have better luck with the other neighbors," Mamie said quietly as they moved down the hall.

Otto knocked briskly. Noise could be heard on the other side of the door but no one answered. After another minute, Mamie reached out and rapped the wood. "Hello? Mrs. Barrett?"

A lock rattled and the door cracked open. A young woman stared out at them, her gaze wary. "Yes?"

Mamie stepped forward. "Do you remember me? My name is Marion Greene and I brought you the Porter children."

"Ah, yes. I remember." The woman's accent contained the remnants of an Irish brogue. "Are you here for the children? They're on the fourth floor with my sister."

"No," Mamie said. "We'd like a word with you, if you don't mind. Would we be able to come inside?"

The woman's expression did not change. A baby could be heard crying from deep within the apartment. "What's this about? The children haven't been mistreated—"

"Oh, goodness. Nothing like that. I'd like to see them before I go but that is not why we are here. We merely wished to speak with you. It's about Mrs. Porter and her case."

Mrs. Barrett's brows shot up. "This is about Bridget?"

"Yes. May we come in?"

Mrs. Barrett stepped aside and the door opened. Frank removed his derby and followed Mamie inside, Otto doing the same. She brought them into a tiny kitchen where a small child wailed in a tall chair next to the table. After picking up and soothing the child, Mrs. Barrett motioned for them to take seats.

"Mrs. Barrett," Mamie said, "this is Mr. Tripp, Bridget's lawyer, and Mr. Rosen, a man gathering information in her case."

She nodded, still distracted by the fussy child. "Do you have news about her case?"

"Not exactly," Frank explained. "We're hoping to gather information from her neighbors to help her."

"Oh." Mrs. Barrett bounced the child in her arms. "I apologize. He's starving."

Mamie held out her hands. "I'd be more than happy to hold him while you fix him something to eat."

"Would you?" Mrs. Barrett appeared hopeful at gaining an extra set of hands.

"Of course." Mamie reached over and took the small boy from Mrs. Barrett, cradling him in her arms. Now quiet, the child stared at her, momentarily stunned at the different view. Frank sympathized with the kid. He often felt dumbstruck in Mamie's presence.

Mamie cooed softly to the child while Mrs. Barrett busied herself at the counter. Frank watched, mesmerized. He didn't ever want children—in fact, he always took precautions to avoid creating any during his encounters—but he was unable to look away from this tender, caring side of Mamie. She was so independent, so strong . . . yet she handled this tiny human like she had a few babies of her own.

That reminded him of the wedding agreement—and his stomach clenched. He hadn't been able to think of Chauncey Livingston without wanting to punch something since drafting that damn agreement. *One grandchild every other year for the next eight years.* Chauncey would be the one to caress and pleasure Mamie. Bring her orgasms and plant his seed in her. Watch as she grew round with society babies. The idea of it sickened Frank. Chauncey did not deserve her—

"You might want to ease up on your hat," Otto leaned in to whisper. "And stop staring."

Frank loosened his grip on the derby, noting the brim was already beyond repair. Dash it all. At least Mamie's focus remained on the child so she hadn't witnessed his lack of control.

Mrs. Barrett returned with the food and Frank breathed a sigh of relief. Now, they could get to business. Unfortunately, Mamie pleaded to feed the boy, which Mrs. Barrett was only too happy to allow. Frank angled away, determined not to look.

Otto opened his notebook. "How well did you know the Porters, Mrs. Barrett?"

"In passing. Her better than him. He was a mean one. Yelling, more often than not."

"At whom was he yelling? Mrs. Porter? The children?"

"Mostly her, it seemed. They fought something awful."

"With words? Or did it ever get physical?"

Mrs. Porter pressed her lips together and seemed to withdraw, shrinking. Frank had seen it many times with witnesses uncomfortable with the line of questioning. Before he could open his mouth, however, Mamie beat him to it. "Mrs. Barrett," she said, never taking her eyes off the small child. "We need to know. It could help Bridget's case."

"Yes," Mrs. Barrett said. "Quite often it turned physical."

"Did Mrs. Porter ever complain to you or show you any bruises?" Otto asked.

"No, absolutely not. Bridget wasn't one to complain. A wife doesn't . . . Well, besides, what can anyone do about it?"

"Did she ever seek help from the police?"

Mrs. Barrett made a dismissive noise. "The police came once. Someone in the building must've summoned them. But they just told Mr. Porter to sleep it off. Ordered Bridget to stop antagonizin' him."

Frank's fists clenched. The police had said the same to his own mother all those years ago, that she was to blame. As if any woman had control over the situation when a man in her life decided to grow violent. "How often?" he croaked. "How often did it happen?"

"Almost every weekend, I'd say. Mr. Porter received his pay on Friday afternoon and went straight to the gin shops. Came home in the early morning. That's when the noise started."

"Other than what you heard through the wall, you never saw anything?" Otto asked.

"No, but I can tell you this: she loves her kids. She would do anything in the world to keep them safe."

A SUBDUED MOOD hung over the group as they exited the tenement. They had interviewed several more families but no one had heard or seen anything useful. Mamie had also checked in on the Porter children—who missed their mother but were otherwise well cared for—then she, Frank and Otto trudged down the steep staircase to the ground floor.

The early evening breeze carried the scent of sausage and fish, with a hint of horse droppings. Mamie hardly noticed, however, too upset over the interview with Mrs. Barrett. Learning of Bridget Porter's day-to-day life had broken Mamie's heart.

*Almost every weekend. Mr. Porter received his pay on Friday afternoon and went straight to the gin shops.*

What anxiety and fear Mrs. Porter must have lived with on a daily basis, a dread of the horrors to come. Horrors no one had helped her with, not the police or her neighbors. So she'd taken matters into her own hands.

Mamie vowed to do whatever possible to see the woman acquitted. Turn over every stone, follow every lead. She'd find a way to pay Frank's retainer, Otto's fee. Hire a hundred more investigators . . . whatever it took.

She stared up at Frank. "We should talk to the area gin shops, to confirm—"

"Slow down. Otto'll handle that," he said and turned to the investigator. "You know what to do. Just keep me informed."

"Of course." Otto tipped his derby at Mamie. "Nice to meet you, Miss Greene."

"And you, Mr. Rosen. Thank you for all you are doing on this case."

"No need to thank me. The coppers may turn a blind eye to this sort of thing, but the judges don't. I'll get enough evidence for her defense. And you've got the very best attorney in the city ready to argue her case. Don't worry about a thing, Miss Greene."

He strode away after that, leaving Mamie and Frank on the walk. The crowds had thinned now that dusk and suppertime loomed, and she became aware of just how alone they were. Until this moment, she hadn't given Frank much thought, not since he'd accosted her in the vestibule. But she was unable to look away and her skin grew tight as they stared at one another. It was as if every cell had woken up and started to vibrate. Lord, he was devastatingly handsome, his face crafted in sheer perfection.

There was more, however. He oozed competence and charm, a man who could handle himself in any situation. It was . . . seductive. Her heart agreed, a demanding pulse she felt in every part of her body.

He slipped his hands in his pockets and peered at her from under the brim of his hat. "I suppose yelling at you for trudging down here on your own is a waste of breath."

Why was her mouth so dashed dry? She swallowed. "We covered that already."

"I figured as much. So, what now, Miss Detective?"

"What do you mean?"

"I feel as though I need to keep tabs on you before you visit any more dangerous neighborhoods."

She frowned. Just when she'd started to soften toward him he had to annoy her. "If you must know, I'm planning to return home. There's a party tonight and I must ready myself for it. Are you headed to the office?"

"Yes, but not until after I drop you at said home."

A carriage ride with Frank . . . all the way uptown? She nearly gulped. "That's unnecessary. I'll locate a hack."

"Nonsense. What sort of employer would I be if I allowed that?"

"A reasonable one?"

He took her elbow and began leading her toward Canal Street. "Mamie, it's nearly dark and you're an unescorted woman in the Sixth Ward. That's begging for trouble."

"The only trouble I ever seem to find is *you*, Frank."

"Please, Mamie? I won't be able to enjoy my evening if I'm worrying over whether you made it home safely or not."

Well. That certainly doused any ire over his high-handedness. She hardly knew what to say, other than to inquire about his evening and what he hoped to enjoy later. A woman?

Lord, that notion lodged behind her ribs like a fist-sized rock.

She remained silent, bothered by her irrational jealousy. Hearing of Chauncey's longtime mistress hadn't given her a second thought, but the hint of Frank's possible liaison sat in her stomach like spoiled herring.

What was happening to her?

She was the responsible one, the daughter who maintained the status quo. The oldest, who would carry on the family legacy in the absence of a son. She wasn't adventurous like Florence or ambitious like Justine. Her father had said she would marry Chauncey and bring the two families together, and Mamie had agreed as long as her sisters could choose their own husbands.

For years, that had been enough. Until this very month, in fact. Before the other night at the Bronze House, she'd never once considered reneging on the agreement with her father.

Then Frank Tripp landed in her life and upended it.

Now, she was scheming a way out of impending marriage and fantasizing about Frank. Inappropriate fantasies that had turned a fire into an inferno. A proper lady might not discuss what happened in her bedroom, alone under the covers at night . . . but what should have satisfied these urges had only fueled a raging desire for *more.*

She had a suspicion that Frank was the "more."

They arrived at his brougham and he assisted her inside. She settled near the far wall, trying to put as much space between them as possible.

It didn't work. He ended up pressed tight to her side. She sucked in a breath.

*Only ninety blocks to go.*

She'd never survive it.

Heat spread along her side where they touched and each one of his movements echoed in her limbs. She couldn't avoid feeling him, her nerves so very attuned to his long frame. Even the rise and fall of his chest affected her, the tips of her breasts hardening into points beneath her clothing.

She exhaled. *You've ignored this pull between you for weeks. One more night won't kill you.*

"You've gone quiet," he said. "Should I be worried?"

*Yes. I think I'm losing my mind.*

After clearing her throat, she asked, "Why didn't you tell me about the unusual clauses in the marriage agreement?"

"Ah." He stared out the brougham window, his fist clenching the knob atop his cane. "I wondered when that might come up."

"Well?"

"Mamie," he said with a sigh, "I cannot discuss my work for your father. You know that."

"Not even when that work pertains to me?"

"Especially when it pertains to you."

"Why?"

He didn't reply, merely shook his head.

"Frank, answer me. Why did you not warn me of what was to come?"

"That wasn't for me to do. Your father—or Chauncey—should look out for your interests."

"That's rich. You've been chasing me about New York City for months looking out for my interests. I cannot turn around in this town without running into you, looking out for my interests. Suddenly, you're finished?"

He shifted toward her and there was a flash of something in his gaze, something dark and heady. An emotion he normally kept tightly leashed. Goose bumps broke out along her flesh.

"I am attempting to do the right thing," he said, his voice a low growl. "Can you not see that?"

Do the right thing? What did he mean? "I thought we were friends."

Instead of answering, he pressed his lips together and looked away.

Disappointment crashed through her, an avalanche of sharp pebbles in her chest. Every time she thought she might understand him, something happened to change her mind. He was the most maddening man. "Fine. I'm tired of never knowing where I stand with you. One day you smother me. The next, ignore me. Keep your agreements and your attentions, then. I don't need them."

"You should marry Chauncey."

She blinked at his words. "Why? So you may collect your fee on the agreement?"

"No, I collect my fee whether you sign the agreement or not. You should marry Chauncey because that is precisely with whom you belong."

He still wouldn't meet her eyes. Was he trying to convince her . . . or himself?

*I am attempting to do the right thing.*

The heaviness in her chest lifted. Was Frank attracted to her? Her sisters had been telling her as much for days, but she hadn't believed it. She'd never known him to tell an outright truth.

Perhaps the truth was in what he didn't say. Perhaps there was a chance she wasn't alone in whatever was happening between them. Perhaps she could have the future she wanted after all, one for herself. Not a loveless marriage and status quo.

There was only one way to find out.

Her heart pounded against her ribs, blood rushing in her ears. She blurted the first thing that came to mind. "I do not wish to marry Chauncey."

FRANK BLINKED. HAD he heard her correctly? His head swiveled until he met her gaze. "What?"

"Chauncey. I do not want to marry him."

"But . . . Because of the agreement?"

"No. I never wished to marry him but our fathers arranged it long ago. The agreement merely brought certain matters to light."

"Such as?"

There was a long pause. Would she be honest with him? In that moment, he fervently hoped so. He wanted to know her better.

*You sound like a schoolboy.* He grimaced and remembered his purpose. This was about Duncan, one of his biggest clients. Mamie might reveal something, some obstacle to the marriage, which Frank could smooth over on behalf of his client. That was all.

"Such as Chauncey's mistress and how he doesn't plan on giving her up after marriage."

*"What?"* The word was a sharp report throughout the tiny enclosure, but he hadn't been able to hold it in. "He actually told you that?"

She nodded. "And I'm glad he did so. I'd much prefer to learn it now than after the wedding."

That fucking bastard. All Chauncey had to do was marry Mamie—this gregarious, vivacious and stunning woman—and he wanted someone *else*? Was he a complete idiot?

Frank knew the answer to that question.

He shook his head and swallowed his blistering monologue on what he thought of her fiancé. "Such arrangements are not uncommon in upper class marriages."

"True, but that doesn't mean I wish it for my marriage."

That made sense. Probably few wives did. A hundred words burned his tongue, begging to be spoken. How she deserved better. How archaic these unhappy society marriages were. How he'd give his right arm to kiss her at this moment.

However, he kept his lips firmly closed and his thoughts to himself. This was not a woman he should charm into bed. This was a dangerous woman, the daughter of a powerful client, a woman who could bring down everything he'd worked to achieve since leaving that shack on Worth Street.

He couldn't marry Mamie. The idea was laughable. And if he couldn't marry her, then he couldn't touch her. Or kiss her. Or lick her . . .

*Christ.*

His cock twitched at the mental image of his face between her legs. He shifted, trying to put more space between himself and Mamie, but there was no room to be had. Why hadn't he brought the larger carriage today?

"Anyway," she said, still pressed tight to his side. "I informed my father of Chauncey's plans and he told me not to worry."

Duncan knew? What the hell? "But that would violate the infidelity clause."

"Exactly. However, my father believes Chauncey will come around. And if he doesn't, then he said I stand to receive a large payout."

Frank rubbed his tongue along the backside of his teeth. None of this seemed right. Duncan should end the engagement, then take Chauncey into the nearest abandoned alley and beat the unholy shit out of him. Instead, her father was using her like a . . . commodity. Trading her future happiness for, what? Why was Duncan so eager for this marriage to take place?

*I wish to know your intentions toward my daughter.*

Duncan had started the agreement process that day, after learning of Frank and Mamie's dinner outing. Was her father so concerned Frank was making a play for Mamie that he'd trade his daughter's happiness for it?

*My daughter is not for you.*

Of course. Get the girl married before the downtown scum ruined her. He clenched his jaw, his back teeth grinding together. Just because he earned his living off men like Duncan Greene didn't prevent Frank from feeling resentful every now and again.

But there was his past, circumstances that must remain buried. He couldn't have his upbringing revealed to the entire city.

"He's right," he forced out. "It's an obscene amount of money, far more than Chauncey could ever pay himself." Not that such logic would stop Chauncey from doing as he pleased. Logic and Chauncey weren't exactly playing on the same team. "No doubt he'll come around."

"You sound like my father," she muttered, and Frank strove to suppress a wince.

"Because we're both right."

"But what if you are wrong? I've lived my life doing what was expected of me—"

A bark of laughter escaped his mouth. "Hardly."

She put up a palm, her lips twisting into a self-deprecating smile. "Only in the last year or so. Before, I was ready to abide by my promise—" She snapped her jaw shut, biting off the words.

He couldn't help but ask, "What promise?"

"To marry Chauncey," she answered vaguely, but he suspected there was more. Then she heaved a sigh. "Have you ever felt like you wanted more than was expected of you?"

He stared out the carriage window. Fancier houses and cleaner streets greeted them on the north side of Thirty-Fourth Street. A tightness he hadn't realized existed loosened in his chest at the sight.

Yes, he knew what it was like to want more out of your future. He pictured his twelve-year-old self, tallying the books at the saloon surrounded by gin, piss and blood. Only death and corruption had awaited him outside on the Lower East Side streets. Escape had been his salvation.

A glib answer leapt to mind but this was Mamie. He couldn't lie to her . . . not about this. "Yes, I have."

"And did you regret taking your own path instead?"

"Not for one moment. But our situations are hardly the same."

"Because I'm a woman?"

"No." He angled toward her. God, the sight of her this close up nearly stole his breath. Every rotted part of his soul yearned to gather her up and show her how much fun the unexpected could be. Instead, he forced himself to stick to the topic at hand, which was why she should marry Chauncey.

"Because you are Marion Greene, daughter of Duncan Greene and upper Fifth Avenue princess. Your father is one of the most powerful men in New York City and your family can be traced back to the days of Dutch rule. You and Chauncey make sense. In fact, it's the only thing in your life that does make sense."

"Are you trying to convince me of all that . . . or yourself?"

The question caught him off guard, his body rocking slightly at the impact. "You, of course." *Liar.*

"If you honestly believe Chauncey and I make sense together then you don't really know me." Her brows lowered. "Or, are you so beholden to my father that you cannot give an honest answer?"

Either way, he lost. The man inside him wished to claim her for himself, but doing so would cost him everything he'd built. "Mamie . . ."

She threw up her hands. "I see. God forbid we upset the great Duncan Greene."

"No, that's not it," he lied automatically.

"No?" Her gaze narrowed and her mouth hitched. "Prove it."

He snorted. This was ridiculous. He was Frank Tripp, king of Manhattan courtrooms. The lawyer who wrapped juries and judges around his little finger. And now this one woman was challenging him? "And how do you suggest I do that?"

She leaned in closer, orange and spice wrapping around him, a sweet and fiery mix that shot sparks through his groin. He fisted his hands in an effort to restrain himself as the tip of her tongue emerged to swipe across her lips, moistening them. That plump flesh parted and she whispered, "Retrieve your dollar."

# Chapter Nine

Mamie shouldn't enjoy surprising him . . . but she relished his reaction. His jaw fell open, his gaze falling to her bosom where she'd tucked the bill earlier. He sucked in a sharp breath and she suppressed a smile. *You cannot lie now, Frank Tripp.*

"You can't be serious." His voice cracked.

She'd never been more serious in her life. Her suspicions about Frank's attraction to her were confirmed, an attraction he was determined to fight. If he wasn't afraid of her father then why not pursue her? After all, he knew what type of marriage she and Chauncey would embark upon. Why should only Chauncey have a lover, a woman he refused to give up after the wedding?

Why was Chauncey the only one allowed to find happiness with another?

Frank was one of the city's most sought-after gentlemen. The newspapers were full of his escapades and liaisons, women surrounding him wherever he went. The two of them were clearly attracted to one another, so where was the harm? At least then she wouldn't remain resentful toward Chauncey.

Frank was safe, the perfect choice. Logical, even. He was a rogue, not a man a woman set her cap for. Therefore, there was no chance they'd develop deeper feelings toward each other. It would remain a light and breezy affair before she married. Purely a physical arrangement.

If only she could convince him to say yes.

"Absolutely serious. In fact, I fail to see the harm."

"The harm?" His lids went wide. "Of me sticking my hand down your dress?"

"Do you not wish to?"

She held perfectly still and awaited his answer. Perhaps he wasn't actually attracted to her. Perhaps she'd misread his actions.

She did not think so, however.

His eyes closed briefly. "Yes, I want to . . . I shouldn't, though."

"Because of my father?"

It was a cheap accusation, guaranteed to annoy him, but she wasn't going to give up. She'd worked to master roulette, craps and other games of chance. She knew what it meant to risk a little in hopes of earning a lot.

She was willing to bet on Frank.

"Because it's inappropriate, Mamie. You are unmarried. Those things should be saved for your husband."

"Chauncey?"

He visibly winced—and satisfaction flooded her like a righteous wave. Was he picturing her and

Chauncey together? "If that is who you marry, then yes."

"It's absurd. Why must I save myself for marriage? No such restrictions exist for Chauncey. He's expected to have mistresses."

"Because that is the way the world works. Consequences exist for you that men don't need to worry about."

"The women they're with need to worry about it, however."

"Those women aren't Duncan Greene's daughters."

Back to her father. Could he ever forget, even for one second, who she was? "So women like Mrs. Porter, women like Chauncey's singer, they don't matter? They deserve the consequences?"

"Don't twist my words. You are asking me to engage in illicit behavior with you and I am refusing."

The bigger mansions began to appear out the brougham glass. Vanderbilt's French chateau. The Bostwicks. The Astors. Places in which she had dined and danced. Where she'd rubbed elbows with the city's wealthiest and most influential residents. It was a life built on money, greed and maintaining rules created almost a century ago.

It exhausted her.

Women were marching in the streets downtown, demanding the right to vote. Demanding temperance laws. Demanding better treatment for the city's underprivileged. Uptown, however, the streets were quiet. Clean and spacious. There were no calls to action here, no angry mobs. Social visits were made between two and four o'clock, drives in the park at five. Dressed for dinner at eight o'clock, dancing until two. Perhaps if she'd never ventured downtown, if she had stayed in her gilded bubble, she would've happily married Chauncey, mistress or not.

However, the world was bigger than these forty blocks. Mamie had seen it with her own eyes, and there was no going back.

Which was how she knew Frank had to agree.

"You're no stranger to illicit behavior," she told him. "I've read about your conquests for years. If you are not attracted to me, then I won't ever ask—"

"Christ. I cannot believe we are having this conversation," he muttered, rubbing his eyes with the heels of his hands. "I should have let you hire a hansom."

"Yes, you should have." She lifted a shoulder. "You only have yourself to blame."

"I have no issue with illicit behavior when both parties willingly consent. However, you are betrothed—"

"Not yet. Nothing has been signed, as you well know."

"Semantics. You told me yourself the understanding has been in place for ages. If anything became public you would be ruined. Your father would be furious. Chauncey would be humiliated. What you are suggesting is the height of irresponsibility."

"I'm no stranger to irresponsibility. Perhaps you should allow *me* to worry about how this might affect my future."

"And what of mine? Taking you to bed jeopardizes my career."

"Because of my father?"

"And all his Fifth Avenue cronies I represent.

Your father carries great influence, Mamie. These men tend to stick together."

She knew that to be true. Her father had ruined a family's standing because the eldest son had offended Florence. Duncan had turned all the husbands and wives against the family, ensuring they were cut from the social lists, and the family moved to Albany three years ago.

Perhaps Frank was not the best man for this job.

If he wanted her beyond reason, passionately—like the men in the novels Florence hid under her bed—he'd overlook her father and the potential consequences to his career. But it seemed he didn't desire her in that way. After all, he could have any woman he wanted. Just because she was desperately attracted to him didn't mean the feeling was reciprocated.

Disappointing, but not devastating.

There were other men in New York City, ones not attached to her father in any manner. Mamie merely needed to encounter one who met her criteria. Handsome, successful, generous, kind and funny. A man who made her feel safe. Who encouraged her to be herself, not just Duncan Greene's eldest daughter.

"Fine." She watched the familiar neighborhood pass as they rode.

"What does that mean, fine?" he asked after a beat.

"It means I'll find someone else. My partner in illicit behavior need not be *you*."

A sound of disbelief erupted from his throat. "You cannot mean that."

"Do you honestly believe you are the only attractive man in Manhattan? Please. Handsome men are as plentiful as the horse droppings here."

"Not sure how I feel about that comparison but, thank you?"

She chuckled. "Cannot allow compliments to go to your head. Besides, you're perfectly aware of your effect on the female gender."

"You are attempting to distract me and I'm not about to let this go. You cannot engage in an affair."

"I'm a young, unmarried wealthy woman in the greatest city in the world. I may do whatever I please—and whatever I do is hardly your concern."

"So, we're back to this?"

"I suppose we are. You cannot track me all the time, Daniel Boone."

"No, but you are my employee. Perhaps I'll hire a few Pinkertons to watch over you."

Was he jealous? She angled to see his face. "Why do you care if I sleep with a man before or after I marry Chauncey?"

His lips were flat and white, unhappiness etched in the depths of his eyes. "Why does it matter to you, my reasons for objecting?"

"You're answering a question with another question. Stop using your lawyer tricks on me."

"I am using reason. I apologize if you confuse them for the same thing."

Very well. She'd be direct instead of vague. That seemed to be the only way to deal with Frank. "Are you attracted to me?"

"Mamie—"

"Answer the question, Frank. If my father were not Duncan Greene, would you try to get me in your bed?"

"Yes," he growled. "I've already told you I want you."

"I thought it was necessary to hear it again."

"Why?"

The carriage slowed as they arrived outside the stone mansion she shared with her family. "For when I try to seduce you."

*FOR WHEN I try to seduce you.*

*Seduce. You.*

So distracted by Mamie's departing words moments ago, Frank nearly tripped going up the steps outside his home. That woman was dangerous. How was he supposed to concentrate on anything ever again after hearing her say such a scandalous thing?

And his cock thought seduction a dandy idea, thickening and making a nuisance of itself.

But he was more than his cock and balls. He was the best damn lawyer in the state. Perhaps the East Coast. He'd risen from filth to own a mansion designed by McKim, Mead & White, for fuck's sake. His determination could easily withstand an intelligent, gorgeous, voluptuous, daring—

"Good evening, sir," his butler announced when Frank entered the vestibule.

He exhaled and shook off the lingering talons of desire. "Evening, Barney."

The butler grimaced ever so slightly at the shortened version of his given surname, Barnaby. Frank couldn't help it; he liked to keep the proper man on his toes. "You are home early," Barnaby commented as he took Frank's derby and walking stick. "Shall I keep the carriage ready for any plans tonight?"

"No, I'll be staying in. I have work to catch up on. Have some supper sent to my office, will you?"

"Of course, sir."

Frank hefted his leather satchel and continued to the office in the back of the house. Familiar sights and sounds greeted him, as well as the smell of lemon polish used by the staff on the wood. He loved this house.

Hours later, the fire in his office had started to burn low when Barnaby knocked. "Sir, Superintendent Byrnes is here to see you."

Frank tapped the end of his pen on the rosewood desk. Byrnes, here? Frank wasn't handling any big cases that would attract the superintendent's attention. "Send him back."

A big burly man of Irish descent, Thomas Byrnes was considered by many to be a tyrant. Yes, he had reorganized and sharpened the city's police detectives, but some of the interrogation methods he used were cruel and coercive. Byrnes would sometimes beat a suspect until he confessed, a technique he called the "third degree." On two separate occasions, Frank had barred Byrnes from questioning a client without him present. Likely that hadn't endeared him to the superintendent but Frank hardly cared.

Byrnes walked in, clothed in a bespoke suit of navy check. An impressive mustache covered the lower half of his face. "Evenin', Tripp. Hope you don't mind the intrusion."

Frank was already on his feet with his coat in place. He held out a hand. "Superintendent, this is a surprise. I didn't realize I had anything pending under your purview."

Byrnes unbuttoned his topcoat and lowered himself into the armchair across from Frank's desk. A gold watch chain dangled from his silk vest. If not for his rough accent Byrnes could pass for any uptown swell in New York. "You don't—not directly anyway. However, it turns out there is a little matter I need to discuss with you about a case."

"Oh?"

"I hear you are representing a Sixth Ward resident for murder."

Frank paused. There was only one current client who fit that description. "Bridget Porter?"

"Yes. That's her."

"Mrs. Porter is indeed my client. Not certain how that concerns you, though."

"It's about her dead husband. And one of my detectives."

"Who's the detective?"

"Edward Porter."

"Porter, as in . . ." A heavy weight settled in Frank's stomach.

"Cousin to the deceased, Roy Porter."

Frank sighed and tapped the end of a pen on his journal. He was beginning to understand why Byrnes had paid this call . . . and he didn't like it. "Let me guess? The detective isn't too fond of his late cousin's wife."

Byrnes hooked a thumb in the tiny pocket of his vest. "Now, we all know marriages have squabbles, Tripp. That ain't a matter for the police or the courts. These things should be handled quietly, internally—"

"So why didn't Edward step in to prevent dear-old-Roy from beating the tar out of his wife every weekend?"

"I cannot say. But Roy's dead and there's a woman responsible. She murdered him in cold blood and deserves to pay the price."

"Hardly cold blood and you know it."

Byrnes held up his palms. "If it was such a problem then why not have her husband arrested? There are plenty of judges who dislike the men who perpetuate these crimes. A few will even take the husbands out back and horsewhip them to bring them in line."

Frank had also heard similar stories and applauded those judges. "That only helps if the husband is arrested. I'm beginning to understand why Mrs. Porter's complaints would've fallen on deaf ears, however."

"We look out for our own, that's true, but our policemen are honest, good men. They wouldn't turn their backs on a citizen in dire need."

As a connoisseur of a deft turn of phrase, Frank recognized the specific word choice on Byrnes's part. So, who determined *dire* need? What about just plain old need? "You said yourself marital squabbles aren't for the police, that they should be handled internally. Where was Mrs. Porter to turn, then?"

"Come now. You know the department doesn't have the time or resources to break up every argument between a husband and his wife. However, if her life was truly in danger then the police would've stepped in."

Frank doubted it, not with her husband's cousin on the force. Roy Porter could have avoided any number of misdemeanors or felonies by dropping his cousin's name. The police force was so ripe with corruption—bribes, blackmail, torture—that "we look the other way" should be engraved on the badges. "What would you have me do?"

"Let the court appoint another attorney. Your talents are wasted on such a trivial matter."

In other words, let Mrs. Porter hang.

In previous years Frank would have agreed. It was a terrible idea to anger Byrnes, who was vindictive and petty to those who had wronged him. Moreover, these quid pro quo deals were common in New York City. Frank couldn't begin to count the number of men who owed him favors at this point.

And still . . .

Mamie's face came to mind, the fierce light in her gaze as she'd insisted on Frank's help for Mrs. Porter. The way she'd cradled the baby to assist Mrs. Barrett. How she stole money and redistributed it downtown.

*Mr. Tripp is the very best attorney in the city. He'll get you acquitted, I promise.*

Shit.

He couldn't let Mamie down.

His leg bounced under the desk as he contemplated all the repercussions of what he was about to say. Developing a conscience was a damn nuisance. "I can't do that, Byrnes. I mean to keep the case and see that Mrs. Porter is acquitted."

Byrnes's lips flattened, his mustache twitching in barely repressed anger. "I've always taken you for a smart man, one who knows how these things work. Do not give me cause to rethink my opinion."

Frank pushed away from the desk and rose. "I suppose we are both full of surprises tonight."

Byrnes heaved himself out of the chair and buttoned his jacket. He said nothing else, just leveled a hard glare at Frank before turning on his heel and striding out of the room.

That had gone . . . poorly.

Frank had just made an enemy of the entire New York City police department.

"FLORENCE, I NEED your help."

It was almost midnight when Mamie strode into her sister's suite. Florence tended to stay awake all night and sleep until the afternoon. She claimed the routine was better for her complexion. *More like better for her scandalous lifestyle.*

Florence was reclining on her bed in her night-clothes. She quickly shoved something under her pillow and sat up, scowling. "Have you lost the ability to knock?"

Mamie raised a brow as she approached the bed. "And what was that, a love letter?"

"None of your concern, nosy. Why are you up so late? I thought you had a headache."

Mamie had complained of the ailment as a way of avoiding the Van Alan's party tonight. She had too much on her mind to stand around eating canapés and drinking champagne. "I preferred not to go. Was it gay?"

"It was positively awful, full of Daddy's cronies and their wives. Not a single handsome man in attendance."

Mamie perched on Florence's mattress. "That does sound terrible. I apologize for deserting you."

Florence settled into her pillows, her long wheat-colored hair framing her face. "Chauncey was there."

"Was he?"

"Yes. He and Daddy were off in a corner for a few minutes. Chauncey appeared unhappy with whatever Daddy said."

Had that been over the infidelity clause? "That's what I need your help with."

"Who, Chauncey or Daddy? I fear I have little help to offer with either. Men are positively baffling."

"It's even worse than you know." Mamie launched into the entire story of the marriage agreement, their father, and Chauncey's mistress.

Florence's face had gone red by the time Mamie finished, the tendons in her neck standing out in sharp relief. "He actually told you he refuses to give up his lady friend? Said that, aloud? I hope you slapped him."

Mamie's lips curved. Florence had always been the feistiest of the Greene girls. "No, I told him I'd speak with Daddy about having that clause removed from the agreement."

"God, Mamie. I cannot see how you stay so practical in these matters."

Because she had no choice. She was the eldest, most responsible sister. Protecting her two siblings, allowing them to find their own happiness, was her duty. Her father's determination was legendary, a trait she'd witnessed time and time again. And he was determined for this marriage to happen.

One summer when she was twelve, she'd overheard her father chatting with Mr. Livingston, discussing Mamie and Chauncey . . .

*"Kids seem to be getting along,"* Livingston said.

*"Yes, not that it matters."* Her father's voice had been

hard. "We agreed on the marriage when they were born and I won't back out on that promise."

"Even if she doesn't want him? Girls today are much more independent than in our day."

"Not Marion. She'll do as I ask."

"You have two other girls, Duncan."

"No, it must be Marion. She's the oldest and everyone in society knows of our pact. We'd look foolish to call it off now."

"Well, that's a relief. And, rest assured Chauncey won't fight me on it. He's quite fond of her."

"Marion will do her duty when the time comes. The other two may marry whomever they wish, as long as Marion marries Chauncey."

Over the years, her father had repeated much the same to Mamie each time she expressed hesitation over marrying Chauncey. He would never bend, and she didn't wish to disappoint him.

So she'd stopped complaining.

"Did you actually talk to Daddy?" Florence asked, regaining Mamie's attention.

"Yes. He refused to remove the clause from the agreement and accused me of being the one interested in infidelity."

"What? That is preposterous. You would never..." She trailed off after she studied Mamie's face. "Wait, you are, aren't you? You are interested in another man. I can see it in your expression. Who?"

"It doesn't matter. What I need to know is *how*."

"How, what?"

"How I might . . . capitalize on that interest."

Florence looked down and smoothed the bedclothes over the mattress. "What makes you think I have any experience in such matters?"

"If anyone in this family knows scandalous behavior, it's you. Let's see." She counted off on her fingers. "Mother caught you with that set of erotic playing cards, you hide racy literature under your bed, and there's all those visits to casinos and dancing halls."

"Visits we've mostly made together, I might add. And I'm not helping you until you tell me *who*."

"I'd rather not say. Just tell me what to do."

Florence tapped a finger against her lips. "Hmm. I know it isn't Chauncey. He hardly inspires seduction." She gasped, her eyes going wide. "It's Frank Tripp. I *knew* it. First he followed you around town then you two shared an intimate dinner at Sherry's."

"It was not intimate, we were in the main dining room."

"If you say so. Admit it, you have a thing for him."

"I do not have a *thing* for him. It's just . . ." She could not voice, even to Florence, her feelings for Frank. She barely understood them herself. It was safer if it meant nothing, just a harmless affair before her marriage. That made it easier to stop when the time came. "If I must marry Chauncey, why should he have all the fun?"

"I couldn't agree more. So, where do things stand with Tripp?"

"He says taking me to bed would ruin his career."

"You've discussed the possibility with him." Florence's mouth twisted into a smirk. "My level-headed sister, not allowing herself to be caught up in the heat of passion. I'm impressed."

"Is that bad, a lack of passion in these matters?"

"No. Frank is a man, Mamie, not a boy like Chauncey. He won't be ruled by his"—she gestured to her crotch—"like younger men. It's clear he lusts after you—I saw it plainly the night at the Bronze House—but he's trying to resist for the sake of his livelihood."

"It's frightening sometimes how much you know about these matters."

Florence threw her head back and laughed. "Can I help it if uptown society bores me to tears?"

Mamie felt the same way, but she had no choice. Not until now. "So what do I do?"

"Catch him off guard, when his defenses are down. Look alluring. Show off your best assets." She pointed at Mamie's bosom. "A low neckline and a little lip paint. That's all you need to have him salivating."

"What if he resists?"

"Then you keep at him, chipping away. A little touch here, a brush of your hand there. Bite your lip. Stare at him through your lashes. That's what the heroines in the steamy novels do."

"And it works?"

"Every time."

Hmm. Failure would be humiliating but she was willing to try. "Thank you. I'll attempt to work up the nerve."

Her sister made a disbelieving noise in her throat. "I've never known you to lack nerve, Mamie Greene. Are you so worked up over Tripp that you're scared?"

"Don't be ridiculous. I've never seduced a man before, is all."

"Which brings up another point: If you're so un-emotional about Chauncey, then why marry him? Why not see if someone else, like Tripp, is more suitable?"

Because life had dealt her a different hand. She might avoid marrying Chauncey, but it would not be because of Frank. "Daddy warned me away from Tripp and said he'd never approve of anything between us." Florence opened her mouth to argue so Mamie quickly continued. "And the understanding with Chauncey's family has long been established. I've practically grown up with Chauncey. I know precisely what I'll be getting."

"Apparently not. You just learned you're getting his mistress in this marriage as well."

True, but it seemed unlikely Chauncey hid anything else. "Beyond that, Chauncey is as clear as glass."

"In my experience those are the ones you need to worry most about."

A laugh bubbled up in Mamie's throat—and then she remembered Frank's comment about Chauncey and opium dens. Perhaps she didn't know her potential fiancé as well as she thought. Nevertheless, Florence's choice of words did not escape her. "In your experience?"

"You're not the only one out having fun at night."

She frowned, unhappy at the thought of Florence in danger. Yet she knew better than to try to stop her younger sister. The Greene girls could be stubborn when the mood struck. "I hope you are taking care."

"Always do. So, when will you seduce Frank Tripp?"

The *when* hadn't occurred to her. "I don't know. The next time I see him, I suppose."

"No, no, no. Must I write it down for you?" Florence straightened and pointed at Mamie. "You must catch him off guard. My guess is he'll try to ignore you as a way of resisting you. Chances are you won't see him at any point soon."

How could he ignore her when they were trying to save Mrs. Porter? Weren't there case-related matters to discuss or more investigations to undertake?

"I think you should sneak into his house," Florence continued. "Hide in his bedroom and surprise him."

"That's crazy. First, he won't ignore me because I hired him to represent a friend. Second, what you are suggesting is breaking and entering. The man could have me arrested."

"But he won't. You'll see. He'll ignore you and you'll have no choice but to sneak into his home."

# Chapter Ten

*What a goddamn week.*

Frank threw down his pen and stood to stretch the sore muscles in his back and shoulders. It was nearly midnight and he'd been working at home since the end of a long and boring dinner at Delmonico's. The group had included the firm's other partners and several important clients, which resulted in plenty of backslapping and bawdy jokes. Frank used to love those outings . . . but the hollowness of it had grated on his nerves tonight. There were a hundred pressing items requesting his attention, but the partners had insisted on his attendance.

So here he was in his office, working, with no end in sight. He had briefs to read, arguments to prepare, forms to sign. Investigation notes to peruse.

That reminded him of Mamie.

Unable to sit still, he strode to the sideboard, poured a healthy glass of whiskey, and finished it in three swallows. The burn hardly registered. Thoughts of Mamie haunted him, a constant temptation slowly driving him insane.

He'd kept busy these past four days, trying not to contemplate her promise of seduction—trying and failing. Every time he slowed down or closed his eyes he saw her lying on his bed, dark hair spread on the pillow, her legs parted slightly to give a glimpse of the paradise awaiting within . . .

Christ.

Heat wound through him and he reached for more spirits. Perhaps drunkenness was the key to forgetting her.

He'd just downed a second glass when the sound of the door caught his attention. Spinning on his heel, he watched a cloaked figure slide into his office. *What the ever-loving hell?*

He clutched the heavy crystal glass, ready to use it as a weapon, if necessary. "Who are you and what are you doing—"

The instant she reached for the hood, he knew. Dear God, he *knew.*

It was Mamie. Here. Alone, in his home.

He squinted at the empty glass in his hand. Was he really seeing her or had the whiskey affected him more than he'd thought?

"Hello, Frank."

That voice. Low and soft, the sound rolling through him like warm honey. His brain momentarily shut down when she lowered the hood of her cloak. Dark hair curled about her face, a stark contrast to the deep red painted on her lips. She was stunning. A goddess. Temptation incarnate. He craved her like his next breath . . . but he had to keep his control.

Exhaling sharply, he struggled to remain still. "You shouldn't be here. Have you gone mad?"

The edges of her lips curled and she started toward him. He immediately took a step backward.

"I'm here for two reasons," she said.

Several options flashed through his mind, all of them prurient and each one more delicious than the last. He swallowed. "No reason is sufficient enough for you to sneak into my house at this hour."

Once at the sideboard, she poured whiskey into a crystal tumbler. "You have been ignoring me."

Yes, he most definitely had.

"That is absurd," he said. "I've been busy. It's not as if we had an appointment I forgot."

"Yet you have ignored the two cables I sent you, asking for updates on Mrs. Porter's case."

Was this a trial? "There are no updates, which is why I didn't respond. Otto is digging up information for use in her case. When I have news I'll contact you."

"Fine, but that was merely the first reason I'm here." She put her lips on the crystal rim and took a long drink. He watched her lick the residual whiskey from her lips, the sight of her tongue causing his heart to pound.

"What is the second reason?" His voice sounded odd to his own ears but he couldn't quite focus on the conversation. Her mouth was too distracting.

"Our billiards game. Or, have you forgotten?"

"Game?"

"Our agreement for Mrs. Porter's case. Best of seven, here at your home. Promised to be the most memorable night of my life, I believe."

Why had he made such an idiotic request? He should have accepted the case without provision, instead of trying to flirt with her and concoct a clever way to spend time with her. *Non compos mentis*, clearly. He certainly was stupid around this woman. "I changed my mind. No payment necessary."

One dark brow shot up. "You'll help her out of the goodness of your heart?"

"I am quite magnanimous, you know."

"More like you're scared to play me."

He couldn't help it, he snorted. "Definitely not. It's more about protecting your reputation. Any number of people could have seen you waltz in here."

"Yet, no one did. Your discreet and efficient staff forgot to lock the front door. I had my hood up the entire time, beginning in the hansom I hired."

"Fine, but your family will be wondering where you are if you're gone for too long."

"Not tonight. My parents are in Boston for a wedding. Just my sisters and I are at home."

Stood to reason she had a rebuttal for every one of his points. The woman would've made an outstanding lawyer. "That does not change the fact that your presence here is highly inappropriate."

She placed her glass on the wood and stepped closer. He could smell her then, her special mix of sweet and spicy, a scent he now associated with stubbornness and longing. She drew near enough where he could see the tiny lines around her mouth. His skin buzzed with electricity, an awareness that jumped and hummed along the surface of his body, from the tips of his fingers to his toes. God help him if she ever put her hands on him. He might very well combust.

Her head tilted back and they locked gazes. "One game, Frank. Nothing more than billiards, I promise."

He wanted to believe her. However, a bigger part of him hoped she hadn't given up on seducing him.

*Stop it. You have no right to touch this woman.*

Logically, he was aware of all the reasons her presence here was a terrible idea. And yet he couldn't bring himself to say the words to force her away. He waited, mute, his mind frozen between his sense of responsibility and his desire.

"Do you wish for me to go?"

He blinked at her simple, straightforward question. For once, he didn't think about the words or the meaning behind them. This time he went with plain honesty. "No."

Her mouth curved into a satisfied smile. "Good. Now, show me the billiards room."

She turned and started for the exit, the cloak billowing behind her like a figure from a gothic novel. As he followed, he reminded himself this was no story, no fictional romance. This was the daughter of a client, an unmarried wealthy woman who was promised to another. He had to retain his wits and keep his distance.

*One game, then send her on her way.*

Yes, that was what he'd do. He was stronger than this weak man affected by a pair of red lips and orange blossoms. He could resist temptation and focus on the game. The sooner they finished playing the sooner he could put her in a hack and send her uptown.

No problem whatsoever.

\* \* \*

MAMIE HAD LIED.

She had no intention of playing one game and going home. If all went well she'd stay a considerable amount of time longer.

The odds were not in her favor. Frank had been adamantly against this visit, worried as always about her father and Mamie's reputation. Could he not see how tired she was of being Marion Greene, the daughter who must carry on tradition and responsibility? She'd never admit it to him, but Frank often felt like the only person outside of her sisters who treated her normally, growling and sniping at her without regard for her pedigree.

Just for tonight she'd try to make him forget about her father, her family and her impending marriage.

His billiards room was an elegant space, with green patterned wallpaper that closely matched the baize of the massive oak table. A gasolier hung from the ceiling to cast a warm glow over the Eastern rugs and dark wood surfaces. Smaller chairs lined the walls along with side tables, seats for spectators and guests. She could easily see him entertaining here, regaling friends with his stories and charming ladies out of their drawers

No need to think about those other ladies at the moment.

She unbuttoned her cloak, shrugged it off and threw the heavy garment over a chair. When she turned, he paused in the act of switching on a lamp, arm frozen, his gaze locked on the neckline of her dress. Excellent. She'd worn a revealing gown of blue silk that belonged to Justine. Her younger sister's clothes were a size smaller than Mamie's, which meant her breasts nearly spilled out of the dress.

It seemed Mr. Tripp was not immune to her bosom, after all.

She removed her gloves and walked over to the row of cue sticks on the wall. She ran a fingertip along the smooth wood. "So, what shall we play?"

He reached over her shoulder and snatched a cue. "Fifteen ball, if that's acceptable. Do you know the rules?"

"I do, yes." She hid her smile as she selected a cue. No doubt he believed this an easy win for him. Frank had no idea how skilled she was when it came to billiards.

He gestured to the table. "Let's roll to see who breaks."

They each placed a ball side by side at one end. Lifting their cues, they struck at the same time, sending their balls careening across the table, where they bounced off the bumper and traveled back toward the starting place. When the balls finally stopped rolling Mamie's rested closest to the start. Frowning, he held out the cue ball. "Nicely done."

She let her fingers brush his hand as she clasped the ball . . . and was rewarded when he inhaled sharply. *A little touch here, a brush of your hand there.* Perhaps Florence had been right. "I got lucky."

He racked the game balls inside the frame while she readied her break shot. Through her lashes, she watched the fine muscles of his shoulders shift and bunch beneath his shirtsleeves. He wore no coat this evening, cuffs rolled up over his delectable bare forearms. Dark hair lightly coated the surface of his skin and she could see veins and tendons shift as he moved. Why was that such an appealing sight?

"Have you been working long this evening?" she asked.

"Yes, for a few hours after I returned from dinner."

"Ah. Entertaining a lady friend?"

He paused in placing the rack on the wall. "Would that bother you?"

"No. With your reputation I nearly expect it."

"Reputations are exaggerated to sell newspapers, Mamie." He strode to a small table where several decanters were lined up. "Another drink?"

The glass she'd poured in his office remained half full. There was no need to become inebriated, not when she hoped to outwit him tonight. "No, thank you."

Leaning over, she took aim, brought her arm back and let fly. The cue ball smacked into the other balls, which all shot in every direction. It was a clean break, and two striped balls disappeared into pockets.

When she looked up, Frank's eyes were glued to the bodice of her dress, his gaze gone dark. She straightened and he seemed to shake himself. He turned away, gave her his back and took a long drink.

"Do you have a mistress?" she blurted. It was what she'd been trying to ascertain earlier.

The instant the words left her mouth he began choking and sputtering. Bending over, he wheezed for breath. "Damn it, Mamie." He gestured at his chest. Drops of whiskey soaked his necktie and vest. "Happy?"

She tried not to smile. "Quite, though I wasn't intending to ruin your clothing. I am merely curious."

"No mistress. I find tying myself to one woman works best only for short periods of time. It's why I know I'll never marry. I have no intention of failing at fidelity."

She sank another ball. "Perhaps you won't fail."

"Everyone fails eventually. I have no fewer than six active divorce cases at all times, sometimes more. Wives who cheat, husbands who cheat. Remember Mrs. Phillips from that night at Sherry's? Women like her are more common than you'd ever believe."

Well, she'd believe women often approached Frank in the hopes of catching his eye. Wasn't that what she was doing here, playing pool at midnight?

Hmm. The comparison did not sit well with her.

She concentrated on the table. So far, she'd made four shots, plus the two balls she sank on the break. Winning this game would be child's play. Lining up, she drew back her arm.

"Have you been intimate with Chauncey?"

Her body jolted and the cue caught the edge of the ball, sending it off at a wild angle. She'd missed her shot. "Dash it. You did that on purpose."

The side of his mouth hitched, so handsome and sinful that her lower half tingled. He raised his palms. "I plead the fifth."

Huffing, she edged away to give him access to the table—but not too far. She had a plan . . .

He rubbed a tiny cube of chalk over the tip of his cue, never taking his gaze off the table. "I think you have underestimated your abilities at pool," he murmured. "It seems I must prepare for a fight this evening."

Oh, but so was she.

When he found his shot, he moved to the proper position. Mamie followed and rested her hip against the wooden edge about six inches from Frank's cue. Just as his arm started forward, she said, "Chauncey and I have kissed, of course."

His arm stuttered and the cue wobbled. The tip missed the ball entirely and dug into the baize. "Oh, for God's sake," he snapped, then straightened to glare at her. She was close enough to see the shadow of his beard coming in, dark stubble over his jaw and around his mouth. It made him appear slightly piratical, the most handsome devil in New York. Something deep in her abdomen clenched.

His eyes narrowed. "When?"

"Ages ago. In our youth." It had been a disappointment, actually. Chauncey had been all tongue, no finesse. She sincerely hoped—for the singer's sake—his technique had improved over the years.

She smothered a satisfied smile and stepped away, ready to resume her domination over the game. The next three shots were clear in her mind when she took aim. This time, she waited, certain Frank would retaliate.

He remained silent, just sidled up next to her. Then he leaned over and put his hands on the rail beside her, his fingers resting casually on the bumper. He took up space but didn't exactly crowd her. His long arms were straight, his torso slightly hunched, and her peripheral vision could no longer see anything else. With no coat to cover the view she could make out the outline of his back and ribs, the tapered waist and hips. The hard backside highlighted so perfectly in those trousers . . .

She swallowed. Good Lord, her heart was racing in her chest. She could barely breathe, her lungs straining beneath a corset laced tightly to accommodate the smaller dress. The smell of whiskey and sandalwood surrounded her, a scent she could happily now drown in.

What was he doing to her?

It was almost as if . . . he wished to distract her with his physical presence.

It worked. Her skin crackled with awareness, the ability to hold a cue steady now impossible.

This was not in her plan. He was supposed to be overcome with lust for *her*—not the other way around. How could she seduce him if he remained unaffected by her?

This would not do.

"Would you help me line up my next shot?" she asked in her deepest, throatiest voice. "I can't quite reach."

FRANK WAS HOLDING on to his wits by a thread. A thread so thin it was nearly air, but a thread nonetheless. He remained in control. Barely.

His cock had been half-hard since the moment Mamie took off her cloak. The dress was indecent. Scandalous. Her breasts spilled out over the top, perfect creamy skin every which way he looked. He wanted to lick and suck all that delectable skin, leave marks on her with his mouth.

Christ, a flash of bosom and she'd turned him into a slavering beast.

He hadn't expected her to proceed so boldly with

this seduction plan. Of course, everything Mamie did was bold and unexpected . . . so he really should have known better.

Now she hoped to tempt him by asking for help with a shot. Interesting. Did she believe he'd be stupid enough to stand behind her, cover her back with his front, and lean over her? Press his hips into her backside? The only way he would do that was if they were fucking—and he was definitely not fucking Mamie Greene tonight or any other night.

He would win this battle of resolve. One did not escape Five Points and become a top attorney in New York City without having an iron will. Let her try and break him. She would never succeed, not even in that dress.

"Of course." He reached under the table and found the bridge, a stick with a brass head designed for hard-to-reach shots. "Here you are."

She covered her surprise well. He could see her adjusting, rethinking. "Will you show me how to use it?"

Clever. He had to respect the change in direction. Various responses leapt to mind. He should refuse. Touching her, even in the most innocent manner, would be the height of insanity. Her fingertips had brushed his palm earlier and he'd shivered, lust so thick in his blood he could barely remain standing.

While he deliberated, she lifted one brow in challenge. The woman never backed down . . . and why did he find that so dashed appealing?

"Fine," he said before he could think better of it. "Which ball?"

"The seven, there by the other corner."

He placed the bridge flat on the table in front of

the cue ball. "Now, place the shaft of your cue in one of the grooves. Line up the shot and go."

"Like this?" She followed his directions, her movements awkward, and he could tell the cue was at the wrong angle. She'd never sink the ball.

"No." He pointed. "Move it over two places. Now, hold the bottom of the cue using your thumb and first two fingers. Like you were throwing a dart."

She tried but she wasn't sighting the shot properly. Without thinking, he wrapped his fingers around her forearm and moved her aim slightly higher. "There you are. Nice and even." Together, they pushed the cue stick forward. The cue ball drove the seven into the pocket cleanly. "Well done."

Her eyes sparkled up at him. "Thank you for your help."

"My pleasure," he murmured, mesmerized by her red lip paint. The upper bow of her lip and the full bottom were a deep red, the color of a fine burgundy. He longed to kiss that color right off her lips. Smear it between them until he stripped her down to the natural flesh . . .

"You may let go."

He still had hold of her forearm. The warm, soft skin and fine bones sank into his fingers. "No."

"I . . . Did you say no?"

The word had come out before he could stop it. They stood inches apart and his feet were rooted to the floor. The tips of his shoes brushed the hem of her skirts. Every angle, every ridge was visible at this distance and he needed to study her awhile longer. To memorize her. "I cannot seem to move."

She shifted slightly to face him, her breasts a

whisper away from his chest. "That may prevent us from finishing the game."

"Do you care?"

They both knew tonight had not been about the game, not for either of them.

Those sinful lips twisted. "No, I don't."

This was madness. Intimacy with Mamie was dangerous to all he held dear. Yet despite the reasons he should resist, everything inside of him ached for her. He was helpless against this pull, this dark force that kept drawing him to her. Perhaps if he indulged his desire, just this once, he could move past it. Satisfy this obsession to regain his focus and resolve. Mamie would then marry a man from her social circle and things would go back as they were.

Yes, absolutely. Why hadn't he considered this before?

He let his cue stick fall to the floor, forgotten, and cupped her cheek in his free palm. "You came here tonight to seduce me."

She nodded, not even bothering to deny it. "Yes, I did."

"It looks as if you have succeeded."

Her lips parted, her tongue darting out to moisten them. "Have I?"

Instead of answering, he removed the stick from her hand and tossed it onto the baize. Then he put his hands on her waist and lifted her onto the edge of the table. Her fingers clutched his shoulders to steady herself, but she said nothing, merely watched him with steady dark eyes.

He'd never wanted anything as badly as this, as *her*. Maybe escaping his childhood home, but nothing since then. Nothing had consumed him like this dizzying craving for Mamie.

"I want you to be sure," he said. "If you change your mind at any time—"

"I won't. And I'm sure." Her hands slipped around his neck and she drew him closer. "I am quite sure, in fact."

He bent slowly, giving her every chance to stop him. "Good, because I am going to kiss you now."

"Please," she breathed, her lips rising to meet his.

At first, it was a gentle sweep. No gnashing of teeth or smashing of lips; rather, a test. A deliberate brush of two separate mouths to taste the other. Then again. His nose slid against hers, their breath mingling. It was a moment where nothing else mattered but the exploration.

Her fingers tightened in his hair and he moved closer. He pressed harder this time, more insistent, and her mouth moved eagerly, picking up his demand with her own. Her kisses were unhesitant, bold, exactly her personality, and he was suddenly drowning in the sweet drag and pull between them. She tasted of expensive whiskey and fire, and he could not get enough. Their tongues tangled, slick and hot, and he couldn't remember whose tongue had started this but he never, ever wanted to stop kissing her. She was driving him wild with flicks and swirls. The fingers twisting in his hair. The breasts skimming his chest. His clothes felt too hot on his body, his skin too tight. He'd give anything to take her upstairs, strip them both down and worship her until sunrise.

But that would not happen. Not tonight, not ever. Mamie, for all her boldness and begging, was innocent. At least, he assumed she was innocent. Chauncey had kissed her . . . Had he dared more? The thought didn't sit well with Frank and he had to remind himself that she belonged to Chauncey, not him. *She is not yours. She will never be yours.*

So he stood to the side, kissing her at an angle, to prevent his hips from coming into contact with her. His cock throbbed in his trousers, but he didn't wish to frighten her. No, he would hold his own need in check and focus on Mamie. She had achieved her goal of seducing him and he'd ensure she didn't regret this . . . no matter if it killed him.

She arched closer, her breasts pressing into him, and he couldn't wait to touch her any longer. "Shall I stop?" he asked against her mouth.

"Absolutely not." She kissed him again, her mouth opening to give him her tongue.

Damn, this woman. She surprised him at every turn.

He broke off to place deep kisses along her jaw, across the smooth column of her throat, tasting her with his lips and teeth and tongue. She tilted her head to give him access, her pulse racing beneath the fine skin. A needy gasp escaped her lips when he gently bit the flesh where her neck met shoulder.

Bending, he brought his mouth to the swells of her breasts. A woman's bosom usually didn't fascinate him this much, but something about Mamie's shape—the round hips and ample chest—along with her audacious personality drove him wild. He pressed tiny kisses along the mounds, bringing his hand to her ribs just below the weight of her breast. Her back bowed in a silent plea for more and so he sucked, drawing the sensitive skin into his mouth as best he could, sinking in his teeth ever so slightly.

"Oh, God." Her voice was the thinnest whisper. "What are you doing to me?"

"Shall I stop?" he rasped, soothing the mark with his tongue.

"Don't you dare." She grabbed his face and dove for his mouth, their lips colliding, tongues dueling. The kiss transformed and exploded into a fiery blast of lust and heat. Air bellowed out of his lungs, his chest heaving, as he struggled to keep his wits. His neglected cock screamed for friction, desperate and hard in his trousers. He would give almost everything he owned to sink into Mamie's warm, snug channel.

*Stop thinking about that. You are merely worsening the situation.*

He needed to take care of her. His pleasure could wait until after she left, as soon as he discovered what she sounded like, what she looked like—what she *tasted* like—when she climaxed. He had to know. It was the beginning of a long list of things he wanted to discover about her, such as what she enjoyed for breakfast and which side of the bed she preferred. Those things would never be his to learn, unfortunately; her husband possessed that right. So Frank would take what he could, just for tonight.

However, he didn't wish to force this on her. She had to be willing. Would this fearless and daring woman admit to craving relief?

He took her jaw in his palms and stared into her hooded gaze. "Do you ever pleasure yourself with your fingers?"

Confusion quickly morphed into embarrassment.

Her eyes slid away. "I hardly think that's any of your business."

"Because you think I'll judge you? I use my hand for my own pleasure every day. Does knowing that make it easier to answer?"

"You do?"

He nodded. "At least once, occasionally twice."

She bit her lip. "Fine, yes. Sometimes I do. Why?"

Swallowing, he put the mental image of her fingers between her thighs out of his mind. For now. "I wish to touch you like that. Will you let me?"

# Chapter Eleven

*T*heir kisses must've melted her brain because it took her a moment to process his request. *You planned to seduce him. What did you think that meant?* Clearly she hadn't considered all the particulars. "You mean . . . ?"

His knuckles grazed the tops of her breasts, causing her to shiver. "May I pleasure you? Make you come?"

She blinked a few times. "Here?" Heavens, they were in his billiards room, where anyone could walk in.

"My staff are abed. Even still, they know not to disturb me. We're safe here."

"Are you always this direct when discussing intimacies?"

The side of his mouth kicked up, a rogue in every sense of the word. "Yes, I try to be. One should understand the expectations in every encounter. Things are clearer that way, less messy."

Hmm. When the whole business started, she'd assumed they would be consumed by passion. Swept away and caught up in the moment. Like their kissing a few moments ago. Couldn't they just return to that and see what transpired?

"So may I?" He slid a finger under the bodice of her dress and expertly found her nipple, rubbing back and forth. She gasped.

*God, yes. More, please.*

"My purpose tonight was to seduce you," she said as he played with her. "I hardly think I'd deny you now."

He leaned in, his mouth close to her ear as his thumb wriggled under her neckline. Then he rolled her nipple between the pads of his fingers and she moaned. "Wrong," he whispered. "You came here tonight for *me* to seduce *you*. You wore this dress to drive me wild and now you've gotten your wish. But never think you cannot stop me at any time. If you change your mind, I will understand."

She was panting now, every sensation centered where he manipulated the tip of her breast. Sweet Lord, that felt fantastic. "I won't change my mind."

"Hmm. Even if I loosen your dress, just enough to suck your pretty nipples into my mouth?"

Heat flooded her, the strong thrum of arousal beating in her blood. "I still won't change my mind."

"What if I lift your skirts and use my fingers on you, slipping them inside you . . . pumping them inside your slick channel?"

She clutched his shoulders, dizzy with the idea of it. Wetness pooled between her thighs, her body eager for the attention. "Won't change my mind. No."

"Is that so?" He pinched her nipple and she cried out from the overwhelming pleasure coursing through her. It was like an electric current ran directly from the tip of her breast to her sex. He nipped her earlobe. "What if I put my face between your legs and use my mouth on you, sucking and licking, until you come on my tongue?"

"Oh, my God." The image of it—his dark head between her thighs, his mouth moving on her most intimate flesh—was illicit and naughty and utterly arousing. Her belly fluttered with longing and lust. She had no idea if this was a common act in the bedroom but she hardly cared. She trusted Frank. He wouldn't hurt her—and he'd promised to stop whenever she asked. She wanted his secret kisses with every fiber of her being. "Yes. I mean, no. I won't change my mind."

He chuckled, a deep sound of satisfaction. "My brave Mamie. You are a gift from heaven."

His fingers slid out of her dress and she nearly wept at the loss. If she asked nicely, would he put them back and return to feeling her breast? Before she could open her mouth, however, air washed over her legs. She opened her eyes and found him concentrating intently on her skirts. Rigid jaw, flushed skin . . . Hmm. Perhaps he wasn't as unaffected as she'd thought.

"Lovely, lovely girl." Her skirts were past her knees now, the lacy edges of her drawers and silk stockings visible. Their gazes caught and she could see the desire swirling in his hooded blue eyes. "Open your legs for me."

She parted her thighs slightly and watched as his hand disappeared under layers of fabric. Fingers skimmed the inside of her knee, along her inner thigh, then continued to the part in her drawers. She jumped when he touched bare skin.

"If it's too much, let me know and I'll stop."

Instead of speaking, she tilted her face and kissed his jaw, the whiskers rough under her lips. He paused, his breath coming hard and fast, and she relished the reaction. As he had before, she used her teeth to scrape across his skin. He growled in his throat—and took her mouth in a savage kiss. Gone was the earlier finesse. This was raw and bruising, his tongue thrusting deep to twine with hers.

And she loved it.

His fingers continued their exploration and found her center. There was no time for embarrassment, however, because he stroked through her folds with deliberate and sure movements, sending sparks along her legs. When he circled the hard bundle of nerves at the top, she nearly jumped out of her skin at the strong sensation. So very different than when she performed this herself.

Pleasure built as he continued to work that one spot. He didn't let up, kissing her fiercely and rubbing between her legs until she whimpered, her muscles tightening. Then he slipped a finger inside her channel, filling her, his palm now pressing against the tiny nub begging for attention. She broke off from his mouth and sucked in air. It was all too much. Too strong, too fierce. Too glorious to resist. The orgasm overtook her then, starting at her toes and rushing up to sweep her away. Light burst behind her lids as her limbs shook, and her cries rang in her own ears.

When the trembling stopped, Frank withdrew his hand and returned to kissing her, but sweetly. He sipped at her lips and nipped gently with his teeth. "You are so beautiful right now," he said. "And I'm not nearly done with you yet."

Before she could inquire what he planned, he moved between her legs and dropped to his knees. He pushed her skirts higher and studied her sex like a starving man staring at cake. Was he . . . with his mouth? It should've been embarrassing but she felt incredibly powerful in that moment. This beautiful man desired her. Wished to please her. How had she gotten so lucky?

His hands glided over her thighs as he leaned in. "Have you changed your mind?"

He was close enough for his breath to tease her sensitive flesh. Tingles erupted under her skin and she clutched the edge of the table. She had no idea what was ahead but she didn't wish to turn back now, not until she experienced all this entailed. "No."

"Thank God."

His mouth descended and his tongue swiped through the folds. He closed his eyes and groaned, almost as if he were in pain. "Fuck, that's good."

The profanity hardly registered, not when she was still reeling from that one lick. Good heavens, that was intense. She barely had time to recover before he did it again, the bliss stealing her breath. Leaning back, she braced herself on the table. Frank shifted slightly, settling in, and his hands slid under her bottom to hold her. Then he used his lips and mouth to taste her, the flat of his tongue scraping across the swollen tissues. She lost the ability to speak. Instead, she moaned and panted, barely able to focus under the onslaught of pleasure. At times, she wasn't sure she would survive it.

When he sucked on the hard button at the top of her folds, she nearly came off the table. He held on to her, not letting her go as he continued to play her body masterfully. The buzz inside grew and grew, rising and expanding, more rapid than before, and soon she screamed out, another climax dragging her under.

She floated, unaware of her surroundings, wrapped in white-hot bliss, for what seemed an eternity. After returning to earth, she found herself lying on her back, the tin ceiling above her. Mercy, that had been unlike anything she imagined. *I had been right to trust him.*

Frank rose stiffly, his eyes screwed shut. His lips had compressed into a flat, white line. Was he all right? Concerned, she levered herself up. "Are you hurt?"

He grimaced. "Fine. I just . . ." He waved a hand in the direction of his groin and she understood. A large bulge pushed insistently against the cloth of his trousers. "Give me a moment."

"Should I . . . ?" She hadn't the first idea what to do, but shouldn't he enjoy this encounter as well?

"No, absolutely not. Tonight was for your pleasure. I hope I was successful."

Successful? She was a boneless mess, barely able to form words. "Yes, I quite enjoyed it."

He took a handkerchief out of his pocket and used it to wipe the inside of her thighs. Embarrassed, she tried to cover her legs with her skirts. "That's not necessary."

"Perhaps I'm not ready to do away with the view quite yet."

The comment made her smile. "You may see it again. This needn't be our only billiards game."

He kissed her forehead. "Let me get you a hansom."

They walked to the front entrance, Frank strangely silent. Was he struggling with his . . . frustration? She missed his teasing and sniping at her. Had their relationship changed for the worse after the evening's intimacies? She hoped not. They should remain friends, at least.

After she'd donned her cloak, he left her in the vestibule to hail a hack on the street. She folded her hands and waited, the glow from their earlier encounter fading rapidly. Had something gone wrong? Had her inexperience offended him? Any previous rendezvous had been limited to kissing. Perhaps Frank had expected more from her?

*No, he said tonight was about her. So what happened?*

Perhaps she was imagining things.

He returned, not meeting her gaze as he held open the door. "Come on."

A sleek black hansom waited at the curb. He escorted her along the walk and assisted her up the steps. When she settled inside, he picked up her hand and pressed his lips to her knuckles. "Thank you for tonight. There can be no further billiards games, however. Let's consider this one a draw."

Before she could speak, he closed the door with a snap and knocked on the side to signal the driver. The wheels began rolling, taking her away from his home and leaving Mamie to wonder just what she'd done wrong.

* * *

FRANK RUSHED THROUGH the entrance of police headquarters. Barely thirty minutes ago he'd received a tip that Byrnes planned to interrogate Mrs. Porter. Based on previous experience, Frank knew Byrnes wouldn't wait for Mrs. Porter's attorney to be present for questioning, so he'd dropped everything and hurried downtown. He had to stop this before Mrs. Porter said something she'd later regret—or was physically harmed.

He darted by the front desk, ignoring the calls of the desk attendant, and went straight to the rooms where interrogations were conducted. After a few wrong doors, he finally found Mrs. Porter waiting in a room alone, her wrists chained to the table.

She looked up, her eyes wild and terrified, her hair mussed. When she recognized him, she slumped over the table. How long had she been here?

Closing the door, he crossed the room and knelt by her side. "Are you all right? Have they hurt you?"

"No," she whispered, her forehead resting on the smooth wood. "But I've been here a long time."

"How long?"

"I don't know. They brought me over from the prison this morning."

Christ, it was afternoon. "And no one has been in to check on you?"

She shook her head. "They told me I had to wait until Byrnes arrives. Who is he, another lawyer?"

Anger tore through Frank with lightning speed. "He is the superintendent. He hopes to intimidate you, no doubt. Leaving you here to scare you into making a confession."

"I didn't say a word. I swear, Mr. Tripp."

"I believe you. Now, let me retrieve a matron who can at least bring you food and take you to the facilities."

A tear leaked from the corner of her eye. "Thank you, Mr. Tripp."

Frank went into the corridor and grabbed the first officer he found. "Bring a matron here now, before I—"

"Mr. Tripp, how nice of you to visit headquarters today."

Superintendent Byrnes had rounded the corner and was flanked by several policemen. His cronies, no doubt, cops so corrupt they made Boss Tweed look angelic.

Frank pointed directly at Byrnes. "You are violating my client's rights. I want a matron to see to Mrs. Porter in less than two minutes, or I will get a judge down here—an honest one."

"Now, there's no need for that. They were merely waiting on me. Due to some urgent police matters I was unable to arrive until now."

What a fucking lie. Byrnes had come running the instant he heard Frank was in the building.

"Matron, Byrnes. Right now."

The silence stretched as Byrnes studied Frank with flat, hard eyes. Frank didn't back down, however. He was right—and Byrnes knew it.

Byrnes broke first. The superintendent looked away and jerked his chin at one of the junior officers. The officer hurried in the direction of the women's wing. "There, I've summoned your matron. Let me speak with your client and we'll get her back to the Tombs."

"You're not going in there until she's eaten and used the facilities."

"We're not runnin' a hotel." The officers surrounding Byrnes snickered at this. "She's a murderer, Tripp, not the Queen of England."

"Accused, Byrnes. And even so, you have no right to treat her worse than an animal."

Byrnes took a few steps closer, so near that Frank could smell his foul breath. "Must be why all the ladies love you. Sneakin' in and out of your big house at all hours. Wonder if their fancy fathers would approve?"

Frank froze, though he tried to not reveal his shock. Was Byrnes referencing . . . Mamie? Were the police watching Frank's house?

Damn it. If they had witnessed Mamie leaving last night, there was no end to the destruction that information would cause. Even if he never allowed her to visit again he had to protect her reputation. An unmarried lady visiting his house after hours? If it were made public, she'd be ruined, her father furious. Chauncey would beg off the marriage, no doubt, leaving Mamie's future in peril. At that point Frank could certainly bid adieu to his law practice. He'd probably have to move to Colorado or California to avoid retribution from her father. Change his name once more and start over.

The thought made him sick. *I won't back down. New York has always been my home and I'll be damned before I'm run out of town.*

He had to brazen it out. Admit nothing. No one could know her identity for certain. Rolling his shoulders, he said, "I'd be careful about throwing accusations around. Things are often not what they seem."

"And other times they are precisely what one suspects."

Movement behind the superintendent caught Frank's eye. A matron had arrived, her keys jangling as she hurried along the corridor. He stepped away from Byrnes. "Second door on the right," he told her. "Food and facilities, now."

She gave him a nod then continued to Mrs. Porter's room.

Frank addressed the wall of blue uniforms in front of him. "Once Mrs. Porter has been readied, I'll let you know. Then, and only then, may you interview her."

Without waiting for comment, he spun on his heel and went to see his client. The matron was helping her stand, as Mrs. Porter's legs had cramped from sitting for so long.

Thirty minutes later Mrs. Porter was properly attended to and fed. Frank had given her an idea of what to expect from Byrnes while she ate. When she finished, they called for the superintendent. The matron departed, leaving Frank and Mrs. Porter alone.

"I'm nervous," Mrs. Porter said while they waited.

"I won't let anything happen. I'll do my best to protect you, and we don't have to answer every question. Trust me, all right?"

"I do trust you. Miss Greene wouldn't have recommended you if you were not trustworthy. She is so smart."

Yes, she was. He admired the friendship Mamie had developed with Mrs. Porter. Had she befriended the other women she helped as well? For her prickly exterior, Mamie Greene certainly had a soft and generous heart.

The door opened and Byrnes barreled in. Another policeman, a sergeant named Hamm, joined them. Mrs. Porter straightened, her back stiff, but Frank tried to remain relaxed. A nervous lawyer made for skittish clients and overly confident policemen.

"Are we allowed to speak with her now, Tripp?" Byrnes folded his arms over his chest. "Or should we come back?"

"Now is fine." He gestured to the seats on the other side of the table. "We're happy to cooperate."

The other two sat. "Mrs. Porter, I am Superintendent Byrnes. I'd like to ask you a few questions about your husband's murder. Would that be acceptable, madam?" She nodded. For the next thirty minutes, he inquired into every second of the day her husband had been murdered. Mrs. Porter answered clearly and carefully, all of her answers matching her previous statements. She maintained she acted in defense of herself and her children.

"Have you ever met Edward Porter?" Sergeant Hamm asked.

"My husband's cousin?"

"Late husband, but yes, his cousin. Have you met him?"

"A few times."

"Do you know what he told us? That according to your late husband you were angry that he went out and spent money at the gin shops. That you two fought quite often over it."

"That's hearsay," Frank said. "Nor is it a question. If you have one, ask it."

Byrnes drummed his fingers on the table. "Do you know what Edward Porter does for a living, Mrs. Porter?"

She glanced at Frank then back to Byrnes. "He is a police detective."

"That's true. And he is ready to testify to what he knows at your trial. Do you really think a jury will believe your word over that of a Metropolitan police detective?" He paused. "They won't. Not for a minute. Now, would you like to rethink your story? Tell us what really happened with your husband."

"Don't answer that," Frank told her then stared down Byrnes. "If all you're doing is threatening her with the testimony of her husband's cousin, then we're done here. Our plea hasn't changed and Mrs. Porter's version of events has been well documented."

Byrnes's gaze narrowed on Frank. "Perhaps the lady would like to speak for herself, Tripp."

"She already has, on multiple occasions. Unless there's a new line of inquiry, this interview is concluded."

Byrnes stood and summoned the matron, who quickly arrived to lead Mrs. Porter out of the room. Frank waited until his client had been safely removed before he started to leave as well.

Byrnes stepped in front of him, blocking Frank's path. "You aren't doin' your client any favors by not letting her talk to us. She's nothing but Five Points trash who's going to lose in court."

He ground his teeth together. Mrs. Porter was *not* trash. She was a decent woman who'd been forced to inflict violence to protect herself and her family. "We'll see, won't we?"

Byrnes leaned over to spit on the floor right by Frank's shoe. "Yes, I suppose we will. I'd say the next few weeks should prove very interesting for all involved. Very interesting, indeed."

The two men brushed by him and disappeared, leaving Frank to wonder over the meaning of those parting words.

MAMIE STIFLED A yawn even as her feet moved across the dance floor. Mercy, this ball was never-ending. She'd tried to stay home but her mother had insisted Mamie attend, saying she and Chauncey must be seen together at all the important social events.

Being an almost-fiancée was exhausting.

"What's wrong?" Chauncey asked as they executed a perfect turn. "I thought you loved a rousing waltz."

Normally, she did. But not after staying up late the previous evening to engage in illicit activities. A shiver went through her as she remembered all that had transpired in that billiards room.

Discounting Frank's strange behavior at the end, the night had been astounding. Life altering. Unlike anything she could have imagined. No wonder men and women were constantly sneaking off from these parties to find stolen moments of pleasure. Now, she finally understood.

"Mamie?"

She shook herself and addressed her partner. "My apologies. I didn't sleep well last night. May we get some fresh air instead of dancing?"

"Of course." Ever the gentleman, Chauncey led her to the set of French doors at the edge of the ballroom. Brisk spring air met them on the terrace, and goose bumps broke out on her exposed skin. "There, is that better?" he asked.

"Yes, thank you." She strolled toward the railing. "I wasn't quite in the mood for dancing."

He leaned to rest his elbows on the stone beside her. "I cannot blame you. It's awfully hot in there. Besides, I wished to speak with you privately."

"Oh? What about?"

He glanced around, presumably to ascertain they were alone. Deciding they were, he said quietly, "The agreement. Your father is unwilling to strike the clause we discussed. He said I would thank him one day for insisting on it. Have you any idea what he's talking about?"

Mamie frowned. Was her father so convinced she would be unfaithful, then? "I intend to honor our marriage vows," she said. *Before the wedding is another matter altogether.*

"Yes, but what about me? The situation from the other day?"

Right. His mistress. "I asked, Chauncey, but he sees no reason to delete the stipulation. Really, I tried."

"I cannot pay the penalty, Mamie. Not until after I come into my inheritance. You must do something."

Why was this *her* problem to solve? "You are welcome to not sign the agreement."

He looked at her as if a horn had sprouted in the middle of her forehead. "Are you saying you don't wish to get married?"

"I haven't said that. But it's clear your priorities lie elsewhere. Why should we make each other miserable?"

"You think I'll make you miserable?" He was aghast now, brows climbing to his hairline. "Mamie, I had no idea you felt this way."

She hadn't, not until last night. Before her "billiards game" with Frank she'd mostly been resigned to marriage with Chauncey. Now, she wasn't certain. Chauncey didn't excite her. He was boring and childish. Justine and Florence wouldn't wish for her to sacrifice her happiness for theirs, would they? And perhaps her father could be made to see reason with all three marriages. He'd forbidden her to pursue Frank, but there were plenty of other men in New York City who might excite her.

*My brave Mamie. You are a gift from heaven.*

Would she ever forget the way Frank had looked at her last night, with glowing hot eyes full of reverence and heat? As if she were the most beautiful, sensual creature in the world. And the things he'd done . . . No other man would ever excite her as much.

Unfortunately, Frank didn't want her. He'd made that quite clear at their parting.

*Thank you for tonight. There can be no further billiards games, however.*

That dimmed her spirits a bit. Had he hated the experience? She could have sworn he'd been excited. Dash that complicated and confusing man.

Chauncey awaited her answer, so she said, "Why shouldn't we marry someone we love, instead of someone to whom we've been promised out of obligation?"

"*Love?*" He practically spit the word. "I thought you were more practical than that. You know our people don't marry for love. We carry on with our traditions and values. We're going to merge two great families. Love is for . . . well, the lower classes."

God, that snobbery revolted her. Had she ever been that closed-minded? "Perhaps we deserve more than a lifetime of responsibility and merging. Wouldn't you like to be happy with your . . ."

"I cannot *marry* her." He shook his head. "I don't understand this. You have always accepted our situation. Now you sound like some . . . trouser-wearing suffragette. Next thing I know you'll be out riding a bicycle!"

Mamie thought bicycles appeared like great fun, but she didn't bother pointing that out now. "Why can't you marry her? Who would stop you?"

"My father, for one. He'll disown me if I don't marry you. How will I live without any money?"

*Find a job,* she wanted to say. But that would only confuse Chauncey further. He had no idea what hard work was or how to live on his own. Not like Frank, who clearly enjoyed working. "Plenty of people get by without trust funds. I volunteer with a few charities downtown and you should see how hard some of these families work—"

"Wait, you aren't actually going downtown, are you? Mamie, that's too dangerous for a woman like you."

A woman like her. Well, if she'd held out any hopes that Chauncey would support her Sixth Ward charity endeavors, those were gone now. "I'm not in any jeopardy, I promise."

"So you are going downtown? Good God, think of the scandal if that were discovered."

"Perhaps you'd rather marry someone else, then."

"It cannot be anyone but you. I must marry you or else I'm ruined."

"So you wish to marry me merely to gain your inheritance?"

Chauncey dragged his hands through his hair, looking as undone as she'd ever seen him. "This is maddening. I feel as though you've been replaced by a stranger, someone completely unfamiliar with the way things have always been done."

*Because I am different. Last night changed me. I know what I'll be missing if I give up passion.*

"I'm trying to ensure we both do not make a huge mistake."

"It would not be a mistake." He drew himself up and held out his palms. "I would prefer to strike the adultery clause, but if I must put off my relationship for a few years while we grow our family, I'm willing to do that. I think we should finalize things before you become any more confused."

Confused? Quite the opposite. She was finally seeing things clearly. "Is this all worth it?" She swung her hand toward the huge stone house behind them. "The parties, the houses? The yacht? Are those things worth trading your happiness for?"

He shoved his hands in his pockets and stared out at the gardens now shrouded in darkness. He waited so long she wasn't certain he would answer. Just when she'd about given up, he said softly, "If I don't have those things then who am I?"

"You are *you*." She placed her hand on his arm.

"You are still the same person, Chauncey. With or without these trappings."

"No, I'm not. Without all this I'm no one. I'm absolutely nothing." He spun on his heel and returned to the ballroom, into the world of glittering jewels and costly dresses. The world of privilege and exclusion.

Mamie remained on the terrace, not sure where she fit in any longer.

# Chapter Twelve

There was a man in New York City, a powerful and dangerous man, one who frightened even the most hardened criminals. This man oversaw much of the city's underworld from a throne in the Lower East Side, not far from where the Porters lived. Many knew his name, thanks to legendary tales of his cunning and brutality retold as folklore. Parents invoked the name to keep small children from acting out, a bogeyman that would come and steal the bad ones away.

Jack Mulligan

Frank had met him. Jack had once asked for Frank's help in representing his brother on a smuggling charge. The younger Mulligan had been caught unloading over one million dollars' worth of stolen French silk and lace at the docks. Every lawyer Mulligan had consulted said the brother should plead guilty and serve his time, which Jack refused to allow. Frank took the case—even though losing meant putting himself in danger.

But nothing risked meant nothing gained in Frank's opinion. He'd been young and eager to prove himself. To make his mark. Taking an unbeatable case and beating it . . . the opportunity had been too great to resist.

In the end, he'd convinced the jury the brother was a somnambulist and therefore couldn't be held accountable for his actions while asleep, all corroborated by a physician. The brother had been acquitted. Perhaps that was the moment where Frank had sold his soul for wealth and glory, yet he'd never regretted it. His reputation as the solver of unsolvable problems had been solidified. Plus, a grateful Mulligan had promised Frank a favor in return.

Now he meant to call in that favor.

"Are you certain about this?" Otto asked. The investigator had insisted on tagging along when he'd learned of the errand. "If you need something, I can help—"

"I wouldn't ask you to do this." Frank dodged the line clustered around an oyster cart. "Not when you hope to gain a spot on the force someday."

"You really think Byrnes is having your house watched?"

"I know he is."

"I take it he noticed a guest of the female variety, one he recognized."

Frank kept quiet and continued on. Hard to say if Byrnes knew for certain Mamie had visited Frank's home . . . but he couldn't take the chance. Duncan Greene would tear Frank's balls off if he learned of what happened on that billiards table—after he turned all of New York against Frank.

God, but when he closed his eyes he could picture her, head thrown back and mouth open in absolute bliss. Body trembling and her moisture flooding his tongue. As long as he lived, he'd never forget how beautiful, how bold she'd been.

He must forget, however. She belonged to someone else. Even if the marriage agreement hadn't yet been signed it soon would be.

They turned onto Great Jones Street where the New Belfast Athletic Club, Mulligan's headquarters, came into view. It was a large building, unassuming, with a boxing club and saloon in the front and a dance hall in the back. One could easily find the city's most dangerous men here at any time of day.

Jack Mulligan commanded the city's criminal class with ease. Ten years ago, he'd accomplished something no one thought possible: uniting the remnants of the most powerful gangs into one organization. Even enemies like the Dead Rabbits and Whyos had made peace and joined Mulligan. It was nothing short of miraculous . . . and Mulligan oversaw the entire operation.

At the club's door, two young men who couldn't have been more than twenty years old stood guard. "You don't look like members," one of them said as he raked Otto and Frank with cold, dispassionate eyes. "You best move along."

"Mulligan's expecting me. I'm Frank Tripp."

"Wait here." He disappeared inside, leaving the three of them on the stoop. The other guard hardly blinked, his face serious. A gun peeked out from the waistband of his trousers. Frank suspected it wasn't the only weapon on the young man's person.

Long minutes later the man returned. "Tommy'll take you up to the third floor."

Tommy opened the door and ushered Frank and Otto inside. A bare-knuckled boxing match was taking place in a large ring, where men stood around and shouted at the two combatants. Various bets were scrawled across a chalkboard on the wall. In the back was a narrow wooden bar, hundreds of liquor bottles and a few empty wooden tables.

They followed Tommy to the stairs. Two floors later, the guard crossed to an ornate oak door with a brass knob. He knocked twice. "Enter," a voice called from within and Tommy pushed open the door.

Jack Mulligan rose from behind a huge walnut desk and started toward them. "Hello, Tripp. I was surprised to get your note."

He held out a hand, which Frank promptly shook. "Thank you for seeing me. This is my investigator—"

"Otto Rosen." The two men pumped hands. "I've heard of you."

Otto frowned, which made sense. Not many men would rejoice at gaining Mulligan's notice. "Mr. Mulligan, sir."

"Just Jack will do. Have a seat, gents." He nodded at Tommy, who stepped out and shut the door behind him. Mulligan was known as a smart dresser and today was no exception, with an elegant blue suit that would look right at home in the Union or Metropolitan clubs. A gold pocket watch chain sparkled in the light from the gasolier. "Would either of you care for a drink?"

"No, thank you," Frank said, and Otto declined as well.

Frank had been here a few times before, always summoned by Mulligan. On each visit, Mulligan's desk had been littered with paperwork, as it was now. Running a criminal empire must require a huge amount of time and organizational skills. "You should hire a secretary." He pointed at the mess.

Mulligan's mouth hitched. "Haven't been able to find one I trust. If you think of someone, let me know."

A job where one was privy to Mulligan's secrets? That was a sure-fire way to be killed or get kidnapped. Plenty of men would love to know what went on inside these four walls. "I will. Thank you for seeing us. I know you're busy."

"Never too busy for you. Your note intrigued me. Something about Byrnes."

Mulligan had a memory like none other. No doubt he remembered every word Frank had written.

"Byrnes and I are a bit at odds over a case. In hopes of intimidating me, he's taken to monitoring my home as well as any guests who visit."

"Fucking bastard." Mulligan's lip curled. "Thinks he's above the law, that he can bully and beat anyone into a confession just because he wears that badge. The bad news is that he's untouchable at present."

Frank held up a hand. "This is more about another detective. I'm representing a woman who has been accused of killing her husband—"

"Mrs. Porter," Mulligan supplied. "I heard you'd taken the case. Knew her husband, a lowlife scum. And?"

"Are you aware that Porter's cousin is a police detective?"

"No." Mulligan's brows lifted. "Where was this paragon of virtue while his cousin was running up debts and taking a fist to his wife?"

"Good question. Nevertheless, Byrnes plans to have the cousin testify at the trial, to paint my client as a shrew and murderess. I need a way to discredit him. I need information on Detective Porter."

Otto nodded to himself, now understanding why this wasn't a job Frank had asked him to undertake. This was defaming a police detective— and Byrnes by association. Involvement would not endear one to the police department.

"I see." Mulligan stroked his jaw thoughtfully. "You know I love to poke at the coppers whenever I can, Byrnes especially. Also, I hate men who beat women. Cowards, all of them. I'll see what I can find out."

Frank breathed a sigh of relief. If anyone could unearth the type of secrets to discredit a policeman in court, it was Mulligan. "Thank you. I appreciate it." He rose and held out his hand. "Consider us even then."

Mulligan came to his feet and gripped Frank's palm. "Not necessary. This one's on me. As I said, I'm gonna enjoy every minute of it. Come on. There's something I want to show you downstairs."

THE GROUP DESCENDED the stairs and entered the New Belfast Athletic Club. The din ceased immediately as Mulligan walked in, every eye swinging his way. It was as if the men stood at the ready, should

Mulligan require anything. Knights ready to serve their liege.

Mulligan waved a hand and told them to resume the match. The two boxers went back to pummeling one another and Mulligan clapped Frank's shoulder. "Shall we have a drink?"

It was less a request than an order. Though he itched to leave, Frank nodded. "Sure."

Otto openly studied the men in the room as they crossed to the bar. Likely Otto knew most of them, either from the streets or his investigations, which might explain why the investigator's fingers hovered near the pistol tucked in his pocket.

At the glossy oak bar Mulligan asked the bartender for three glasses of a German pilsner. "You'll like this," Mulligan promised Frank over the noise of the boxing match. "They brew it just a few blocks over."

And gave Mulligan a cut of the profits, no doubt.

"Surprised you don't drink something stronger," Frank said. "Like whiskey or gin."

Mulligan shook his head. "I like to keep my wits about me. Easier to stick with beer."

That made sense. Mulligan must sleep with one eye open, considering his vast number of enemies.

Tall glasses of straw-colored beer arrived, the head dense and foamy. The three men toasted and drank. The pilsner was delicious. Hoppy with a little zing of citrus. "I can see why you like it," Frank said.

"I'll send you a barrel."

"That's not—"

Too late. Mulligan had already turned and was having a word with the bartender. Frank glanced at Otto, who just shrugged.

"One of the boys'll deliver it to your house," Mulligan said when he faced them. "Either of you care to place a wager?" He tipped his chin toward the ring.

Frank watched the clearly exhausted boxers. One was superior physically, but the other was smaller and quicker. "I wouldn't know who to pick. They're opposites but seem evenly matched."

Mulligan's mouth curved as he took in the fight. "It's been going on the better part of four hours. Sometimes it's not about strength but about outlasting the others."

Were they talking about boxing . . . or how Mulligan had taken over the gangs in Five Points?

"Ah, here's my brewer now."

At Mulligan's words, Frank turned—and sucked in a breath. A man was walking toward them, a slight limp to his gait, and it was a man Frank recognized. He hadn't seen him in more than fifteen years, but he'd know Patrick Murphy anywhere.

His brother.

Jesus. Patrick looked exactly like their father, the resemblance so striking and disconcerting that Frank actually took a step backward. The hard shell he'd built up around his past cracked and memories of his childhood came flooding back. The small shack on Worth Street had been home to too much violence and strife. Hunger and fear. There wasn't much he cared to remember from those years, yet Frank couldn't seem to forget them.

Two years older than Frank, Patrick had gone to work in a factory as soon as he turned nine. That had left Frank alone in the house with their parents most of the time, until he'd learned to escape to the saloon down the street.

Stone's Saloon had been his refuge. The owner, Mr. Stone, paid him to run errands, clean and eventually do the books. When Frank proved adept at the accounting, Mr. Stone had arranged for him to go to a boarding school. That start had enabled him to get out of Five Points. Frank Tripp was born.

Patrick approached to have a word with Mulligan and sweat rolled between Frank's shoulder blades. So his brother worked here, now? A few years ago Patrick had been arrested on a burglary charge. Frank had paid the bail and convinced the prosecutor's office to drop the charges. He'd insisted it be done anonymously, that Patrick never find out his involvement. Part of him had hoped the arrest would scare his brother into going straight.

Apparently not.

"Tripp, I'd like you to meet Patrick Murphy, the genius behind the German pilsner you are drinking."

Frank blinked. His brother, a genius? Behind the pilsner?

He glanced at Patrick's outstretched hand before meeting his brother's eyes. Recognition slowly dawned on his brother's face and his mouth slackened. Patrick immediately withdrew his hand and his expression darkened. "Well, if it ain't Frankie, all grown up. Down here to slum it with us hooligans?"

"Hello, Patrick. You're looking well."

His brother snorted. "As if you cared." He turned to Mulligan. "I'll speak to you later, Jack. Right now I need some fresh air."

Patrick limped away, the impairment reminding Frank of the factory accident that almost took his brother's life at the age of eleven. The loss of income had caused their father to go into a drunken rage for two days, beating on their mother until she couldn't stand. Instead of worrying about his injured son, Colin Murphy had cared only that his gin money would disappear.

Frank exhaled and cast a quick glance at Mulligan. The leader's gaze showed no surprise over the exchange, merely a quiet curiosity. Had he known of Patrick and Frank's history? It seemed unlikely, as Frank had gone to great pains to distance himself from his past. He'd buried those secrets deep.

But Mulligan had ways of learning information that other men couldn't. After all, wasn't that why Frank was here?

"Still want the pilsner?" Mulligan asked. "I'll give you an old barrel, one you can be certain Patrick hasn't spit in."

Now it was all Frank could think about, that he'd be drinking his brother's spit. "Thank you but I'll pass." He set his glass down on the bar top. "I need to be going. Appreciate your help, Jack."

"Don't mention it," Mulligan said with a smirk. "After all, you're practically family."

With those words ringing in his ears, Frank hurried from the club, Otto at his side. So Mulligan knew. How? Frank had been so careful in burying his past and distancing himself from the Murphy clan. He'd never told a soul the real story of his upbringing, not since leaving Five Points.

Mulligan had orchestrated that meeting tonight

between Frank and Patrick. Why? For his amusement? Or, rather some darker purpose?

Frank's throat tightened with the terrible possibilities.

They walked a block before he trusted himself to speak. "I need a favor," he told Otto. "The brewer."

"I gather you know him," the other man said.

"I do, but from a long time ago. Almost fifteen years." He stopped and moved to the edge of the walk, where he and Otto could talk. "Dig up what you can on him. I'd like to know what he's doing with Mulligan, if this pilsner thing is legit."

"All right. I can do that, if you're certain."

Frank dragged a hand through his hair. Did he really wish to do this? He'd left home and never regretted it. Sent his mother money but nothing more. Why did he suddenly care?

The image of Mamie cradling Mrs. Barrett's son popped in his mind, her willingness to help these women, near strangers. *He spent their funds on gin and women. Came home and treated her like trash. What kind of man is that? Not the one who courted her, I can guarantee it.*

Frank's present was full of gray areas, blurred lines between good and bad. Murky legal waters only he could navigate. In his memory, though, his childhood had been very black-and-white, with clear villains. There hadn't been a need to reevaluate those impressions as an adult . . . not until Mamie.

Mamie was full of compassion and generosity, risking her own personal safety and standing in society to bring money to these families. She'd fought for them, even with him, and he was beginning to see that perhaps his judgment had grown clouded in certain areas.

Perhaps he hadn't always been fair.

No, he didn't work with middle- or lower-class clients. Instead, he helped the richest New Yorkers avoid trouble, legitimate or not. His law practice demanded it, as he didn't work for free. Other than Mrs. Porter and springing his brother from the Tombs a while ago, Frank had avoided any case that wouldn't pay him handsomely.

So, was he a bad person because of it?

He rubbed the sudden tightness in the back of his neck. Damn Mamie Greene and her do-gooder stubbornness. He didn't need to feel guilty over the choices he'd made in his life. It was too late to change them anyway. He'd have Otto find out what he could on Patrick and then be done with the Murphies forever.

"Just learn what you can and let me know. I'll pay double your normal rate."

Otto's brows shot up but he didn't comment. He merely tipped his derby and walked away, leaving Frank alone on haunted, familiar streets.

MAMIE WAS IN her room, counting money, when her mother knocked. "Marion, are you there?"

She quickly stashed the few hundred dollars she'd saved, money that would be redistributed to her tenement ladies next week. When all evidence of the secret cache had disappeared, she called, "Come in, Mama."

Catherine Greene was a blond beauty. Florence, the middle Greene sister, was the spitting image of their mother, though their personalities couldn't have been more opposite. Their mother followed the rules, never bucked convention. She paid calls and hosted dinners, never complained about the hours Daddy worked, and ensured the Greenes appeared at all the important social events.

Mamie had once asked her mother if she'd ever longed to do more with her life than be a society wife. "Why on earth would I leave the top of the mountain to begin climbing once more?" Mama had replied.

Mamie stopped asking her mother questions after that.

"There you are," Mama said as she approached the bed. "Your father wishes to see you in his study."

"Oh." Apprehension slithered down Mamie's spine. After her conversation with Chauncey two nights ago, she'd been nervous about where things stood. It felt as if a hammer blow might fall at any moment. "Do you know what about?"

"Nothing terrible, I'm sure. If he were upset he would not have sent me."

True. Her father wasn't one to delegate a dressing down. "All right." Mamie slid off the mattress, shook out her gown and adjusted her bustle. When she felt put together the two of them walked downstairs. Her mother chatted about wedding plans the entire way and by the time they reached her father's office, Mamie's stomach had knotted into a ball.

They entered without knocking. When she stepped into the room she nearly stumbled. Standing by her father's desk was Frank Tripp.

She purposely didn't look at him for more than

a passing glance, yet her brain memorized every detail. Handsome, tall and a strong jaw. Wearing a brown suit that showed off his wide shoulders and tapered waist. Dark hair that had been oiled back, causing his cheekbones to stand out in sharp relief. Full lips she'd felt on her mouth, her neck . . . and other places.

Oh, yes, she'd seen quite a bit in that quick glance, enough to weaken her knees as she approached her father's desk.

*He doesn't want you, Mamie.*

Right. As delicious as the other night had been, he'd made his intentions perfectly clear. She lifted her chin and wiped any trace of expression from her face. No matter how much his departing words had stung the other night she refused to let him notice. She had her pride, after all. "Hello, Daddy. Mr. Tripp."

Frank executed a neat bow. "Miss Greene."

Her father gestured to one of the chairs in front of his desk. "Marion, we need to discuss your marriage agreement."

Mamie clasped her fingers together and tried not to panic. It was merely a discussion, nothing to get hysterical over. "I'll stand, if you don't mind. What about the agreement?"

"We've heard back from the Livingstons. Chauncey has signed the agreement."

The air actually left her lungs and she couldn't breathe for a long second. It seemed everything in the room froze as the weight of those words sank in. Chauncey had signed. Now only one outstanding signature remained before the agreement was binding. *Hers.*

She wobbled, actually dizzy, and wondered if she was going to faint. Everyone stared at her, so she drew herself up and tried to appear calm. "With the clauses intact or has he made amendments?"

"With the clauses intact. He has asked for leniency on the time allowed to pay the penalties, should they be necessary, and I've agreed."

"I see." She dug her nails into her palms, grateful for the sting. The sharp bite of pain kept her from fleeing the room in terror.

Chauncey's reservations over the infidelity and progeny clauses must have resolved themselves, perhaps when she'd suggested forgoing the marriage altogether.

*God, why had she opened her mouth?*

"So you need me to sign?"

Her father lifted a shoulder. "Not exactly. I am your legal guardian and would therefore sign on your behalf."

Oh. Then it was done? With two strokes of a pen her entire life had been turned upside down.

*You knew this day was coming. You have no reason to complain.*

Yes, but she'd hoped to find a way out of this. After the other night, after *Frank*, it was clear she'd be miserable in a loveless marriage.

She tried not to let her gaze drift to the man responsible for her epiphany. "I see. Then I'm uncertain why I'm needed."

Her father dropped into his chair and gestured to his lawyer. "Frank, perhaps you'd best explain."

Frank cleared his throat. His eyes held no teasing warmth, no blazing lust. His expression was flat, just a shade above bored. "Mr. Livingston has asked for your full participation. Legally, your father may represent you, which makes the agreement binding. But Mr. Livingston prefers you consent of your own free will. That you understand the terms and initial the agreement yourself."

"Why?" her mother asked, voicing the question before Mamie could.

"He said there had been some doubts expressed. He is ensuring those doubts have been satisfied."

Their conversation from the other night. She didn't know whether to be grateful to Chauncey or furious with him for raising the issue.

"What does that mean, doubts?" Her father scrutinized her face. "Doubts from you?"

"Of course not," her mother said. "The two of them have known one another for ages. What on earth would cause either of them to doubt the match?"

Mamie couldn't answer. She didn't trust her voice at that moment. Part of her feared she might confess everything if she started speaking, like a dam that crumbled under the pressure around it.

The silence in the room felt heavy, the weight of everything unsaid hanging in the air. She didn't dare look at Frank. Instead, she focused on her father, who appeared none too pleased about this latest turn of events.

He sat forward in his heavy leather chair. "Marion, I asked you a question. Why does Chauncey believe you are experiencing doubts about this marriage?"

"I discussed this with you a few days ago," she lied. "The clauses in the agreement."

"Those were Chauncey's issues and he's now conceded them."

"They pertain to me as well. I do not wish to produce children on your timetable."

Frowning, her father drummed his fingers on the surface of the desk. "Fine. Tripp, strike that clause from the agreement."

Frank took a pen off the desk, flipped to the correct page, and drew a line through the clause. "Just need you to initial the change." He handed the pen to Mamie's father. "Mr. Livingston will also need to initial the change, but I cannot foresee his objection."

Her father scrawled his initials and then held the pen toward Mamie. "There. Now we're ready for your signature and this can all be put behind us."

Hardly. This felt like the beginning of a long unhappy road, not the end. She stared at the pen in her father's fingers, the moment stretching. She tried to think of every reason to march forward and sign.

Her promise to her father.

Her sisters.

Not disappointing her mother or Chauncey.

Tradition and status quo.

None of those reasons caused her feet to move, however. She stood rooted to the floor. *I wish for more than a loveless marriage to a man in love with someone else.*

"Marion," her father said, his voice sharp with impatience. "Sign this now."

"No."

The word had escaped her mouth before she could stop it. Her mother gasped while Frank massaged the bridge of his nose between two fingers. Mamie didn't drop her father's gaze, however, not even when his skin flushed with anger. He rose slowly from his chair and put his hands on his hips. "Did you just refuse?"

*Think, Mamie.* How could she possibly make him understand? Then a realization occurred. He wouldn't understand. This was a business transaction for him, a way to blend his family with the son of his closest friend.

She needed her mother.

Spinning on her heel, Mamie locked eyes with her mother. "Mama, I need more time. I just . . . *please.*"

Mamie hardly ever asked her mother for anything; she'd been the dutiful eldest daughter for so long. She wasn't like Florence, who was demanding and troublesome. Or quiet and stubborn, like Justine. Mamie had never been rebellious, not with her parents. She prayed her mother understood the desperation behind the request.

Her mother's gaze softened and she rushed forward to wrap Mamie in an embrace. "Oh, my darling. Of course. There's no rush, is there, Duncan?"

Mamie breathed in her mother's familiar rosewater scent while she awaited her father's reply. *Please, give me more time to figure a way out of this mess.*

"Catherine," her father started. "She's had *years.* It is past time to get this over with."

"One or two more months won't hurt. Will it, Mr. Tripp?"

Mamie snuck a glance at Frank, who shook his head. "No, madam. She may sign when ready."

"There, it's settled." Her mother released Mamie and linked their arms together. "Two more months—"

"One," her father snapped. "One more month,

Mamie. Then you'll be signing, if I have to force your hand to do it."

Mamie let out the breath she'd been holding. A month. It wasn't much, but four weeks was better than nothing. "All right."

"And it goes without saying, but if there is another man behind this postponement I will ruin him. I'll burn everything he cares about to the ground if he dares to get in the way of preventing this."

She swallowed and merely nodded once. She didn't trust her voice.

"We're done here. You ladies may go," her father said. "Tripp and I still have a few more things to discuss."

Mamie bid her father good night and quickly left before he changed his mind. She didn't dare address Frank, lest she compound her father's belief that the attorney was the reason for her reticence.

Besides, she planned to see Frank later tonight anyway.

# Chapter Thirteen

An awkward silence filled Greene's office after Mamie and her mother departed. Frank's head spun, his thoughts too jumbled to make sense of what had just happened. Before leaving, Mamie had defied her father and somehow convinced her mother to agree. Beyond being impressed at her maneuvering, he was dashed relieved. Which was ridiculous, considering where things stood.

*Let's see, the police are watching my house. Byrnes may blackmail me at any moment—or worse, tell the world what he saw. Mulligan somehow has learned of my darkest secret, one I've kept buried for fifteen years. Mrs. Porter may be found guilty and subsequently electrocuted.*

And yet, despite all that terrible news, the knot in his stomach had eased considerably when Mamie postponed her engagement by a month.

He was definitely in deep over this woman.

"Have a seat, Frank." Duncan indicated one of the chairs across from his desk.

Frank walked over, lowered himself down, and braced for an unpleasant conversation.

Duncan sat and folded his hands on the desk. "You and I have known each other a long time. I've trusted you with some of my most personal matters and you've never disappointed. I am asking for you to be totally honest with me." He paused and stared directly into Frank's eyes. "Are you aware of any reason why my daughter is unwilling to marry Chauncey Livingston?"

"No."

The quick emphatic denial must have appeased Duncan's worst fears because he relaxed slightly. "I believe you."

Thank Christ. Frank did not wish to find himself in the middle of this family squabble. If he had to lie to protect himself then so be it. That was better than ruining Mamie's life as well as his own.

"Nevertheless," Duncan continued, "has she said anything to you about her feelings on the wedding?"

Frank considered his words carefully. Under no circumstances could he admit the truth, but he'd learned a crumb could often buy him time when cornered. "At dinner, she discussed her charity work and how she'd encountered many different women in the city. I think she's discovering the world is bigger than upper Fifth Avenue."

"What does that mean, exactly?"

"Young girls today are more independent, with jobs and apartments of their own. The number of divorce cases I've handled in the last year—"

Duncan put up his hand. "I don't want to hear about your divorce cases. And I fail to see how these loose lower-class shop girls have anything to do with *my* daughter."

"It's in the wind, Duncan. Women are marching in the streets downtown and suffragettes are pushing lawmakers for change. Mamie is likely caught up in the causes of her generation, which puts marriage fairly low on the list of priorities."

"No, I don't think so." He drummed his fingers on the desk. "Being a wife doesn't mean she cannot undertake a cause. If that were her concern I could talk her out of it."

*Good luck with that.* Mamie was as stubborn as they came. "Perhaps," he said. "But she's very—"

"It's another man, I'm certain of it."

Frank swallowed. "How can you be certain?"

"Because of here." He pointed to his stomach. "My gut. It's right every time. And my gut is telling me that some man has caught her eye and been filling her head with lies."

"Well, she only asked for more time, not to put the wedding off entirely. So perhaps she wishes to enjoy a few more weeks of independence. You know how busy the betrothal parties and fittings can be."

"It's not that. She was bothered by the infidelity clause. I think I'll have her followed, see if I cannot—"

Panic caused Frank to blurt, "No, you shouldn't do that."

"Why the hell not?"

He tried to think of a compelling case, one that would prevent Duncan from following through on this idea. Money was certainly no impediment to hiring a team of Pinkerton detectives so Frank would need to go with morality. "Because she will resent you for it. Your daughter is stubborn and proud, smart and resourceful. She'll realize you're spying on her and that will only serve to drive her away. I know she's always been your favorite, but this could ruin your relationship with her. Forever."

"You're saying I should trust her."

"I am. If you give her the month, she'll sign the agreement. She and Livingston belong together. Everyone knows it."

Duncan rubbed his jaw. "You are quite confident of my daughter's opinions, especially from only one dinner."

"Most young women are the same," he said and lifted a shoulder, hoping to sell the world's most egregious lie. No other woman Frank had met was like her. Stealing money and redistributing it downtown . . . befriending tenement wives and helping with their children . . . learning to gamble in Tenderloin dives . . . Who else could compare with his beautiful little thief?

*You're in love with her.*

He froze. Love? Good God, where had that come from?

No, not love. Lust. Most definitely lust. That was all—and any further dissection of his thoughts and feelings was out of the fucking question.

Still, the single shocking word reverberated in his head, like he was on the witness stand and his brain was questioning him.

*Whereas you've chased her about the city for months.*

*Whereas you are jealous of Chauncey Livingston, a man more useless than a glass hammer.*

*Whereas you have risked your career to help her friend.*

*Whereas you took liberties on a billiards table and cannot get the taste of her out of your mind.*

*Whereas you would do anything she asked, anything at all, just to see her smile.*

Damn it all.

"You do know young women," Duncan muttered as if trying to convince himself. "All right, I'll back off. For now. However, if I notice any behavior that's out of the ordinary for her, I'll be signing this agreement in her stead. Chauncey will just have to live with it."

"Noted."

They both stood and Frank blew out a silent breath of relief. Somehow he'd avoided disaster today. He collected the copies of the unsigned marriage agreements and placed them in his satchel, trying not to think on what this all meant. "Shall I let the Livingstons know of the delay?"

Duncan grimaced behind his prodigious facial hair. "No, best for me to handle that. I'm supposed to see the eldest Livingston tonight anyway."

"Excellent. Enjoy the rest of your day, then." He lifted his satchel and prepared to leave.

"Frank, one more thing." Duncan put his hands on his hips. "My daughter *will* marry Chauncey Livingston, even if I have to pull her down the aisle kicking and screaming to do it."

Did Duncan still suspect Frank had designs on Mamie? Apparently Frank hadn't been as convincing as he'd hoped.

He dipped his chin and forced out, "Of course. I'll do everything in my power to ensure the marriage happens."

"See that you do."

\* \* \*

NIGHT HAD LONG fallen when Mamie tiptoed out of her bedroom and along the corridor. She and her sisters always snuck out via the servants' stairs, as they were far from her parents' bedroom and unused at this hour. Through the kitchens, out the rear, around the side of the house and . . . freedom.

When she was halfway down the stairs, noise sounded behind her. A servant? Her father? Panicked, she pressed tight to the wall and held her breath. She was fully dressed, clearly not just on her way to the kitchen for a small bite. Dash it all.

Footsteps on the stairs. There was nowhere to go but to the bottom and hope the darkness provided a hiding spot. As quietly as she could, she descended the rest of the steps. Then she darted around a corner and tried to calm her racing heart. A minute later, whoever was on the stairs reached the ground floor. Mamie carefully took a peek—and saw her fully dressed sister creeping toward the empty kitchen.

"Florence," she hissed. "What are you doing?"

Florence spun and put a hand to her heart. "You scared me half to death," she whispered. "What are *you* doing?"

Mamie came forward and took her sister's arm. When they were in the kitchen, she asked, "Are you going out?"

"Yes. Are you?"

Mamie nodded. "Shall we share a hansom?"

"If you're going downtown, then yes."

Holding Florence's hand, Mamie led them out the back door and around the house. Once on Fifth Avenue, they crossed over and flagged a passing hansom. The entire business lasted less than five minutes.

"Now," Mamie said as they settled inside. "Tell me where you're going."

"The Bronze House. I think I know where *you* are going. You're visiting Frank Tripp, aren't you?"

Was she that obvious? Mamie didn't confirm her destination. Instead, she said, "How will you get in? We were barred from entering that casino ever again."

"I have my ways." Florence's sly smile was evident in the dim interior light. "Let's just say the owner and I have become friends of a sort."

"Mr. Madden?"

Florence nodded. "I am learning so much. Remind me to give you my winnings for the tenement ladies. I think I have six hundred dollars squirreled away in my suite."

"Six hundred dollars?" That would feed a lot of families. "How did you win so much?"

"Talent. And you never said whether I was right about your errand this evening. That was Mr. Tripp's address you gave, wasn't it?"

"Yes." Mamie brushed her skirts, smoothing the fabric. "I'm going to see Frank."

"Ha! I knew it. I take it my advice on seduction was successful."

Mamie didn't comment on that. Instead, she thought it might be time to confer with her sister about the ramifications of refusing a marriage to Chauncey Livingston. "Chauncey signed the marriage agreement today. Daddy is still set on the marriage taking place, despite my objections."

"Oh, he would never make you marry someone

against your wishes. You've always been his favorite."

Because she'd always done as he asked, played the part of dutiful society daughter. "He told me I would sign the marriage agreement, even if he had to force my hand to do it."

"He's bluffing."

Florence sounded certain, but Mamie didn't share her sister's optimism. "What if he isn't?"

"Then run away."

*"Run away?"*

"For whom are you living your life, you or Daddy? What's the worst that happens if you refuse?"

A strangled noise escaped Mamie's throat. "At best, he disowns me."

"Then you marry whomever you'd like. How is that a deterrent, exactly?"

"You say that, knowing I'd be kicked out of the family."

"Maims, you'll always be my family, no matter what happens with Daddy. I certainly don't plan on letting him choose my husband. Would you still be my sister if he disowned me?"

"Of course," Mamie said without thinking. "I would never turn my back on you."

Florence held out her hands as if to say, *See?*

Then there was the promise she'd made. "There is another concern. If I marry someone other than Chauncey then Daddy might force you to marry Chauncey—or some other man of his choosing."

Florence threw her head back and laughed. "I would leave and join a traveling sideshow before I'd marry Chauncey. Being a Greene with all the trappings and trimmings of society means absolutely nothing to me."

Mamie believed her. If any of them was fully capable of starting a new life somewhere, it was Florence. She was wise beyond her years, self-sufficient and absolutely fearless.

Florence sobered and studied Mamie's face. "Have you been worried about that possibility? Is that why you agreed to marry Chauncey, so I wouldn't have to?"

"No, of course not." Not exactly anyway. "I just didn't mind the idea so much when the marriage was first discussed."

"Before Frank Tripp, you mean. That's another reason I like your knight in shining armor. I hope he sweeps you off your feet."

"He won't. He keeps telling me to marry Chauncey."

"Likely because he's worried what Daddy will do when he finds out about the two of you. Convince him you're worth it, dear sister."

No, Mamie couldn't. Their father would ruin any man involved with her. The guilt would kill her if Frank's career and social standing suffered because of their acquaintance. Perhaps in five or ten years her father would be more understanding— not that she expected Frank to wait that long.

Besides, Frank had repeated there could be nothing between them, that he had no interest in marriage. The man certainly wasn't head over heels for her, writing sonnets and sending her gifts. She'd never change his mind . . . but she did have one month to enjoy whatever this was between them in secret.

In the meantime she'd find a way out of this arrangement with Chauncey. Under no circumstances could she marry that man. She'd be absolutely miserable as a society wife and everything told her Chauncey would make a terrible husband. He'd already warned her he wouldn't be faithful. He'd shown no backbone in standing up to either of their fathers, and had caved on the marriage agreement the second she'd expressed doubt about their union.

Not to mention a man like Chauncey would never understand her causes. He'd nearly had apoplexy when she'd mentioned her downtown charities to him the other night. The truth would likely give him a stroke.

Most importantly, she didn't *feel* anything for him. Her heart didn't beat hard around him, her chest tightening like a bowstring. She didn't long for Chauncey's fiery kisses or whispered promises. She didn't crave his rough yet gentle touch, or wish to explore every inch of his body. Only one man brought forth those desires—and it wasn't her almost-fiancé.

Marriage to Chauncey would be like a lifetime of cloudy days after first experiencing sunshine.

So tonight, she planned to confer with Frank on ideas to extricate herself from this agreement. There had to be a way. And if kissing happened as well . . .

The carriage slowed. "Be careful," she told Florence. "I don't like you out on your own."

Florence rolled her eyes. "Bald Jack hardly leaves my side whenever I'm there. Madden won't let anything happen to me."

The way she said it, with such confidence . . . "Are you involved with Madden?"

"No. I don't think he has much interest in women. I can't . . . Well, I can't figure him out."

"Isn't he dangerous? Florence, it's one thing to visit his casino but another altogether to become entangled with him."

The carriage stopped at the curb. Florence pushed open the door. "Don't worry about me. I'm in no danger from Madden or anyone else in that place."

"You'll be in danger if Daddy learns of these outings," Mamie warned as she crawled over her sister and stepped out of the carriage. "Don't let anyone recognize you there."

"I won't." Florence shooed Mamie with her hands. "Stop badgering me. Go forth and have fun. Give Sir Frank my best."

The hansom door closed and the wheels began to turn. Mamie didn't know what to think about her sister going to the Bronze House and developing a friendship with Madden. No good could come of it, that was for certain.

There wasn't time to dwell on that now. She was too exposed, standing here on Fifth Avenue in the middle of the night. Hurrying up the walk to Frank's house, she climbed the steps and tried the latch. Locked. Dash it. Frank must've spoken to his staff after the last time she'd snuck in.

There had to be a rear door or window unlocked. Moving silently around the side of the house, she looked for a way in. She rounded the corner and approached the terrace. Perhaps she'd find the terrace doors open.

Her feet whispered over the stone steps. She held

her skirts to keep them from rustling and moved to the door. Just as her hand fell on the latch she heard a noise behind her.

Startled, she spun around—and a figure emerged from the dark edges of the terrace. "What are you doing here?"

*Frank.* Oh, thank heavens. He didn't appear happy to see her, unfortunately. His long legs stalked toward her, his body clad in only a shirt and trousers. His feet were bare, which she found oddly arousing. "Mamie, it's the middle of the night."

Blowing out a breath, she leaned against the glass panes. "I came to talk to you about earlier."

"Did you?"

A light from inside the house illuminated his rugged handsomeness. His eyes were locked on her, not wavering for a moment as he drew closer. She shivered at the intensity in his hooded gaze, the grim set of his mouth. He looked as if he'd decided on a course of action but wasn't too pleased about it.

*Please, God, let that course of action involve kissing.*

He kept coming until he stood directly in front of her. Then he jammed his hands into his pockets, as if he were trying to keep from touching her. "Your father is already suspicious enough. Must you tempt fate by coming here?"

"What did he say to you after I left the room?"

"I talked him out of hiring a Pinkerton to trail you around New York City."

Shocked, Mamie's equilibrium wobbled for a brief second and she rocked against the glass. Heavens, that would be nothing short of disastrous. "Why would he want me followed?"

"Because, my little hedonist, he believes there is another man involved. One who is trying to woo you away from Chauncey."

"That's ridiculous."

He braced his arms on either side of her head, trapping her against the door. Her skin prickled, a rush of excitement filling her as she breathed him in. He smelled of cigar and springtime, a heady combination of man and earth. He was real and raw, polished veneer over a core of pure steel. She wanted to lean into him, feel all that heat and strength for herself.

"Is it?" he whispered. "Because I'd say he's exactly right in this case."

She licked her dry lips, moistening them. "Are you trying to woo me, then?"

"Come inside and perhaps you'll find out."

AGAINST HIS BETTER judgment, he took her upstairs.

Frank never took women to the second floor of his home. It was his private space, one he didn't like to share. Growing up, he'd never had a room to himself, let alone a bed. With so many people in one tiny space, there'd been nowhere just for him. Once he could afford to live alone, he made a habit of using only hotel suites or the woman's home for liaisons.

And now, here was Mamie, standing in his bedchamber like she belonged.

*I like her here.*

He might never recover. He'd have to sell the house and start over just to erase the memory of her in this room.

*Or maybe I'll keep her forever.*

"I thought you were angry with me," she said, turning to take in the space. "The way you said there would be no more billiards games the other night worried me."

Not angry, merely resolved to resist her. After his meeting with Duncan, he'd vowed to forget her. To shepherd her and Chauncey into the marriage agreement then move on.

That was before she'd appeared on his terrace, skulking about in the dead of night to see him.

And also before he'd spent the last six hours thinking about her, how he'd never kiss or touch her again. How he'd encounter her and Chauncey around town, watching them smile and laugh in Delmonico's or at the Metropolitan Opera House. How he'd always regret losing the smartest, strongest and kindest woman he'd ever known.

And as soon as he saw her tonight he knew he couldn't do it.

He couldn't let her go, not without a fight.

They stared at each other for a long time, tension coiling around them, winding, as they both waited. He was lost for her, drowning in craving and *need*, and the force of it frightened him. The urge to cross the room, tear off their clothes and slide inside her had his hands shaking.

No, he must pause a moment and calm down. He couldn't frighten her, too.

Then the side of her mouth hitched and she crooked a finger, beckoning him.

*God, yes.*

He closed the distance between them in four steps and cradled her face in his palms, brushed the soft skin of her jaw with his thumbs. "Does that mean you'd prefer to play billiards tonight . . . or would you rather stay here instead?"

"That depends." Her fingers wrapped around his wrists. "Will we be playing another type of game?"

The words, along with the heavy-lidded gaze she gave him, punched through his chest like an arrow. Lust uncoiled in his gut, heat that wound its way along his shaft and through his balls. "Perhaps. Would you like that?"

"If you let me win."

He dipped his head to whisper, "In this particular game we both win."

He heard her swift intake of breath just before he sealed his mouth to hers. Her lips were soft and luscious, just as delicious as he remembered, and he deepened the kiss. All of his frustration and longing over the past few days combined and he was instantly, insanely desperate for her. He loved the way she kissed, her mouth greedy and fierce, tiny sounds of pleasure escaping her throat as if she couldn't help herself. With some women, kissing was a quick prelude to other more intimate acts. With Mamie, he could do this all night and expire a happy man.

She wrapped her arms around his neck, moving closer, her breasts molded to his chest, and he had to touch her. Opening his mouth, he slipped his tongue past her lips to seek hers then let his hands drift to her sides. She was breathing every bit as hard as he, their lungs bellowing as if they'd run a race, and he slid a palm across her ribs until he reached the underside of her breast. He wanted her naked and underneath him, her supple body welcoming

his, breasts swaying while he pumped atop her . . .
Fuck, that mental image threatened to unravel him.

But that was not his decision. It was hers.

And this had to be discussed with a clear head.

Breaking off from her mouth, he rested his forehead on her temple. "Christ, Mamie. I lose my mind every time I'm around you."

"I feel the same. It's like I need to crawl inside your skin to get close enough." Her fingers tightened in his hair. "I hardly recognize myself."

"We need to talk about this."

"Must we?" She angled her face and kissed his jaw, her lips dragging over his rough whiskers. She'd end up with beard burn on her creamy skin if this went further.

"I would have shaved if I'd known you were coming," he murmured.

"Then I am glad you didn't. I adore it. Feels like the real man underneath the smooth lawyer."

His imagination instantly went to the other places where she could feel the real man. *Stop. This isn't helping.* He let out a shaky breath.

Stepping back, he put distance between them. "We should discuss what you'd like to happen."

"Is it unclear? Because I assumed coming up to your bedroom was a definitive sign of what I would like."

Oh, his little innocent. She had no idea the number of depraved acts that could occur in his chambers. "Not entirely. For example, are you hoping for what I did the other night . . . or are you hoping for more?"

"More," she instantly replied, and his cock pulsed, more desire rushing to his lower body.

God, this woman.

She came toward him. "You're a man of words but I'm a woman of action. There are times when words are unnecessary." Her hands found his chest, palms gliding over his ribs and pectoral muscles. Fire trailed across his skin where she touched.

He swallowed and tried to remember what they were talking about. "I don't wish to hurt you."

"If you do something I don't care for, I will tell you."

Holding his gaze, she plucked the stud from his collar, tossed it on the ground and slid the collar free from his shirt. His breathing hitched as she started undoing his shirt buttons. Every brush of her fingers against his chest and stomach was pure torture. It seemed the ability to move had deserted him. He could do nothing but breathe and struggle to maintain his control while she attempted to shred it.

She bit her lip, fighting a smile. "You're enjoying this," he said.

"You're quiet for once. How could I possibly complain?"

He huffed a laugh—and couldn't remember the last time he'd actually laughed while intimate with a woman. He charmed them, yes. Complimented and pleasured them. But no one taunted and teased him like Mamie. Or drove him to the brink of insanity, as she was currently doing.

She pushed his suspenders off his shoulders and pulled the tails of his shirt out from his trousers. In one quick movement, he whisked it over his head. She wasted no time in unfastening his trousers and shoving them over his hips. He stepped out of them, leaving him in just a thin undergarment that hid nothing from her roving eyes. If she looked below his waist she'd hardly be able to miss the erection tenting the cotton.

"My goodness," she whispered as she skimmed her fingers over his shoulders and biceps.

"Do I pass muster?"

"As if you were worried you might not."

He had been, actually. Bedding an inexperienced woman was new for him. Had she seen an unclothed man before? Would he scare her? So when she reached for the buttons on his undergarment, he stilled her hands. "I believe it's my turn."

Lifting her hands in surrender, she took a step back and waited. Undressing women was a lesson in patience. So many hooks and tiny buttons, tapes and laces to protect all that lusciousness from prurient gazes. Normally, he conducted this process in a logical, straightforward manner, his excitement in check as he went along smoothly.

As he started on Mamie's clothing, however, his fingers felt clumsy. Awkward and anxious. The idea of having her naked in mere moments made him stupid. Three buttons broke in his haste, and she had to help with the skirts because he fumbled with the ties. His heart was pounding as each layer landed on the floor, more of her bare skin revealed. Each beat echoed along his shaft, his cock hard and ready.

*Keep it together. You must make this experience perfect for her.*

"Damn," he said when the strings of her corset twisted and knotted in his haste.

"Oh, dear. Do we need scissors?"

He dropped to his knees to better see the problem. "I hope not. I cannot remember ever being this inept."

"A word of advice," she said over her shoulder. "Never remind the woman in your bedroom of how many others have come before her."

The string pulled free and he set to work loosening the laces. When he worked enough slack into the garment, he moved to face her. "No other woman has ever flustered me like this. You've turned me upside down—and if I don't kiss you soon, I may—"

She launched herself at him, this glorious, adventurous woman, and their mouths crashed together. It was messy, but he was too desperate to care about finesse. Why had he ever considered her audacity a defect?

He unclasped her corset as quickly as he could manage and dropped the heavy thing to the floor. Soft, full breasts spilled onto his chest, and their hips met as she pressed closer. He groaned, overloaded with sensation. Tonight was definitely going to kill him before it was all through.

And that's when she took his hand and led him to the bed.

# Chapter Fourteen

*H*er poor lawyer.

He was rattled—and nothing pleased Mamie more. His reaction made her feel special, not just another face in a long string of women who'd visited his bed. She sensed he was holding back, taking this slow for her sake. The consideration, while thoughtful, was unnecessary. She was absolutely burning alive, desperate for him. Desperate for more of the mind-numbing bliss he'd given her the other night.

It was time.

Without breaking their kiss, she led him toward the massive walnut poster bed in the middle of his room. She still wore her chemise, drawers, stockings and shoes, and Frank was clad in just his undergarment. Lord, the sight of him nearly unclothed should be photographed, painted and sculpted by artists everywhere. The cloth clung to every ridge, muscle and curve, showing off his hard angles and long limbs, with bulges in all the very best places.

In fact, divesting him of the rest of his clothes was her top priority.

She wasn't nervous about the act itself. Not with Frank anyway. She trusted him, knew they shared something extraordinary—a spark she certainly lacked with Chauncey or any other man. Furthermore, based on what happened on the billiards table, she was certain he would take great care with her, ensuring she enjoyed every minute.

When the backs of her knees hit the mattress, he lifted her like she weighed nothing and placed her on the edge. His hands moved swiftly, removing her shoes and stockings, then sliding the chemise up and over her head. He kissed her again, angling them down until she was flat on the bed, his body partially atop hers. Before she could complain about his remaining clothing, he cupped her bare breast with his hand, gently testing and shaping the flesh. He tore his mouth away from hers. "I've been dreaming about these beauties," he murmured before bending to take her nipple into his mouth.

She gasped. The pressure was unlike anything she'd experienced, her nerves stretched like electric wires, shocks of pleasure traveling to every part of her. By the time he switched to the other breast, she was shaking, restless, her hips moving impatiently. "Frank," she breathed. "Please."

He licked the underside of her breast, scraping his teeth across the tender flesh, as his fingers found the tie of her drawers. She helped him push the garment over her hips then kicked the cloth onto the floor. Before the silk had even dropped he was turning her more fully on the bed and moving between her knees. Then his head dipped and his mouth was there, licking and sucking the very heart of her in an erotic rhythm that sent her soaring. Her back bowed off the mattress, a moan escaping her throat as she closed her eyes and let her thighs widen in surrender.

A large hand closed around her wrist and lifted her palm to her breast. *Yes, that felt even better.* Without thinking, she plumped and molded the heavy mound, rolling the nipple between her fingers. Touching herself alone had never yielded results quite like this, where her limbs trembled and her body raced toward the pinnacle at breakneck speed.

The tip of his finger played at her entrance, dipped inside. She rose up to meet the pressure, craving it, demanding it, and he dove in, filling her. His lips wrapped around the bud at the top of her sex and drew it into his hot mouth, suckling. Then he added another broad finger, stretching her tissues, and the orgasm rushed up like lightning through her limbs, an electric charge pulsing in bursts to steal her reasoning.

When she regained herself, Frank was still between her legs, moaning as he lapped up the additional moisture and whispering praise about her beauty, her taste and the way she'd responded to him. She relaxed, floated on a cloud of bliss and listened to the deep rumbling of his voice. He gentled with his attentions but didn't pull away.

After a moment he easily slipped two fingers back inside her. She twitched, her body more sensitive, but his clever digits curled and pressed a secret spot that caused her hips to buck. "Oh, God," she said, startled.

His gaze, bright and hot, watched her intently

as he repeated the ministrations deep inside her. Desire exploded in her lower body once more, stronger, faster—and her lids fell closed. He then began sliding fingers in and out of her channel, a sweet friction that left her aching every time he withdrew. A third finger joined as his tongue swirled. She could feel her muscles tightening, the fever expanding, as his clever mouth and hands worked.

When she was mindless and panting, he stood at the side of the bed. His cheeks were tinged with red, a flush on his neck. Wild blue eyes raked her nakedness as his fingers hurried to undo the buttons of his undergarment. He pulled his arms free then shoved the garment to his waist and down his legs. When he straightened she had a brief glimpse of a thick shaft in a nest of black hair before he crawled toward her. Bare skin met hers for the first time, and the crisp satiny hair of his chest and legs teased her everywhere.

He braced himself on his arms above her with most of his weight supported by the bed. The heavy length of him rested on her thigh. "We may stop if you don't wish to continue."

"I don't wish to stop."

"You know what this will mean, don't you?"

Her brows knitted. "No, what will it mean?"

Reaching for her hip, he rolled onto his back and pulled her atop him, her legs straddling his hips. His erection, hard and insistent, was directly under her core. He cupped her face and stared up at her, as serious as she'd ever seen him. "It means you're mine."

He took her mouth and kissed her, robbing her of the ability to respond. His hands moved over her, touching as much as he could reach. Stroking. Petting. For a man who'd just ripped off the remainder of his clothing he seemed to have infinite patience, content to drive her wild.

She, on the other hand, was burning alive. She knew about the mechanics of intimacy with a man—Florence did own a set of erotic playing cards, after all—but she hadn't expected to feel this insane craving and blind desperation for another person. How *necessary* his touch felt. Her body had a mind of its own, seeking fulfillment, and she rocked her hips over his shaft.

He bucked underneath her. "Christ, Mamie. I need to be inside you. Take me in, for God's sake. Please."

Oh. Now she understood. Was this . . . with her on top?

"Yes, my lovely girl. Just like this. It's supposed to be easier for you this way."

Never mind how he'd so easily understood what she'd been wondering. That was a thought for another time. Reaching between them, she gripped his shaft firmly—and he hissed through clenched teeth. She dropped her hand and started to retreat.

His fingers clamped onto her hips. "No, Mamie. You're perfect. It's perfect. Make it more perfect, please."

She tried again. This time he watched, head bent to see her lift him and rise up on her knees. "That's it," he said. "Put the head inside then drop down a bit at a time, whatever you can—"

His jaw clamped shut, words bitten off, because she'd taken his advice and started working him inside her channel. The smooth crown slipped in, and from there it was a matter of breathing and adjusting every few seconds. There was no pain, merely pressure, and she suspected his fingers had done much to prepare the way. Frank remained still, a light sheen of perspiration coating his skin, his glorious chest rising and falling, as she controlled the pace.

Soon he was fully seated and they both gasped. He felt huge and hard, taking up all the available space in her body. It was almost too much, her walls stretched around him, gripping his shaft. Then suddenly it wasn't enough. She squirmed slightly, unsure what to do but ready for more.

His big palms guided her hips, rocking her. Soon she caught the rhythm and reveled in the way he watched her, hooded lids shielding his hot gaze. Any awkwardness over the position or her bouncing breasts disappeared. They moved together as one, both reaching and straining, grasping at each other, nails biting. Each stroke caressed the swollen nub he'd loved with his mouth earlier and she only wanted more, more, more . . .

"God, yes. Faster." He levered up to take the stiff tip of her breast into his mouth, sucking hard.

White sparkly fire washed over her and the pleasure crested. Her muscles squeezed and pulsed around him and he took over as her rhythm faltered. His hips churned through her orgasm, then he stiffened, growling deep in his throat. Dimly, she felt his shaft thicken as he pumped inside her.

She collapsed on his chest and tried to catch her breath. Good heavens, that was . . . unexpected. For her first time, she'd expected messy, awkward and painful—and tonight hadn't been any of that. It had been sweet and passionate. Energizing and exhausting. All because of this maddening, charming and beautiful man.

He was still hard inside her, his hands rubbing her spine in long sweeps. A fire burned low in the grate and gave the room a soft orange glow that matched Mamie's mood. Warmth settled into her bones and she closed her eyes, content to stay here all night.

"I meant what I said earlier," he whispered into her hair. "You're mine, now."

She smiled and pressed her lips to his sternum. "For the next few weeks anyway."

He shifted until they were lying on their sides. "No, my little stubborn rose. I mean mine, as in forever mine."

SHE BLINKED AT him, so adorable in her confusion. But after what occurred here tonight, how could she doubt him?

No way was he giving her up. Not now, not after he'd been her first—and only—lover. He'd just come inside her, for God's sake. She might have conceived a child tonight.

*And why did you not withdraw, as is your habit? Are you trying to force her hand?*

No, he wouldn't do that to her. To be honest, he hadn't been able to help himself. The orgasm had taken him by surprise, rushed at him so furiously he hadn't been able to pull out in time. That had never happened before, not once. After watching his father's philandering ways as a boy, he'd always been careful not to sire any children. He'd failed tonight with Mamie, but would take more care in the future.

Besides, he meant to marry her.

The idea had settled in and taken root the second she'd arrived tonight. He wouldn't give her up. A lifetime to repeat tonight's activities with her? Fuck, yes. Having Mamie would be worth any price to his career or social status.

Not that he would give up either of those things easily. Duncan Greene might try to ruin him, but Frank was tougher than these men. He remembered what it was like to have nothing—and he'd be damned if someone would take it all away from him now.

Wasn't he known for finding impossible solutions? This was no different. He'd figure out a way to appease Duncan, keep his past a secret, maintain his position and marry Mamie.

He would be the luckiest man in the city.

Her brows dipped. "I don't understand. Forever?"

He gave her his most charming smile. "Yes, Mamie. You don't think I would sleep with you and not marry you, do you?"

She sat up, one hand trying valiantly to cover both of her ample breasts while locks of disheveled brown hair fell onto her shoulders. "Marry? *Me?* What has come over you? Have you hit your head?"

His smile slipped a fraction. "Why so skeptical? Am I not capable of marriage?"

Her jaw fell open and she scrambled off the bed. Leaning down, she grabbed his shirt and threw it on. The garment was much too large and baggy, but lust instantly spread in his groin once more. Jesus, he'd never seen anything more appealing than the sight of Mamie wearing his clothing, with her nipples visible through the thin material and her bare legs peeking out from under the hem.

He couldn't wait to take it off her.

She put her hands on her hips. "First, you told me you'd never marry, that you didn't wish to fail at fidelity."

He dragged his gaze back to her face. "I'm able to change my mind, you know."

"Of course you may, but not with me. You heard my father. He'll ruin you. He'll destroy you and refuse to bless our union."

"I have money saved, investments. He cannot take it all."

"I can't allow that to happen. I'd never forgive myself—and some day you would resent me for it."

"Impossible." He stretched out on the bed, folded his hands behind his head. "I would never hold any of this against you."

"This is unbelievable," she muttered. "You're not supposed to change your mind."

"I thought you would be happy. Now you needn't marry Chauncey."

She covered her mouth, turned her head and fixed her stare at the wall. "Where is this coming from? Because of tonight? If you feel guilty because of my maidenhead, there is really no need. There's no obligation of marriage between us, especially when you stand to lose everything."

Ah, he was beginning to see why she was so rattled by his change in attitude. Rolling to his side, he swung his legs over the mattress and stood. In two steps, he was on her. "My dear." He cupped her head and gazed into her eyes. "This is not about your maidenhead or any obligation. It is about you and the fact that I cannot let you go. I realized it only tonight, after spending a miserable evening thinking of that damn marriage agreement."

"This is insane. *You* are insane. You should be committed."

"I am in my right mind, I swear." He kissed her forehead. "Now, come back to bed so I may show you how much I adore you in my clothing."

"This was a mistake." She winced, then gestured to her middle. "And I'm *leaking*. I have to go." Bending, she began gathering up her clothing.

"Sorry about that. I got carried away."

"Good. I'm relieved to hear you say that. Now we may drop the marriage issue altogether."

"No, I'm sorry for spending inside you. I normally withdraw. But I meant what I said about marrying you."

"Then I'll choose to ignore it."

He shook his head. She made no sense. Marriage solved everything. "I don't understand. You no longer need to marry Chauncey and I've said your father's threats don't concern me. What else could be wrong?"

Holding her underthings to her chest, she spun to face him, her chin raised. "The reason I don't wish to marry Chauncey is because I prefer to have a say in my future—not have it dictated to me by the men in my life. Never once have you asked me what I want. You assume I will jump to marry you because you have deigned to choose me. Well, no thank you."

"So you'll marry Chauncey instead?"

"Why is it you or Chauncey? Why must I choose any husband?"

"Because your father will do it for you unless you marry me."

"So, what? We elope?"

"If you like." He didn't care for weddings, hadn't attended but a few. City Hall would suit him just fine.

"The romance of this proposal is positively overwhelming. I think I'd better sit before I swoon," she said, sarcasm dripping in her voice.

He dragged a hand over his jaw. "Better than Livingston, telling you he planned to keep his mistress during your marriage. Are you saying that was romantic?"

"Definitely not."

"Then what's the problem?"

"I cannot marry you. I cannot marry anyone at the moment."

A band tightened across his chest, the air squeezing out of his lungs. This had not progressed as he'd hoped. "Because of your father."

"He is one of the reasons." She picked up her dress and shoes. "Not to mention, you never really asked me."

She carried her clothing to the bathing chamber adjoining his suite. Damn it. He'd bungled this. The first woman he'd ever considered taking as his wife and she was walking away from him. *Do something, idiot.* "Will you marry me?" he called after her retreating back.

"No," she answered immediately, then disappeared inside the bath and shut the door. The lock engaged, the sound like a gunshot in the empty room.

Failure stung like needles under his skin. He

hated this feeling, this helplessness churning inside him. He hadn't expected her to say no.

His argument, he'd thought, had been a good one. Marriage to him prevented the need for her to marry Chauncey, and he would gain the most vivacious and beautiful woman in New York as his bride. Duncan would pose a problem at first, but one Frank could manage.

He'd continue to lie about his past, adding in a tragic tale to explain the lack of living relatives to Mamie. It wasn't a perfect situation, but what was the alternative? For Mamie to marry Chauncey in a month?

No, absolutely not.

Mamie belonged to Frank, not that foolish peacock. He had to find a way to convince her. *The romance of this proposal is overwhelming.* True, it had been a bit on the practical side. A good thing, then, that Frank knew how to charm women.

Indeed, he would woo her. Show her he was serious, that he cared for her and really did wish to marry her. And he wouldn't stop until he won her over.

After all, he'd escaped that shack and become the best lawyer in the city. He had a big house on the city's most desirable street. Any night he wished he could dine at the popular restaurants, attend the sold-out performances or relax at any of the exclusive clubs. He hadn't risen to this level of success by sitting back and waiting for things to happen. No, he'd worked hard—and then worked a bit harder—until he got what he wanted.

And he wanted Mamie Greene.

"I won't stop asking you," he shouted at the closed door.

"And I won't stop turning you down," she shouted back.

He reached for his trousers and smirked. "Challenge accepted," he said under his breath. "We shall see who wins, Marion Greene."

THE NEXT MORNING Frank bounded out of his house later than usual. After he'd seen Mamie home safely—much to her annoyance—he hadn't been able to sleep. His mind kept turning over the problem of how to win her over. Flowers were too tepid. Jewelry too traditional. Mamie was unique, unlike other women who needed material things. A woman out stealing money to support families downtown would not find a bauble or bouquet flattering.

He had to think grand.

And he also needed to think quickly. He had less than four weeks to convince her. That was not a lot of time.

His town carriage waited at the curb. After nodding a greeting to his driver, he climbed up. Perhaps he'd read some reports on his way downtown.

He sat—and recoiled in surprise. A man waited inside, one he hadn't seen but once in fifteen years. "What are you doing in here?"

Patrick's mouth twisted. "Now, is that any way to greet your long-lost brother?"

Frowning, Frank leaned toward the window. "Wait a moment," he called to his driver. "Stay here until I say."

Smith, his driver, tipped his hat and said nothing. Frank would need to learn how Patrick gained access to the carriage, but that could wait.

He tried to relax and appear as if Patrick's presence hadn't unnerved him. "Well?"

Patrick stretched out his legs and folded his hands. Uncanny how much his brother resembled their father, with his sharp chin and dark blue eyes. It was a face that still haunted Frank's dreams.

"Care to tell me why you're havin' a man tail me?"

Frank fought to hide a reaction. Clumsy of Otto to let Patrick spot him. "I don't know what you mean."

"Don't lie to me, Frankie. The man who was with you in the athletic club, he's been following me and digging into my life. The only person who would've asked him to bother is you. So tell me, why have you suddenly developed an interest in your family?"

"Ridiculous. I wouldn't bother to have you followed, not with the company you're keeping."

Patrick's gaze narrowed, a flash of anger appearing before he masked it. "So high and mighty. You always thought you knew everything, and I can see that's not changed in all these years."

"Enlighten me, then. Tell me you're not one of Jack Mulligan's thugs."

"I've watched you from a distance." He glanced down and brushed lint from his clean but well-worn trousers. "Important fancy lawyer in your big house on Fifth Avenue. I always wondered why you didn't move away when you left home. Why you've stayed in New York City when it's clear you could live anywhere you wished. Then I got pinched and locked up in the Tombs. Imagine my surprise when someone sprung me, paid my bail and managed to get the charges dropped. Not many could accomplish such a feat, not even Jack. I realized then it was you."

"No, it certainly was not—"

"Then there's the money," Patrick said, interrupting. "Ma gets two hundred dollars every month, no note, no receipt. Just an envelope of cash. She hid it for a long time and didn't tell me. The old man's been dead going on eight years, so why keep the money a secret from me, the only child who's bothered to stick around?"

Frank said nothing. A giant lump rested in his throat. Where was Patrick going with this?

"You couldn't leave us alone, could you? That's why you didn't move away. You think we need you, that we're these poor, pathetic creatures who exist beneath you. Like you're some white knight ridin' to our rescue in a Brothers Grimm tale."

Anger sparked in Frank's chest, eclipsing any surprise over the information Patrick imparted. "You were arrested for stealing, Patrick. Were you so eager to spend time in jail, then?"

"I was caught taking something back that belonged to *me*, something a lot of men have tried to take the last few years. I just happened to retrieve it at the wrong time and was noticed by a roundsman. Doing a few months in the Tombs would be worth it, seeing as how I was successful in getting my property back."

"So I should've let you rot inside the prison, with the disease and vermin—not to mention Mulligan's enemies."

"You still don't understand. We don't need you. The Murphies wrote Frank Murphy off ages ago, when it was clear you were ashamed of your background. What kind of last name is Tripp anyway?" He scoffed a deep laugh. "Not very creative, are you?"

"Fuck off," he growled, unable to help himself.

"No, fuck *you*, Frank Tripp." Patrick leaned forward, his face taut. "Fuck you for lording your wealth and privilege over us, like we should be grateful for any crumbs you deign to throw."

"That's not what I am doing. I'm trying to help."

Patrick's mouth twisted into a bitter, cynical line. "Let me tell you about your *help*, then. Do you know what happens every month when Ma receives that envelope of cash?" He paused for an answer, but Frank said nothing. "She breaks down and cries for hours. *Hours*, Frank. She's never spent one cent of that money, just shoves it in her mattress. When I asked her why, she said, 'That's Frankie's money. I'll give it back to him when he comes home.'"

Frank's tongue grew thick with emotion. He cleared his throat. Twice. "I wanted to ease her burdens."

Patrick shook his head. "Living way up here, with your fancy house and fancier women, all these servants . . . you think money is the most important thing in the world. What you don't understand is that you broke her heart when you left. She doesn't need money from you. She would rather know her son than have a hundred thousand dollars."

"You're wrong. She was grateful when I left."

"Because you were going to school. She wanted a better life for you—we all did—but she didn't know you were never coming back."

Frank clenched his jaw and stared out the window. Was that true? He could still picture her the day he left.

*She was in the kitchen, his father asleep in the back room. Frank knew to keep quiet, not to wake his father, especially not so early in the day. Colin had stumbled in around dawn, one of the working girls helping him inside. They'd been loud and drunk, reeking of gin. Frank had peeked from his pallet on the far side of the room to find his father's hand down the front of the woman's dress, their mouths tangled. He'd rolled to face the wall and crawled beneath his pillow.*

*It was then he'd decided to take Mr. Stone up on his offer.*

"Ma, Mr. Stone says I can go to a boarding school he knows of out in New Jersey."

*She paused stirring the soup on the stove.* "Who'll pay for this school?"

"He will."

*She had stared at him, hard.* "And what does he expect in return from you?"

"Nothing. He says I'm good at doing the books, that he should have been paying me more all along. I think this is his way of making amends."

"Frankie, no one does a good deed out of the kindness of his or her heart. He must want something from you."

"No, it's not like that. He said I should go and get a degree. Get out of this neighborhood."

*A voice boomed from the back.* "Shut up, you stupid cow. Can't you see I'm sleepin'?"

*Frank flinched and his eyes darted to where his father slept.* "Why do you let him talk to you like that?" *he whispered.*

*His mother pulled him deeper into the kitchen, hugged him and kept her voice soft.* "Go, my darling boy. Go take on the world and never look back."

"But she told me . . ." He trailed off. It hardly mattered now, not after all this time.

"Stop following me and stop sendin' her money. You've been gone for fifteen years. Leave us alone. We're doing just fine without you."

"Indeed, fine," he said, not bothering to conceal his sarcasm. "You're in Mulligan's gang and our mother still resides in the shack on Worth. Sounds dandy."

"You arrogant son of a . . ." Patrick's jaw hardened. "I work for Mulligan, but not in the gang. I'm a brewer, for God's sake. Part owner in my own brewery. And if you'd bother to see the inside of that house on Worth Street, you'd notice quite a lot of changes from the old days. But you haven't bothered, have you?"

Frank remained quiet. They both knew the answer to that question.

Patrick reached over and threw open the door. He put one foot on the step and then turned. "We don't need to be rescued. Not by you. Not by anyone. Leave us the hell alone."

# Chapter Fifteen

❧

The first gift arrived that next afternoon.

Mamie was having tea with her sisters and mother when their butler, Williams, arrived. "Miss Marion, a delivery has arrived for you. We've left it in the entryway."

"Ooh." Florence sent Mamie a knowing glance before she jumped up and hurried toward the door. "What could it be?"

Mamie had confided vague details about last night's activities to Florence, who thought Mamie was insane for turning down Frank's proposal. No matter how many times Mamie explained her reasoning, Florence said she was letting their father win.

Mamie preferred to believe she was saving Frank from the wrath of Duncan Greene.

She put those thoughts aside for now and chased after her younger sister. Their mother and Justine followed as well, everyone headed toward the front door. What sort of gift had arrived? Flowers? Chauncey hadn't sent a gift before, but perhaps he was worried she'd never sign the—

She stopped short. In the entryway was a bicycle, with its gleaming metal and small leather seat. Large wheels and flat handlebars. A glossy red ribbon had been tied to the front.

She blinked and tried to make sense of it. Chauncey definitely hadn't sent this. He viewed bicycles as feminine acts of rebellion. That meant . . .

"Look, there's a card," Justine said, strolling forward when Mamie paused. "Open it, Mamie, and tell us who it's from." Lifting the card from the ribbon, she walked it over to Mamie.

Swallowing, Mamie opened the card.

*For my little rebel.*

Warmth settled in her belly, a squishy tenderness far more drastic than anything she'd experienced before. Only one person could've written that card. How had he known? She hadn't told him of her conversation with Chauncey, who believed the bicycle was something only troublesome women enjoyed. Yet somehow Frank had chosen the perfect gift, something meaningful as well as fun.

She adored it.

*I won't stop asking you.*

Was he attempting to soften her up with gifts? If so, he would end up disappointed. She was Duncan Greene's eldest daughter and all that entailed. For Frank, any association with her meant the end to his social standing, his career and his wealth. She couldn't let that happen to him.

And besides, he'd assumed marriage a foregone conclusion once the topic had been raised. No ring, no proposal. Not even an *I love you.* Just a calm, logical decision about his life that now happened to include her.

No, thank you. That wasn't how she wanted her future decided.

"Chauncey is so very clever," Justine said. "This is an extraordinary gift."

Mamie shot a glance at Florence, who merely smirked. Then Mamie tucked the card into a pocket within her skirts. No need to correct the youngest Greene sibling on the giver of said gift at the moment. She couldn't very well tell her mother that Frank Tripp was wooing her.

The front door swung open. Their father appeared, his face softening as soon as he saw the group gathered in the entryway. "Well, I am certainly lucky today. All my girls are in one place."

"Daddy, look! Chauncey sent Mamie a bicycle." Justine went and kissed his cheek. "Isn't it great?"

He handed his satchel, cane and derby to the butler, then ran a hand through his hair to smooth it. "That certainly is smart. Well done, Chauncey," he said as he examined the bicycle. "You know, I've seen them in the park but never ridden one myself. Have you tried it out, Mamie?"

"No, not yet." She had practical knowledge of how the machine worked, but hadn't actually ridden before.

"You and your sisters should take it out. The weather is beautiful. Just keep an eye out for streetcars."

Their mother had agreed, shooing the girls out into the spring air to try out the new toy. It had been an absolute gay time. Both Florence and Justine planned to ask their father to purchase more bicycles for the family.

"Chauncey would succumb to a fit of the vapors if he saw you riding that," Florence whispered as she and Mamie watched Justine pedal along the path. "How could anyone believe it's from him?"

Hard to say. Must have been wishful thinking, since Chauncey hadn't ever bothered to send her anything. Not one note, not a single flower. Nothing in all the years she'd known him.

She didn't cable or write Frank to thank him. The bicycle was lovely—and quite thoughtful, if she was honest—but it didn't alter anything. She would find a way out of marriage, any marriage, and the solution wouldn't involve her growing affection for a certain Manhattan lawyer.

Another gift arrived the following night.

She returned from dinner and found a book resting on her pillow, a red ribbon marking a specific page. She assumed one of her sisters left the volume behind, likely because they wanted her to read a particular section. Of course, there had been the time Florence snuck an erotic playing card in Mamie's copy of *Wuthering Heights*. Never had a jack of clubs startled a woman so completely.

Was her sister playing another joke?

After summoning her maid, Mamie kicked off her slippers and placed her wrap on the dressing table chair. Then she removed the jeweled pins from her hair, one by one, anxious to put this evening behind her. Dinner had been a long formal affair with several of her parents' friends. Fielding repeated questions about Chauncey had tired her out. Neither of her sisters had been required to attend, which left Mamie no buffer whatsoever from the storm of curiosity.

Her maid knocked then entered. As she began bustling about to get Mamie prepared for bed, Mamie asked, "Did my sister leave that book behind?" She pointed to her pillow.

"No, at least I don't believe so. Miss Florence departed just after cocktails began and I was in here after that, tidying up. There was no book on the bed then."

That was odd. Perhaps Justine was to blame.

By the time Mamie was changed, combed and clean, she'd nearly forgotten about the book. She crawled beneath the bedclothes and reached to examine the novel.

*How to Master Sleight of Hand Tricks.*

The meaning was not lost on her and she didn't bother to hide her smile. He was helping her better learn how to lift money from the pockets of unsuspecting swells. It was considerate—and a tacit approval of her charitable activities. Lord knew Chauncey would never encourage that behavior.

*See, Frank is perfect for you.*

She pushed that ridiculous notion aside and settled deeper into her pillows. It didn't matter how well suited the two of them were, or how the idea of kissing him again sent fire licking through her veins.

Or how beautiful his eyes were.

Or how well he could use his tongue and mouth when—

Ahem.

She must forget all that. Frank had too much to lose in the face of her father's wrath. She would not have him ruined because of her. No, whomever she eventually married, if ever, must operate outside the circle of New York high society and have no connection to the Greene family. Someone who loved her and would allow her to make her own decisions. Frank was not that person.

If only it didn't hurt quite so much.

She rubbed her sternum, attempting to alleviate the ache there. The dashed pain hadn't ceased since she'd left his house two nights ago. Would it ever go away?

She sighed and stared at the book in her hands. Had he written a note? She flipped to the cover page.

*For my little finger-smith.*

A chuckle escaped her throat at his inscription. *Clever man.*

How on earth had he managed to get the book in her room? Unless he'd used a ladder, there was no chance he had come through the window. She couldn't picture him skulking about the servants' quarters, either. When would she ever figure him out?

*Never, remember? You and Frank have no future.*

And she merely had to keep reminding herself of that fact.

THE KNOCK SOUNDED exactly on time. Thank God for those who respected punctuality.

Frank threw down his pen on his desk and rolled his shoulders. After a long day of meetings, he had a busy night of work planned. "Enter," he shouted.

The door opened and Otto Rosen appeared. Frank stood as Otto closed the door behind him. "Good evening. Thank you for coming."

Otto nodded and removed his hat. "Of course. I think I have all the information we need."

"Excellent. Have a seat. I want to have a quick word before Miss Greene arrives."

"Ah." Otto's brows rose. "I wasn't certain if she was joining us."

"She is, but there are a few matters I'd like to discuss out of her earshot. First, let's start with Patrick Murphy, Mulligan's brewer."

Otto shifted uncomfortably. "Not much to say there, unfortunately. I tailed him for a few days but I suspect he spotted me."

"He definitely spotted you."

"He did? How do you know?"

"He told me. So, there's no need to continue digging into his life." Patrick had made his wishes perfectly clear the other morning. Frank had no intention of meddling in his brother's affairs any longer.

"How did he find you?"

"I couldn't say," he lied. "I suspect he's smarter than he lets on considering he's one of Mulligan's thugs."

"He's not running with Mulligan, if that's what you think. Yes, he and Mulligan have a partnership when it comes to the beer but he's not a criminal, not from what I could learn."

Hmm. That fit with Patrick's version. Yet it didn't fit with everything Frank knew of the Murphies. Had Patrick gone straight? "Had you discovered anything useful before he spotted you?"

Otto removed a small notebook from his pocket and flipped through the pages. "Let's see . . . Lives on Worth Street with his mother and his family. She's older and he appears to be taking care of her."

Frank smothered a grimace. Patrick was taking care of their mother? Was she ill? He didn't like the idea of his mother growing too old to be self-reliant. Why not use the money he sent each month to hire help?

*That's Frankie's money. I'll give it back to him when he comes home.*

The back of his neck ached with what he suspected was guilt. He pushed all those feelings aside to contemplate later. "What else?"

"Worked in a metal factory as a boy and got some shards in his leg. The injury became infected and he was forced to quit."

It had been much worse. In fact, Patrick nearly died. The surgeon had wanted to cut off the boy's leg, but their mother had insisted she could cure her son.

*I won't give up on him,* she'd told the surgeon.

Now, where had that memory come from? Frank hadn't thought of that day in a long time.

"And the brewery?" he asked.

"Makes a decent living at it. Murphy started there as an apprentice and then bought the previous owner out as time passed. He married a German girl from the neighborhood. The beer is well regarded in Five Points and beyond, and they're expanding out into Brooklyn."

Christ. How had all this happened without Frank's knowledge?

*Because you never bothered to look.*

"Siblings?" he heard himself croak.

"Two sisters. Both married. One lives in New Jersey and the other in Astoria, Queens."

Frank shot to his feet, too shocked by this news to sit still. He dragged a hand through his hair and faced the wall. His sisters . . . alive and married? When he'd been nine, the fifteen-year-old twins, Laura and Sarah, left home to work for a fancy brothel uptown. He'd heard his parents discussing it. The girls hadn't returned and Frank had assumed . . . well, he'd assumed any number of things had happened to his sisters, all of them bad.

Did Patrick see them? Were they happy? Frank had loved his older sisters fiercely. They were smart and beautiful and had kept an eye on him for most of his youth. When they left, he'd felt lost. Abandoned. Like Five Points ruined anything and everyone who resided within those shabby, dangerous blocks.

Had he been wrong?

"Are you all right?" Otto's brows had lowered. Frank nodded, swallowing his shock and composing himself. He was very good at composing himself, at donning a mask of affability and charm when it suited.

"Of course. Just a cramp in my leg from sitting too long. Anything else on Murphy, or shall we move along?" He lowered himself into his heavy leather chair and folded his hands. *Relaxed. Calm. Reassuring.*

"Nothing else. Like I said, he spotted me fairly early on."

*The Murphies are clever, son. We're smarter than the whole lot of 'em.*

His father had said this so often that Frank

couldn't recount the number of times he'd heard it. He hadn't believed it, not when his father's breath had reeked of gin. To this day Frank couldn't smell gin without gagging. "Have you unearthed anything we can use on Detective Porter?"

"No, but I'm still digging. Perhaps Mulligan will have more luck."

That was the answer Frank expected. People were hesitant to speak ill of the police in the city, mostly for fear of retribution. The officers were seen as corrupt agents of Tammany Hall, self-serving and biased. Reform had been discussed for years but so far those were empty threats. "Check in with Jack tomorrow, will you?"

Otto nodded and wrote in his small notebook. "Happy to, but he may not wish to speak to anyone but you."

"I'll see him if I have to, but I'd rather focus on the preliminary hearing. I have five days to put my thoughts together."

"You could waive it."

"No. Mrs. Porter's children deserve to have this wrapped up as quickly as possible."

"You're certain you can get her charges dismissed."

"Absolutely. If I weren't I would've pled this out already for a reduced sentence."

Otto pursed his lips and flipped his notebook closed. "Hate to see Miss Greene's face if you lose this case."

So would Frank. "We're not going to lose."

A knock on the door sounded just before Mrs. Rand's face appeared. "Sir, a Miss Greene is here to join you."

"Show her in, please." Frank stood and straightened his cuffs.

Otto rose a bit slower, a smirk on his face. "You are so done for. Does she know how you feel?"

"Shut up," he murmured as Mamie entered. She was dressed practically, with a white shirtwaist and navy blue jacket that hugged her upper half. A matching blue skirt swirled below to the tops of her leather boots. He thought about all the soft skin under that clothing and how he'd love to run his hands over her. Place her on his desk and slide inside her slick heat . . .

Fuck. He had to stop these prurient fantasies or else he'd embarrass himself in front of Otto.

"Hello," Mamie said.

Frank's secretary hovered. "Sir, did you need me to stay late?" She sent a pointed glare in Mamie's direction.

He often worked late hours at the office and preferred to be alone. Even if that weren't the case, Mrs. Rand had an infirm husband at home and she needed to relieve the nurse who cared for him during the day. "No, that's unnecessary. Have a good night, Mrs. Rand."

She departed and closed the door, giving the three of them privacy. "Thank you for coming," he said and gestured to Otto. "You remember Mr. Rosen."

"Of course." Mamie came forward and shook Otto's hand. "Nice to see you again."

"And you, Miss Greene."

It was not lost on Frank that she hadn't shaken *his* hand. "Have a seat and let's get started. The reason I asked to see both of you is because the preliminary hearing is in five days."

Mamie smoothed her skirts. "What happens at this preliminary hearing?"

"The prosecution will attempt to prove they have enough evidence to proceed to trial. I will try and poke holes in their case. The judge rules on whether we proceed to a jury trial."

"Which would take place months from now."

"Correct, but I'm doing everything in my power to get Mrs. Porter released as quickly as possible."

"I know." She nibbled her lip and her attention seemed far away. "I'm merely thinking of her children. It must be awful for them."

"I'll speak to Mrs. Porter," he said. "To prepare her on what to expect. I do have some disturbing news, however. Katie Porter is on the witness list for the prosecution."

"Oh, no," Mamie gasped. "How could they do that to a five-year-old child?"

"She's the only witness, Mamie. If she testifies that she saw her mother strike her father with the pan, then that helps the prosecution's case. For now."

"Children make unreliable witnesses," Otto said.

"True." Frank would have to think on how best to cross-examine the young girl. "Mamie, you know these children. Is she capable of testifying in court?"

"Yes. She's shy but quite smart. Though I'm not sure what she'll say. I haven't asked how much she saw that morning."

"I'll need you to assist with this. These children know you, and you'll be able to ease her worries better than Otto or myself. We need her to tell the truth but in a way that puts her mother in the best light possible."

"You want her to lie?"

"Absolutely not. But we need to know what she saw." Now he had to break the bad news to her. "This means you'll need to be at the proceedings as support. You will have to attend the hearing."

MAMIE WASN'T FOLLOWING. Frank seemed to brace himself, ready for her to argue, but she didn't understand how helping Katie at the trial was problematic. She was willing to do anything to get Mrs. Porter out of jail faster. "All right."

"I don't believe you realize what this means."

She cocked her head at Frank, aware of Otto's presence beside her. She attempted to keep the frustration out of her voice. "Illuminate me, then, if you please."

"Your presence will be noticed. By anyone present."

"And?"

"And reported in the newspaper. And noted by members of the police force. And commented upon by anyone who recognizes you."

Oh. That meant . . .

A cold shiver went through her and she blinked a few times at the stark wall in Frank's office.

"Otto," Frank said and stood. "I'll cable you later and let you know how we're getting on."

Their voices drifted on, but Mamie wasn't paying attention. She was thinking of her father and how he'd react to the news of her involvement in this. Her prediction? Not well.

*You were willing to appear in court before you slept with Frank Tripp. Daddy's reaction shouldn't matter.*

Yet she knew the conclusions her father would draw upon learning of this trial. Conclusions that reinforced what he already suspected: Mamie was involved with Frank Tripp.

Dash it all.

Well, there was no help for it. If Katie was to testify, then Mamie was the best person to assist with the girl. She'd visited the Porter children many times, always bringing treats, and Katie had even begun giving Mamie smiles. If Mamie had to suffer her father's anger and disappointment to free Mrs. Porter, she would do it. Gladly.

Her father would recover. Mamie was not marrying Frank. They may have developed a special . . . friendship, but not one that led to marriage and Frank's ruin. Nor would she marry Chauncey. All she needed to do was remain strong and not let her father bully her into doing what he wanted.

The same went for Frank. No matter how hard he tried, she had to resist him and his well-chosen gifts.

The back of her neck prickled with awareness a half second before he appeared. He leaned against the desk, his gaze wary. Her heart fluttered as she took in the long legs encased in fine wool. The tapered waist and broad chest. He wore a yellow silk vest with his dark gray suit, and the color brought out the vivid hue of his irises. Would she ever become immune to the sight of him? Doubtful, considering her memories of the other night.

*You're perfect. It's perfect. Make it more perfect, please.*

He'd turned her into a quivering pool of desire

that night. The way he spoke, the things he'd said.
The feel of his mouth on hers, his hands . . . The
care with which he'd touched and pleasured her. It
had all felt so *right*.

Frank's appeal went deeper than his looks, however. It had to do with his intelligence and determination. His confidence, the ease with which he
moved and breathed.

*It's called privilege. He's wealthy and moves in the
same social circles as you.*

Privilege her father would strip away if he discovered their secret.

She could not allow that to happen.

"I see you understand my meaning," he finally
said.

"There's no help for it. I'll lie and tell my father
Mrs. Porter is a friend."

He crossed his legs at the ankles. "He will ask
how you met."

"Through my charity work downtown."

"What charity work?"

"Helping needy families."

"You know he's going to be furious."

She struggled to suppress a wince. "With both
of us, undoubtedly. He'll question why you've allowed my involvement at all."

"I'll handle your father when the time comes."

She narrowed her gaze and studied him. What
was he up to? "I don't care for the sound of that.
What do you mean?"

"I mean, I will deal with him." He lifted a shoulder. "I'll make my intentions known."

"Sorry, intentions toward what?"

"Not what. Whom. More specifically, *you*."

If she'd been drinking, she would've choked. "*Me?* Have you lost your mind? You cannot tell him about us."

"I won't tell him everything, merely explain my feelings for you." His jaw hardened, determination etched on his face. "I meant what I said, Mamie. I'll not give up until you marry me."

This again. "I have stated my objections to the idea. I wish you would respect them."

"Once I convince your father to support us, I know you'll change your mind."

She made a disbelieving sound in her throat. "He will never agree to your suit over Chauncey. Never. Chauncey's father is my father's closest friend. The pact for the marriage was made years ago."

"We shall see." He smirked ever so slightly, as if he knew something she didn't.

"What are you planning? I hope you're not going to harm Chauncey."

"Does that seem like something I would do?"

"If it suited your purposes, yes."

"Such a low opinion of me." He shook his head ruefully. "And here I thought my gifts would help with that. You received them, yes?"

Heat rose under her collar. It had been rude to not thank him for the gifts. "I did. They're lovely. The bicycle is quite the spectacle."

"And what of the book?" He uncrossed his legs, pushed away from the desk, and moved closer. "Have you been studying?"

"Perhaps." She had . . . not that she would admit it to *him*.

"Liar. I know you've practiced." He bent, placed his hands under her elbows, and lifted her out of the chair. When they were face-to-face, he kept holding her, his palms sliding to clasp her hips. Her heart raced, the silly organ excited at the idea of having him near. The heat from his touch sank into her flesh, a brand to remind her of all the wicked things from the other night. Wicked things she could not forget, no matter how hard she tried.

"I've missed you," he said quietly, his thumbs stroking her hip bones through her clothing. "Have you been thinking of me?"

The ridiculousness of the question, so needy and unsure, was not lost on her. It was quite unlike him. "No," she lied.

"Hmm." He didn't appear to believe her. His hand came up to her throat, where gentle fingers swept over the pulse hammering beneath her skin. "Someday you'll admit the truth."

*Never.*

"So stubborn," he murmured. Then he watched, his gaze hooded, as his thumb brushed her bottom lip. "I've done little else besides think of you. My daily routine has increased to three sessions, in case you were wondering. Soon, I won't be able to separate my hand from my cock at all."

She bit her lip to stifle a chuckle, even as her body suffused with warmth. "And what are you thinking about during these three sessions?"

"Pleasure. Yours, mine. *Ours.*"

Her fingers skimmed his chest, the digits desperate for another chance to map his sharp angles and thick muscles. "That sounds fairly generic. I pity your imagination."

"You believe I lack imagination? My dear little

innocent, my depraved thoughts would send you screaming from the room."

She could barely breathe, the air thick with wanting. Run screaming? Not dashed likely. Besides, she was dying to know what constituted *depraved* for her high society lawyer. "Try me."

The edges of his lips curled and he pulled her flush with his body. The hard length of him pushed insistently between them. His mouth rested near her temple, and air from his mouth teased the fine skin. "At the moment I am fantasizing about bending you over my desk. With everyone just on the other side of that flimsy door, I'd push up your skirts. I could fuck you through the slit in your drawers, keep things neat and tidy. But I want more. I want you whimpering and begging instead. So I untie your drawers and let them fall to the floor, your naked, glorious heart-shaped bottom tilted up toward me. I kneel behind you, spread you apart, and tongue your folds. I'd tease your clit until you were wet and ready, grinding on my face. Then I'll stand and unfasten my trousers—"

She launched herself at him, her mouth slamming into his, their lips clashing in a brutal kiss. *God*, what he'd said . . . She was a melted, trembling mess of need. Where had he learned to speak like that, use words like that? Rather than shock her, however, it had turned her inside out. Between her legs ached, her body thrumming with the beat of her heart.

Blunt fingers dug into her skin, his kiss desperate and wild. So unlike the polished man who'd presided over their earlier meeting. She loved seeing him undone. Her hands threaded his hair, her grip firm as she pressed closer. This was madness, kissing him in the early evening with the entire office outside, but she couldn't seem to stop herself. His mouth was firm and coaxing, his touch a drug she could not function without.

When he broke off from her mouth, a sound of protest left her throat. They stood there, panting, for a long second, before he closed his eyes. "I shouldn't have started this. Not here."

"Because the door is unlocked?"

"No. I turned the lock when Otto departed. I shouldn't have started because I cannot possibly concentrate on work with you here, and I have too much to do yet before I can leave." He took a step back and gestured at the erection in his trousers.

"Session number four, then?"

He dragged a hand down his face, groaning through a laugh. "It seems I must, unless you have plans to visit me at home later tonight."

"I have an event with my family. The Kirkland Ball." Likely it wouldn't end until one or two in the morning.

He appeared crestfallen at this news. "You are dangerous to my peace of mind, Marion Greene."

A heady power swept through her, the knowledge that he was equally wound up, longing for her as she did him. This was all new for her, so it was a relief to realize he shared this overwhelming lust as well. Her gaze drifted to the front of his trousers then to the desk. Craving and desire burned in her veins, a crackle that demanded satisfaction from this one man, a man she could not marry. However, they could enjoy the most of their short time together.

And really, where was the harm? They were two consenting adults who desired one another and the office building had been nearly deserted when she'd arrived. Was what he said earlier even possible?

Did people do that . . . on a desk? Then, she remembered one of Florence's erotic playing cards. Substitute a sofa for the desk and Mamie suddenly understood how it worked. And the position had looked quite pleasurable, if the faces of the partners had been anything to go by.

*I want you whimpering and begging.*

Yes, but she'd have him whimpering and begging as well.

"This fantasy of yours," she started and strolled toward the desk. "Have you ever done it that way before?"

"Here?" His voice broke in the middle of the single word. A telling sign, she thought.

"Or at home. Anywhere with a desk."

"No, I haven't." His throat worked as he swallowed. "That's a bit advanced, Mamie. I hope you aren't thinking we could do that now."

Advanced? Meaning, she couldn't handle it? A tiny spark of anger flared at the base of her spine. "You know, whenever you tell me I cannot do something it merely makes me want to do it all the more."

"I know, but damn it. You're Duncan Greene's daughter and I can't—"

"Not this again. I'm tired of only being Duncan Greene's daughter." She held her skirts, perched on the edge of his desk, and pushed up onto the wooden surface. Papers crinkled beneath her backside. "When will you begin to see *me*?"

"*Get off that desk.*" The skin of his neck flushed a deep scarlet above his collar, his chest rising and falling rapidly with his breath. Mamie hid a smile. He liked her here.

"No, I think I'll stay. Besides, there's hardly any difference between this desk and a billiards table."

"Perhaps I could spare time for a hotel. Let's go now. There's one a few blocks away. That would be more appropriate for you."

"Again with your decisions of what is appropriate for me. It's very, very tiresome, Frank." She dragged her skirts up slowly, inch by inch, revealing her calves, until the delicate lace cuff of her drawers peeked out below her knees. "When will you learn? I decide what I want, no one else. No man—husband, father or otherwise—will make my decisions for me."

"Oh, Christ," he muttered, his bright blue stare focused on her legs. She widened her knees until her thighs were splayed open, still covered by her skirts, and he inhaled sharply.

"Still wish for me to get down from here?" she rasped.

"God, no." He stalked toward her while removing his jacket. The garment hit the floor and then he was on her, his big hands cupping her face as his mouth slammed against hers.

*Sweet victory,* she thought and kissed him back.

# Chapter Sixteen

$\mathcal{H}$e'd surely go to hell for defiling Duncan Greene's daughter in his office, on his desk . . . but Frank couldn't help himself. Mamie was too tempting, too stubborn, and he was too weak to resist her. *I've always been too weak to resist her.*

His hips wedged between her thighs and he pulled her as close as the position would allow. He kissed her hard, his hands moving everywhere at once, his brain unable to decide where to focus first. Desire raged in his blood, his faculties overcome with lust. *So hard. So desperate.*

He thrust his tongue in her mouth, needing to taste her, and she met him eagerly, tasting him right back. He groaned and, without thinking, rolled his hips into the cradle of her thighs. She broke off from his mouth to gasp, her head thrown back in abandon. "Do that again," she pleaded in that husky voice he loved so much.

God help him, he did. He pressed the ridge of his cock to her core and dragged, the result a heavenly friction that had him seeing stars. *Fuck.*

He shoved the tiny jacket off her shoulders and

down her arms. Even still, she was too buttoned up, too closed off from his hands and mouth. "I want you naked," he said, kissing his way down the soft skin of her throat. "Spread out like a feast in my bed again." He'd been able to smell her on his sheets for days and her scent never failed to get him hard as stone.

"I'd like that, too. I didn't even get a chance to explore you the other night."

His cock jerked as he pictured lying on his bed, naked, while Mamie touched and licked him everywhere. It scared him how much he wanted that. "I am at your service, madam."

She hummed in the back of her throat. "Is that so?" Her fingers went to the waistband of his trousers and began working on the buttons. "Then may I explore you now?"

Could he stand it? He was practically ready to spend from just a few kisses and humping her pelvis. This couldn't end too quickly, not when she'd granted him this unbelievable fantasy. "Mamie . . ." His voice drifted off as he watched her fingers. He needed her to both hurry up and slow down at the same time. *I am losing my mind over her.*

She pushed apart the placket then grabbed the fabric of his shirt to lift it out of the way. With his vest and suspenders still on, however, the effect was a lot of cloth in awkward positions. "You could help," she said and brushed the back of her hand over the outline of his erection. His knees damn near buckled as pleasure shot up the length of his shaft.

He was beyond banter, past playing. His ability to form words had deserted him the second her fingers landed on his waistband. Quickly and efficiently, he removed his necktie and vest, lowered his suspenders, and drew his shirt over his head. She observed this quietly, biting her lip, her eyes serious and intense. Her fingers traced his sternum through his thin undergarment when he finished. "Mercy, but you are the most handsome man I've ever seen."

He opened his mouth to return the compliment but her hand trailed south, toward his groin, and his jaw snapped shut. Dainty fingers unfastened the tiny buttons of his undergarment, which was all that separated her touch from his bare skin. Frank held his breath, anticipation crawling over him like a live electric current, and hastily undid a few buttons himself.

When his cock was released from its confines, Mamie wrapped a hand around the shaft, delicately, politely, as if afraid of hurting him. "It . . . looks so different close up," she whispered. "Feels soft and hard at the same time."

He panted, chest bellowing, as her gentle touch mapped him. "Grip it tight, sweetheart. Be as rough as you like. You can't hurt me."

"Like this?" She clenched her fist then jerked. Hard.

"Fuck," he growled as pleasure exploded in every part of his body. "Yes, exactly like that."

She did it again and his lids closed in exquisite bliss. He dropped his forehead to her shoulder and tried to keep from coming after a few pumps like a teenage lad. But Jesus, it wasn't easy. Nothing was ever easy with Mamie . . . and he loved it that way.

His hands sifted through the fabric at her hips. "May I touch you?"

"You are touching me," she teased. "And besides, I'm enjoying having you at my mercy."

"So you don't want me to make love to you on the desk? Sink deep inside you and make you come?"

Her rhythm faltered and her free hand began helping move her skirts out of the way. "God, yes. Please."

In seconds, he found the part between her drawers and reached hot, wet skin. "You're soaked. I think you enjoy seducing me."

Her teeth closed over his earlobe and gently bit down. "I think you're right," she whispered in his ear.

His balls tightened at the delicious twinge of pain and moisture leaked from the head of his cock. *Not long now. Hurry, damn it.* He slipped a finger inside her, stretching her until he could squeeze in another digit. Then he kissed her, swallowing her gasps and moans, working her clitoris with the palm of his hand, until she dragged him closer. "Now, Frank. Please."

She guided the tip of him to her entrance and he pressed forward, taking care to go slowly. It wasn't lost on him that this was only her second time and he'd rushed her a bit tonight, considering the circumstances. He'd be damned if she didn't enjoy it. *So tight, so hot. Don't come yet.*

Deeper and deeper, inch by agonizing inch. Sweat broke out on his forehead. The urge to thrust nearly overwhelmed him.

Then her fingernails dug into his hips and he was lost. He drove into her sheath, filling her, and they both exhaled sharply. "You feel so good," he told her. "I don't know if I can last."

"Please move. I need you to move."

The desire to pleasure her overrode everything else. He lifted her knees and spread her wider, and she braced herself with her hands on the desk. Then he drove deep, with enough force to raise her slightly off the wood. "Oh, God," she breathed. "More."

He couldn't stop then, her pleas ringing in his ears, as he rocked his hips and dragged his cock in and out of her sex. It was pure heaven, unlike anything else he'd experienced, probably because he wanted this woman more than anything else on earth. If this was what he had to look forward to for the remainder of his life, he'd die a happy man.

Her walls contracted as her limbs tensed, the look of rapture on her face so alluring he had to bite the inside of his cheek to avoid spilling right then. He shifted a hand to brush his thumb over her clit. "Come, you beautiful girl. Come right here on my desk, in my office, where anyone walking by might hear you cry out—"

Her body began to spasm then, her core milking his shaft, and he couldn't hold off any longer. His lids slammed shut as his hips faltered, the orgasm upon him then, fierce and strong, his knees buckling as semen shot from his cock. It was pure dizzying bliss, wave after wave of mind-numbing pleasure, his body emptying into hers.

They stood there, catching their breath, for a long moment. He'd finished inside her again, which was not a habit he wished to make, not without discussing it with her first. Children hadn't been a part of his future, nor had marriage, but then he'd met Mamie. He liked the idea of starting a family with her when she was ready. He wanted to experience everything with this woman.

She shifted. "Ouch."

"Oh, apologies." He'd been standing here like a dolt, inside her, waxing poetic, not even considering her discomfort. The wood had to be hard. Stepping back, he tucked his semihard shaft back in his underclothes then helped her down from the desk. He smoothed stray strands of hair off her forehead. "Have I romanced you enough?"

She chuckled. "Any more romance and I might very well expire."

"You know what I mean. Have I romanced you enough to agree to marry me?"

Her lips twisted into a reluctant smile. "Frank, I cannot marry you. The sooner you accept it, the better off you'll be." She pointed to a closed door on the far side of his office. "Is that your washroom?"

He nodded and let her go clean up without arguing. In the end, he would emerge victorious from their battle of wills. For now, he would enjoy the fight.

NOT LONG AFTER, once Mamie had been seen off in a hansom, the door to Frank's office opened. The other partners of the law firm walked in, en masse. Frank studied their grim expressions and braced himself. "Evening, gentlemen. Were we scheduled to meet and I forgot?"

"Frank, we have a problem," James Howe said without preamble.

William Travers, the most even-tempered of the

bunch, said nothing, merely walked to the chairs opposite Frank's desk and sat.

Charles Thomas pointed directly at Frank. "You have turned the police force against this firm."

Frank leaned back and rocked in his chair. "That's ridiculous. What on earth makes you say so?"

"Evidence in my murder case has gone missing," Charles snapped.

"And I was counting on police testimony in a trial next week to help my client. They've now recanted." James put his hands on his hips. "And I cannot get any of the detectives to speak to me in any official capacity."

"Two witnesses have disappeared, and one of my clients was beaten unconscious in a holding cell last night." Charles looked at William. "This cannot go on. He has to drop this case."

William held up his hand and faced Frank. "You had a run-in with Byrnes over this Porter case."

Not phrased as a question, so his partners already knew. "One of Byrnes's men is the cousin of the deceased. Byrnes asked that I step aside and allow the court to appoint someone."

"Also advice we gave you weeks ago," Charles said. "You told us not to worry—and now look at what's happened."

"Charles, please." William never took his gaze from Frank. "Let's hear why this case is so important."

Frank laid it out as best he could: the abuse, friend of Marion Greene, self-defense, the children. When he finished, William stroked his beard thoughtfully. "This case is a request from Duncan Greene?"

Frank shifted in his chair. "No, not specifically."

"What does that mean, *not specifically*?"

"Duncan has asked me to watch out for his interests, and I have interpreted that request to mean his family. Marion, specifically."

"Are the two of you romantically involved?"

Frank paused. That was not something he wished to discuss, not even in the privacy of his office with his three partners. All of them were adept at keeping secrets, but admitting the affair felt like a betrayal of Mamie's trust.

"Christ, you are," Charles said. "She's betrothed to the eldest Livingston boy."

"The marriage agreement has not been signed," Frank couldn't help but add.

"I cannot believe you are ruining this firm over a woman." Charles stared furiously at Frank.

"Now, no one is ruining anything," William said. "Does Duncan know about you and Marion?"

Frank shook his head. "Not yet."

William blew out a breath. "I've spoken to Livingston about this. Everyone considers the marriage a foregone conclusion."

*Except me and Mamie*, Frank wanted to add.

"Let me understand this," James said. "You have pissed off Byrnes and every detective in the police department, and you're about to upset two of our biggest and most prestigious clients. Am I missing anything?"

"I am doing the right thing by our client, Mrs. Porter," Frank said. "She deserves to be acquitted for this crime."

Charles's face turned a deep red. "You are jeopardizing our livelihoods for a low-class murderer who belongs locked up on Blackwell's Island."

"She's not insane. She was a woman defending herself and her children from a violent drunk."

"No one cares!" Charles blurted. "That happens daily down in Five Points. Those people are animals."

The words scraped across Frank's nerves like a straight razor. Two months ago, he might have agreed; but, after all he'd seen and learned, from Mrs. Porter and her children, Mrs. Barrett, to his own brother, Frank knew better. Merely because they struggled and lived in a tenement didn't mean they were bad people.

And Frank had met plenty of blue-blooded criminals who'd committed despicable acts . . . and never paid the price. *Because you've helped them. You craved the money and power, turning your back on those less fortunate.*

"She is not an animal," he said. "She is someone who needs help and I aim to give it."

"At what expense?" James asked, his voice cracking in outrage. "Ours? This firm's?"

Frank looked at the faces of the men he'd considered colleagues and friends. They were everything he'd aspired to become when he escaped Worth Street and went to school. Rich beyond his dreams, welcomed at every club and restaurant in town. Meetings with the mayor and state senators. Beautiful women whenever he desired.

Now he saw these men for what they were: cold, calculating. Elitist. Mercenaries, ready to do anything for a buck.

*Before I decide to help this woman, I wish to know what's in it for me.*

Shame crawled across the back of his neck. Had he really said that to Mamie?

"Charles, James," William said. "Give us a moment, will you?"

Their jaws tight, the other two partners stormed out of Frank's office. The door slammed shut and silence hung over the room like a dark cloud.

"Now, Frank," William started. "I've always felt like a bit of a father to you. When you first started here at the firm, right out of school, I knew you had a special gift when it came to dealing with difficult clients. As you know, I'm the one who recommended you for partner. And while your intentions with Mrs. Porter are noble, nobility is not what this firm is about. If you want to save the world, I'm certain some legal aid society would be happy to have you."

"What are you saying?"

"If you antagonize Duncan Greene, do you think any other man of his stature would hire you? Would hire us? Why would they, when they know we don't have their best interests in mind."

"I do not plan on antagonizing Duncan. Whatever is between his daughter and me—"

"Wrong. You are well aware of what he thinks about his daughter and her impending marriage to Livingston. Working on this case, pursuing her, whatever you're doing right now . . . all of that will upset him. And you're too smart not to realize that."

Frank ground his back teeth together. Of course he realized it. He was merely at a point where he didn't care. Mamie was worth it.

"Equally distressing is this situation with Byrnes.

You need to set things right, quickly. Whether that means wrapping up the Porter case, apologizing to Byrnes, sending a case of whiskey to police headquarters, I couldn't say. But you'd best fix it before this firm suffers for your rash behavior."

"Or?" He wanted the partners to spell out the consequences. What did they plan to do if Frank continued on his current path?

William shook his head. "You don't want me to answer that."

"I do, actually. Are you saying you'll force me out?"

"Yes, since we're speaking plainly, that is exactly what I'm saying. I haven't spent the last forty-six years building up this firm from nothing only to lose it because one of my partners went and forgot his place. If it's you or this firm, I will choose the firm every time. So, were I you, I would remain an asset here and do my best not to become a liability."

Frank pounded a fist on the desk. "More than half of last year's revenue came from my cases, William. You need me more than I need you."

"The bit about the revenue is true, but only because the others cut back on hours and let you handle the load. If you leave, the rest of us will take up the slack." He rose and slipped his hands into his pockets. "And it's worth noting if word gets around that you've made enemies of Byrnes, the police department, Livingston and Greene—which it certainly will—no other firm would dare touch you in this town. You might as well move out to California and start all over out there, because your career will be finished on the East Coast."

* * *

THE TREES OF Washington Square Park were just beginning to bud, the smell of spring heavy in the air. Mamie walked along the path with the Porter and Barrett children. She'd gone downtown to visit and offered to take the older children to the park to give Mrs. Barrett a break. The children had been enthusiastic for the trip after being cooped up inside for most of the day.

The Barrett boys asked Mamie for permission to explore on their own, and Henry slid closer to them, his hopeful expression indicating he wished to explore as well.

"Henry and Katie, would you like to join the boys?"

Katie immediately shook her head. "I'd prefer to stay with you, if you don't mind."

Henry's face fell. Knowing she had to speak to Katie privately, Mamie asked, "Would you mind if Henry went with the other boys, then?"

She hesitated then nodded. "As long as he doesn't get lost."

Mamie understood. The girl's family had been torn apart, and her brother was all she had left at the moment. "Boys, stay together. Do not wander off and keep an eye out for each other. Katie and I will wait by the fountain."

The boys ran off, not bothering to even say goodbye. Mamie took Katie's hand and they strolled toward the giant stone fountain, which was dry right now. The girl was quiet, so Mamie tried to think of a way to start off this difficult conversation. "Did you know this fountain came from Central Park?"

"It did?"

"Yes, it was at the Fifty-Ninth Street entrance. They moved it down here to replace the old broken fountain. Isn't it pretty?"

In the late spring and summer, water sprayed high from a spout in the middle, the droplets falling into the huge round basin. Rows of seats lined the inside of the basin for New Yorkers to cool off during the hot months. "Shall we sit?"

"Are we allowed?"

"Yes, most definitely. In the summer this fountain is crowded with people."

Katie sat stiffly next to Mamie on the top step. Mamie took a deep breath and decided to forge ahead. "How are you and your siblings faring?"

"All right. The families we're staying with are nice."

"I know this is a difficult time for all of you, but I promise I'm doing everything in my power to help your mother."

Katie stared at her toes. "I miss her so much."

Mamie wrapped an arm around the girl's slim shoulders. "It's going to turn out all right. You'll see."

"I hope so."

"Has a man asked you to come and speak to the judge?"

"I think so. I might have heard him talking to Mrs. Barrett about it. What will I have to do?"

Hadn't the prosecutor explained any of this to the little girl? Mamie tried to keep the annoyance out of her voice. "Your mother will meet with a judge in a few days. This is when everyone says whether or not there is enough evidence to send her to prison for a long time. If the judge thinks there's enough evidence, then a trial will start."

"I don't want her to go to prison."

"Neither do I. The problem is they may not believe your mother about what happened with your father."

"Why?"

"They're used to people lying, even in front of a judge. So you need to tell the judge the truth about what happened that day, as well as what it was like in your household."

Katie frowned, her expression serious. "What will they ask me?"

Mamie couldn't lie. The girl had to be prepared for any bad memories stirred up by her testimony. "They will ask you about your mother and father, what they were like and their relationship with one another. They'll ask you about the day your father died, about what happened."

"I don't like thinking about any of that."

"I know, sweetheart. That's perfectly understandable. But we need someone to tell the truth."

Katie thought about this for a moment, her gaze unfocused and distant. "They won't believe me. My daddy's cousin is a policeman."

So she knew about Detective Porter. "All you have to do is tell the truth. Your mother's lawyer will help prepare you for what to expect."

"What about Mrs. Barrett? Will she mind that I'm helping?"

They didn't have a choice, as Katie was on the prosecution's witness list. "I'll speak to her when we return and make sure."

"Will you come with me?" Katie dragged in a shaky breath. "I don't want to go alone."

"Of course. I'll be there the whole time, I promise." She squeezed the girl's shoulders. "We'll see Mr. Tripp tomorrow. He's your mother's attorney and he's very good at his job. He'll tell you exactly what to expect."

The boys returned and Katie joined them to walk around the edge of the fountain's basin. Mamie enjoyed watching the children as they ran and laughed. She'd let them play a few minutes longer then take them for ice cream.

Suddenly, the hairs on the back of her neck stood up. She looked over her shoulder and discovered a man standing almost directly behind her. He was tall with a ruddy complexion, a nose that suggested he was no stranger to spirits. He wore a derby low on his forehead. "Nice to see children in the park, especially at this time of year," he said.

Mamie swallowed, instantly alert. A quick glance in her periphery revealed no one close enough to intervene should this man have violent intentions. The children were far away, thank heavens. "Do I know you?"

"No, but I know *you*. I'm a friend of Edward Porter's."

The police detective and cousin of the deceased. Was this man also a police officer? Her heart began to race, blood rushing in her ears. "What do you want?"

"Nice of you to take an interest in the wee urchins," he said, ignoring her question. Instead, he tipped his chin toward the kids playing in the empty fountain. "The city is so dangerous for children."

Was that a threat? Her blood chilled. Yet, as the daughter of Duncan Greene, Mamie had learned to stand her ground. She wouldn't let this man intimidate her or harm these sweet children. "They are not your concern. Have you something to say to me? If so, I wish you would say it and leave."

The man's face tightened and he leaned in. "You and your . . . *partner*, Mr. Tripp, you've made some terrible enemies lately. If you knew what was good for you, you'd back off. Let the courts handle this."

The way he spat the word *partner* was not lost on her. Did he suspect that she and Frank were lovers? They had been careful. How would anyone possibly know? "I don't care for your tone or your words, sir."

"You'd best watch yourself, Miss Greene. I don't think your father would appreciate how you are spending your days . . . or your nights."

Speechless, she sucked in a breath and could only stare as he sauntered off down the path.

THE DOOR OPENED and Mrs. Porter appeared, her hands shackled in irons. Dark circles sat heavily beneath her eyes, her skin pale. Frank rose, Mamie and Otto beside him, as the matron brought Mrs. Porter forward and helped her into a chair.

They had come to see Mrs. Porter and discuss the preliminary hearing. The sooner this moved forward, the sooner she could return home. If they went to trial, so be it. But Frank hoped to get the charges dismissed as quickly as possible.

Especially with the police now making threats against the Porter children.

Moments ago, as they had waited, Mamie confided in him about the outing to the park, the man who'd approached her. Angry beyond reason, Frank nearly put his fist through the wall. Had Edward Porter no shame whatsoever? And what of Byrnes? Threatening children was disgusting, even for the superintendent.

"Good morning, Mrs. Porter," Frank said when she'd settled. Then he addressed the matron. "Please remove the irons."

"I was told—"

"No doubt you were. I'm afraid I must insist, however." He held the matron's stare. Mrs. Porter was no danger to anyone, and he'd rather she were comfortable.

The matron grumbled under her breath but did as Frank asked. After telling them she'd wait outside, she departed.

"How are you?" Mamie reached across the table to clasp the other woman's hand.

"Tired. It's hard to sleep here."

Frank nodded. Most of his clients in prison had said the same, that the noise, unfamiliar surroundings and worry caused chronic insomnia. "I'm doing my best to move this forward quickly. That's actually why we are here." He gestured toward Otto. "This is Mr. Rosen, the investigator working on your case."

"Ma'am," Otto said with a dip of his chin.

She nodded once but said nothing in return.

"Your preliminary hearing is in three days," Frank said. "That's what we need to discuss."

"Preliminary hearing?"

"Yes. It's basically where the prosecution shows the cards they're holding to the judge. We'll try and convince the judge to dismiss the case, while the prosecution will argue for a jury trial."

She closed her eyes and swallowed. "What will I do?"

"Nothing. The burden of proof is on the district attorney. You won't testify. However, I wanted to discuss our strategy with you first, so you won't be surprised in court."

"All right."

He leaned back in his chair and kept his arms loose, not folded or crossed. People generally found this posture trustworthy and calming. The last thing he needed was to put his client on edge. "If this does go to a jury trial, we intend to argue you were forced to strike the deceased with a pan to protect your children. It's a clear case of self-defense."

"That's correct," she said when Frank paused.

"That won't be mentioned at the preliminary hearing, however. The other side will argue that you killed your husband without just cause. Also, they intend to put Katie on the stand, as she is their best witness to say what happened that morning."

"No." Mrs. Porter's eyes grew wide and her back stiffened, as if she'd seen a ghost. She looked at Mamie then back at Frank. "They cannot ask her to do that."

"I understand it's upsetting," he said. "But we don't have a choice. The prosecutor may call whomever he wishes to testify."

"Why can't I just tell them?"

"You will, if we go to trial."

She rubbed her brow, her head bent. "I don't un-

derstand. Why can't I just tell them at this preliminary hearing?"

"Because this isn't a trial. We don't offer a defense at a preliminary hearing. We just poke holes
at the prosecution."

"What about my neighbor, Mrs. Barrett? I suspected she knew what was happening. Not everything, but she could guess what it was like, living
with Roy. She could testify instead."

Frank gentled his voice. "We'll ask her to testify
at the trial, I promise. We'll do everything we can
to prove you were justified in killing him. But for
our purposes, we just need to weaken the prosecutor's case."

When she lifted her head there were tears gathered in her eyes. "I cannot ask Katie to suffer on
my behalf. I want her to forget what happened that
day, not remember it."

"That's completely reasonable," Mamie said,
squeezing the other woman's arm. "However, I
spoke with Katie and she understands what will
happen in court. She wants to do whatever she can
to get you home as quickly as possible."

"She's a good girl. I know this has been hard on
her." Mrs. Porter's chin wobbled. "I would spare her
from any bad memories, if I could. I never wanted
for them to understand what he was really like."

Yet, Frank thought, children always knew. They
were far more perceptive than adults gave them
credit for. His mother had tried to lie about what
was happening with their father, but the Murphy
children were painfully aware. And they'd escaped
as soon as possible—all except Patrick, apparently.

"Miss Greene will be in court to lend Katie support," he said. "She'll make sure to help her through the process."

"If I just plead guilty and go to jail, then she wouldn't need to testify."

"Would you really do that?" Frank asked. "Who would take care of your children, then?"

Mrs. Porter wiped her eyes and turned to Mamie. "What would you do, Miss Greene?"

The question seemed to surprise Mamie, who sat back and blinked. "Me? Well, I don't have children. I'm not really qualified to answer."

"But if you did have children, what would you do in my place?"

Mamie considered this, chewing her lip for a moment. "I think . . . I would let her testify. Telling her story might help her to feel a bit more in control of what's happening. As far as her own memories, I cannot see how this experience would make them better or worse. The memories are already formed in her mind."

Mrs. Porter dragged in a heavy breath. "You're probably right. I just do not want her hurt."

"Nor do I," Frank said.

"Mr. Tripp and I will watch out for her." Mamie folded her hands and tilted her head thoughtfully. "But before you agree, I thought you should be aware of what happened—"

"Miss Greene," Frank snapped, his body instantly on alert. "May I see you outside a moment?"

Mamie shot him a confused look. "Now?"

"Yes, right now." He raised his brows meaningfully and rose. "Please."

She excused herself and followed him into the corridor. Frank closed the door behind them as

Mamie rounded on him. "What on earth has gotten into you?"

"Were you planning to tell her about the man in the park?" he asked quietly.

"Yes, why?"

His suspicion had been correct. "You cannot share that with her. It'll only upset her and she'll decide to plead guilty."

"Then that is her decision, Frank. She should have all the information before making up her mind."

"Not when it is information she cannot control and will merely cause her pain."

Mamie crossed her arms over her chest. "We cannot hide this from her. A policeman threatened her children. She has to understand what's happening outside these walls to her loved ones."

"Absolutely not. Trust me, I've dealt with people who are imprisoned. It can be very difficult for them to hear of problems with friends and family, especially when they're powerless to help. Giving Mrs. Porter bad news about her children could cause her to plead guilty and go to prison, in which case we lose."

"I understand you're worried about the case but what about *her*? What about her children? She has a right to know. Testifying may put Katie at further risk."

"And we will tell her later, after it's over."

Her brows knitted. "That is quite a callous attitude."

"Perhaps, but I am here to win cases, Mamie. That's why you asked me to represent Mrs. Porter in the first place. I'm trying to keep her from going to prison."

He did *not* want to lose—nor did he want this case to drag out for months. Between Byrnes and the firm's partners, he needed to wrap this up quickly, get Mrs. Porter's charges dismissed and move on with his life. That meant convincing Mamie to marry him and not making an enemy of Duncan Greene. None of that could happen until Mrs. Porter's case was behind him.

"And I am here," she said, "to look out for Mrs. Porter's best interests—and that includes her children." She put her hands on her hips. "She is your client. You should also be looking out for her best interests."

"I am, with regard to her legal troubles. Not her personal life."

"No matter the cost? Even if it puts Katie in more danger?"

He didn't care for the way she stared up at him, as if she'd never seen him before. As if she'd just learned he enjoyed kicking puppies. He put out his hands, pleading with her. "You make it sound as if I don't care what happens to Katie. I do—but my primary concern is keeping Mrs. Porter from the electric chair. The only way to do that is to proceed as planned. Then Mrs. Porter can leave prison and keep her family safe."

"It's wrong to keep that information from her. I don't care how you justify it. It's wrong."

"And having her put to death is better?"

A policeman strode down the hall and walked past, rendering conversation impossible. Mamie pressed her lips together, her lids narrowing dangerously as she waited. When they were alone again, she stepped closer. "I do not like this at all.

I vehemently disagree about keeping Mrs. Porter ignorant of what's happening." Her finger pointed at his chest. "Hear me now. If something happens to any of the three Porter children, I'm holding you personally responsible. And you will not like the consequences."

She moved around him, skirts swishing, and started down the corridor. "Where are you going?" he called after her.

"To a place where I won't be required to lie."

# Chapter Seventeen

Frank pushed open the heavy wooden door of the Little Water Street Brewery. He'd come downtown tonight to meet with Jack Mulligan, who'd provided Frank with a stack of information on Detective Edward Porter, none of it good.

Turned out Detective Porter was deep in the pocket of some of the most corrupt men in the city. Powerful men who didn't appreciate having their names associated with words like *bribery*, *fraud* and *murder*. If necessary, Frank would use this information to help Mrs. Porter's case, those powerful men be damned.

Plus, there was another surprise Mulligan had uncovered, one so useful Frank wasn't telling a soul about it yet.

In the meantime, he had a lot to do. Plans to make, a hearing to prep for. He should be in a room with Otto, discussing facts and strategy.

Or, he should track down Mamie. He hadn't seen her since she departed the prison in a fit of pique, and he needed reassurance she wasn't angry with him. She may not have liked it, but he was right.

Worrying Mrs. Porter over things beyond her control was not healthy.

And yet, despite all that, his curiosity had carried him someplace else entirely after his meeting with Mulligan.

The brewery was housed in an unassuming brick building. When he entered, the sight of large round copper kettles greeted him, sort of like the gin stills he used to see in back alleys as a child, only much grander in scale. The inside air was warm, with a sweet malty aroma. Cases of full bottles were stacked along the wall, ready for delivery. And Patrick was part owner of all this? Frank couldn't wrap his head around it. His brother, a brewer.

Several men were on the far side of the space, gathered around the kettles. At Frank's approach, one of the men elbowed a taller man next to him and pointed.

The taller man turned. It was Patrick, with a pencil and journal in his hands. He frowned at Frank then murmured something to the other two men by his side. The others walked away and Patrick slipped the pencil behind his ear. "I thought I was clear the last time we saw each other."

Frank held up his hands. "I'm not here to cause trouble." He looked around. "I found myself curious about the brewery. Perhaps I could buy you a beer and we could talk."

A muscle jumped in his brother's jaw, indecision in Patrick's eyes. "Why?"

Hell if Frank knew. There was no good answer for that. He'd turned his back on his family fifteen years ago. Why now? Why seek out some connection when it would only do harm? Still, something in him needed to try, at least to get some answers to questions that nagged at him. "Because I like your pilsner."

Patrick spun and began to walk away, his slight limp reminding Frank of his brother's childhood injury. "You can buy a glass anywhere in lower Manhattan."

"Patrick, I . . ." He hurried after the other man until he caught up. "I want to know my brother. Can you spare me a few minutes, please?"

"Didn't think you fancy uptown swells knew the word *please.*"

"If I say it again will you sit down with me?"

Patrick cursed and came to a halt. "Are you going to leave if I say no?"

"Absolutely not. If I took no for an answer I'd never win a case."

The side of Patrick's mouth hitched. "You always were the most stubborn of all of us. Fine. Come with me."

Frank followed his brother deeper into the building. Patrick stopped at a door with a metal handle and pulled it open. A blast of cold air escaped as his brother disappeared inside. He quickly returned, two brown bottles in his hand. When the cabinet was sealed tight once more, they set off down the corridor and ended up in an office. Patrick dropped into the chair behind the desk and motioned for Frank to take the empty chair on the other side. He popped the tops off the bottles and held one out to Frank. "Do you need a crystal glass or can you stand to drink out of a bottle?"

"I'm fine with the bottle." Frank accepted the beer and took a long drink. "Truthfully, it's very good."

"Don't sound so surprised," Patrick grumbled and leaned back in his chair. "And I know it's good. I spent five years of my life perfecting it." He put his mouth on the lip of the bottle and drank.

"Why beer? Why a brewer?"

Patrick made a noise that almost sounded like a laugh. "Alcohol is in our family's blood, wouldn't you say?"

Frank nodded grimly. Sad, but true. "And you're married?"

"I am. Rachel's her name. We have two daughters."

God, he was an *uncle*. A flash of Mamie cradling Mrs. Barrett's baby went through his mind and emotion clogged his throat. "Congratulations." He meant it. He never wished Patrick any ill will. He'd never wished *any* of his family harm, except for his father. He swallowed another mouthful of pilsner. "What happened to Colin?"

"You don't know?" When Frank shook his head, Patrick said, "I figured you would've kept an eye on him, even after you left."

"No. I just wanted to forget."

Patrick grimaced. "We all felt that way." He took a drink then sighed heavily. "Fell onto some train tracks and got run over by a train. Killed instantly, they said. He was drunk at the time, of course."

"She had to be relieved." No need to spell out who *she* was.

"Not at first. She was . . . lost. She'd spent her whole life under that bastard's thumb. When he died she was torn up. Worried about money. It took almost a year before she realized she'd be all right, that the pain was over."

Frank had a similar experience when he went off to boarding school. Always flinching when someone reached out to him. Looking over his shoulder for a threat. It had taken a long time before the sense of danger left his system. "And what of Laura and Sarah? I thought they went to work somewhere in the Tenderloin."

"That's just what Mama told him. The old man had started to talk about using them as a source of income, loaning them out to his friends, so Mama let him think she'd sent them off to a high-class brothel. She protected them."

Stunned, Frank could only blink. Almost everything he'd believed his entire life was a lie. He downed more pilsner. "Where did they go instead?"

"A garment factory uptown. They didn't have it easy, that's for certain. But had to be easier than earning money on their backs."

"And they're married now?"

"They are. To good men who take care of them. I don't see them often, maybe once or twice a year." Silence descended and Patrick sipped from his bottle. Then, he said, "Why now, Frankie? Why show an interest in your family after all these years? Back then, you couldn't get away from Five Points fast enough."

How could he even explain it? In the past few weeks, his whole life had turned upside down. No, longer than that. Ever since the first time he chased after Mamie in an attempt to keep her out of trouble. The instant she had smiled he'd felt it deep in the pit of his stomach. When she'd opened her mouth—challenging him, taunting him—he had felt it in an even lower, more personal, part of his body. The woman was enticing and maddening. He was never letting her go.

And that had changed everything.

He wasn't certain how much of that to share with Patrick, however. "I . . . met someone. She's opened my eyes to a few things. Likes to point out when I'm wrong. I never thought any good would come from that household. I thought it was best to start over and try to forget."

"I can't blame you. God only knows what would've happened to you before Colin died. I just . . . it's not easy seeing you. The fancy lawyer in his fancy suit, hobnobbing with all the uptown Knickerbockers . . ." Patrick set his bottle on the desk. "Maybe it's better for all of us if you just stay gone."

"Have you told her you've seen me?"

"No, I haven't said a word. She's not in great health and I fear it would only upset her."

Frank absorbed that, his thoughts in a tangle. Perhaps Patrick was right. Perhaps it was best for everyone if Frank went back to ignoring his family. His whole life had been built around the lie that he was a blue blood himself. If the truth were discovered, he'd no longer be able to hold up his head in this city. Mamie would never marry him. And even if she forgave him for lying, her father would ship her to a convent before he'd allow her to marry a man raised in Five Points.

He stood and held out a hand. "Damn fine beer, Patrick. You should be very proud.".

Patrick rose and shook Frank's hand, his expression wary. "Take care of yourself, Frankie."

MAMIE SNUCK OUT of the kitchen door, the cool spring evening wrapping around her. The note on her pillow had been simple: *Meet me in the gazebo at midnight.*

As angry as she was with Frank, she couldn't refuse the request. She wanted to see him. Alone, in the dark. Where she could pretend there weren't a hundred reasons why they could not be together.

She became a different person with him, a confident and bolder woman. One who lifted her skirts on a desk at the end of a workday. Her cheeks heated even in the chilly air. Mercy, the feel of him inside her had been glorious.

The gravel path whispered beneath her feet. She didn't spend much time in the gardens, though her mother insisted it look pristine year-round. A bevy of gardeners attended to every path, shrub and stick because nothing less would do for the Greenes. That time and money could certainly find a much better use in the world, considering all the suffering.

When she reached the gazebo at the back of the property, she stepped in, a welcome smile breaking free for her vexing and handsome lawyer.

Only it was not Frank who stood there. Chauncey waited instead.

Her smile dimmed significantly and she folded her hands. Thank goodness she remained fully clothed and hadn't decided to attend this rendezvous in a state of undress. "Hello, Chauncey."

"Mamie." He crossed the wooden floor and leaned in to kiss her cheek. "Stunning, as always."

He was a bit disheveled and she could smell spirits on his breath. Brandy, if she wasn't mistaken. "Thank you. I was surprised to get your note. A bit late for a call, don't you think?"

"I haven't seen you this week around town. Have you been ill?"

"No, merely busy." With Frank, Katie, Mrs. Porter. There hadn't been time for balls and dancing.

"With what?" Her expression must have shown her shock because he followed up with, "Forgive me, but our families wish for us to be seen together at as many events as possible. You've ignored my requests for an escort and have not been out. I grew concerned."

She couldn't decide whether she was touched or annoyed. "There have been some friends in need recently. My schedule should return to normal in a few days." After the preliminary hearing and Mrs. Porter was released from prison.

Chauncey's brow furrowed. "What am I supposed to do in the meantime?"

"I don't understand. What are you supposed to do? About what?"

"Never mind that. Let's sit and visit, shall we?"

She exhaled and debated this request. Though she was exhausted, perhaps this was another opportunity to press her case about ending the marriage agreement. "Fine."

They both sat on the wooden bench that ran along the interior of the gazebo. The night was quiet, the occasional rustle of underbrush the only sound. Mamie had fond memories of tea parties out here with her sisters as a young girl. Justine had always brought stale bread to feed to the birds and squirrels.

Chauncey took her hands between his. The simple contact startled Mamie, then she forced herself to relax. It was merely Chauncey, a man she'd known all her life. They had danced many times, and she'd taken his arm in escort. The bare touch had been unexpected, that was all.

"Mamie, have you thought any more about signing the agreement? My father prefers to finalize everything as soon as possible."

She tried for a diplomatic answer. "I'm still not convinced we'd suit."

"That is ridiculous. We grew up together. Our families are the same station. We're of the same world, you and I."

"There's more to compatibility than just an address, Chauncey."

His hands tightened on hers. "Are you worried about my . . . lady friend? Because I assure you that will not be a problem."

She didn't wish to say it, but she did not give a fig about his lady friend. It was time to stop dancing around the subject. She had to be honest with him—or as honest as possible, under the circumstances—because she was not signing that agreement. "I just don't believe I'm cut out for marriage."

"Not cut out for marriage?" His brows shot up to his forehead. "Why not?"

*Because I've fallen in love with someone else.* "I like my independence. Why should I turn my life over to you just to make our families happy?"

He nodded once, his lips pressed tightly. "It's as my father said. You're nervous about the physical aspect of our marriage."

Mamie blinked up at him. "I . . . No, that is clearly not what I—"

She broke off as he leaned in, his hands clamping her upper arms to hold her close. "We'll be compatible. I'll show you. I'm a very good lover, Mamie. Everyone says so."

Oh, God. Was he . . . ?

Before she could protest or try to edge away, Chauncey had his arms around her and his lips pressed to hers. Stunned, she froze while his mouth worked over hers. The lack of response didn't seem to bother him, however, because he pushed his tongue past the seam of her lips and into her mouth. The wrongness of it hit her and she tried to push against his shoulders, to move him off her. What was he thinking, attacking her like this?

Turning her head to the side, she was able to break their kiss. "Chauncey, stop. This is a bad idea."

He began licking her throat, his grip not loosening for one second. "No, this is what you need." A large hand covered her breast. "Once I've had you then you'll see. I know how these things go. Sometimes girls like you just need a little coaxing."

Fear, cold and sharp, slid through Mamie's veins. "You're wrong. I don't want this. Chauncey, stop." She pushed harder but couldn't budge him.

"Relax. Stop fighting me. It'll go easier if you stop fighting." He pushed her down on the bench, following to lie atop her. "I know what I'm doing, Mamie. You'll see."

Her legs were trapped in her skirts, her body at an awkward angle and weighted down by Chauncey's bulk. She tried to buck him off, but he wouldn't move. Panic filled her lungs, her breath coming fast and short. Was he planning to take her by force to show off his prowess? Had he gone *mad*? "Please don't do this. Get off me."

"Shh. You just need to get used to it. The first time is always difficult."

"No, absolutely—"

He clapped a large palm over her mouth, his fingers digging into her cheek, and she felt him working at her skirts with his free hand. She yelled beneath his grip, a muffled shout of terror and anger that didn't faze him. Instead, he nibbled her throat as she struggled and pounded on his shoulders. She couldn't *breathe*, couldn't draw in enough air.

*Oh, God. Please make him stop.*

Chauncey didn't seem to notice. "You don't need to be scared," he told her. "You're going to like this, I promise. I'll show you."

Air hit her legs and she did the only thing she could think of: she bit the palm of his hand as hard as she possibly could, her teeth sinking deep. The reaction was instant. He released her and howled in pain, cradling his injured hand. She scrambled backward as he fell to the gazebo floor.

She didn't wait. She ran as fast as she could for the safety of the house, with no effort to keep silent, gravel flying as she ran. Once at the house, she flung open the kitchen door, charged inside and turned the lock. She stood there a moment, trying to catch her breath. What had just happened? One minute, she and Chauncey were talking, and in the next he attacked her.

It had been so unlike him. *I know how these things go. Sometimes girls like you just need a little coaxing.* Clearly she didn't know Chauncey as well as she'd thought. Was there a chance he had forced himself on other women? The idea sickened her. She rubbed her forehead and hurried toward her room, her mind spinning.

*You're safe. It's over. You're safe. It's over.* She repeated this on her way through the quiet house. Even still, her heart thundered, the organ not quite certain the danger had passed.

When she entered her bedroom, it took a moment to comprehend the light on her side table was switched on. And there was a man lying in her bed. She blinked at him.

Frank sat up, his eyes instantly concerned. "What's happened?" He was on his feet and coming toward her in a flash.

She swallowed and tried to relax. "I'm fine."

"The hell you are. You're white as a sheet, sweating and all disheveled. What's wrong?" He wrapped his arms around her, pulling her to his chest. He'd shed his topcoat, leaving him in a shirt and vest, and she pressed her face to the warm skin of his throat. She breathed him in, and his heat sank into her bones, easing her tremors. His hands stroked her back and they merely stood for a long moment. She was incredibly grateful he didn't press her for information, though she imagined the effort was killing him.

He kissed her temple softly. "I'm trying not to worry because I see you're safe. Was it the police again?"

"No. Must we discuss it?"

"You should know me well enough by now. I examine things and pick them apart for a living. There's no chance you are keeping this from me. What had you so frightened?"

She didn't wish to think about it any longer. Chauncey's advances would upset Frank, and she'd rather avoid any more anger tonight. "It was nothing. Just noises in the night. I think the kitchens are haunted."

His chest rose and fell with a deep exhale. He led her to the bed and lay down, tucking her into his side and holding her close. "A ghost, really? Is that the best you can do?"

"Would you believe I saw a mouse?"

He snorted. "No. Tell me, love."

The endearment caught her off guard and melted her insides along with her resistance. "I received a note asking me to come to the gazebo at midnight. It was unsigned, but I thought it was from you."

Frank's breath hitched. "Who was it from?"

"Chauncey."

"I see."

"He'd been drinking. Talking about all sorts of nonsense about our marriage."

"Hmm." His fingers slipped into her hair and massaged her head. Her body grew lethargic as her heartbeat slowed.

"I told him I had no interest in marrying him. He thought I was just nervous about the physical aspect of a marriage. Can you imagine?" A soft laugh escaped her lips. Then she yawned, the entire encounter leaving her drained.

"No."

She closed her eyes and burrowed closer to him. "I can tell you this, his kissing skills have not improved a bit over the years."

"What did he say, exactly?"

*So tired.* Her limbs each felt as if they weighed a ton. She stifled another yawn. "That I merely needed some coaxing. That everyone says he's a good lover and he'd show me I had nothing to worry about."

Frank was silent and sleep tugged at Mamie's brain. "I thought you would be angry," she mumbled. "The good news is that I bit his hand and he released me. That's how I got away."

"I'm proud of you." He kissed her forehead. "Sleep, my little warrior."

"Promise me you won't say anything to Chauncey about this." When he didn't respond, she said, "Frank, you cannot mention this to him or anyone else. If you do, then everyone will assume you're jealous. That will only complicate matters."

The fire crackled and the rise and fall of his chest lulled her to sleep. She let herself drift, darkness descending in her consciousness. Before she succumbed, Mamie thought she heard him say, "I am indeed very, very angry . . . but not at you."

GROWING UP DOWNTOWN meant many things. Like running to buy delicious hot corn from the girl on the corner. Knowing which alleys and blocks to avoid because of the gangs. Playing in the street while dodging streetcars and carts.

And learning how to fight.

Frank hadn't used that skill in years. As a rule, he preferred using words rather than his fists. However, he planned on putting his Five Points roots to use today by beating the *ever-loving fuck* out of Chauncey Livingston.

Mamie had scared him half to death last night. He'd never seen her so frightened, her eyes wild and her body trembling. Chauncey had dared to assault her, kissing her against her will. Had he tried more before she bit him? If she hadn't hurt him, how far would Chauncey have gone? In his efforts to "coax" her, would he have stopped before raping her?

It didn't matter because he'd touched her, even when she'd said no. Whatever had happened in that gazebo, Chauncey would come to regret it.

Frank had asked Otto to locate Chauncey as soon as the spoiled prick emerged from his home today. Chauncey's first stop? The Union Club, where he'd no doubt attempt to nurse his post-assault hangover.

Frank arrived at the large stone mansion at Twenty-First Street and Fifth Avenue. Several broughams and carriages lingered nearby, with liveried drivers awaiting their charges. He was a member of all the social clubs worth belonging to in the city. The Union was the oldest and most conservative of the clubs, where not even money and a pedigree were enough to gain admittance. Any hint of a scandal would prevent membership. Frank never cared for the privileged atmosphere here.

The attendant at the front tipped his hat and

pulled open the door. Frank thanked him then checked in at the desk.

"Good afternoon, Mr. Tripp. Welcome back. Shall I take your coat and hat?"

Frank handed over his accessories. "Afternoon, George. I need a private word with Mr. Chauncey Livingston. I wonder if you can give me the use of a room for a few moments."

"Of course. Would you like me to send word to Mr. Livingston to join you there?"

"Please." He reached in his coat pocket and withdrew two crisp one-hundred-dollar bills. "I would appreciate if you did not tell him it's me." He slipped the money to the attendant.

"Not a problem, Mr. Tripp."

"And one more thing, George. I was never here."

The attendant did not miss a beat. He nodded and put the money in his pocket. "I understand. Your things will remain close at hand and I won't mark you down in the book."

"I appreciate that."

The club kept a few well-appointed bedrooms on the upper floors for members. Some were rented out to bachelors, others were used on a nightly basis. Frank never had the need, but he couldn't very well break Livingston's face in the middle of the club's library or dining room.

When he was shown to the room, he removed his topcoat and placed it carefully over a chair. Then he unfastened his cuff links and rolled his sleeves up to the elbows. He heard Chauncey's cultured voice complaining from down the hall. "I don't understand. Why can't you tell me where we're going? I was in the middle of a dashed good cribbage game down there."

Frank's muscles tightened in readiness.

The door opened and Chauncey, the picture of childish annoyance, stomped in. When he saw Frank, he frowned. "Tripp. What do you want?"

"Thank you," Frank said to the attendant. "That will be all for now."

The man nodded and the door closed, leaving Frank alone with Chauncey. "Livingston, this conversation is long overdue."

Chauncey was elegantly appointed in a bespoke brown suit and his hair was neatly oiled off his forehead. Frank knew all about Chauncey and his devil-may-care attitude. The Livingston heir had been given everything he'd ever wanted in life, and it showed by his petulant, entitled demeanor. The lower class was far beneath him, the middle class there to serve him. He dabbled in every vice the city had to offer, never suffering any consequence whatsoever.

That ended today.

Chauncey looked Frank up and down, as if searching for clues. "Conversation about what? I have no legal business with you."

"This isn't about business." He closed in. "This is personal."

The other man took a step back. "What do you mean?"

When he was within reach, Frank snatched Chauncey's necktie and shirt in his fist. He leaned in until they were nearly nose to nose. "I mean Mamie. Specifically, you putting your hands on her like it is your goddamn right."

"Now, look here. I don't know what she told you, but nothing happened." Chauncey tried to step back but Frank held fast.

"Only because she bit your hand and got away, you morally bereft piece of shit. If she hadn't, God only knows what you would have done to her."

"I wouldn't hurt her. I've known Marion all my life. Whatever she told you, she's—"

Frank shook Chauncey hard. "Do not dare call that woman a liar. If you do, I will knock every tooth from your head."

Fear and confusion washed over Chauncey's face, but he quickly masked it with bluster. "This is outrageous. How dare you take me to task for something that is absolutely none of your business? Release me or I'll sue you for assault."

"This is my business. Mamie is my business— and anyone who hurts her will pay the price. Do you understand?"

"No, I don't understand—" His eyes went wide just before his expression darkened. He twisted away, slipping out of Frank's grip. "It's *you*. You're the one turning her against me, against the engagement. You are having an affair with her."

"Mamie and I are friends. I am not turning her against anyone or anything. If you would listen to her, you'd know that."

"That's a dashed lie. Her father's been saying for weeks there's another man, but I didn't quite believe it. Not until this moment." Chauncey put his hands on his hips. "Have you fucked my fiancée?"

Fury erupted in every part of Frank's body, a white-hot heat that scorched his skin. Instead of shouting, though, he laughed because he knew it would put Chauncey off guard. "See, just when I was beginning to think I could reason with you." Quick as a whip, he shot out his right fist and punched Chauncey square in the nose. Cartilage crunched upon impact and blood sprayed before Chauncey hit the floor.

He rolled on the ground and clutched his face. "Damn it! You broke my nose."

Frank kneeled and pressed on Chauncey's hands, adding more pressure to the broken nose, until Chauncey howled. Frank eased up and when he was sure the other man was listening, he growled, "Do not come near her ever again. If I find out you've touched her, I will destroy you and every single thing you care about."

He rose and took out a handkerchief to wipe the blood from his hands. Drops of red spattered his navy silk vest, but the fabric was dark enough to hide the stains. Nevertheless, he'd need to drive home and change his clothing before returning to the office. Clients generally preferred their attorney not be covered in blood. At least, he assumed.

He tucked the handkerchief in his pocket and left, with Chauncey still writhing in pain on the expensive carpet.

# Chapter Eighteen

𝕸amie watched as Frank patiently explained to Katie the process by which she would testify in court. The three of them, plus Otto, were at an ice cream parlor near Frank's office in the late afternoon. Mrs. Porter's preliminary hearing was to take place in a few days.

Katie showed no signs of fear, as if she'd resolved herself to speaking and doing the best job possible. After illustrating what the experience would entail, Frank asked his own questions to ascertain her version of events from the day of her father's death.

Katie had previously confided to Mamie a bit about the Porter household, awful, terrible stories that broke Mamie's heart. Katie recalled her father's yelling, the times she'd hid because her father was hitting her mother and the fear they'd lived with on a daily basis.

Mamie couldn't say she was sorry that Roy Porter was dead.

For a man who had no children of his own, Frank was quite comfortable with Katie. He didn't condescend to her. Some adults treated children like babies; however, a girl like Katie had seen too much, heard too much, to be treated as if she were made of glass. The five-year-old was incredibly brave, in Mamie's opinion.

She hadn't expected that of Frank. Honestly, she hadn't known how he would interact with children. He'd looked uncomfortable and eager to leave in the face of Mrs. Barrett's fussy child last week. But perhaps she'd been wrong about his uneasiness.

*Tell me, love.*

Her face heated as she recalled his words. That night, he'd held her until she had fallen asleep then slipped out of the house unnoticed. Not long after, a jewelry box had magically appeared on her nightstand. Nestled inside was a silver charm bracelet, the only charm a bow and arrow. A reference to calling her his "little warrior," no doubt.

More heat slid through her. Goodness, at this rate, she'd burst into flames before suppertime.

She did wonder, however, how he'd managed to gain such unfettered access to the Greene household. Crafty, crafty man . . .

Movement at the table brought her out of her own head. Otto was leading Katie to the counter.

"Are we finished?" she asked Frank as he retook his seat.

One side of his mouth tipped up into a wicked grin and her heart skipped a beat at that knowing look. "Having trouble paying attention, Miss Greene?"

"Not at all."

"Then you know precisely why Otto has taken Katie to the counter?"

"To order more ice cream." It was a guess but a logical one.

"Wrong. He's convinced her to try an egg cream soda, which has no ice cream in it at all."

She decided to let this go. Conceding the point would only swell his head. "Thank you for the bracelet."

"Did you like it?"

"Very much so." Desperate to touch him somehow, she surreptitiously squeezed his gloved hand. When he winced, she immediately let go. "What's wrong? Did I hurt you?"

He reached for her with his left hand. "Just shut a desk drawer on my right hand and it's a bit tender. Nothing to worry about."

"Thank goodness. We cannot have you injured right before the preliminary hearing."

"I'm fine."

"Will you be ready in two days?"

"Of course. I'm always ready."

The braggart. Still, he was adorable in every way . . . and the most handsome man in New York City. "I have every faith in you, Mr. Tripp."

"Save your praise for after Mrs. Porter is released." He leaned down closer to her ear. "And for when I've got you alone in my bed again."

Sparks spread over the surface of her skin, coalescing between her legs. *Speaking of bed . . .* "You never did tell me why you came over the other night." She didn't like to think about that episode with Chauncey. It still both frightened and angered her.

"To ensure you weren't annoyed with me. You left the prison in a huff after we met with Mrs. Porter."

"I was not in a *huff*. I do not *huff*. And I maintain not telling Mrs. Porter is a mistake. She should know the risks when it comes to her own child."

"I promise to keep Katie safe." His blue irises blazed with sincerity, but how could he possibly watch over Katie at all times?

"Short of moving in with the children, I cannot see how that is possible."

"I've hired Pinkertons to watch the building around the clock. Does that help?"

Her mouth fell open slightly. She hadn't considered this possibility. Her chest pulled tight, emotion clogging her throat. He'd hired guards for the Porter children. He was a blue-blooded, silver-tongued rascal, but Frank Tripp was also a good man. The best man.

*Her* man.

*You're in love with him.*

Yes, she supposed she was. The thought of giving him up, of not seeing him again, caused her stomach to cramp painfully. Somehow, she had to convince her father that Frank made her happy and she'd have no other. She would never marry Chauncey, definitely not after the other night and not after finally accepting these feelings for Frank. Her father would see reason eventually and agree to not ruin Frank's career.

Because she was going to marry this man.

"If we weren't in public, I would kiss you right now."

His leg slid to find hers under the table. "Would you, indeed? Where would you kiss me?"

She glanced at the nearby tables to ensure the other patrons couldn't overhear. Then she licked her lips and inched closer. "In the very best places."

He exhaled slowly, never breaking his gaze with hers. "Damn. Now I won't be able to stand up for another ten minutes."

"If I am supposed to apologize, I'm afraid I won't do it."

"Never apologize for tempting me. I could be dead, buried six feet under the ground, and still crave the taste of your skin."

She had to take a sip of water because her mouth had gone dry. "Perhaps we could discuss your condition later. Say, nine o'clock at your place?"

"Are you asking me for a liaison, Marion Greene?"

"Not if you continue to tease me."

He put up both palms. "Consider the teasing stopped. Let's say ten. That way, I may take my time with you and not worry about staff still moving about the house."

She liked the idea of that. "Ten it is."

Frank opened his mouth to say something else but promptly shut it when Katie and Otto appeared at the table. "Well, Miss Katie," he said. "What do you think of the egg cream soda?"

"It's delicious." Otto placed the tall glass in front of her and she grabbed for the straw. "Did you know there's actually no egg in here?"

Frank leaned in and stage-whispered, "There's no cream, either. That's milk." Then he winked.

Katie giggled and Mamie's heart melted into a puddle on the marble floor. The man was absurdly charming.

"I'm afraid Otto and I must return to my office," he told Katie. "I'll leave Miss Greene to see you home. Get some rest, all right? No staying up late dancing and drinking."

Katie giggled around her straw. "I will."

"Good girl." Frank ruffled her hair then shot a glance at Mamie. "Until later, Miss Greene."

A dark thrill shot down Mamie's spine at the promise in those words. "Mr. Tripp." Then she dipped her chin toward Otto. "Mr. Rosen."

"Good day, Miss Greene." Otto looked as if he were stifling a smile but said nothing more before following Frank out of the ice cream parlor.

Then, despite the cool temperatures inside the shop, Mamie had a desperate need to fan herself.

MAMIE'S BODY STILL tingled as she crept toward the servants' door behind her house. It was just after midnight and the imprint of Frank's fingers lingered on every part of her. His breath continued to whisper over her skin. His warmth tattooed into her flesh.

With any luck, she'd feel him for *days*.

The kitchens were dark as she entered, her skirts softly rustling in the quiet. She didn't bother locking up behind her, just in case Florence was out on the town.

She moved around the large worktable, snatching an apple from a bowl as she passed. God knew she'd worked up an appetite tonight with—

The light switched on, startling her. She gasped and the apple fell from her hands as the dim yellow glow illuminated the kitchens.

Her father stood by the wall. "Care to explain where you've been?"

She pressed a hand to her chest, trying to calm her racing heart. "*Daddy.* You scared me half to death."

"Undoubtedly. Now imagine how I felt discovering my daughter had snuck out of the house to go God knows where."

"I went for a walk in the gardens," she lied. "It was such a nice night that I thought—"

"Do not lie to me," he snapped. "You're disheveled and you have a love bite . . ." He made a vague motion to his neck.

Her hand flew up to her throat as if to feel it. Had Frank actually left a mark?

"No, you don't actually have a mark." His mouth tightened, his mustache twitching in the way it did when he was furious. "But the fact that you thought you might tells me all I need to know."

"Daddy, you're wrong. Whatever you are thinking, I swear it didn't happen."

"Who is it?"

She hated lying to him but, at the moment, could see no other option. *Deny, deny, deny.* "There is no other man. I'm nearly engaged to Chauncey."

"Yet you won't sign the agreement, and whoever's bed you just left is the reason why. I want to know who, damn it. *Right now, Marion.*"

She couldn't tell him. No matter her feelings for Frank, this was not the way for her family to find out. Not in anger and deception. She wished for her father's blessing, needed time to convince him that she and Frank made sense together. After all, Frank's background wasn't so different from Chauncey's. Though he worked as a lawyer, Frank was from a prominent family in Chicago. And he made her *happy.* Surely that would matter to her father when the time came.

Straightening her spine, she said, "I was out for a walk. That's all."

Her father shook his head and stared at his shoes. "You've left me no choice. Follow me to my office."

Her stomach plummeted as she trailed him into the main part of the house. *Perhaps he merely wishes to be comfortable while he yells at you.* Honestly, what else could he do? He had no proof and she wouldn't admit to anything improper. They were at an impasse, so she would listen to his lecture, apologize for worrying him, and go to bed.

He threw open his office door and held it for her. She walked in—and nearly tripped. Mr. Livingston, Chauncey and a big, thick man she didn't recognize all came to their feet and turned her way. *Oh, no. This is bad.*

Then she noticed the black circles around Chauncey's eyes, how his nose was red and swollen. What on earth had happened to him? He stared at her sullenly, arms folded over his chest.

*Very bad, indeed.*

"Sit down, Marion." Her father strode past her and moved his bulk to the chair behind his desk. She walked a bit slower, taking one of the chairs opposite. Mr. Livingston sat in the other empty chair, leaving the stranger and Chauncey to stand.

Her father addressed her. "You know Chauncey and Mr. Livingston. The man you don't know is Superintendent Byrnes of the Metropolitan Police Detectives. The superintendent has some information he's gathered on you, according to Mr. Livingston."

Mamie gasped. "You were *spying* on me?" The police had been watching her. Good God, what had they observed? The prison, the tenements . . . Then it hit her. *Frank's house.*

No, she'd been careful. Hadn't she? Frank had driven her home in his brougham tonight to keep her hidden and safe. Her father may suspect but couldn't prove anything. She straightened and swallowed the panic bubbling in her throat. "You had no right to do that, sir."

"We were conducting an investigation, miss," the superintendent said. "I thought it prudent to inform the interested parties of what I've learned."

"Daddy, how could you allow this?"

Her father's eyes narrowed as he drummed his fingers. "You have changed in the last few weeks, Marion—and not for the better, I might say. I think we were all eager to learn what had caused such a shift in your personality."

"All you had to do was ask me."

"If there had been a chance of receiving a truthful answer, I might agree. However, you haven't been honest with me and you haven't been honest with Chauncey."

She looked over at Chauncey. His face was gruesome. Whatever happened to cause those injuries must have hurt considerably. Not that she could work up any outrage on his behalf. She couldn't forgive him for assaulting her in the gazebo.

"So," her father continued. "Byrnes, you have a report for us?"

"Yes, sir. I do," the superintendent said. Instead of speaking, however, he turned on his heel and walked out of the room. No one spoke, and she could feel Chauncey's angry gaze burning a hole in the side of her head.

Ignoring him, she tried pleading with her father. "Daddy, I don't understand what is happening.

Perhaps this could all wait until the morning when we've all had a chance to rest."

Her father remained silent, his stare fixed on the door. The clock on the mantel chimed the half hour, the rhythmic clang startlingly loud in the quiet. Then the door opened and she looked to see what had been keeping—

She froze in horror, the room tilting on its side for a brief second. Frank walked in behind Superintendent Byrnes, her lawyer's face decidedly grim.

Oh, Lord. This was worse than bad. This was an unholy disaster.

She had to do something, *say* something, but she could only watch, dumbfounded. The words tripped over themselves in her brain, fragments and pieces that could not form sentences. Frank . . . here . . . Chauncey . . . police . . .

"Tripp, I believe you know everyone here," her father said flatly as the two men approached the desk. "Byrnes, let's get this over with."

"Of course, sir." Byrnes produced a notebook and began reading. "On several occasions, Miss Greene has been observed traveling downtown to the Sixth Ward, where she visited families living in four different tenement buildings. It's my understanding she brings money to these families as a way of supplementing their incomes."

Mamie opened her mouth to explain but her father gave one shake of his head. A muscle jumped in his jaw, a well-known display of his extreme displeasure. She clamped her lips shut and folded her hands in her lap.

"On two occasions she has visited the women's section of the Tombs to see a prisoner, a one Mrs.

Porter. This is the wife of one of the families Miss Greene routinely visited and Mrs. Porter has been arrested on a murder charge."

The superintendent cleared his throat. No one in the room moved, and Mamie didn't dare glance at Frank.

"The lawyer representing Mrs. Porter is one Mr. Frank Tripp. He took the case at the request of Miss Greene, against the advice of his partners, I might add, who are all vehemently opposed to the idea of their firm being associated with anything of this sort."

"I should say so," her father muttered.

Mamie hadn't expected that. Had Frank's partners asked him to drop Mrs. Porter's case? He hadn't mentioned it. Her eyes darted to him, but he stared straight ahead, hands in his pockets. She couldn't tell what he was thinking.

"Miss Greene is apparently helping with Mrs. Porter's case, as she is close to the Porter children. The preliminary hearing is scheduled with Judge—"

"Never mind that," her father said. "Stick to the relevant issues."

"I apologize." The superintendent's neck flushed. "Miss Greene has visited Mr. Tripp at both his office and his home, most recently this evening, when she arrived at approximately ten o'clock and departed at twelve-oh-five this morning."

Shame washed over her. Not because of her relationship with Frank—she didn't feel an ounce of regret over *that*—but because it was no one's business outside of hers and Frank's. Chauncey and Mr. Livingston certainly should not be privy to such personal information. Bad enough her father was here to learn about it.

Frank's lids fell briefly, his expression pained, and guilt nearly overwhelmed Mamie. She had to salvage this before her father and the superintendent ruined everything. "We were discussing the case," she said to the room.

"Duncan, this is an egregious breach of trust for my son," Mr. Livingston said. "He expected her to remain chaste until their wedding, not run amok in New York City."

"Never mind that Chauncey hasn't bothered to remain chaste," Mamie said. "He has a mistress he refuses to give up."

"That is hardly relevant," her father snarled, pointing a finger at her. "It is your behavior we are discussing here, not Chauncey's. And considering how very badly this is going, I would cease speaking altogether, were I you." He gestured to the superintendent. "I was told you had information about Mr. Tripp's background."

Frank jerked and she watched his throat work for a brief second. Then he adopted an easy smile and addressed her father. "Duncan, I can't see how my background has any bearing on tonight's discussion. I have already offered to do the right thing by Mamie. I wish to marry her."

The offer did not appease her father. "I made my feelings on that quite clear the last time we spoke regarding my daughter. Byrnes, please continue."

Byrnes's mouth hitched in a satisfied smile, one that had Mamie's chest squeezing in dread. "Yes, thank you. As you all know, Mr. Tripp claims to come from a prominent family in Chicago. However, I have learned that he actually grew up on Worth Street in Five Points, with his real surname as Murphy."

THE ROOM ERUPTED in chaos, with the two Livingstons expressing their extreme displeasure to Duncan, who merely glowered at Frank, but Frank paid them no attention. He concentrated on Mamie. Her brows had knitted in confusion, her eyes vacant. She was likely doubting the revelation, thinking it improbable that lies of this magnitude could ever perpetuate.

And yet, they had. Frank had ensured it over the years, doing everything he could to bury his lower-class past. Goddamn Byrnes. Somehow the superintendent had learned the truth and was using it to destroy Frank before the preliminary hearing.

When he neither refuted the story nor defended himself, her shoulders sank. Knowing Mamie, she was now wondering what else he'd lied about. A fair question, he supposed, given the circumstances. But he'd never lied to her about his feelings or his desire to marry her. Those things had been quite real.

Not that she'd believe him now.

Pain seared through his chest, a burning panic that far eclipsed the humiliation of having his shameful secret paraded in front of Duncan and the Livingstons. He couldn't lose her, not now.

Not when he'd just discovered how she smelled in the moonlight.

Not when he'd learned how sensitive her neck was, how she loved to be kissed there.

Not when he'd lay the world at her feet to see one of her smiles.

Not *fucking now*, damn it.

"Have you nothing to say for yourself?" Duncan barked, breaking into Frank's thoughts. "Any way of explaining this?"

"It's true." He kept his focus trained on Mamie as he forced the words out. "I was born Frank Murphy and raised in Five Points, the youngest of five children. I left home at fourteen for boarding school as a charity case. After, I attended Allegheny College and then worked under a lawyer until I passed the bar."

"I knew it!" Chauncey shouted. "I knew he was nothing more than a dirt-dwelling thug. Look at what he did to my face."

Mamie's brows pinched together as she took in Chauncey's injury. Then she seemed to shake herself, looking more like the determined woman he knew. "Mr. Tripp only hit Chauncey because of me. Chauncey tried to force himself on me the other night in the gazebo and—"

"I did no such thing!"

The room quieted as Mamie's declaration settled. Duncan's expression grew fearsome as he slowly stood up, his attention now entirely on Chauncey. "You tried to *force yourself* on my daughter?"

Fear briefly flashed on Chauncey's face before he hid it. "We were kissing and got carried away. Nothing happened—and it's no worse than what she's been doing with him!" He pointed at Frank.

"You're a liar," Frank growled, his muscles clenched and ready for battle. "You told her she merely needed coaxing and that you'd prove what a good lover you were."

"Now, hold on," the elder Livingston said. "You

cannot fault Chauncey for anticipating their wedding vows. He was only trying to help the process along."

"By *forcing himself on her*?" Duncan roared. "What sort of man has to resort to physical violence to romance a woman?"

"I didn't hurt her," Chauncey protested. "We merely kissed, is all."

"Because I bit your hand when you covered my mouth to keep me quiet. Only then was I able to get away," Mamie pointed out.

"Let me see your hand," Duncan ordered Chauncey.

Chauncey swallowed, his left hand curling into a fist at his side. "She's going to be my wife," he said. "I fail to see what the problem is with getting things started earlier than expected."

"The problem," Duncan said and closed the distance between himself and the young man, "is that she is my daughter and I won't have any man—not even one she plans to marry—force himself on her. Let me see your goddamn hand. *Now.*"

Chauncey withered in the face of Duncan's anger. Duncan was intimidating at the best of times; at worst, he was downright fearsome. Chauncey slid his left hand forward, where a bluish bite mark was clearly visible on the palm. At the proof of Mamie's terror, Frank wanted to destroy Chauncey's face all over again.

Duncan's expression darkened even further. Chauncey must have feared for his life because his voice trembled as he said, "It was only a harmless bit of fun."

"Now, Duncan," Mr. Livingston said. "You remember how girls are at this age. They want to experiment but have to maintain the cloak of respectability. I suggested Chauncey should try to influence her a bit. Goose things along. We can't blame him. He thought she was a virgin. Little did everyone know she'd been giving it away for free to *him*." He tilted his chin toward Frank.

Duncan's right eye twitched as he faced his friend. "You . . . You told him to force himself on my daughter? *My* daughter, the girl you've known since I first held her in my arms?"

"Chauncey wasn't going to hurt her, for God's sake," Livingston said. "You are overreacting."

"I am *overreacting*?" Duncan's eyes nearly bulged from his head. "You told your son to assault my daughter and I am overreacting. Do I have that right?"

"The boy's done nothing wrong. She's made him wait, for God's sake, while she was parading all around town with her lover instead. And you know if she has one, there's likely more. What kind of girl are you raising?"

Duncan's nostrils flared, his chest rising and falling rapidly. Frank was about to intervene, calm everyone down, when Duncan said, "Get the hell out of my house. Both of you. Get out and never come back."

Livingston's jowls worked as his mouth opened and closed. He struggled to his feet. "You cannot possibly mean that."

"I do. I absolutely do. There'll be no marriage between your son and my daughter. In fact, if I catch him anywhere near her, I'll break a hell of a lot more than Tripp did."

"You'll regret this," Livingston said. "After you've calmed down you'll change your mind."

"Not in a million years, Richard. I know we've been friends a long time but I won't ever forget this."

Livingston huffed and told Chauncey to get moving. The two men stormed out of the room, not bothering to close the door behind them. "Superintendent," Duncan said tiredly as he lowered himself into his chair. "I believe we're done here."

Byrnes looked reluctant to leave, probably because he wished to revel in his destruction, the bastard. "Of course, sir. Thank you." The superintendent gave a short bow and departed.

Duncan dragged a hand over his face. "Christ, what a mess."

Frank couldn't agree more. And it would only get worse from here. Livingston and Byrnes would relish telling everyone in Manhattan about Frank's background. The scandal would forever change Frank's life. The partners at the firm would be furious. He'd lose his club memberships. No one in society would speak to him. His career as high society's favorite lawyer was over.

Yet, that wasn't what hurt the most.

What really hurt was the way Mamie avoided looking at him, as if she couldn't stand the sight of him. He cared about nothing else in this calamity but seeing Mamie's eyes sparkle once more. He'd beg, plead—even get down on bended knee, if necessary. He would do whatever it took because he had to put this right.

He couldn't lose her. Not now.

"Duncan, I'd like a moment alone with your daughter, if you don't mind."

The older man sighed. "I suppose there's no harm in that, at least not now anyway. Mamie?"

Mamie nodded. "Daddy, I'm so sorry about all this."

"I'm the one who is sorry. I thought Chauncey . . . Well, I was being selfish, wasn't I?" Duncan's face softened and he swallowed hard. "Mamie, you may not come to me with skinned knees and bee stings any longer, but I'm always here for you. *Nothing* will ever change that."

She wiped her eyes. "Thank you."

He rose, came around the side of the desk and planted a kiss to the top of her head. "I love you, Marmalade." Then Duncan approached Frank. "You and I will speak tomorrow," he said quietly. "And I expect you to respect my house."

"I will, sir."

The answer must have satisfied Mamie's father. He walked out of the room, leaving the door open behind him.

# Chapter Nineteen

Silence descended in Duncan's office, the hiss and pop of the dying fire the only sound. Frank had anticipated Mamie's anger, for her to yell at him about his deception. Yet she merely waited, quiet, her body perfectly still. A shell of indifference seemed to surround her and he wasn't certain how to break through.

He lowered himself in the chair next to her and cleared his throat. "Marmalade?"

She lifted a shoulder. "Florence's childhood nickname for me. I thought he'd forgotten it."

More silence. "I'd like to explain. To tell you why."

"It doesn't matter."

"It does matter. Mamie, will you please look at me?" She met his eyes, her expression flat. A stab of pain that he suspected was guilt erupted under his ribs. "The world, *this* world"—he gestured to the room—"judges one's background very harshly. I knew I'd never be accepted if I told the truth."

"Yes, but I am not everyone. You know my work downtown, how I truly feel. I'm not one to sit in judgment of another's upbringing, especially when mine has been so privileged. Yet you continued to lie to me, even after . . ."

After they'd slept together. Yes, he understood. "How was I supposed to tell you after all this time?"

"Easily. 'Actually, Mamie,'" she said in a deep voice. "'I was born in Five Points.' There, see how easy that was?"

"Be serious—"

"I am being serious." She shot to her feet and put distance between them. It was only a few feet, but it felt like miles to Frank. "You've lied to me about your family, your birthplace. Your parents in Chicago and your grandfather's copper mine . . . All lies. I don't even know who you are!"

He rose. "You know *exactly* who I am. I'm still the same man who found you in casinos at night, who represents Mrs. Porter and who held you after Chauncey attacked you. A man who loves you beyond all reason and logic."

She covered her mouth, tears pooling on her bottom lids. "Yet that man couldn't be honest with me about where he'd come from, the experiences and people who shaped him. You know, I suspected you were lying about your background when we had dinner at Sherry's that night. I should have trusted my gut. I'm so stupid for trusting *you* instead."

"You are *not* stupid. I may have broken your trust, but I'll make it up to you."

This did not appear to reassure her. She asked, "Do you have family in the city?"

"Yes. My mother and brother. My two sisters live just outside the city."

Mamie squeezed her eyes shut, which caused two fat tears to roll down her cheeks. "Do you see them? Talk to them?"

"I've spoken to my brother recently for the first time since I left home."

She winced. "And the others?" He shook his head and her shoulders dropped. "You haven't spoken to your mother or your sisters in all these years? I cannot . . . I cannot wrap my mind around it. How could you walk away from them?"

Her judgment rankled, and Frank's neck grew hot. "Mamie, my father was Roy Porter. No, he was *worse* than Roy Porter. All of us kids suffered his abuse, and my mother the brunt of it."

"So that means you run away and never speak to them again? My God, your mother . . . She must blame herself."

*That's Frankie's money. I'll give it back to him when he comes home.*

Emotion clogged his throat. No, his mother had urged him to go. She'd known he wouldn't survive in Five Points. And he'd succeeded beyond his wildest dreams. He'd clawed his way to the top of New York's elite, where he'd thrived. Made enough money that he'd never be able to spend it all. Partner in a prestigious law firm. His name in all the newspapers. The city's most desirable debutante in his bed . . . Frank Murphy never would have had *any* of it.

And now Frank Tripp had lost it all.

He didn't care. Not a bit of it mattered except for Mamie. He could lose everything, but he couldn't lose her.

"Is Tripp your legal name, or is it still Murphy?"

"I legally changed it to Tripp when I turned eighteen." She winced at that statement, so he begged, "Please, Mamie. Let me explain."

She made a scoffing noise. "You mean, let you attempt to talk your way out of this. That's what you do, isn't it, Frank? But I am neither a judge nor a jury. I am the woman who cared about you. Who loved—"

When she bit off the words, he rocked back on his heels as if he'd been struck. "Do not use the past tense. Please. I love you madly."

More tears rolled down her cheeks and she looked away. "I cannot love a man I don't know. Worse, you've been lying for so long I suspect you don't even know yourself." She wiped her face. "You've broken my heart—and I'm not certain who to blame."

Before he could say anything, she hurried toward the door with her head down. He hated that he'd hurt her, that she was upset. Why wouldn't she listen to him? "Mamie, wait."

She ignored him, disappearing into the darkness, taking everything he'd ever wanted with her.

"You CANNOT STAY in bed all day."

Mamie ignored Florence's voice and burrowed under the bedclothes. She didn't care. She absolutely would stay in bed all day.

Suddenly, the pillow was ripped away from her face and bright light assaulted her eyes. Her sister had opened the curtains, dash it. "What are you doing in here?"

"Getting you out of bed. Come on, now. Rise and shine."

"Why?" She tried to roll over, but Florence's hand stopped her.

"For one, because it's not like you. Marion Greene is not a moper."

"I am allowed to change."

"Yes, that's true. But we Greene girls are made of stronger stuff. A little tiff with our intended is not the end of the world."

Mamie rolled over and glared at her sister. "It is not a *little tiff* and he's not my intended."

"Pff. It is and he is. Now, I understand you're upset for not knowing his background, but surely you understand why he lied. You have seen how the world views people from the supposed wrong part of town."

"I understand why he lied to everyone else, but not to me." Love required honesty and trust to thrive, and Frank had given her neither. So whatever they'd shared had merely been lust, not something lasting and real.

And God, how that *hurt*.

"Fine. The second reason you have to get up is that you promised Justine she could join you downtown today."

Mamie groaned. She'd forgotten. *You cannot abandon Mrs. Porter and the children merely because Frank broke your heart.*

Now she'd need to appear cheerful all day. The thought made her slightly nauseated. "Any chance Justine doesn't know what happened last night?"

"Daddy told all of us at breakfast. And it's in the newspapers."

Mamie sat up, her heart in her throat. "It is? They printed that Frank and I . . ."

"No. Goodness, no. About Frank's background, his real family. Did you know his brother brews beer?"

"Out of that whole story, that's what you find most interesting?" Sometimes Mamie didn't understand her younger sister. "And no, I did not. Frank didn't tell me any details about them."

"So, you love him?"

"Frank's brother?"

Florence smirked. "Nice try. You forget, I'm the one who told you to seduce him."

Mamie sat up and pushed the hair out of her face. "Then I have *you* to blame for this entire mess."

"You're being too hard on him. You two barely got to know one another before you called it off. Think about Chauncey. You've known him for years, yet he tried to attack you in the gazebo. You never really know someone, Mamie. We must go by his or her character instead. Chauncey is an overprivileged, entitled brat. He's been given everything and worked for none of it."

"And?" Mamie asked when Florence gave her a meaningful look.

"And Frank had nothing, built himself up into a powerful, wealthy man. He knows what it means to work hard for something. He has integrity."

Yes, Mamie supposed he did. Frank started from humble beginnings; it couldn't have been easy to leave his family and strike out on his own at such a young age.

Still, he should have told her. After everything they had done and said to one another, he should've been honest. How could she ever forget the sting of his betrayal? It felt all encompassing, a pain that started in her heart and reached every vein and pore in her body.

A knock sounded at the door. Both girls looked up as their parents walked in. Her mother's eyes brimmed with concern while their father appeared disheveled, as if he'd repeatedly run his hands through his hair.

"My darling girl," her mother said and sat on the bed. She wrapped her arms around Mamie. "I am very upset with your father for not waking me last night. I should have been there for you."

Mamie sagged into her mother's familiar embrace. "Thank you, but there wasn't anything you could do."

"A mother doesn't need to do anything to be helpful. A mother exists to ease her child's pain. When your father told me what happened, I knew you must be hurting."

"I assumed you would be angry with me."

Her mother leaned back. "Mamie, you are my most practical, most level-headed daughter—"

"I beg your pardon," Florence said, shoving her hands on her hips. "I would like to point out that I have been advising her throughout this entire escapade."

"Encouraging recklessness, no doubt," their father said. "Run along, Florence. Give us some privacy."

Florence grumbled under her breath but left nonetheless. "As I was saying," her mother continued. "You are my practical, level-headed daughter. You've never been given to flights of fancy or changing your mind. He's obviously the reason you asked for more time before agreeing to marry Chauncey."

"Yes." No need to deny it now.

"Well, I apologize for not seeing it before. Chauncey always seemed like a good fit for you, and you never questioned the match. So I thought you were happy with that choice."

"Chauncey was Daddy's choice," Mamie reminded her mother. "And he promised to let Florence and Justine choose their own husbands if I agreed to marry Chauncey."

Mama's jaw fell open and she frowned at her husband. "Is this true, Duncan?"

He had the grace to look sheepish. "I wasn't planning on holding her to that promise. I just didn't want her getting ideas in her head about other men."

"You used her love for her sisters as a weapon. How could she possibly understand you were not serious?"

"She is the oldest and I thought Chauncey would make a good husband. The betrothal had been in place for eons and I didn't want any reason to call it off. How was I to know what the boy was really like?"

"You and I will have words in a moment," Mama said, her tone laced with steel. "Mamie, do you wish to marry Frank Tripp—oh, I suppose it's Murphy, isn't it? Is he what you want?"

Mamie rubbed the bridge of her nose between her fingers. "I don't know. I cannot forgive him for lying."

"Well, you must decide. Reputations are a tricky thing, and if you don't marry him then we will send you to Paris or Rome for a year. You'll weather out the scandal there."

Paris or Rome for a year? Away from her family and friends. Away from Frank . . . Her stomach clenched. That sounded positively unbearable.

"If he is what you want," her father said, "then I will get him for you. But before I meet him this afternoon, I must know your wishes."

She didn't like the idea of her father strong-arming a marriage for her. Again. Besides, she wasn't ready to forgive Frank, this relative stranger that she'd been intimate with. "I cannot give an answer yet. But, whatever happens remains between him and me. I ask that you not pressure him into marrying me."

"He ruined you," her father growled. "We should force him to do the right thing."

"Duncan, stop. She either decides to marry him quickly or we'll send her to relatives abroad. I won't have her in a miserable marriage. I would rather she was happy, as we are."

Her father's gaze melted at that, a small smile on his broad face, the one he wore just for their mother. "Fine," he said, holding up his hands. "But the two of them need to decide soon. Byrnes and Livingston will have Mamie's involvement in this all over town by afternoon tea."

A SNIFFLING MRS. Rand handed Frank two empty boxes. "I cannot believe you are quitting."

Fired, more like it. Yes, Frank had officially resigned from the firm this morning, but it had been made clear by the other three partners that he was no longer welcome here. He couldn't really blame them, not after the headlines today. The newspapers made him out to sound like some sort of grifter, a man who'd created a persona to flimflam the upper-class elites. He'd never have another client who resided above Forty-Second Street.

He wished he could feel angry about it . . . but he felt nothing. He'd been numb since Mamie walked out last night.

*I cannot love a man I don't know. Worse, you've been lying so long I suspect you don't even know yourself.*

Those words haunted him. He'd had everything in the palm of his hand only a few hours ago. Now, he had nothing.

He took the boxes. "I'm sure you've read the morning editions. There's no need to pretend with me."

"I don't care if your name is Tripp, Murphy or Carnegie, you're the same man I've been working with for four years. You're a great lawyer and you should not let those old buzzards run you out."

The side of his mouth hitched. "I'm going to miss you, Mrs. Rand."

She waved her hand and hurried from his office. He heard her blowing her nose at her desk as he looked around. There wasn't much in his office to pack. No family photos. No mementos. No artwork or certificates of merit. Just blank walls and papers. God, that was pathetic.

He wouldn't even take any files. All of his cases had been turned over to the partners, save one: Mrs. Porter. No lawyer at the firm would take it on, so he'd filed a motion to withdraw from the case this morning. That way, Mrs. Porter could find a new attorney, one not tainted in scandal.

"Well, well, well . . ."

Frank's head snapped up at the voice and found

Julius Hatcher, his longtime friend, strolling into the office. Julius removed his derby. "I spend two months in London and look at what I return to."

Heat worked its way up Frank's neck. "Shut the door. If you're going to shout at me, I'd rather the whole building not hear it."

Julius did shut the door, but then he came over and shook Frank's hand. "And why would I shout at you?"

Frank faced the man he'd known since law school, when Frank traveled to Manhattan on breaks for debauchery. "For not telling you all these years."

Julius shook his head and lowered himself into an empty chair. "I suspected something was amiss when you never went to visit this supposed family and the family never visited you. But you know my background. It's hardly pristine. Who was I to judge?"

"Maybe that's why we always got on so well."

"Perhaps. So, Miss Marion Greene . . ."

Frank sat in the chair behind the desk and squinted at his famously reclusive friend. "That wasn't in the newspaper."

"Indeed, it wasn't, but I do have my ways of learning information."

"Your wife, I suppose. And how is the Lady Nora?"

Julius's mouth hitched into a smile. "Wonderful. However, let's not lose the topic at hand. Word is you've ruined Miss Greene, broken up her engagement to Livingston."

"I . . ." He couldn't even deny it. Yes, he'd done those things. "I want to marry her."

"What's the problem, then? Her father?"

"No. She's the problem. She says she cannot love a man she doesn't know."

"She's hurt because you lied to her."

Frank nodded once. "Won't even let me explain." He dragged a hand through his hair. Was it too early in the day to start drinking? *You've lost everything. Might as well get drunk.*

"I don't understand. You had good reason to cover up your past from what I read. She has to know, with a family like hers, that society never would've accepted you otherwise. Your career wouldn't have thrived had the truth been known."

"She doesn't care about society. If she did, she would've married Livingston." Frank then explained about Mamie's involvement with the tenement families, Mrs. Porter and the Porter children.

Julius's eyes sparkled with amusement. "Stealing money from those fools stupid enough to gamble in casinos? Oh, that is absolutely priceless. I adore her already."

"You would. She is beyond reckless, just like you were once."

"And you. Don't play the choirboy around me. I've known you too long."

Fair enough.

"So, friend," Julius said. "Now that you've wallowed in your pity this morning, what do you plan to do about all this?"

"I haven't a clue. The firm forced me out and Mamie won't talk to me. Thought I'd spend the afternoon getting as drunk as absolutely possible. Care to join me?"

Julius's head tilted. "That hardly sounds like

you. Where's the man who could unlock any legal puzzle with his mind? Who would argue and fight for his clients to the very last second? You're not one to give up. Ever."

Frank slowly spun a pencil on the surface of his—the firm's—desk. "I suppose that was when I had something to lose." Hard to fight when one had nothing.

"My, we are feeling sorry for ourselves today." Julius leaned forward. "Frank, the clients you have, the firm you work for, do not define you. The address of your house, the clubs you visit . . . Those things do not make up who you are inside. I've seen you treat debutantes and street urchins alike with the same amount of respect and courtesy. This," he said, gesturing to the office, "is merely the gilding on the man you already are."

"And who is that?" he snapped. "The son of a violent alcoholic? The boy who grew up in filth and terror? Who relied on the kindness of charity until he was nearly seventeen? I don't want to *be* that man. I never did."

"Don't you see? All that only makes the man you are now more remarkable. We may try to outrun our past, but it always manages to catch up with us. Take this from me, it's a lot easier to make peace with your inner demons than to fight them."

Julius's middle-class childhood had contained violence and tragedy, something he'd never shied away from. Frank had always admired that. "None of that will help with Mamie. She'll never forgive me."

"You can't predict that. The greatest gift the world has been given is a woman's capacity for understanding and forgiveness—though she may make you work hard for it this time."

"I don't even know where to begin," he mumbled.

"Then start at the beginning."

Frank frowned at his friend. "What does that even mean?"

"I have no idea, but I have every confidence you'll figure it out." He stood and put on his derby. "By the way, I've already told your partners that my business stays with you. Whatever your last name, you'll always be my attorney—and my friend."

THE STREET HAD changed considerably since the last time he'd stood here. Where there had been dirt now there were buildings. The bare ground paved over with cobblestones. And where once stood a shack of untreated wood was a house painted white. With a second floor.

Frank stood on the opposite side of Worth Street and tried to take it all in. How had they managed it? Patrick? His sisters? Frank's money would have helped, but his mother hadn't spent it, at least according to his brother.

*Start at the beginning.* Wasn't that what Julius had said? Mamie claimed Frank didn't know himself. So here he was, trying to figure himself out now that he was no longer Frank Tripp, the attorney to New York City's elite.

He watched the house for a long time. There was movement inside, but he couldn't make out the identities of the figures. Supposedly Patrick lived there with his family and their mother. Was there laughter? Were the children happy? Frank couldn't imagine it.

*I'm glad you're dead,* he said to the ghost of the man who'd terrorized that piece of land. At least Colin Murphy could no longer hurt people.

Suddenly, the door opened. Patrick appeared on the stoop, shut the door behind him and put his hands on his hips. His gaze locked on Frank. "Are you going to stand there all day or come inside?" he shouted.

Fuck. He hadn't realized his vigil was so obvious.

Still, he hesitated. Was he ready to go inside? *He's not there. It's different now,* he told himself. But there were memories. And memories were often not improved upon by reality.

Sometimes, the reality was worse.

Mamie's voice echoed in his head. *You've broken my heart—and I'm not certain who to blame.* If he hoped to win her forgiveness, he had to start here.

Patrick waited patiently, as if aware of Frank's struggle. Swallowing hard, Frank thrust his hands in his pockets and started forward. When he reached the steps, Patrick met him and held up a palm. "If you're here to upset her, then I won't allow you inside."

"I don't know why I'm here, but it's not to hurt anyone."

Patrick's gaze narrowed on Frank's face. "See that you don't. I may have a bad leg but I'm still able to pummel you, uptown boy."

Frank resisted the urge to laugh at his older brother. "Understood."

Patrick turned and opened the door. He went through first, leaving Frank to follow. "She's in the kitchen," he said over his shoulder. "Come with me."

The house was tiny but clean. Decorated with feminine touches and personal items. It was homey. Warm. Well lived in. Absolutely nothing like its former shell that had contained three small, unkempt rooms.

They crossed through a parlor then a dining room. The smell of freshly baked bread grew stronger as they traveled. Patrick paused at the doorjamb at what had to be the kitchen. "Wait here."

He disappeared inside and Frank took a few deep breaths. Then he heard a chair scrape and an older woman with his mother's features suddenly appeared in the doorway. Her eyes grew round as she took in the length of him then filled with tears. "Oh, my heavens. It's my baby boy."

She threw herself against his chest, her arms wrapping tight around him, and Frank had no choice but to reciprocate the embrace. She was slighter than he remembered, her dark brown hair now streaked with gray, but it was definitely his mother. "I knew you'd come back," she whispered into his vest. For a long moment, he held her as she cried and his own eyes filled with moisture. It had been so long.

"The last time we did this I wasn't taller than you."

"And now look at you. All grown up." She pulled away and wiped her face. Then she reached up and placed her palm on his cheek. "You're just as handsome, though. And that suit! It must've cost a fortune."

"Ma," Patrick called. "Stop fawning over him and both of you get in here."

The side of her mouth kicked up. "He's always

fussing after me. Well, come on and meet Rachel. That's Patrick's wife."

Frank nodded and followed her. The kitchen was clean and bright, a rack of pots and pans hanging from hooks on the wall near the black iron stove. There was a sink with a faucet, which implied running water indoors, and Frank tried not to remember going out to the well to draw water as a boy. In frigid temperatures, the trip had been nothing short of miserable.

And don't get him started on the outhouse.

"Hello." A tall woman with dark eyes approached and held out her hand. "I'm Rachel Murphy, Patrick's wife."

"Nice to meet you. I'm Frank, Patrick's brother," he said as they shook.

"I know. I've heard quite a bit about you."

"Oh?" He shot a quick glance at his brother.

"Thank you for helping with his arrest a few years ago," she said. "We were all worried sick before he was released. It was like magic." She smiled brightly.

"Or a lot of money," Patrick said under his breath.

"Ignore him," Rachel said. "He's grateful but also proud."

"A common Murphy trait, I'm afraid. And it was my pleasure to help."

"Come sit down," his mother urged. "I want to hear all about your life as a big city attorney. According to Patrick, the newspapers sure do love to talk about you."

Especially today. Had his mother seen the morning's rags? Big city attorney no longer. More like disgraced man with useless legal knowledge.

Rachel went to stir something simmering on the stove. "Shall I put on tea?"

"I'm afraid we're all out of champagne," Patrick said to Frank. "Will tea do?"

"Patrick," their mother snapped. "Mind your manners."

Frank had to smother a smile. Some things never changed. "Tea is just fine."

Tea was soon poured and Frank learned about his two nieces (both attending school this morning), how Patrick and Rachel met (in Brooklyn), and the rebuilding of the house (completed by Patrick and some friends). He kept asking them questions, partially out of curiosity and partially out of a need to keep from talking about his own miserable life.

"That's enough about the brewery," Ma said when Patrick had gone into detail regarding his expansion plans. "I want to hear about Frankie. Let him talk for a change. Tell us, are you married? Do I have more grandbabies?"

"No and no. I . . ." He sighed. "Well, there is someone I plan to marry but she's not exactly interested at the moment."

"And why not?" His mother set down her mug on the table. "You are handsome and successful. What more does she want in a husband?"

"Have you seen the newspapers today?"

Ma shook her head. "I never bother reading them. Patrick and Rachel tell me all I need to know. Why? What's happened?"

Patrick leaned over and whispered in his wife's ear. She nodded then left the room, Patrick on her heels.

Frank turned his mug in slow circles on the wood,

thinking how best to begin. "I quit my job a little over two hours ago. Well, it was quit or be fired."

"Whatever the reason, they were fools to let you go."

The unwavering, unflinching support from this woman he'd turned his back on half his life ago staggered him. He didn't deserve that unconditional support, not even from his mother. "Ma, when I left, I changed my last name. I never told anyone where I came from. I . . . made up a childhood in Chicago where I had wealthy parents and every advantage money could buy. The truth was discovered recently and revealed to the entire city. It's caused quite the scandal."

She put her hand on his arm. "You thought that would upset me? I found out about Frank Tripp when Patrick was released from prison. He was angry, but I was so proud. Look at all you've done. How far you've risen. And you helped your brother when he needed it. How could I blame you for changing your name? You wanted so desperately to leave, to be anywhere but here."

That was true. He had wished to be anywhere but here. "I still felt guilty, leaving you and the others here with him. It . . ." He blew out a long breath. "Why did you stay with him? Why didn't you leave?"

Pain flashed in her gaze for a brief moment. "Where would I go? How would I support us? What if he took you all away from me? You don't understand. Women are stripped of choices in small ways every day. Makes it easier for them to convince us we have no choices whatsoever when the time comes."

He stared at the wall, unseeing. "I would have helped you. Patrick, Laura, Sarah—we all would have helped you."

"And put you at further risk than you already were? No, I could never do that to you." Her chin trembled. "Not once did I regret letting you go off to boarding school. I let you go because you were too smart to stay behind, caught up in the gangs and the troubles down here. I missed you, yes. And there were times we needed you. But seeing you rise so high, everything you've accomplished . . . Why, Patrick says you live in a mansion on Fifth Avenue. No mother could ever regret a path leading to who you've become."

"But that's just it. I don't know who I am anymore. I've lost nearly everything and I haven't the faintest idea how to fix things."

"This is about a woman. The one not interested in marrying you at the moment."

He took a sip of tepid tea. "Yes. She hates that I lied to her."

"My darling boy, words often lie but our actions do not. Your father professed his love for me daily, but his actions told a very different story. So what have you done to show her that you love her?"

"I've sent her gifts," he said, the only answer he could think of.

"But that's just money," she said with a sad shake of her head. "I'm talking about finding something she cares about and showing her you care about it, too."

"She cares about helping people."

"Good. Now, what can you do to aid her in doing that?"

The idea was so obvious, it hit him like a thunderbolt. "You're right, and I think I might have a way. Thank you, Ma."

"You're most welcome."

He had the urge to leave, to put the wheels of his plan immediately in motion, but he didn't wish to cut this visit short. He wasn't ready to say goodbye just yet. The reluctance surprised him. "Do you think I could bring her down to meet you sometime?"

His mother drew in a shaky breath, emotion causing her eyes to glaze over. "I would like that very much."

"Good. I'd like to stay and meet my nieces, but I have a case to argue and a lady to win back. I will return, though. I promise."

"I know." She clasped his hand and squeezed. "I was certain you'd come back when you were ready. And I can see you're ready."

# Chapter Twenty

The courtroom was packed.

Mamie hadn't expected that. She had thought this would be a quick few hours with the attorneys, two or three witnesses, and a judge. Instead, the room was nearly full to capacity.

That's what happened when one of the city's most famous attorneys caused the biggest scandal of the year, she supposed.

From her seat near the back, she could see him, this tall and dashing dark-haired man in a striped navy suit at the front of the courtroom. His hands were in his pockets but his shoulders were tight, a subtle reminder that he was mortal. Aware of the spectacle he'd caused and . . . what? Regretted it, most likely. How long would he have carried out the deception? Until he died?

*I would have married a man without truly knowing him.*

The idea gave her shivers.

She missed him, yes. Her body ached for him and her heart yearned for him. But her brain . . . Her brain told her she'd been duped, that he hadn't cared enough to tell her the truth about himself. And that hurt.

She was confused, angry and crushed. Perhaps a year in Rome would help clear her mind and give time for the scandal to die down. Being a ruined woman wouldn't be so terrible. Her sisters would forgive her and her parents still loved her. New York society might turn its back on her but she never cared much for society anyway. She'd played the dutiful daughter to please her parents, but that was no longer necessary.

*I'm free.*

Free to do whatever she wanted. Go wherever she wanted. Be with whomever she wanted.

Her gaze strayed again to Frank, alone and remote on the other side of the room. She could feel the stares of those seated around her, those who'd learned of her ruination at the lawyer's hands. It had been spread all over New York by the Livingston family, as a way of preserving their dignity over the broken engagement, she supposed. Mamie was too devastated to care.

A police officer near the bench asked everyone to rise and announced Judge Smyth. The judge came in and took his place behind the massive wooden dais. When everyone was seated, a matron led in Mrs. Porter. Mamie's friend was wearing clothes Mamie had brought her, a white shirtwaist and a navy skirt. Her eyes darted around nervously until she spotted Mamie in the crowd. Then she seemed to relax, nodding her head in acknowledgment. Frank came to meet his client, helping her settle into the chair next to his.

Mamie clasped her hands tight, her heart racing as the judge addressed Frank. "Mr. Tripp, you have filed a motion to withdraw as the attorney of record. Is that true?"

"Yes, your honor." Frank's voice, deep and familiar, filled her head and caused her skin to prickle. It reminded her of whispers and promises, lies and endearments. Everything that made up this complicated man. "However, the defense wishes to withdraw that motion from the court."

"You wish to withdraw the motion?"

"Yes, we do. I will continue representation for the defendant."

"Mrs. Porter, this is acceptable to you?"

"Yes, your honor."

Frank had tried to back out of representing Mrs. Porter? This was news to Mamie. Why would he give up the case? Because of the scandal?

"Then the motion is withdrawn," the judge said. "Proceed, Mr. McIntyre."

The prosecutor stood up and called his first witness, the sergeant Mamie remembered from the murder scene. After being sworn in and identified, the prosecutor asked about what Sergeant Tunney had seen the day of the murder. The facts were as Mamie knew them, that the sergeant had arrived to a dead body and a wife covered in blood.

"And was Mrs. Porter crying?"

"No, she was not." He looked quite smug at that fact.

"Upset in any way over the loss of her husband?"

"No."

"And why do you believe that was?"

"Objection," Frank called out. "Speculation."

"Sustained," the judge said. "Sergeant Tunney, do not answer that. Mr. McIntyre, please move on."

The sergeant testified to the position of the body and the evidence of the heavy pan used as the weapon. When the prosecutor finished, the sergeant appeared quite pleased with himself. As if he were untouchable, the same attitude as the day of the murder. As angry as Mamie was with Frank, she rooted for him to take this sergeant down a peg or two.

Frank stood and buttoned his topcoat. She could see only the back of his head and part of his profile. Even still, he took her breath away. *You're perfect. It's perfect. Make it more perfect.* Heat crawled through her, slow and painful. Goodness, she'd never forget those words as long as she lived, even if they hurt to recall.

"Sergeant Tunney," Frank began. "You just testified that you have been employed by the municipal police force of this city for the last nine years. Is that correct?"

"Yes."

"And you were promoted to the rank of sergeant how many years ago?"

"Three."

"You are stationed at the 20th Precinct, correct?"

"Yes. West Thirty-Seventh Street."

"It's unusual for a sergeant from the 20th Precinct to go all the way down to the 6th Precinct on a domestic murder case, isn't it?"

"We go where we're needed."

"Yet in your three years as a sergeant you haven't personally handled a case in the 6th Precinct, have you?"

"No."

"So you weren't *needed* on any cases or murders in the 6th Precinct before this?"

"No."

"You must have had a very good reason for going down to Roy Porter's apartment, correct?"

"As I said, we go where we're needed."

"One of your fellow officers at the 20th Precinct is a Detective Edward Porter, isn't that right?"

"Yes."

"Were you aware that Detective Porter was a cousin to the deceased, Mr. Roy Porter?"

"Yes."

"And would you call Detective Porter a friend?"

"Objection," the prosecutor said. "What is the relevance of these questions?"

Frank addressed the judge. "Your honor, the relevance is the participation of Sergeant Tunney in this case and his personal reasons for doing so."

"Overruled. Please answer, sergeant."

"Yes, I know him."

"Would you say you're close?"

"I'd say we're colleagues."

"Isn't it true that you were best man at his wedding two years ago?" Frank asked.

Tunney said nothing, merely glared at Frank.

"Sergeant Tunney?" Frank prompted.

"Yes."

"I see. You've investigated many murder cases, have you not?"

"Yes, I have."

"In fact, your conviction rate is quite high, isn't it?"

"I like to think I'm good at what I do."

"So you must have a good understanding of the

key elements of any successful murder investigation?"

"I don't know what you mean." Tunney was obviously going to make Frank work for his point.

"I think it's clear what I mean. Your suspect must have an opportunity to kill the victim, correct?"

"Yes."

"And motive is central to any investigation, am I right?"

"Obviously."

"Thank you. And means are also critical. Wouldn't you say that's true?"

Tunney shifted uncomfortably. "Yes."

"How did Mrs. Porter allegedly murder her husband?"

"Mrs. Porter killed her husband with a cast iron frying pan."

"And what did your examination of this so-called murder weapon reveal?"

Tunney looked uneasily at the prosecutor, then back at Frank.

"Sergeant Tunney, please answer the question," the judge said when it was clear Tunney was stalling.

The sergeant cleared his throat. "Unfortunately, we didn't have a chance to examine the murder weapon as thoroughly as we'd hoped."

"Oh?" Frank inquired. "Was the murder weapon not found at the scene?"

"Yes, it was there, as plain as day."

"I can't help but notice that the murder weapon hasn't yet been presented to the defense. May we see the murder weapon, Sergeant Tunney?"

"It's not available."

"And why is that?"

"We . . . misplaced it."

"You *misplaced* the murder weapon?"

"Not me, personally," Tunney said, indignantly.

"The police department misplaced the murder weapon, then."

Tunney said nothing.

"When did you notice it was missing?"

"A few days after the arrest."

"And you didn't bother to tell the court?"

"We were hoping it would turn up." Tunney tugged at his collar, as if he weren't getting enough air.

"And did it?"

"No," said Tunney, averting his eyes.

"Leaving only your claims of its use in this case, and nothing for the defense to examine." Frank paused for effect. The damage was done. "Nothing further for this witness, your honor."

Frank sat at that point, finished, and the prosecutor attempted to undo some of the sergeant's damage with follow-up questions. It failed. The crowd cast disapproving glances toward the sergeant as he stepped down. One point for Frank.

Detective Edward Porter was then called in. He swore to tell the truth, deliberately not glancing in Bridget Porter's direction. He sat and the prosecution began to ask questions about the deceased's character. From Edward's answers, one would think Roy Porter had been a saint.

When Frank finally stood, Mamie perked up. Would he be able to discredit the detective's testimony?

After some preliminary questions about his

background, Frank asked, "Sergeant Tunney has just testified that you asked him to go downtown and oversee your cousin's murder scene. Do you often ask Sergeant Tunney to oversee specific cases for you?"

"No, not often."

"How many times would you say you've asked your friend to get involved in a case at your request?"

"I don't know. Maybe once."

"One time before Mrs. Porter's case?"

"Yes, I think so."

"Do you remember the nature of that case?"

"No."

The judge took notes, his brows knitted in concern, as Frank continued. "Yet you asked your friend to go downtown and oversee the scene of your cousin's murder. Why?"

Porter pressed his lips together. "Sergeant Tunney is an exemplary officer and I wished for the case to be handled by the best."

"Because the deceased was your cousin?"

"Yes."

"So you must believe that the detectives of the 6th Precinct are not exemplary officers, that they would proceed in a manner not to your liking on this case, correct?"

"Objection," the prosecutor called.

Frank held up his hands. "Withdrawn, your honor." He paused, as if to consider his next question. "You married two years ago, is that correct?"

"Yes," Edward said, a bit confused.

"But you'd been engaged once before, had you not?"

"Objection," the prosecutor said. "Relevance."

"The question is quite relevant to the defendant, your honor."

"I'll allow it. Please answer as to whether you have been engaged before, detective."

"Yes," Edward said coolly.

"To whom were you engaged?"

Edward jerked his chin toward Mrs. Porter. "Her."

"Do you mean Mrs. Roy Porter, the defendant?"

"Yes."

A wave of murmurs rippled through the courtroom and the judge banged his gavel to call for order. Mamie blinked, stunned. When had Frank learned that piece of news? Bridget and *Edward Porter*. It was unreal. Had the cousins been jealous of one another?

Frank waited for the crowd to quiet. "And who called off your engagement?"

"She did."

"Why?"

"I don't know," Edward said through clenched teeth.

"You don't remember, or you don't know, Mr. Porter?"

"She never told me."

"How soon after breaking your engagement did she marry your cousin?"

"I don't know."

"Come now. Approximately how long after? Was it two years? Three years?"

Porter stared at the wall for a long second. "Three weeks."

"*Three weeks?*" Frank paused. "It seems your

cousin wasted no time. That betrayal must have been difficult for you, wasn't it?"

"No." Neck flushed with anger, he appeared ready to leap over the partition and strangle Frank. "She fooled him, just as she fooled me."

"What does that mean, exactly?"

He pounded the rail in front of him. "It means she's a whore who deserved every beating he gave her."

Chaos ensued in the courtroom. The judge banged his gavel once more, asking for quiet. Mamie's jaw fell open. The detective's words were cruel and hateful, especially toward a woman he'd almost married.

The witness was excused. Porter climbed down from the stand, his eyes promising retribution to Frank. When he left, the prosecution called Katie Porter and Mamie held her breath.

KATIE WAS SHOWN into court and helped onto the witness stand. The young girl's lip trembled as she stared at her mother and Mamie's heart clenched. Katie must have been terrified, not to mention desperate to see her mother.

On the stand, Katie was asked her name, address and age, which she answered in a clear, albeit soft, voice. No one in the courtroom spoke. Everyone leaned forward, quiet, to better hear her.

The prosecutor asked general questions about the family, the neighborhood. Then he asked if she had been present the day of the murder.

"Yes," Katie replied.

"What happened that morning?" McIntyre asked.

"My father was angry. Mommy told me to be quiet, but I couldn't."

"You couldn't be quiet?"

"No."

"Was anyone else in the house that morning?"

"Just my younger brothers."

"And what happened with your parents?"

"Daddy came in and scared me. Then my mommy hit him and he fell down."

"Did he ever get back up?"

"No."

The prosecution sat and Frank came to his feet. In his hand, he held a glass of water, which he carried over to Katie. She accepted it and took a drink. He left the glass within her reach. "Katie, you said your father came in and scared you. How?"

"He was yelling. His face was red, too. Then he hit Mommy—"

"He hit your mother?"

"Yes."

"How many times? Once?"

"No. More than once."

"What did you do?"

"I started hollering."

"Hollering, as in yelling?"

"Yes."

"What were you yelling?"

"For him to stop hitting her."

Mamie's chest tightened. How terrible for a young girl to witness such violence and pain to her mother.

"And did he stop?"

"Yes."

"Then what happened?"

"He came at me, his fist raised. He told me he would make me be quiet."

"Were you scared?"

She bit her lip and closed her eyes briefly. "Yes. I thought he was going to hit me, too."

"Did he often hit you?"

"No, never." She shook her head. "He only ever hit Mommy."

"How often did he hit her?"

"Objection, your honor," the prosecutor said. "Propensity."

"Overruled," the judge answered.

"Katie, how often did he hit her?"

Katie lifted a shoulder. She didn't meet Frank's gaze.

"Miss Porter, we need you to answer the question," the judge said, his tone gentle.

"A lot," she whispered.

"He hit her a lot," Frank confirmed.

"Yes."

"How often is a lot?"

"A few times a week."

"And did she ever strike him in return?"

Katie's brows shot up, as if she'd never considered this a possibility. "No."

"Not once?"

"No, never."

The prosecutor and his assistant began whispering, but Mamie ignored them. Frank and Katie riveted her.

"I'm almost finished with my questions, Katie. You just said that on the day when your father died he scared you, that you thought he was going to hit you. What did you do at that point?"

"What did I do?"

"Yes. At the moment when you were scared, when he came toward you, what did you do?"

"I ran."

"You ran?"

"Yes. I ran out of the kitchen."

"Where did you run to?"

"The other room. Outside the kitchen."

"Could you see your father from the other room?" She shook her head.

Frank leaned in to whisper loudly, "We need you to actually say the words so the court stenographer may record it."

"No," Katie answered. "I could not see him from the other room."

"And what about your mother? Could you see her from the other room?"

"No."

"So you couldn't see either of your parents. What did you see next?"

"My father on the floor."

"Did you see him fall?"

"No, I saw him lying there."

"Did you see anyone hit him?"

"No, but—"

"So you didn't see anyone hit your father before he fell because you were in another room?"

"That's right."

"That's all, your honor. Thank you, Katie." After Frank went back to his seat, the prosecutor tried to talk Katie into saying she'd actually seen her mother hit her father with the pan, but Katie stuck to her story. She'd clearly been hiding in the other room and hadn't witnessed the actual crime.

When Katie stepped down, an officer led her out of the courtroom. Mamie didn't wait to see what else happened in there. She hurried from the room and went to the outer chamber. Her only thought was about reaching Katie and seeing her home.

NIGHT HAD FALLEN when Mamie found herself once again headed downtown. She snuggled deep into the warmth of the carriage seats and stared out at the barren streets. The area around City Hall was mostly empty, the traders and politicians long gone for the day. *I must be insane for coming down here.*

Earlier, after leaving the courtroom, she'd driven Katie home. The girl had been in good spirits, hopeful her mother might be released soon. Mamie was also hopeful. Frank had been magnificent, easily tearing apart the testimony of the prosecution's witnesses. She'd taken her time in reliving the trial for Mrs. Barrett over tea, not missing any detail in the retelling.

An hour later, Otto had arrived at Mrs. Barrett's apartment with Mrs. Porter in tow. Everyone erupted into tears. Apparently, the district attorney had dropped the case against Mrs. Porter. Between the testimony of Katie and Edward Porter, as well as the missing murder weapon, the district attorney didn't believe he would win against Frank in a jury trial.

Mrs. Porter had left a free woman.

She'd thanked Mamie effusively, hugging her and promising undying gratitude. Mamie was just happy the ordeal was over and that Mrs. Porter could return to her children. Everyone could now get past the awfulness and start healing.

Frank had been absent from the Porter reunion. She hadn't asked after his whereabouts, either. As happy as she was with his performance in court today, she hadn't forgiven him for lying to her.

Then tonight she'd received a note on her pillow.

*I need your help. Please, Mamie. Meet me at midnight. Thirty-Nine Nassau Street.*

*—Frank*

She wasn't altogether surprised he wished to see her, likely to once again offer his apologies. So, why the strange address?

She considered not going. What could they possibly say to one another? The case was over, their friendship—or whatever it had been—in flames. Yes, they had been lovers, but she could no longer be intimate with someone who'd deceived her like that. If he thought to seduce her into forgiving him, he'd be sorely disappointed.

The hansom pulled up to a brick building on Nassau Street. There was no sign or nameplate to give any clues as to why Frank had called her there. Confused, she descended to the walk and paid the driver.

"Miss, are you certain about this address?" He glanced around them. "It ain't exactly a safe neighborhood for ladies after dark."

She nearly laughed. She'd been in far worse neighborhoods than this in the dark. "I'll be fine. Thank you."

He tipped his hat but didn't immediately drive away. Instead, he watched as she approached the door at number Thirty-Nine. A figure appeared from the darkness to meet her. *Frank.* She'd know the outline of those broad shoulders anywhere.

He unlocked the door and held it open. Mamie turned to wave at the hansom driver, letting him know she was safe, then went inside.

Frank locked up behind her and thrust his hands in his trouser pockets. He still wore the same suit from court, his face so handsome it made her heart hurt. Late evening whiskers covered his jaw, giving him a roguish appearance, as if he were about to steal her away on a pirate ship destined for the Caribbean Islands. A dark thrill skated down her spine, one she tried her best to ignore.

"I wasn't certain you'd come," he said.

"I did so only to congratulate you on winning Mrs. Porter's case. You were fantastic."

The side of his mouth hitched. "Thank you. I couldn't have won without you and Otto, however."

She doubted that, but it was kind of him to say. "Why am I here, Frank?"

"I wanted to show you something—and ask for your help."

"Here?" She took in the empty vestibule, the dust and cobwebs haunting the floors and walls. The place looked as if it had been abandoned since the Draft Riots.

"Follow me." He held out his hand, his eyes daring her to refuse. It was a look she'd seen often from him during their early battles, as if he knew she couldn't resist a challenge.

She clasped his forearm instead. A small, but necessary, compromise. "I cannot be gone long so let's get this over with."

He said nothing. Silently, they made their way

up a flight of stairs. The office building was in better shape than she'd initially thought. Brass handrails adorned the marble stairs and crown molding hugged the ceilings. The details were there, they just needed a bit of shine.

At the second floor, he stopped and faced her. "Close your eyes."

"Frank, this is ridiculous—"

"Please, Mamie," he said, his deep voice full of uncertainty and hope. She couldn't refuse that tone, one she hadn't heard him use before. After she closed her eyes, he helped her forward. "Just a few more feet. Keep going."

Then he moved behind her. "Now, open them."

Dim light from an overhead bulb illuminated a glass door with big block letters.

### LOWER EAST SIDE LEGAL AID SOCIETY
### Frank M. Tripp, Attorney

Mamie blinked. "I don't understand."

"Come inside." He turned the knob and led her into a large reception area. Several doors surrounded them, all leading to smaller offices.

"What is this place?"

"My new idea. What do you think?" He propped a shoulder against the wall and folded his arms.

She searched his face. "I don't know what to think. I'm not certain what this is about."

"I am starting a legal firm to represent those without the means to afford an attorney."

"But you already have a firm."

"We've parted ways. They would never allow me to represent more clients like Mrs. Porter. Those kinds of cases hardly draw praise at the Union Club."

"So, how will this work? Because I don't think clients like Mrs. Porter can afford your rates."

He shook his head. "I won't charge them anything. We'll get funding to cover our costs, donations from uptown swells. That way, no one must pick any more pockets. Illegally anyway."

"Charity work. I'm astounded. You are starting a philanthropic organization." It boggled her mind. This man, who'd been so passionate about money and status not that long ago . . . now a philanthropist?

"Yes, I am. And I hope you'll help me."

"*Me?*"

He moved closer, slowly, as if concerned about spooking her, until he was within arm's reach. "Yes, you. I need someone to help secure funding. I need someone on the streets, to help refer clients. I need someone here to hold my clients' hands and reassure them." He stared down at her with his brilliant blue gaze, with no hint of deception or insanity. Just plain honesty and longing. "I need you by my side, Mamie. I don't want to do this without *you.*"

"Frank, this is . . . a lot to take in. And you don't need me specifically. Anyone would be happy to help in such a worthwhile cause."

"I don't want anyone. I want you."

"Why?"

The edges of his lips turned up as if he were sharing a secret. "Because I love you. I love how you show no fear when it comes to the causes in which you believe. I love how you treat everyone the same, no matter their background or status. I love how you care for those in your life, whether they are family or someone you just met. You are passionate and strong, kind and steadfast. You're the only woman I ever want to partner with, and no matter how long I have remaining on this earth I want to spend it at your side. Making a difference, building a future together."

Her throat tightened, emotion building like tiny boulders in her chest. Swallowing, she forced out, "I'm having a hard time wrapping my head around this new man in front of me."

"I'm still the old man, just enlightened. *You* have changed me for the better. I thought I lost everything, but I haven't. I've gained a whole new perspective, not to mention my family. The only thing I don't have is you and I'll fight like hell to win you back. For the rest of my life, every case I win, every person I help, is in your honor, in the hopes of making you proud. I'll understand if you walk out of here and never want to see me again. I'm damn sorry I ever lied to you. Yes, I should've told you the truth about me. But even if you leave, I'll never give up, I can't. You're the most important thing in the world to me."

It was all too much. The legal aid society, the apology and the profession of his feelings . . . She couldn't walk away from him, not now. Her life was not complete without him in it. She threw herself against his chest, her arms squeezing him tight. He caught her, as he always had, this man who'd chased her around every part of the city to keep her safe. Only she didn't need rescuing.

She never had.

He'd been the one in need of saving all along.

"Stop talking," she choked into his silk vest. "Just stop. I will help you. I'd be honored to stand by your side, both in this philanthropy and in your life. I've never been prouder of someone than at this moment. You are the very best man I've ever met, Frank Tripp."

"Frank Murphy Tripp," he corrected and placed a kiss to the top of her head. "And I will never let you down again, I swear it."

"I believe you. You may be a silver-tongued devil, but you're *my* silver-tongued devil. And I'll never give you up."

He leaned in and placed his mouth near the shell of her ear. "I knew you really loved me for my tongue . . ."

Liquid fire raced through her as relief and desire cascaded like a thousand stars inside her chest. She breathed him in, the spice and heat, deep into her lungs. *Glorious, sinful man.* "You know, I may have forgotten your talents in that area. Perhaps you should remind me?"

"Follow me. I have just the desk in mind."

# Epilogue

"*Y*ou are one lucky bastard."

His gaze never leaving his beautiful bride, Frank grinned at the familiar voice of his best friend and best man. "I am, aren't I?"

Julius Hatcher rested against the wall next to Frank. They were standing at the edge of the huge Greene ballroom, hours after Mamie and Frank had married.

*Married.* The word had a nice sound to it. In fact, he doubted he'd ever tire of saying it.

Julius handed Frank a glass of beer. "Your brother has a gift," he remarked. "I've already invested to help take his brewery national."

Frank sipped the crisp pilsner. "You may have to fight Mulligan for the privilege."

Julius made a scoffing sound. "I can handle Jack Mulligan. By the way, that little favor you asked of me, the one for the Livingstons?"

Frank perked up at that. He and Julius had discussed various ways of retribution for Chauncey and his father. The one they'd settled on was sure to be the most humiliating. "Yes?"

"It's finished. The house, the stocks, it's all gone. They're broke."

Frank couldn't dredge up one ounce of sympathy for that family. "Good. Perhaps I'll offer Chauncey a job at the legal aid society."

"Word is he's left for Paris. Probably swiped the family silver to live off before he sailed."

At least Chauncey would never harm Mamie again, even if Frank didn't wish for the man to escape the scandal. "Thank you for that. I don't have the influence I once did when it comes to ruining lives."

"Never thought I'd see the day. Frank Tripp, a do-gooder."

"Believe it. Besides, my wife prefers me this way. And I much prefer her gratitude over yours."

Julius chuckled. "As you should."

The crowd in the ballroom swallowed up Frank's view of Mamie. *Damn.* He couldn't wait to get her alone. For a brief moment, he'd considered eloping with her. However, he hadn't wished to further scandalize her. That meant a huge wedding in front of all New York society—and Frank's family. Of course, there was nothing society loved more than a huge party and the Greenes had outdone themselves today. Not wanting to miss out, the blue-blooded families had attended en masse. Everyone except the Livingstons.

Also here were some of Frank's clients, both new and old. It turned out not everyone above Forty-Second Street had a problem with his background. This had come as a pleasant surprise, even though Frank no longer handled the wealthiest citizens of the city. The legal aid society was up and running, with more cases than they could possibly handle. Just this week Frank had hired three additional attorneys and six legal assistants to handle the caseload.

He'd never been happier.

He and Mamie worked side by side nearly all day. She was a natural, both for raising funds to keep the legal aid society running and convincing those in need to trust Frank. She cared about people. Genuinely liked them.

He couldn't wait to spend every night with her as well.

Catherine and Duncan Greene suddenly appeared with Frank's mother in tow. Julius excused himself with the promise to see Frank later.

"There you are," Catherine said to Frank. "Did you know your mother has never traveled outside the city? We must take her with us to Newport for the summer."

His mother's expression was hesitant, as if she was uncertain how Frank would take this news. He smiled at both women. "I would like that. Ma, do you feel up to traveling?"

"I'm perfectly healthy," she told him. "Stop listening to your brother. One bout of pneumonia and he thinks I'm on death's door."

Frank wasn't so certain, but she certainly seemed to have enough energy lately. "Then you must come with us. Patrick, Rebecca and the girls, too."

"Excellent, then it's settled," Catherine said. "I know it's months away, but the ocean breeze will do you wonders, Genie."

They wandered off, and Frank marveled over Mamie's mother calling his mother by a nickname. *Genie*. He'd always thought of his mother as Eugenia. Strange, the turn his life had taken in the last six months.

"I apologize," Duncan muttered. "My wife is like a bull when she gets something in her head."

"And here I thought Mamie took after you."

Duncan's mouth hitched slightly. He and Frank had made peace of a sort, for Mamie's sake. They would never be close but had learned to let the past go in the last few months. "Welcome to the family, Frank. I didn't for once imagine it, but I can honestly say I've never seen her so filled with joy."

"And I'll spend my life trying to keep her that way. I love her, Duncan."

"I know you do. I'm damn sorry I ever tried to force her to wed Chauncey. It's hard to think you know what's best for your kids and be proven disastrously wrong."

Frank hated to point out that Mamie never let anything get in her way when she wanted something—not even her father. "I didn't plan on falling for her. At first, I followed her around to keep her out of trouble for your sake."

"Probably my fault." He rubbed his jaw thoughtfully. "I've indulged all three of my daughters far too much. Florence, especially."

Frank couldn't argue with that. Mamie had shared some truly astonishing stories about her younger sister.

"Oh," Duncan said, spotting someone in the crowd. "There's Teddy. I want to speak to him about some of this corruption you and Mamie have faced with the police department. I think he's just the man to take on Byrnes and his ilk."

Duncan excused himself and Frank silently wished him luck. The city's police force was rife with corruption. He didn't think anyone could ever set them straight, not even the well-connected and well-meaning Teddy Roosevelt.

Searching the crowd, he finally found her. She wore a cream satin gown that showed off the perfection of her skin. The gown's train had been removed for the reception, and Frank anticipated removing even more fabric from his lovely wife's person. Perhaps now.

As if she sensed his stare, she found his eyes with hers. She was laughing at something the man next to her was saying, her gaze sparkling with mirth, and the sight of her happiness settled into his chest with all the subtlety of a hammer. God above, she was beautiful. It was more than her clothes and appearance, however. Her appeal was wrapped in a thousand tiny things, like the way she stood up for those less fortunate. The ability to always make him laugh, no matter how grim his mood. How she accepted his family with open arms. And not the least of which was her ability to drive him wild with the smallest touch.

She moved toward him, gliding through the well-wishers and relatives with grace, a secret smile on her face. He loved that smile, the one she wore just for him.

*Tonight, she's mine. Forever and eternity.*

Fuck, the idea of it had blood pulsing in his groin. He tried a few deep breaths to calm himself. An erection would prove incredibly inconvenient at the moment. He'd been waiting for months for her to move into his Fifth Avenue home. Finally, this evening, she would live with him. *His*.

"Mr. Tripp," she said as she stopped before him. Her skirts rustled ever so slightly, reminding him of what lay beneath all those layers.

"Mrs. Tripp. How stunning you are today."

"Sweet talker. Are you enjoying the reception?"

"Not particularly. However, I am enjoying watching you enjoy the reception."

She quirked an eyebrow. "Is that why you've hardly taken your eyes off me since we arrived?"

"Perhaps. Or perhaps it's because you spent all those months trying to get away from me and I'm afraid you'll disappear."

"I was never trying to get away," she purred, sliding closer. "Maybe I was trying to lead you on a merry chase to catch your interest."

He clasped her hand. "Well, I've caught you now, my crafty little wife. What shall I do with you?"

"Would it be too bold if I answered, 'Anything you like'?"

"Are you trying to get me to embarrass myself at our wedding reception?"

"No," she said, her fingers rubbing his wrist. "I am trying to get you to *leave* our wedding reception."

Lust wrapped around the inside of his thighs and traveled up his back. "Just say the word and I'll take you home."

"Home. I like the sound of that."

"You do, do you?" He took her arm and tugged her out of the ballroom. "I much prefer other sounds, sounds I hope to hear quite soon. For example, your moans in our bed . . ."

"You'd best cease or I shall melt into a puddle of desire long before we reach home."

"No need to worry. I brought a closed carriage."

"You did?"

"Of course. I've waited my entire life for you. I don't plan on waiting one second longer than absolutely necessary to please my wife."

And, the instant the carriage door closed, he proceeded to show her exactly what he meant.

# Acknowledgments

I'm not going to lie. This book was a *blast* to write. But it likely never would've been written at all if not for the multitude of emails and messages I received about how much you adored Frank Tripp and asking when was he getting his own HEA. I hope you liked Frank and Mamie's story!

The fun part about researching history is that I learn something different for each book. For this one, I learned about Otto Raphael, a prominent Jewish police officer in New York City who became friends with Teddy Roosevelt. Then there's Paul Kelly, the gangland kingpin who ran the New Brighton Athletic Club, and Thomas Byrnes, who was the head of the NYC police detective bureau. Also, the House with the Bronze Door was a real Gilded Age casino for the city's elites. I think it's obvious which places and characters these have inspired.

Now, I'm neither a lawyer nor have I played one on TV, so there were plenty of folks who helped with Frank's legal abilities. My deepest thanks to Hon. Leo M. Gordon, Daniel Campbell, Tina Gabrielle, Christina Ponsa-Kraus, Sarah A. Seo, Claire Marti, Felicia Grossman, Cecilia London, Lin Gavin and Erin from the Heaving Bosoms podcast (give them a listen!). All errors are my own, and forgive me for applying some modern sensibilities in some places.

Thanks to writing pals Michele Mannon, Diana Quincy and JB Schroeder for their spot-on comments and never-ending support. I also must thank the amazing Sarah MacLean and Sophie Jordan, who were so helpful with titles, blurbs, covers and all around support on this project (and the authoring biz in general)!

My deepest gratitude goes to editor extraordinaire Tessa Woodward for helping to make this story (and all my stories) infinitely better. Thanks to everyone at Avon Books and HarperCollins— most especially Elle Keck, Pamela Jaffe, Kayleigh Webb and Angela Craft—for all their work on my books. And thanks to Laura Bradford, who always looks out for me.

A shout-out to the Gilded Lilies on Facebook! Thank you for sharing my enthusiasm for this time period and loving my crazy stories.

As always, thank you to my family for all their love and support.

Finally, the Legal Aid Society of New York City is the oldest and largest legal aid society in the United States. Founded in 1876, the Legal Aid Society continues to serve as "the voice for those who suffer in silence, face oppression, and struggle to access justice because of poverty." To make a donation, visit www.legalaidnyc.org.

**Don't miss all of Joanna Shupe's captivating romances in her Four Hundred series! Available now from Avon Books!**

## A Daring Arrangement

Lady Honora Parker must get engaged as soon as possible, and only a particular type of man will do. Nora seeks a mate so abhorrent, so completely unacceptable, that her father will reject the match—leaving her free to marry the artist she loves. Who then is the most appalling man in Manhattan? The wealthy, devilishly handsome financier, Julius Hatcher, of course . . .

Julius is intrigued by Nora's ruse and decides to play along. But to Nora's horror, Julius transforms himself into the perfect fiancé, charming the very people she hoped he would offend. It seems Julius has a secret plan all his own—one that will solve a dark mystery from his past, and perhaps turn him into the kind of man Nora could truly love.

# A Scandalous Deal

*They call her Lady Unlucky . . .*

With three dead fiancés, Lady Eva Hyde has positively no luck when it comes to love. She sets sail for New York City, determined that nothing will deter her dream of becoming an architect, certainly not an unexpected passionate shipboard encounter with a mysterious stranger. But Eva's misfortune strikes once more when she discovers the stranger who swept her off her feet is none other than her new employer.

*Or is it Lady Irresistible?*

Phillip Mansfield reluctantly agrees to let the fiery Lady Eva oversee his luxury hotel project while vowing to keep their relationship strictly professional. Yet Eva is more capable—and more alluring—than Phillip first thought, and he cannot keep from drawing up a plan of his own to seduce her.

When a series of onsite "accidents" make it clear someone wants Lady Unlucky to earn her nickname, Phillip discovers he's willing to do anything to protect her—even if it requires a scandalous deal . . .

# A Notorious Vow

With the fate of her disgraced family resting on her shoulders, Lady Christina Barclay has arrived in New York City from London to quickly secure a wealthy husband. But when her parents settle on an intolerable suitor, Christina turns to her reclusive neighbor, a darkly handsome and utterly compelling inventor, for help.

Oliver Hawkes reluctantly agrees to a platonic marriage . . . with his own condition: the marriage must end after one year. Not only does Oliver face challenges that are certain to make life as his wife difficult, but more importantly, he refuses to be distracted from his life's work—the development of a revolutionary device that could transform thousands of lives, including his own.

Much to his surprise, his bride is more beguiling than he imagined. When temptation burns hot between them, they realize they must overcome their own secrets and doubts, and every effort to undermine their marriage, because one year can never be enough.

REL 0619

*At Avon Books, we know your passion
for romance—once you finish one of our
novels, you find yourself wanting more.*

May we tempt you with . . .

- **Excerpts** from our upcoming releases.

- Entertaining **extras**, including authors'
  personal photo albums and book lists.

- Behind-the-scenes **scoop** on your favorite
  characters and series.

- **Sweepstakes** for the chance to win free books,
  romantic getaways, and other fun prizes.

- Writing **tips** from our authors and editors.

- **Blog** with our authors and find out why they
  love to write romance.

- **Exclusive content** that's not contained
  within the pages of our novels.

Join us at
**www.avonbooks.com**

**AVON**

*An Imprint of* HarperCollins*Publishers*
www.avonromance.com

Available wherever books are sold or please call 1-800-331-3761 to order.

FTH 1013